The New Hero
Volume 1

Every Age Needs Its Heroes

Edited by Robin D. Laws

Published by Stone Skin Press 2012.

Stone Skin Press is an imprint of Pelgrane Press Ltd. Spectrum House, 9 Bromell's Road, Clapham Common, London, SW4 0BN.

ISBN 978-1-908983-00-8

A CIP catalogue record for this book is available from the British Library.

1 2 3 4 5 6 7 8 9 10

Printed in the USA.

This book can be ordered direct from the publisher at
www.pelgranepress.com

Contents

A Book of Heroes

A Preface

This is a book of heroes.

To assemble a book of heroes is to make a statement on what heroism is—as a literary *construct*, and thus as a reflection of our lived experience.

To do this today is to reflect a time when the hero's position in popular culture has never been more paradoxical. In an age of tentpole movie franchises, continuing character novel series, and television season box sets, the character type I'm about to define as the iconic hero has never held greater sway over our collective imaginations. Yet at the same time, the iron rules underpinning these serial characters have been forgotten, ignored, and misapplied.

From creative writing classes to the pitch rooms of Hollywood, they've been eclipsed by assumptions appropriate to a quite different protagonist type; the dramatic hero. These ideas maintain a hammerlock on our way of thinking about characters and the stories that develop around them.

Dramatic hero conventions arise from the novelistic tradition of psychological realism, which in turn traces its roots back to Aristotelian tragedy. Whether she is felled by hubris, ancient-Greek style, or earns reassuring redemption in the American pop culture mode, the dramatic hero appears for the purposes of a single story. It's always one of transformation. In screenplay jargon, the hero undergoes an arc. She begins in one emotional condition, and from that state faces a crisis that puts her at odds with the world. This confrontation with the world changes her, completing her arc. At the end, the dramatic hero is a different person.

The opposing tradition is that of the iconic hero. The iconic hero exists to drive many stories. Whatever their external details, each of these recapitulates the same classic structure. The iconic hero encounters a disorder in the world. As it does the dramatic hero, the world tests the iconic hero, trying to change her. Where the dramatic hero transforms, either for better or worse, the iconic hero prevails by reaffirming her essential identity. By enacting her iconic ethos, she pushes back against the world's attempts to change her, to introduce into her its disordered state. In rejecting this onslaught, she instead forces change on the world, returning it to a place of order. That return might be incremental, a slight infusion of order into a fundamentally bleak and chaotic status quo or it might be decisive, a return of sunlight and goodness to an environment formerly threatened by fear and predation.

- Employing rigorous deductive logic, Sherlock Holmes untangles inexplicable mysteries.
- Her sharp mind hidden behind a deceptively doddering demeanor, Miss Marple solves multiple-suspect murder mysteries.
- With cold suavity and colder violence, James Bond dispatches Britain's enemies.
- Tarzan upholds the noble values of the jungle against the predatory outsiders who would despoil it.
- Conan uses his barbaric superiority to overturn the false order of corrupt civilization.

- Batman brings justice to cowardly and superstitious criminals, doing for others what he could not do for his murdered parents.
- Storm overcomes the enemies of human- and mutant-kind by wielding nature's untamed power.
- Dr. Gregory House caustically tramples social decencies as he ruthlessly pinpoints the causes of baffling medical conditions.
- Philip Marlowe goes down mean streets, without himself becoming mean.

Where the arc of the dramatic hero offers us the catharsis of tragedy or the uplift of redemption, the restoration of order offered by the iconic hero plays to our primal sense of justice. It is this deeply ingrained impulse toward fairness, and the darker urge for the punishment of wrongdoers, that makes us social animals, and fueled our evolution as a species. Whether they acknowledges the darkness or gloss it away, the pleasure these stories convey takes on a ritualistic quality. It grants vicarious power. It allows us to place ourselves in the shoes, not of a figure who must change or die, but one who wins by staying true to a fundamental self.

Here beats the metaphorical heart of the iconic hero. These stories mirror the everyday struggles of life, as we try to remain true to our best selves in a confusing and pressure-filled world.

The pattern of the dramatic hero is well-studied. It drives the great plays and novels of the literary canon. Filtering from lit classes into creative writing workshops, it has become part of the *lingua franca* of criticism and story collaboration. The iconic hero is a creature of pop culture, born of penny dreadfuls, of pulps and radio plays and comic books and B-movies. He gets his due in academia through the lens of cultural studies, with scant attention paid to the alternative story structure that is his essential root. Hence the vogue for disastrous reboots that hobble classic characters with plodding arcs and unnecessary backstories.

A form that relies so heavily on repetition must be continually renewed and updated to remain vital.

To this end, *The New Hero* challenged fourteen talented writers from disparate creative scenes to invent new iconic heroes and put them through their ritualistic paces in the eternal battle against injustice and disorder.

The wide variety seen in the resulting tales testifies not only to the diversity of their visions, but the capaciousness of the iconic hero formula.

The structural bedrock of the iconic hero story might provide a gateway to a vividly envisioned imaginary world, as it does in Julia Bond Ellingboe's *Ezekiel Saw the Wheel*, set in an American south reeling in the wake of a folkloric apocalypse.

Its formal verities likewise allow the exploration of a distinctive voice. Richard Dansky infuses *The Thirty-Ninth Labor of Reb Palache* with an epic rhythm as inexorable as the sea plied by its battling galleons. In a *Man of Vice*, Peter Freeman channels high Victorian style with a tale of grimly applied justice.

By tackling its structure head on, writers may engage with the classic modes of the pop cultural past. Graeme Davis pays homage to the two-fisted South Seas adventures of yore, and to the wonders of early aviation, in *Against the Air Pirates*. Ed Greenwood embraces his full-throated love of storytelling with his gleefully uninhibited *The Midnight Knight*.

A straight-up hero tale can deliver visceral thrills even as it critiques the uncomfortable elements of the form's past. In *Warrior of the Sunrise*, Maurice Broaddus deploys the tropes and styles of a Robert E. Howard swords and sorcery tale. By casting as his hero an African woman, he upends the racism and sexism that so often mars the tradition he's drawing from. Jonny Nexus, in *On Her Majesty's Deep Space Service*, allows us to enjoy the entitled swagger of his hero, an overconfident upper-cruster, while at the same time wryly jabbing at it. Jeff Tidball likewise adds a twisted perspective to the urban military genre, portraying the hero of *Better Off Not Knowing* as a man with a platoon of voices in his head.

One can see from the range of characters and settings mentioned so far that the iconic hero structure transcends genre trappings. As such, it's a perfect vehicle for the mash-up epoch. Monte Cook demonstrates the principle with his western-informed fantasy tale, *Sundown in Sorrow's Hollow*. Kenneth Hite finds a fresh spin on the alternate history genre with his reality-crossing fugitive hunter, Ray Cazador, in *Bad Beat for Aaron Burr*. The vampire story has broken out from its horror roots to become a genre of its own; Monica Valentinelli's *Fangs and Formaldehyde* delivers the sharp-fanged thrills while showing there are changes left to ring within its boundaries.

As in any fictional form, the heart of an iconic hero story remains the human character. The pathos of Mookie, the sad sack leg-breaker of Chuck Wendig's *Charcuterie* lends an unforgettable emotional solidity to his world of contemporary supernatural menace. Kyla Ward shows how a few deft touches and a lot of mystery can render a character, in this case the smart aleck summoned spirit in *Cursebreaker: The Jikininki and the Japanese Jurist*, instantly memorable. (Kyla's *Cursebreaker* character makes a repeat appearance here, underlining the iconic hero's affinity for serial treatment.)

Authors were asked to tackle the form head on, setting aside parody, ironic riffing, and other forms of premise avoidance. This brings us to our capper, Adam Marek's *The Captain*, which in brilliant and disturbing fashion turns the iconic hero story inside out, while also completely fulfilling it, in a covert and surprising manner.

That's what this book of heroes is all about. Fourteen sparks struck between timeless, primally satisfying tradition and fresh invention.

From the breezy to the mordant, from sunny to pitch-black, our new heroes span moods, modes, and genres. Dive in and you'll find warriors, agents, avengers, and of course the always-obligatory pirate rabbi. On modern city streets, in the space ships of a retro-alternative future, in goblin-haunted fine dining establishments and haunted Japanese hills, they unravel mysteries, rescue the innocent, and dispense bare-knuckled justice.

Never mind the story arcs.

It's time to meet the new heroes.

– Robin D. Laws, Feb 2011

Ezekiel Saw the Wheel

Julia Ellingboe

I know early in the day that something will call on me. I sit on my porch, dressed to the nines in a fiery red suit and button shoes of alligator hide. Not a curl falls out of place, even in the dead dripping heat of the Charleston summer. The sky is blacker than blue, the clouds hover menacingly low. It's just too hot to move, too hot to change into something less formal and confining. Besides, I like to greet my favorite time of night in my finest. Duppies, as the Caribbean immigrants call the spirits that haunt the last sliver of daytime, float about the fog. It is eerily beautiful, like moonlit jellyfish drifting on a sleepy ocean current. Duppies are harmless things, for the most part, but like all haints, it doesn't take much to anger them, and it's difficult to predict what it will take. Sometimes it's a crack in the sidewalk trespassed, other times it's a curious glance and wordless desire tossed carelessly into an alley, or a whistled song imperceptibly out of tune. Tonight it's nothing but complacent duppies. Perhaps I am wrong, no one will call on me, and I dressed up for my own vanity.

I am what the old folks call a Reader. 'Psychic' is the common term, but in the Southern Territories, we're still called Readers. Moreover, I am a Gifted or Touched Reader, born able to read people and catch glimpses of their future, rather than having learned it from playing with divining tools like tea leaves or bones. Most Gifted Readers become Rootswomen or Witchdoctors, some become Charlatans, and others work with such people in order to give the appearance of staying out of trouble. In this day and age, with the world split open, Heaven and Hell in chaos, and the dead walking among us, everyone claims to be a Reader, and the real ones are in high demand. Most gifted Readers have a specialty. Some can read babies, some read animals. I read the dead just as I read the breathing.

In Charleston, everyone's strongly encouraged to attend church to offset the blemish of gambling's sin. Due to a long and intimate association with the Devil, I am banned from all church activities in the Territory of Carolina. I am also banned from the gambling halls, since everyone in Charleston knows my association with the Devil began in a gambling hall. So I am denied access to God's houses and the Devil's playground. No church and no gambling halls make for a lonely Sunday morning and evening. My porch goes vacant on Sunday while my aunt attends church. I miss cards. I'd play hours of canasta—or any card game—if someone deigned to join me.

On the upside, I like this time of evening because no one's actively avoiding me. I savor the hours of sitting out of the eyeshot of scorn. I watch duppies and haints float by in the swirling fog in peace, waiting to read a wayward ghost and direct it to its descendants. That's the idea, at least. No dead thing has stopped to chat in weeks. Now it's late and Aunt Sungila still hasn't come yet. Not one to pass up some juicy and true gossip, I bet she cut out with her friend Opal Teal just after the collection plate passed their laps, and are chatting like brooding hens on Miss Opal's porch. Aunt Sungila might not be home until I'm long in bed. I expect to have the porch to myself as long as I want it.

If I had the appetite, I would finish off that pecan pie she baked this afternoon, but my boredom cares little for food. Instead I shuffle a deck of cards and lay out a spread of Solitaire. After a few rounds, I take off my hat, blow the beads of humidity off the ostrich plume, and lay it next to me. As I lean over to unlace my shoes, a hairpin falls out of my hair and rolls across the porch. I leave it there for now. Hatless, shoeless, I undo the top buttons of my blouse, and hike up my skirt. Comfortable at last and a little vulnerable to scandal and other haints. I'm inviting trouble, I suppose, because nothing else invites me. I close my eyes and listen. There's a lot out there, but nothing wants to talk, wants to be heard, or needs direction except me.

From down the road, a horse trots at a leisurely pace. The fog converts to rain, which bears down on the roof. Something vexes the dog next door. The air smells of the ocean, musty wet porches, and what's that? Chicory and salted pork. A last meal. I open my eyes as a handsome young man's corpse in an old army uniform dismounts a red saddled horse. First Civil War, Confederate. An old one.

'You Ivy Greene?' He says plainly in an old Charleston drawl.

'I am. And you are?'

'Lieutenant Jeremiah Weed.'

A Horseman of Revelation, maybe War given his uniform and red bridled horse. The Horsemen like their whiskey and bourbon so much they take the name of it. He approaches the porch, and looks at the blue steps. Hesitating at first, he taps the step with caution and lets out a laugh like a rattling gourd. 'You fooled me, Miss Ivy. I thought you had built a little moat around your house. Trying to keep us out?'

'How can I help you?' I ask. Even the Horsemen like to be read, so I've heard. Lieutenant Weed takes off his kepi and walks up cautiously, as if he still expects a flood from the blue steps. He stands in front of me. Now he looks imposing. I can smell death on him. The dead and things from Hell don't usually scare me, but he is of grave concern as he towers over me on my porch, and I am shoeless, hatless, and alone.

'I have a message from an old friend,' he chuckles, 'your former paramour.'

It's one thing to have an association with the Devil. Everyone boasts an association with the Devil these days. Even the most sincere churchgoers claim to have met and chatted with him at least once. It's an entirely different matter to have seduced him and proudly walked about the crumbling world on his arm. No good could ever have come from the courtship. Accepting a message from the Devil, delivered by a Horseman of Revelation is a small but not insignificant example. One doesn't quit the Devil easily, with a clean conscience, and no consequences.

I try to keep my eyes on him, but there's something else out there that has yet to reveal itself. Lieutenant Weed runs an invasive dead finger across my jawline. He smells of chicory, salt pork, bourbon, freshly turned grave, and Hell.

'Tell me your message, then go before—' I look back to where Lieutenant Weed once stood, and where three more cavalrymen now sit atop three handsome red-eyed horses. One has a black bridle and the rider is all bones. He holds out a constant, hungry, begging hand. I read 'Famine' from him. Flies swarm around the head of the second man, and putrid, stinking flesh drips from his body. He sits atop a white bridled horse. Pestilence. The third man slumps over a pale horse with no bridle. A continuous stream of blood drips from his limp arm, and a sword sticks straight up from his back. Death.

Lieutenant Weed smiles a rotted tooth grin, and follows my gaze off the porch. He turns back to me and laughs breathlessly. A gold tooth pops out of his mouth and into my lap. He doesn't seem to notice, thankfully, and I brush it into my pocket with the subtlety of a thief. 'That's my cavalry, in case you plan to finish your threat, Madame. Soldiers, meet Miss Ivy Greene. Miss Greene, meet Lieutenants Jim Beam, Jack Daniels, and Elijah Cross.'

I stifle a laugh at their names. They all politely nod, except Lieutenant Cross. Lieutenant Beam keeps his hand out. I run my finger across the grooves of Weed's tooth in my pocket. I give no expression to my face or voice. 'Hello, gentleman. Please tell me your message and leave. I have a long day tomorrow.'

'I'm sure you do, Madame. Your man's in town, and expects you to be his table at the Sunday Driver Bingo Hall tomorrow night.'

'I don't have a man,' I reply, irritated, briefly dropping my poker face. 'And I'm not permitted in any gambling establishment in Carolina Territory, Lieutenant Weed, even if I'm just there to meet someone.'

I stand up, stretching backwards to avoid Weed's groping fingers, then take a step back toward the door. The other Horsemen, now close behind Weed, follow my steps into the house. I read no malice from Lieutenant Weed. I read amusement. I step away faster. I do not wish to mess with an amused Horseman.

'They'll make an exception for you, just this once,' Weed continues. 'You can do something for your city, little lady.' And with that, he slams the butt of his rifle up side my head and knocks me senseless.

Frank and I met at the Sunday Driver Bingo Hall on Market Street. That's how the Devil introduced himself: Frank. The name certainly rolls off the tongue easier than 'Prince of Darkness' or 'The Man Who Waits at the Crossroads'. Lots of women have nice regular guys named Frank, suitable lovers who bring them flowers, rub their feet in the evening, and write bawdy love songs about them. My Frank—the Devil, rather—did those things, too. Naturally he was handsome and soft-spoken, and made no effort to conceal his identity. At the time we met, he was just 'The Devil', a supernatural being who had come to make our lives a little more chaotic. He's got a great public face, and charming as, well, all Hell. Up until a few years ago, few really believed we were in the midst of The End Times, because the agents of Hell and Heaven are so personable.

Frank once mused that New York fell so quickly because when Gabriel came to warn of Armageddon, everyone just wanted to hear him sing and play renditions of Coltrane's 'A Love Supreme' on his trumpet. He told me that he didn't even bother to send Flatterers, demons skilled at stroking the ego, to tempt Gabriel to listen to his fans. He didn't need to. Next thing you know, Gabriel gives up warning people and takes to singing at open mic shows in the East Village. Of course, the Devil is the Prince of Lies, so I take that account with a grain of salt, but it is a reasonable reflection of our times. Demons, ghosts, even angels walk among us and indulge in the whims of the living so much that we just don't take them seriously.

I didn't take his Devil nature seriously at first either. I just wanted to test my gift as a Reader and see if I could read and beat the Devil at cards. Now any Reader worth her salt can cheat the Devil. It takes a special Reader, daring and foolish like me, to charm him and let herself be charmed. I beat Frank in five consecutive rounds of poker, and not through honest means. I read him deeply. I found his vulnerable spot. I read that he was lonely in his mission of destruction, and his loneliness melted something in me. He took a liking to me, and I to him.

Five years in gambling halls all over the Southern Territories, garden parties at his villas in Hell, the scorched beaches of South Texas, even the ruins of Disney-world, those were good times. The fact is, despite being a great boyfriend, the Devil is the Ruler of Hell, and Supreme Leader of Evil and all. And he's the *Devil*. When I introduced the idea of us settling down, taking our relationship to the next level, and perhaps his giving up Armageddon, he tried to steer the conversation to me selling him my soul. I ended the relationship then and there, returned to Charleston to find my Aunt Sungila, and lay my mischief to rest. Aunt Sungila took me on as an apprentice Rootswoman. Honestly, my heart isn't in it, and most breathing people will not let me read them. It's only been a couple of years since the Devil and I split up. People remember seeing us around town together, even though I never did anything wrong, the Devil is a bad crowd.

I come to in the living room, on Aunt Sungila's sofa, just as the clock strikes eleven. Someone has draped an afghan over me, carefully folded my spectacles, and put them on the coffee table. Has the Devil been here? It doesn't feel like it. I lay under the afghan, staring at Sungila's herb shelf over in the kitchen, my heart full of regret. If my head didn't hurt so much, I'd get up and make some lavender tea. I'm the Pariah of Charleston, but the Devil wants me bad enough to send the Horsemen of the Apocalypse to invite me to dinner. I fall asleep troubled, lonelier than ever. Readers often go crazy because we distance ourselves from people. I've heard that before the End Times, few people believed Readers, psychics, telepaths, whatever we were called, could read heads. These days, folks believe alright. Folks believe and don't fault me for my Gift.

They fault me for keeping the wrong company. I was the Devil's girlfriend when the mountains swallowed Asheville, Knoxville, and the Eastern Territories lost contact with the West. The distancing works both ways in my case.

Aunt Sungila wakes me up some hours later. I open my eyes cautiously. I feel her eyes boring holes into my forehead, where Lieutenant Weed's rifle must have left an ugly mark. She looks displeased. As I sit up she hands me an ice pack.

'Put that on your head, Ivy.' She instructs flatly. 'Looks like you had a party here last night.'

'No ma'am.' Confused, as I put the ice pack on my head, I scan the room to see what gives her the idea I had a party. Sure as day, while the parlor looks tidy, on the table I spy several stacks of poker chips, and bottles of Elijah Cross, Jack Daniels, Jim Beam, and, naturally, Jeremiah Weed on the table. Strewn all over the floor is a deck of playing cards with a black fiddle on their backs. They knocked the daylights out of me, and then drank whiskey and played cards at my parlor table? Classy.

'Auntie, you know I—'

She holds her finger to her mouth and turns to the kitchen. I hear nothing. She looks back at me and her eyes narrow. 'You're gonna be late for work, child.' She pulls the afghan off of me. 'Get your shoes and your hat and get on! Keep the ice on your head to keep down the swelling.'

'But I need to change my clothes.'

'No, you don't!' She shouts with fire in her voice. 'No time. If you lose that job, I'll see to it that you spend the next ten years in the Georgia Penal Colony. You put me in danger by bringing folks here for what I'm sure you thought was a harmless game of poker or euchre, or whatever it is you play.'

Stunned, I fasten my shoes, straighten my blouse, button my jacket, and run out the door with Sungila sweeping a broom at my heels. It's not until I'm just about to the harbor do I realize that not only did I forget the ice pack, but that Aunt Sungila's neck was bare. She always wears a mojo hand with a trick to prevent me from digging in her head. I'd read her if I could. The Sungila who shooed me out of her house was not the real Sungila.

Aunt Sungila, confident in my Gift and concerned that idle hands might lead me to mischief, helped me get a job working for the Harbor Patrol. They needed someone to read the influx of dead immigrants and refugees. And Laverne Archer, the Head Reader, is married to the preacher at Aunt Sungila's church. Giving me a job was a compromise for not having to let me into church.

As I walk to work, I think about the few things I've wondered about Aunt Sungila. First, she's often gone over night. Second, it's not the first time I've seen a Sungila I didn't believe to be the real Sungila, even though she gives off an inner psychic impression of Sungila. Third, Sungila looks the same as she does in photos taken before I was born, before the world split open. She hasn't aged in thirty years at least, and I have no idea how old she is. The worry fades some. Whatever posed as Sungila back at the house probably got me out of there for my own good. That's all I need to know for now. I'm used to not knowing much about Aunt Sungila, and probably better off not knowing.

A few years ago I used my gift at the poker table. Now I use it to inspect ships for haints, hags, and plat-eyes (incorrectly called zombies up North.) On occasion, I read breathing passengers, and Aunt Sungila has me read her clients when she can't figure out what's going on with them. Rather, I read the ones who will let me. At the Harbor Patrol, the breathing are the least of our worries, though. The dead come, with alarming frequency, to settle old scores, open old wounds, or to engage in their tricky side and mess with folks. Some angry and nasty old things, now nastier and angrier than when they first came here, creep the streets of Charleston, hell-bent on breaking down what the living try to hold together as the world crumbles. The silence of these past few weeks gives no comfort.

Despite the abundance of dead in the city, most believe that Charleston won't fall anytime soon. Everyone and everything loves to gamble apparently. We have plenty of gambling establishments to keep the peace, and enough Conjurers to protect the living and banish the unruly dead. New Orleans thrives for similar reasons. Demons, ghosts, nameless horrors from Hell all play cards, and will set aside their mission to destroy the world if they can sit at a table and throw a few chips in the pot. All the breathing of Charleston, Gifted or otherwise, hold the world together with gambling, magic, and an uneasy acceptance that they share the town with the dead.

I arrive to work disheveled and wrinkled, even under my suit. I am a shameful sight. I sulk to my desk and look over the list of today's arrivals. Nothing much. A passenger ship from Jamaica, likely full of duppies and breathing refugees from a hurricane that tore up Kingston last week.

'You're late, Ivy, and inappropriately dressed.' Laverne Archer, the Head Reader, snaps as she walks in. She's late, too, but it's probably unwise to mention it.

'Yes, I know, Laverne.' I answer. 'My Aunt didn't return home last night from church and I stayed up waiting for her.'

'Really? And did she beat you for asking too many questions about her whereabouts?' Laverne reaches for my face where Weed's rifle met my head. I draw back. I read that she found out I was late by 'practicing' on the receptionist. Laverne's not very good at reading, not particularly smart, but she's sneaky. She needs to touch people to even read the surface of someone's mind. She's honest enough to know I'm a better Reader than she is, so I interview most of the arrivals, even the live ones, while Laverne files, bosses me around, and gossips about me to the other people in the office.

'Oh, that. No.' I catch and hold her gaze, and float the impression that something terrible has happened and I'm not ready to talk, but I'm probably easy to read if caught off guard. 'That's not important. It'll go away in a few days.'

'Uh huh,' she replies. She'll try to grab my arm in a couple of hours, I'm certain, and leave a greasy fried chicken hand print on my jacket. I wish I liked Laverne Archer. I wish we could be friends, since she's the only other Reader I see on a regular basis, even if she's not a good one. I wish she'd share some gossip with me, or invite me to her weekly bridge game and share the recipe for her chocolate cake that she brings to the Harbor Patrol office on people's birthdays.

After two hours of searching for busywork, not a single vessel drops her anchor and releases her passengers. The radios are still down from the hurricane, and the shipping lanes have been off for the past week. The Harbor Master pops in at some point, and even he is unconcerned. I spend a while in the ladies' room in front of the mirror, fretting about the angry bruise on my head from Lieutenant Weed's rifle butt. I know I'll see Frank soon, and against my better judgment, I'd like to look my best. Then again, Frank's man inflicted it. I feel foolish.

At noon, I ask Laverne with some reluctance if she wants to get some lunch at the farmer's market. She eagerly agrees, until I look her dead in the eye and say, 'I ain't telling you nothing, and if you so much as flick a mosquito off my shoulder, I'll put a picture in that busy head of yours so horrific, you won't sleep for a month. And you know they say I lived in Hell. It might be true. I've seen things only the damned see.'

Laverne glares at me, but agrees to find lunch without calling my bluff. I can't plant anything in anyone's head, and she probably knows that. Maybe she wants to know something else.

'People would probably like you more, Ivy, if you didn't follow up your politeness with ugliness,' she says in a falsely friendly tone.

As we walk down the boardwalk, Laverne greets nearly every person we pass. She asks about one woman's baby who's been sick. She inquires about people she hasn't seen at church lately. A few folks politely, uncomfortably greet me. One man tells Laverne that he'll reveal some auspicious and important news when she's not busy. I read him quickly. He got a dog. Several people think 'why's Laverne with her'? Or 'Miss Sungila should just stop pushing her niece on fine people like Laverne Archer.'

As we sit in the park across from the harbor, Laverne says quietly, 'I saw your auntie leave church with Opal Teal last night. I was late today because Magpie Williams stopped me on my way to work and told me Opal didn't come home last night. What did Miss Sungila say when she came home?'

'She threw me out of the house.' I want to tell her all of it, the way I would if we were friends, about the Horsemen, and how a Sungila who wasn't quite Sungila put an ice pack on my head and shooed me out the door, but as I'm about to start in on the whole story, Laverne's eyes widen and she looks past me, out to the docks.

'Oh,' she gasps. She snaps back to my face in terror. We feel it at the same time. A thousand or more single eyes fix on us. I turn around. Plat-eyes. Row upon row of plat-eyes drag themselves out of the ocean. Plat-eyes shuffle down the cobblestone streets. Plat-eyes stuff food into their gaping maws as cart merchants abandon their wares.

The alarms sound, warning the breathing folks of Charleston of the invasion of plat-eyes. Before the world started to crumble, parents told their children to stay out of the swamps and other bad, dark places, lest the plat-eyes make a meal of them. Plat-eyes, decomposed bodies of people or animals with one single eye that hangs out of a dead socket by a bloody sinew, never appeared anywhere other than in stories, and never appeared in droves as platoons of the Devil. They are hard to kill, impossible to read because they don't think in readable ways, and exist solely to eat the breathing and flatten cities.

I stand enthralled as the plat-eye horde shifts from random mayhem to form organized rows of one-eyed monsters that march towards us. Laverne looks at me with vicious anger. 'Did you invite some friends from Hell, Ivy Greene?' She yells.

'Shh!' Laverne, not particularly smart, calls me by my full name. All the plat-eyes swing around and look at us. At me, really. No one moves, but Laverne continues. She grabs my arms, holds and reads, and shoves me to the ground.

'You're nothing but trouble, Ivy. And you know, no one likes you because you think you're better than we are, not because of some rumor that you probably started about being the Devil's girlfriend. The Devil's got girlfriends in every city left. He's a dog, you know. Being his girlfriend is nothing to be proud of. It's nothing special. And you know what else? I wish we could be friends, too, Ivy Greene, but I would hate to get my greasy fried chicken fingers on your pristine Hell's Whore suit and ruin it!' A plat-eye puts its bony hand on her shoulder and she runs away screaming.

At that, a few of the plat-eyes chuckle. It sounds more like dry beans in a can than laughter. I don't look at them. I keep my eyes on the ground, hoping they'll forget about me in my humiliation, and go back to terrorizing until I can gather my wits and run home. Or somewhere else. Their chuckling and moaning grows louder.

They're multiplying, coming in from the ocean and the swamps. I count to twenty to give my courage time to show up. Instead, a white doeskin gloved hand reaches down to help me to my feet.

It's Frank. I stand unaided.

Now the Devil, if nothing else good about him exists, is a vision of beauty. His skin is as black as espresso (his favorite drink), with malachite green eyes, soft hands with long manicured pianist's fingers, a wide pearly toothed smile. He's almost too pretty and boyish. He sports a carefully trimmed and pointed goatee with flecks of steel gray. He keeps his cloven hooves well-trimmed and filed. Excessively proud of his obviously devilish features, his horns shine and a black silk bow adorns his tail. Pride is one of his favorite sins, vanity comes in a close second. I came to appreciate the care he took not to gouge my eyes when we kissed. The tail I never got used to, but I assumed there would have been something else unsettling, like poor table manners or a former lover's name tattooed on his forearm that I could never abide if he were a man. When we were together, he kept his hair short and slicked back with a peculiar smelling pomade he claimed was just olive oil, vetiver, and sandalwood, but I also pick up undertones of lemongrass and rotten bananas.

Today he wears a crimson suit, impeccably tailored, a crisp white shirt I suspect is woven lotus. He wears a black rose boutonniere with a spray of Baby's Breath. If you stand close enough to the flowers, you can hear babies gasping for air, even over the blaring alarm. He's barehooved. His hair is long and curly, and he wears it neatly tied in a ponytail of four well-oiled coils. I smell the pomade. He hasn't changed much. His goatee is a bit grayer, which seems odd given that he's the Devil, a fallen angel, immortal. I assume he's trying a new look or making a statement. Frank runs a bare hand over the bruise.

'You're looking out of sorts, my lady,' he says in a soft baritone.

'I've been better,' I reply. I look around. The plat-eyes now stare at us as the breathing folks of Charleston flood the streets. They head for the shelters designated for supernatural attacks: churches and gambling halls, so they can get right with God, or make deals with the Devil's representatives. 'What's this all about, Frank?'

Frank offers me his arm. 'I've just missed you. Let's walk.'

I gesture angrily at the plat-eyes, who stand at attention behind us in endless rows that span to the harbor. Frank sighs. 'Don't worry, Ivy. Once we finish our business, depending on what you do, they'll either eat Charleston or go back to Hell.' He offers me his arm again. I walk without taking it.

The Sunday Driver Bingo Hall is a few blocks from the harbor. Hundreds of years ago, at the height of the slave trade, the building was the point of entry and sale for thousands of souls, so of course it's haunted. About ten years ago, a group of Rootswomen managed to guide most of the haints to resolution, but a few still lurk. It's considered lucky if one acknowledges you. One of them blocks our way and points an incorporeal finger at me. He whispers in my head, 'What's in your pocket?' I'd forgotten about Lieutenant Weed's gold tooth. Frank looks at me puzzled. 'He wished me luck,' I say as the haint moves aside and lets us in.

The living and dead fill every table in the place, except one, and more breathing folk pour in behind us. Our table, where we first played, is empty. As we walk through the hall, all attention turns to us. The Horsemen, even Death, Lieutenant Elijah Cross, stand at attention behind the obviously terrified dealer. Lieutenant Weed tips his hat at me. 'I think Jeremiah has taken a liking to you, Ivy,' Frank says grinning proudly as he draws back a chair for me. 'You have way of attracting chaos, and he likes that.'

I smile coyly at Lieutenant Weed and take a deep breath of confidence. 'What are we playing today, Frank?'

'I thought we'd play Blackjack.'

My favorite game. 'What are we playing for?' I ask.

'What do you have in mind?' Frank counters. He wants me to ante up my soul, but a strict metaphysical rule prohibits him from asking for it directly.

'Well, I haven't played cards in a couple of years. I'm sure you're aware that I'm barred from entering the Bingo Hall. I'd like to prolong the time, and get in a few games before you push me to put my soul on the table.' Frank leans in expectantly. What do I have that he wants? He wonders. I fish around in my pocket, squirming and struggling for dramatic effect before I pull out Lieutenant

Weed's gold tooth and slam it on the table. 'A gold tooth. First Civil War Era. Now I'm no antiques expert, but I think it might fetch a good price.'

Frank laughs. 'Okay, Miss Ivy. I've got all night—'

'That's mine!' Bellows Lieutenant Weed. 'She can't wager my tooth! It doesn't belong to her.'

I don't look at Lieutenant Weed. I don't need to look at him to read the same amusement I read from him last night.

Frank turns slowly towards the Horseman, 'Oh come on, Jeremiah.'

'No! It's my tooth! She can't bet something that doesn't belong to her.'

'Well, how did she get it?'

'I certainly didn't steal it,' I say, looking at Frank. 'You don't think I reached into his mouth and grabbed it, do you?'

Frank smiles.

Anger, amusement, and a twinge of affection well up in Jeremiah Weed. 'She's a tricky one. She's got you wrapped around her pinkie finger.' Certainly the Horseman of War would love to pick and join in a good, if not, pretty fight.

'She does not,' Frank protests.

Lieutenant Cross, Death, speaks up in a shivery, wanting voice, spraying blood with each word. 'Then why are we here, Frank? Let's be honest. We're here because she dumped you and you can't let it go.'

'I love her! She belongs with me!' Frank rants. All eyes turn to The Devil. I look away, embarrassed, and feeling a little sorry for him. The Devil's not supposed to love anyone or anything. In the years we were together we never exchanged those holy words, and as much as I wanted, I never expected to hear them. I can read him loud and clear. Absence has warmed his heart.

'You've gone soft, Frank,' Lieutenant Beam whispers.

'I told you three hundred years ago, no more wars over women,' Weed says. 'We're outta here, boys.'

Lieutenant Beam throws Cross over his shoulder and walks out. Lieutenant Daniels shuffles behind them. I stand in front of Lieutenant Weed and offer him his tooth. 'Keep it,' he snaps, smiling. 'You'll just owe me.' He tips his hat at me and touches my forehead. 'I'm real sorry about that, Miss Greene. You know, you really are a sweetheart. You could do better. And, by the by, red becomes you.' He nods at Frank, and follows the Horsemen out the door.

I sit down again. I stare at Frank, Frank stares at the table, chewing on his bottom lip, rubbing his left horn. Neither us knows what to say. What is there to say? Finally, I put my hand on Frank's shoulder. 'Just stay out of Charleston, at least for a few years. Do that for me?'

'Fine. I need to regroup anyway.' He leaves, his tail swaying defiantly behind him.

He has gone soft. I pick up the deck of cards and shuffle it. I don't want to leave and lose a chance to play cards again. Someone here might have heard that I told the Devil to leave Charleston. Some of the folks here believe that.

A young man opens the door and announces that the plat-eyes have retreated, led back to an old warship by a dapper man in a fine suit. The room lets out a collective sigh of relief, and they return to their business.

I motion to invite a couple of the bystanders from the bar to join me. I may not get a chance to enter the Sunday Driver Bingo Hall for a long time, especially if Laverne Archer tells everyone that the plat-eye attack was my fault. I hand the cards back to the dealer. 'What are we playing this afternoon?' He asks.

'H.O.R.S.E.'

Better Off Not Knowing

Jeff Tidball

'I love these greasy spoons.'
John Squad stood in the parking lot of a crappy little diner near the edge of town, taking the last drag off a cigarette and wincing at the voice.

'And I'm starving.'

There was no one else with him in the parking lot. The cab he'd come in was already pulling back out into the road. The voice was in his head.

'You're always starving,' came another voice, a deeper one, *'and you can't eat any more than any of us, so why don't you can it, Puppydog.'*

'Nobody's eating anything,' said Squad out loud, throwing his cigarette down and grinding it out.

The voices knew that tone, and they shut up. Squad went inside.

◇

No surprise it was a crappy little diner inside, too.

The girl Squad was looking for, Becky, was sitting in the corner near the kitchen. She was maybe just legal to drink—maybe just. Small girl, with long hair, dishwater blonde, looking at a video on her phone.

'Guy in the green looks like a greasebag, chief.'

Squad looked left without moving his head while he crossed toward Becky. The guy was looking out the front window, maybe trying a little too hard not to be looking at Squad.

'Could be,' Squad thought back. He stepped up to Becky's table.

'Mr. Squad?' she said.

He nodded just once while he grabbed her backpack off the table. He inclined his head to say she should head into the kitchen.

'I thought we were going to—' she started to say, but Squad cut her off, shaking his head.

Becky started to stand, grabbing her phone. Squad threw a glance back over his shoulder at the guy with the green jacket. He was still looking out the front window.

'Uh-oh, chief.'

'What?'

'He's looking at us.'

'He's looking out the window,' Squad objected.

'He's watching our reflection.'

'We're going out the back,' Squad said to Becky, steering with a light hand on her arm.

'But aren't we—?' she started to say, but Squad broke in:

'We'll talk somewhere else.'

In the kitchen, the short order cook glanced up at them, bobbing his head in time with the music in his earbuds as they passed through.

'Why?' asked Becky.

'People know where we are.'

They came out the back door of the restaurant into the gravel parking lot. There was a dumpster next to the door. It stank of grease.

'Like who?'

'Restaurant full of people for one. Rabbit for another.'

'Isn't Rabbit a friend of yours?'

'He's a guy I owe a favor.'

'Am I going to owe you a favor, when this is over?'

'Maybe. You have a car?'

Becky pointed at a Crown Victoria, a retired taxi cab, parked near the edge of the lot.

'A *Crown Vic, sergeant!*' came a deep voice, enthusiastic. '*I used to*—'

'Shut up,' said Squad.

'I didn't say anything,' shot back Becky. She turned back toward the restaurant suddenly, saying, 'I've gotta go back inside and drop a five on the table. They're going to think I ran off.'

'Be quiet,' said Squad, stopping her from going back inside with a firm grip on her bicep while cocking his head to listen. '*What's that noise?*' he asked. Becky only saw him cock his head, squint his eyes, and concentrate.

All was quiet, inside and out, for a long beat. Becky got bored, pulled her arm out of Squad's grip, and started across the parking lot.

'*That's the mains hum, sergeant,*' came the deep-voiced verdict. '*The sound's too low, though,*' he added. '*That's probably why we can hear it. Band-stop filter isn't damping it down all the way.*'

'Whenever you're done staring at the sky,' said Becky, halfway across the lot, 'you can let me know where we're headed.' Squad looked over at her.

'*Hey, is that a dead squirrel on the back of her car?*'

Sure enough, a squirrel, stone dead, on the trunk of the Crown Vic.

'Don't touch the car!' Squad shouted as Becky reached for the handle. She jerked her hand back as Squad charged for her.

Squad grabbed Becky by the arm, yanked her back toward the kitchen door at an all-out run. She shrieked, a sound that overlapped a gunshot and the explosion of the car's driver-side window.

Becky screamed. Squad nearly lifted her into the air as he dragged her back to the dumpster. He tossed her behind it, taking cover himself, already holding the worn black M1911A1 he'd carried for damn near twenty years.

'Wh—?' Becky began, but a bullet punched into the dumpster and zanged into the wall of the restaurant. The query ended in another scream.

'Did anybody see the shooter?' Squad asked, peeking his head around the dumpster to try to get a clear view.

'You didn't exactly keep the headlights pointed at the road.'

Squad jerked his head back as another round kerranged off the dumpster.

'Muzzle flash on top of the school across the road.'

'Good work, kid,' thought Squad. Squad stuck his head back around again and saw, sure enough, somebody lying up there with a rifle.

'Let's take him out,' came the kid's voice again.

'You gotta be kidding me, Puppydog. That's fifty yards from here.' Squad.

'I could hit him.' The kid.

'Well you don't run the arms anymore, do you?' Commentary from the peanut gallery.

'Shut up,' muttered Squad.

'Why do you keep saying that?!' shrieked Becky. 'I'm not saying anything!'

Squad took a deep breath. 'You seem to be in some pretty deep business, Becky,' he said. He glanced over at her. She was terrified, shaking, but even so, keeping it together remarkably well considering who she was—a small-city kid all of 21, give or take a year.

'You're gonna help me, right?' Becky asked.

Squad didn't answer right away. She started to panic, then, on top of being scared.

'Of course we are, chief.'

'Yeah,' Squad said, barely audible, a little annoyed.

Out of nowhere Becky screamed again. John jerked around and followed her eyes to the green jacket coming out the kitchen door with a 9mm in his hand. As the guy extended the gun John dropped him, two in the chest and one in the head, the Mozambique Drill. The guy fell in the doorway, propping the screen door.

'You think there's a third one, chief? Or can we make a run for the tree line in the vacant lot and keep the restaurant between us and our friend on the roof until we're out of here?

Squad thought about that. He turned to Becky. 'You pretty quick?'

'Pretty motivated,' she said, breathing hard.

'You see those trees?' Squad pointed. She nodded. The empty lot was about twenty yards off. 'Then I'm gonna count to three and then you're gonna run for that tree line as fast as you can. Ready?'

She nodded, getting her feet underneath her.

Squad got ready to throw some bullets in the other direction while she fixed her eyes on the tree line.

'One… two…'

Twenty years ago, John Squad enlisted in the United States Army.

Eight years ago, Sergeant Squad's unit was sent on a top-secret mission that went worse than bad, further than south, more crooked than sideways. The extraction force never came and Squad's men were gunned down to the last, on the run through a Central American jungle. All except Squad.

When Squad came to, the voices of his men lived on, inside his head.

'Never leave a man behind,' they say.

That's a mixed bag of advice.

Five minutes later, John and Becky were on a city bus headed in the direction it was going when they saw it. Using the restaurant as cover had done the trick, gotten them out of harm's way. Out of its immediate way, anyway.

They were sitting in the back, a seat between them.

'So who'd want to electrocute your car, Becky? And failing at that, gun you down in a parking lot?' Squad spoke low, which made his voice sound like gravel rolling downhill in a mason jar.

'These...' she looked for the word in Squad's eyes '...criminals, I guess. These mobsters.'

'Assume I have no idea what you're talking about.'

'Because we don't have any idea what you're talking about.' Dutch Harms. In life, a machine-gunner, ordnance expert, demolitions guy. Also, a wiseass and a womanizer.

She started again, cheeky this time: 'Hi, I'm Becky. It's nice to meet you, Mr. Squad.'

'Cute.'

She told the story straight, though: 'I live with my mom and my baby son. I'm taking journalism at the community college. I did an interview—a practice thing for class, you know?—with this guy at the prosecutor's office and I see a file open on his desk while he was in the john. I read some of it. Why not? The next week these... these goons came around the house, asking what did I think I was doing, did I think I was pretty smart, you know? They said their boss sent them over to make sure I knew I'd better keep what I saw to myself. I was scared they were going to come back and hurt Jakey. Rabbit said he knew someone he thought might be able to help. I—' Becky suddenly choked on a sob— 'They weren't trying to *kill* me... before today.'

Squad grunted, to indicate he'd heard all of that. He looked out the window.

'Ask her what she read in the file.' The quiet voice of Jeremy 'Fax' Steinmeyer, the tight-lipped guy from Intelligence who hardly ever said anything, before he died or since.

'Does it matter?' Thom O'Brien. Squad's corporal, to whom John owed his life a dozen times. The philosophical one, Squad's conscience. It wasn't a challenge; O'Brien honestly wanted to know whether it mattered.

'*I'm pretty sure I don't want to know,*' said Squad, '*unless one of you guys is volunteering to get out and make some room up there.*'

Silence.

Squad turned back away from the window. As far as Becky knew, he hadn't done anything more than look outside for a minute.

'You're going to have to get out of town,' he said.

'What, go on the run? I have a baby.'

'Where's he?'

'With my mom.'

'And she's how you know Rabbit?'

'He's my mom's boyfriend.'

'*I'm with the sergeant,*' said Jim Cragg, a deep-voiced technical guy—apparently a Crown Vic enthusiast—who had called John's Humvee a Warthog until the day he died. '*It's time for her and the family to pack it up.*'

'*It hardly seems fair,*' said Harms, '*for the pretty girl to leave town because of some greasebag mobster's bad behavior.*'

'*If she's going to stay, what about the leverage angle?*' said Thom.

'We're going to need some leverage,' said Squad to Becky. 'You have some paper?'

Becky produced a pad from her backpack.

'Write down whatever it is that you know that got you in this trouble. Whatever it is you read in the file.'

'Right now?'

'Depends on how long you want to ride this bus.'

◇

'*Can we get a smoke in here?*'

Squad absently lit one as he walked down a trash-strewn downtown street, stinking steam rising from the sewer grates. He stopped and looked up at the brick building to his left, squinting.

It hadn't taken him long to track down Jerzy Polowski, although he'd been annoyed to have to go through the exercise.

On the other hand, his vast cynicism was built from a thousand other older little bricks that were each some inconvenience or annoyance, the functional equivalent of Becky knowing enough to put her on a hit list but not knowing enough to give him an address for the local boss who apparently wanted her dead.

Squad stepped over to the building, peered through the dusty windows of an apparently deserted warehouse.

'Phones, mister,' said a junkie, approaching Squad with a massive starter jacket wrapped around his skeleton.

'Get out of my face,' Squad growled.

The junkie recoiled and retreated.

'When are you gonna get a cell phone?' Cragg demanded. *'Pay phones are for throwbacks.'*

'Throwback,' said Squad. *'I like the sound of that.'*

Squad reached up to grab the bottom rung of a dangling fire escape ladder.

'Doesn't bother you, does it, Jim? Me being a throwback?'

Cragg groaned.

'Later on I'm gonna step on a computer and set an answering machine on fire. What's that other word you like, Jim?'

'Luddite,' Puppydog said helpfully.

'Yeah, Luddite,' said Squad. *'I'm a Luddite throwback. And the next time I see a one of those smug punk kids with a smartphone, I'm gonna…'*

Squad scaled the ladder, giving Cragg shit all the way up.

◇

'Ouch!' complained Jerzy Polowski, again, as Squad shoved the barrel of his .45 into the mobster's head a second time.

Jerzy was sitting at a desk in a back room of the warehouse, both of his hands in the air. Sneaking past Jerzy's muscle had been an exercise in embarrassing ease.

'Is he really gonna make you say it again, boss?'

'Can the commentary while the chief's working, specialist.'

'Her name is Becky,' said Squad slowly and clearly, 'and if you don't leave her alone, everything that's written here on this piece of paper is going to get really, widely, publicly public. Are you hearing me? If Becky should happen to catch so much as a half-waft of the B.O. drifting off one of your goon's overripe asses, the newspaper and the city attorney and the President of These United States are all going to know all of this.'

Jerzy turned his head, looked at him blankly, although not without pique. 'Give me the paper,' he said.

Squad extended it, keeping the gun leveled at his head.

The mobster unfolded the ragged paper, torn from a spiral-bound notebook, and squinted while he read.

'The hell does "Certain damning evidence contained in file 10016 at the prosecutor's office" mean?' Jerzy said the Squad. 'The hell is "Lawrence Sootin, esquire"?' Jerzy focused on Squad's handgun for a brief second and added, 'All due respect.'

'*You should have read the letter,*' said Fax.

A moment later, Squad was on Jerzy's desk phone with Becky, still holding the mobster at gunpoint.

'I'm here with your Mr. Polowski,' said Squad into the mouthpiece. 'He's telling me he doesn't know anything about what you wrote down here. It's a little bit of a problem, Becky.'

'*This punk's lying,*' said the kid. Raymond Stiles. They called him Puppydog to jerk him around, because once upon a time, it had gotten a reaction. He didn't know a damn thing, but back when the kid had still been a kid, he could put a bullet through an engagement ring at a full klick. '*Shoot out his knee, see what he says then.*'

'Polowski?' said Becky.

'Everybody on the street agrees that this guy I'm talking to right here, Jerzy Polowski, runs the local rackets,' said Squad. 'And you told me that the boss is the one who sent his goons after you.'

'No, that's Guido. The file was about this guy, Guido Haczyk.'

'*What kind of name is "Guido Haczyk"?*'

'*Shut up.*'

Squad covered the mouthpiece and turned back to Jerzy. 'What does the name "Guido Haczyk" mean to you?'

'One of my lieutenants. What's it to you?' Again, a glance at the gun. 'All due respect.'

'You should really have read that letter.'

'Keep poking me about it, motherfucker!' Squad shouted back at Fax, his rage reverberating off the inside of his skull.

'Is there any other critical news I ought to know, Becky?' asked Squad into the phone, terse.

'I don't think so.'

'Are you sure?'

After a long beat of silence, she said 'Is it important whether I told anyone else about this stuff?'

Squad sighed. Another little brick. Someday he was going to build a castle out of them, and go inside, and everybody was going to leave him the hell alone.

'Yeah, Becky. That might be kind of important.'

'Alright, uh— alright. Hang on a sec, I've got to go out into the garage, Jakey's crying.' Squad waited a moment, could hear Becky handing off the baby. After a moment, she started talking again: 'I know this guy from school, Leon.'

'Let me guess, a Polish guy,' said Cragg.

'He's kind of sketchy,' she continued, oblivious to the commentary track.

'Get right out,' said Cragg.

'There was some stuff in the file that I didn't understand. Some slang, some stuff about, you know, crimes. I thought Leon would be able to help me understand it.'

'Uh-huh,' said Squad. Squad turned to Jerzy. 'Guy name of Leon work for you?'

'One of Guido's, kind of a fag. Wants to be a writer or whatever.'

Squad was about to say something else back into the phone when a short, surprised shriek came out of it and then a hushed, horrified, 'Oh my god,' and then the line was quiet.

'Becky?' said Squad. 'Becky?'

'That's not good.'

'What's going on?' asked Jerzy, wary.

'What just happened, boss?'

'Becky?'

'They're here,' Becky whispered into the phone. 'They're at the house! Those mob guys, and they're with the guy from the file. They've got guns, and— My god, I have to go, Jakey and my mom are—'

'Where are you?' Squad hissed.

'In the garage.' Still whispering.

'Can you get out?'

Becky sobbed once then choked it off.

'Get out, Becky.'

Silence for a long moment.

'Becky, can you get away?'

'Yes.'

'Do it.'

'I can hear Jakey crying,' her voice was small as a dormouse a thousand miles away.

'You've got to get her out of there, boss. If she loses it, she's going to—'

Squad said to Becky, 'Jakey needs you to live. If you go in the house, you're dead. Jakey needs you to live. Leave the house.'

'Ok,' said Becky finally.

'You said your mom's house was in Cloverdale. I'm going to meet you at whatever McDonald's is closest to your house. Are you leaving the house?'

The line went dead.

Over the next sixty seconds Squad said things like 'This fuckhole Leon,' and 'No, right this instant!' and '...faster than you've ever driven this top-heavy piece of shit in your life.'

Jerzy's SUV tore into the lot. Becky was standing next to the massive post that held up the golden arches, leaning on it like she lacked the strength to stand on her own. She was wretched, her face a red, demolished mess of regret and terror.

Jerzy had come around to an intense interest in knowing why a file in the prosecutor's office was full to the brim of one of his lieutenants.

Squad jumped out of the truck before it came to a stop, running across the parking lot, scanning the area for danger.

'*Nothing, boss. It's clear.*'

Squad reached out his hand to Becky, who was sobbing openly at his arrival.

'They h-h-h-have…' she started, but couldn't finish. Squad took her hand and pulled her back toward the SUV.

'It's going to be okay,' he said. 'We know how to deal with shitbags.'

◇

Becky balked at getting into the SUV when she saw Leon inside. He was riding up front, with Jerzy in the back and one of Jerzy's goons behind the wheel.

'They're going to help us,' Squad said to Becky, and demonstrated his surety by climbing in first, taking the middle seat on the back bench and holding out his hand to help her up.

She hesitated. Squad barreled ahead: 'Jerzy is Guido's boss. He's not any happier that Guido's apparently planning to turn state's evidence than Guido is that you know he's going to do it. Get in, Becky.'

Becky blinked.

'*She can't process that in her state,*' said Thom gently. Squad took a frustrated breath, doing his best to swallow his impatience.

'This truck is going to where Guido has your baby. When it gets there, Jerzy is going to kill Guido. Are you alright with that?'

Becky climbed into the truck.

◇

The SUV rolled into the alley behind the drug store where Leon had told them that Guido holed up when he needed to lay low.

Leon looked sick, which is how he'd looked ever since Jerzy had exploded into the room where Leon had been working on a laptop and let loose a fusillade of Polish. He then proceeded to empty a clip of 9mm ammunition into the computer and the table it was sitting on while Leon rolled frantically backward on his second-hand office chair and barfed into his own lap. Shooting up the laptop had pushed Jerzy a notch up the sensibility scale, as far as Squad was concerned.

'If this one moves,' Jerzy said to his driver, indicating Leon, 'kill him.' Driver nodded. Jerzy slid out of the car.

'You stay here,' Squad said to Becky, and followed Jerzy out.

Squad came around the SUV's open tailgate, where Jerzy tossed him an M16. As he reflexively caught the weapon, Squad grinned, a shy thing he immediately tucked back inside the scowl whose outlines made up the more permanent definition of his face.

Jerzy was popping the clip on his own assault rifle, checking the rounds inside and slapping it back in place.

Squad slid the proffered weapon back into the truck to a cacophony of protest— *'Oh, man!' 'No!' 'C'mon, boss!'*—from inside his head.

'I'm good with this,' Squad said, sliding his beat-up army-issue from his waistband.

Jerzy shrugged and shut the tailgate as Becky came around the back of the truck, a monument of determined motherhood.

'I've seen that look before, boss,' said Harms.

'Get back in the truck,' said Squad.

'Are you planning to get my baby back with those?' she asked, looking pointedly at the guns.

'Get back in the truck, woman!' said Jerzy. 'We will take care of this!'

'*She has a point, sergeant,*' said Thom. '*We don't know what's inside that place. You can't establish a perimeter by yourself. Especially while you're keeping your other eye on this loose cannon mobster.*'

'*Although we realize he's your new Luddite best buddy,*' added Cragg.

Squad looked over at Jerzy. 'Get Leon.'

A moment later Squad, Jerzy, Leon, and Becky were wedged into the alcove where the back door of a coffee shop on the next block gave a good view of the drug store's side door, where a black F150 was parked that both Leon and Jerzy had confirmed was Guido's.

Leon had his cell phone pressed to his ear. It was ringing.

'It's, uh, Leon,' he finally said into the handset. 'I, uh— we've got a problem.'

He listened to the tirade of response for a moment, tried to break in, gave up under the avalanche. Jerzy finally reminded Leon of the M16 concealed inside his jacket and Leon found renewed religion about wedging a word in edgewise.

'Look,' Leon blurted, 'Jerzy found out about the arrangement, and there's some more, but I don't want to tell you on the cell.'

Silence. Then some decidedly cranky Polish.

'*Colorful,*' commented Cragg.

Into the phone, Leon said 'I, ah…' He looked like he wanted to die. Jerzy gave him a look. 'I can't get away right now,' he said. 'Is there any way you can meet me?'

The string of obscenity that flew out of the phone suddenly jumped across the street as Guido came out the side door of the drug store, still swearing into his cell phone as he stormed to his pickup truck.

Jerzy emerged from the alcove and stalked purposefully toward Guido, taking his M16 out from under his jacket.

'*Hey sergeant,*' said Cragg, '*ask Becky for her phone.*'

'*Not the time, specialist,*' said Thom.

'*I'm saying you might want to—*'

Thom suddenly understood, and broke in: '*—Cragg's right, Chief, and you haven't got a lot of time.*'

Squad knew the tone, and it had never led him wrong.

Meanwhile, in the street, Jerzy had brought the M16 to his shoulder. He shouted something in Polish to Guido that had the unmistakable character of, 'Turn around you sonofabitch.'

Guido got halfway around before a burst of bullets tore him to pieces.

Jerzy stepped up to his still-twitching body, yelled something else, and put another bullet into his head.

Back in the alcove, Squad was holding Becky's phone. She had her hands over her ears and was shrinking into the far recesses of the doorway. 'Alright,' Squad said to her, 'how do I, uh, get a copy of that to somewhere else?' he asked her.

'Uh…' She was freaking out, unable to summon anything other than horror at having just seen a human being shot to hamburger.

'My wild guess would be the button that says 'Send,' sergeant.'

Jerzy was already walking back across the street toward them, smoke rising from the M16's barrel and action. Squad's callused, sausage-looking fingers hunt-and-pecked at the phone as he came.

Jerzy pointed at Leon, jerked a finger back toward the SUV. Leon humbly turned to head for the vehicle. As soon as Leon's back was turned, Jerzy brought the gun to his shoulder and put a bullet in Leon's brain stem. Becky screamed.

Jerzy turned back to Squad and Becky. 'Sadly, it is check-out time for you and you, as well.' Jerzy, who didn't seem remotely sad, started to bring his gun up again, but Squad held up Becky's phone.

'Did you know these things have video cameras in them, these days?'

Jerzy faltered for a second.

'And I have it on good authority that when you push this little button, the one that says "Send", you can just e-mail some video from the phone to anyone on the Internet. Like, say you had a home movie of some crazy Polish mobster shooting some guys up in broad daylight.' Squad narrowed his eyes and growled: 'You kill us, friends of mine are gonna wonder why they just got that video, and they're going to come looking for you, and they're going to have some leverage, and you're gonna all of a sudden get really popular on…'

'…*Christ, what's that Internet thing with the videos called, again?*' Squad asked.

'*Are you talking about YouTube, chief?*' the kid asked.

'…on YouTube,' Squad finished. 'So instead of pointing that thing at me, get your ass inside that drug store and explain to your wayward thugs that one of them just got promoted, and then come walking out that door with a baby and its grandma.'

Jerzy didn't look too happy, but sure enough, that's what he did.

Jakey and grandma were reunited with Becky, with sobbing and hugging and all that stuff that Squad had never once in his life waited around to see.

Before Jerzy's truck pulled away, everyone agreed that none of them ever wanted to see each other ever again, and that if anyone ever said anything to the police, it was going to be an unwelcome shitstorm all the way around.

And that was that.

Squad walked down the street at dusk in the direction of the Greyhound station.

'*I noticed you never did find that "Send" button,*' said Cragg.

Squad took a drag on his smoke and then tapped his temple with his index finger, leaving a cigarette contrail.

'*Let's keep that between the five of us,*' he said.

Warrior of the Sunrise

Maurice Broaddus

Lalyani surveyed her surroundings, one hand pressed against her hip in stoic resignation, the other clutching her spear. Half of her spear's length was razor sharp iron and had considerable heft, not easily wielded by a man, much less a woman. Pangs of hunger rumbled her insides, but she dared not chance a bite of what little fruit she spied amongst the sickly branches. Fungus encroached into the uninviting copse of trees in slow digestion. The stink of rotting carcasses rose from the murky waters of the fetid pool, discouraging anyone from tarrying too long. A low-laying fog swirled about at the foot of the jutting crag. The Mountain of No Name, a desolate stretch of rock, leered from above the tree tops.

The silence disturbed her, the forlorn and petulant stillness wore on her bones. No bird song, no frog bark, no monkey chatter, no whir of insect, no stir of bushes. The beast had come this way. The muscles in her arms ached from their previous encounter. The scars along her back still oozed, though she paid the pain no mind. She nursed her anger, a newborn to be suckled until it could march on its own. She would kill the beast and then its master, such was the simple order in her world. That was who she was now.

Lalyani, the Outcast.

Her name would be whispered on the lips of griots, in poem, and song, and story—sometimes of her adventures with Dinga Cisse and that Greek dog he called a friend—not that she cared about such things. Most times, however, she preferred to go her own way, to wander The Path anyway it bent.

Unbridled and sure-footed, she had the supple physique of a horse, her legs wide-braced and powerfully muscled. Though lacking a man's height, she held her head high, her shoulders always bent in anticipation of action. A broad girdle of bronze beads over black sable skin made no attempt to hide her full-bosomed figure. Her leopard hide skirt stopped a hand's spread above her knees.

Slinging her spear through her kaross, she groped for handholds along the unnatural ridge of stone before her. The shelf was more wall than anything else; a craftsman had worked too hard to make the imposing edifice appear natural. Her people, the Mo-Ito, were hill denizens, so she climbed the stone spire with keen aplomb. She quickly passed the shattered bones of men scattered along the ridges who had failed their bid to climb the summit.

Hours into her ascent, the cliff wall leveled into a landing. Her hands had grown numb from finding purchase. From the top, she turned westward. The impenetrable forest roof thinned at a kraal. Her breath hitched in remembrance of ...

... how she struggled in Manuto's presence. The chief story-teller and high wizard summoned her to his hut for his final pronouncement. Manuto let loose a weary sigh as if not knowing where to start and circled her. She imagined he often paced the length of his hut, wondering what to do with her. In better days, she teased his over-protectiveness of her, rarely admitting, even to

herself, how much comfort she took in his attentions. Tonight he bore the mien of his position; his word to the chief's ear was law. Her throat tightened in a dry swallow.

'It is time,' Manuto said. A fine sheen of sweat misted his fresh-shaven head.

'Let me see him one last time.'

'No.'

'You dare stand between a mother and her son?' She stood tall and proud, too much iron in her backbone for some. They met eye-to-eye as he drew near to her slender body, her long limbs somehow seeming out of proportion with the rest of her. Despite her exaggerated illusion of fragility, she possessed a tensile strength, a fierce tenacity of spirit, matching both her raw beauty of exquisite cruelty and her air of cold serenity.

'He nears the age of ascent. And there have been … whispers.' Manuto shifted as if in sudden discomfort. 'The tribal code demands that you name the father.'

'I cannot. He belongs to another.'

'He's married?' Adultery meant fatal punishment doled out by the Tribal Avengers. She hated this dance of conversations. It was mostly for the benefit of the two warriors who stood guard outside his dwelling. Or the countless other ears straining to eavesdrop.

'Only to his duty and obligation.'

· He rubbed the keloid along his neck. 'Then Kaala has no mother. He has no father. He is of the tribe.'

'Like mother, like son.' The Mo-Ito were a mixed race people, accepting any who wandered into their community as long as they lived by The Path. Proud and fierce though a near forgotten people now. Lalyani's mother was never named, her father was … gone. Like her, her son would never truly know the embrace of this village. He had to earn his right to be a part of the San tribe. 'What will come of my son?'

'Rest easy in this: when it is time for him to walk the journey into manhood, I will stand beside him.'

Lalyani nodded. She understood this was how things had to be. All choices had consequences and she made hers readily enough.

The time would not be easy for either of them. She had little stomach for the politics of the tribal ways, but she knew what her fate was to be before Manuto gave voice to it.

'You, however, cannot stay here.'

'I know. I will abandon The Path as it has abandoned me.' Hers was a conviction that struggled to find meaning. While many in her tribe found comfort in The Path, she knew only her terror and brokenness. Some questions were best left unasked because no answer would satisfy. And Lalyani questioned. Buried doubts and insecurity, an embraced self-deception, meant she would never know the pain again. But the pain cut through the lies. Pain was the Master-Teacher.

'You may abandon it, but you may find that it is not so easily left behind. The teachings remain in your heart.' Manuto moved to comfort her, his thick arms opening in embrace. She pressed her palm into his chest to halt him.

'Many things remain in my heart that I can no longer feel.'

'Mine as well. The demands of duty.'

She knew this day would come and had steeled herself for it. A few tasks remained before night descended on …

… the wings of sunset. Lalyani dropped into the gardens. Caution lightened her steps as she glided along the cave wall. The honeycombed mountain encircled a small kraal with a series of catacombs. From the upper ridge, she made out the shapes of huts as well as a byre full of cattle. Off to the side of the kraal proper stood a lone leather-thatched hut, shaded by an old, leafy marula tree. Like a breeze through leaves, Lalyani moved along the gentle slope of the cavern, treading close to the kraal without disturbing a thing. Only when approaching the hut did she realize how large it was.

Slits between sheets of cow hide allowed her to study her enemy's master. The cruel tyrant Harlaramu was renowned for his tremendous rages. A gold band pulled the lank strands of his long black hair into a cord revealing a bald pate. Taut muscles rippled under duress, his skin glistened in the heat, his body sticky with greasy charm medicines designed to repel demons. Scars scored his back. Beside him, an overturned pot—with the last trickle of strong beer draining from it—had drowned his heart and dulled his sullen anger. Mad laughter erupted from him as he talked to the shadows, a shifting silhouette against the tricks of moonlight. With a flourish, he whirled to grab whips tipped with shards of broken pottery and began to scourge himself. Ancient, unnatural words tripped from his tongue. The guttural language wailed in higher and higher tones. His limbs flailed in spasmodic gyrations as the spirit talk threatened to consume him, until he fell prostrate as if struck from behind.

For a few heartbeats, he lay on the floor of his hut. He grabbed a fistful of earth and let the dirt trickle from his grasp. Once. Twice. Thrice. Then he struggled to his feet and entered the next chamber. Fearful of being watched herself, Lalyani scuttled along the side to peer into the room. Harlaramu bent over a coterie of small figures. His body obscured the people, but she heard their thin voices. Once he stepped to the side, she realized this was a nursery of sorts. Strapped to curved pieces of wood, small men—she prayed they were of the Pygmy tribe rather than children, though this was no better a fate for those warriors—whose legs were snapped into positions to encourage deformed growth. Their bones canted at odd angles, their limbs pulled and bowed, suspended in agonizing positions. She counted five bodies in restraints. Harlaramu tended to each one, feeding them, stroking them, whispering to them. The sixth body lay on a table. Its ears mangled, still leaking blood. Harlaramu closed his eyes and uttered a prayer. He jabbed a sharpened stone into the creature's mouth, and buried its edge to remove its tongue.

'Now you are truly born,' he said with foul pride. A tokoloshe. 'Hush now and rest. Soon you will be ready to do your master's bidding.'

In that moment, Lalyani's warrior's instinct alerted her that she was …

◇

... *being observed. A team of scouts patrolled the kraal at the behest of the great crone. Lalyani trailed them though, unasked and unwanted. She, too, knew the sting of duty and one of hers was to the great crone. Perhaps a faint sound broke her reflections, but she brought her spear to bear before her mind realized what disturbed her. Someone stole along the forest line. Branches snapped in the wake of a sinister shadow. Lalyani fought down a surge of panic; its familiar fearsome lope caused most men's hearts to pump water. It stooped in a semi-crouch, its head turning from side to side, mouth ajar as if tasting the air.*

Then it turned to her.

Lalyani's eyes widened in surprise as the beast was like no creature she had seen before. A distorted face — the flesh of its previous victim draped its own, giving the face the appearance of a melted candle — worn as a trophy. Baboon pelts stitched together formed its vest. The decomposed head of a woman dangled from around its neck. All sinew and hair, it hunched over, a malformed man short of stature, its ears raised to a point, almost as a wolf. Its jaw yawned and revealed a gullet of protruding teeth. The snapping of branches and crackling of bushes ushered its charge. Mad laughter careened through the forest in its dash. Despite its diminutive size, it hit with enough force to send her reeling the length of several men.

It should have killed her in its initial rush, but like most men in her experience, it had to demonstrate how strong it was first. Now she had its measure. As it sprang forward, she dodged to the side, but its long arms slashed wildly. Its raking panther talons caught her along her back. It battered the wind out of her. She cursed herself, angry at her carelessness. Its eyes glinted with intelligence. Thrown off balance, she stumbled to the ground, but leapt to her feet to face her attacker. It lashed out in frustration. Holding her spear in a two-handed grip, she didn't measure her strength against that of men. She was as strong as she needed to be. It reared in a blur of motion. She tried to side-step it, but its momentum carried them into the forest when it tackled her. The tokoloshe snapped at her throat until it slowly realized it had impaled itself on the point of her spear. Buried in its fur, the spear pierced thick muscle. Her dark grimace gave a rueful stare as it escaped into the …

◇

… shadows of the catacombs. The rocky path left little doubt the direction it traveled; however, it knew the crags and crevices much better than she. She closed her eyes and listened. The cavern echoed with life of its own, the thrum of rock and pressing presence. She stilled even her breath so she could try to sense it. A void in the darkness hiding patiently, waiting for her to near if only a step further. It was stunned into momentary inaction as she sprang upon it. Her spear whipped through the air, beautiful and frightening, catching the beast across the bridge of its nose. The spear point lanced both eyes like overripe boils.

The tokoloshe screeched in tongue-less cries. Blood spurted as it slashed about, seizing her by chance rather than skill. Death was upon her with a snapping jaw and terrible grip. Instinct took over her, her lips drawn back in a crazed snarl, a primal rage burned in her eyes. Reckless, she threw herself into the beast, letting the force of her weight do its work. Its wounds showered her in a spray of blood. She drove the length of her spear deep into its belly, the creature's face tightened in surprise. Its blows grew weaker with each careless swipe until it fell limp along her shaft. She scanned the cavern, her ears alert for any tell-tale footfalls of guards approaching the fray.

Wiping her spear point on its vest, Lalyani stood over its corpse and knew that the great crone …

◇

… rested a little easier in her grand chair. Daubed head-to-toe in white and red clay, the old woman rocked back and forth. Little more than a skeletal figure, a shawl of antelope pelt cloaked her. Her fierce eyes commanded respect once they opened and focused on the young warrior. The great crone summoned her with a gesture of her message stick. A man's head was carved onto the handle of her stick. It was whispered that it was through him that the gods spoke to her.

'Lalyani.' The great crone demanded an austere reverence, one for pomp and pageantry with an ill temper for poor manners and hasty words.

'Mistress.' Lalyani resented the bowing and scraping of her assumed tone.

'I want you to kill a man for me.'

Lalyani demonstrated nothing approaching surprise at the request. Men and women alike from all tribes and status sought her when their needs so required. 'Mistress?'

'Harlaramu. Blood demands vengeance.'

'If I may ask, whose blood cried out?'

'As it was whispered to me, Harlaramu suffered from pains in his head so strong, thoughts were harassed from his mind. Only his personal guard, the Krys, seemed safe around him. One day, driven mad from his pain, he shut his favorite wife into a cave alone except for a cow dung fire so that he might watch her tortured expressions while she suffocated to death. Later that night, he raped his daughters and fed them to crocodiles. Yet the maddening headaches still torment him.' The great crone reached for her cup of wine and drank deep but with all due deliberation. Lalyani hated the way she had to wait on the great crone's performances. 'I trust you knew of the creature that stalked our kraal? The beast comes for me. The weapon of Harlaramu.'

'Ah, so it's a game of kill him before he kills you,' Lalyani said with a smirk.

'You are too stiff-necked. Your insolent tongue will be your undoing.'

'Until then, it amuses me,' she said over a mildly derisive laugh.

'I hope your son will be equally amused.'

Lalyani's eyes focused into a dagger's gaze. 'What say you of my son?'

'No more jokes?' The crone brushed her hair to the side. 'Despite the huffing of the chief, your son will be raised as one of our own. He will follow The Path and perhaps he won't stumble as his mother and father did. He will be the pride of the tribe and will one day lead it to great heights. I will see to his education personally. Once you accomplish your task.'

Lalyani parsed the choice before her. She asked for nothing, depended on nothing, and she expected nothing. All she had was honor and duty. She hated to depend on others—a man, an employer, the world—where she'd be tied to life. When things become precious to her, she was always on guard against someone snatching it from her; or worse, she herself destroying it. Life became about fear of losing. And the compromises she made in order to keep what she had. Better to stay unattached. Free. A tribe of one.

Lalyani nodded.

'You remember how to use the charms.' The woman handed Lalyani what appeared to be a bone wrapped with twine.

'Yes, mistress.' Lalyani held the talisman to her ear. It hummed with the pulse of magic.

'Good, for unprotected I'd be sending you to certain death.'

'The night is my ally and stealth my trade, mistress.'

'I trust in your ability to remain silent.'

'How will you know if I succeed?'

'These bones will know. And you'll be free. You will be of the Baluba tribe, one of the forgotten, and one day, you may even lead those nomads.'

Dismissed, Lalyani …

… crept up the earthen stairs. Weeds sprang up through cracks in the crushed rock that formed the pathway. The cloying moisture of the stones formed a stark dankness with malefic odor. Torches lit the way through the cavern. The walls closed in on her, the passageway narrowing such that only one body could pass at a time. If she knew fear, she pushed it down into the deepest part of her. It was easier for her to act rather than worry, especially in defense of her own. Even if her own would never know of her actions.

Stones steeped in shadows formed the portico of the temple. A series of caged, chattering monkeys screeched in alarm at her approach. Lalyani cursed and then plunged into the deeper shadows of the temple proper. The main chamber was a huge cavity the color of teeth, the walls smooth as if hewn from a single block of marble. From her hiding perch, Lalyani had full view of the passing processional.

Three female agoze, initiates to the dark ways, accompanied the dark priest, Harlaramu. Clad only in a loincloth, a brief garment of antelope hide covered their brown skin. Glazed amber in the eerie firelight, the first carried a macabre drum: a human skull with its top sawed off and skin stretched across. The second illumined the path of the processional with a torch. The last brought a dog to the kneeling Harlaramu. Lalyani stared in horror and fascination as the woman slit the dog's throat. Its spurting blood baptized the shaman. Then the dance began. Harlaramu stomped his foot and held the position until the first agoze began her gyrations. The hollow echo of the drumbeat continued as Harlaramu thrashed about to its rhythm. Faster she twirled about, the frenetic beat riling him to ecstatic exultations until the frenzy dropped him in an exhausted heap. Harlaramu came to a halt between two warriors each bearing heavy swords.

Curiosity suckled at her …

… as she watched from the forest line. The thin barrier of foliage hid her, not that any in the tribe paid her any attention. They had already turned their backs to her. The murmur of the gathered throng formed a melancholy cadence, their chants a dull intoning to call to the spirits of the kraal. The musicians occupied the clearing around the central fire. Dancers pranced along, their frenzied steps

punctuated by yelps. The drummers caught the spirit of their dance, their wide smiles signaled an increase in the music's tempo. Despite the preternaturally cool night, the tension thickened to that of a storm cloud. Abruptly the chanting and music ceased, the settling silence a curtain raised for the final act of the performance. The entire village surrounded them, the crowd turning to face the great throne. Manuto brought Kaala before the tribal council, a group made up of Manuto, the high priest, the great crone, the elder, and the chief, the father of the tribe. Manuto engulfed the boy's small hand in his own, his face a sullen mask, except for his eyes, and led him to the great crone. Kaala had too solemn a face. A young boy lost, wanting to cry out, but choosing not to. He would be a fine warrior one day. His chest puffed out, Manuto searched for Lalyani. The great crone nodded. He released the boy into her hands and she, in turn, presented him to the chief. The father of the tribe stood taller than the others, half his face daubed in crimson clay, his arms crossed along his chest. His impassive stare, without scorn, without judgment, turned to the boy. The chief carved a crescent moon onto his left buttock, the tribal scar. He would be accepted for now, but would have to prove himself during his rites of manhood.

Lalyani turned, head held high and uncompromising, and strode into the forest maw ...

... as if drugged, she swam in darkness, breaking the surface as her eyes fluttered open. Her scattered thoughts took a moment to collect, memories returning in degrees. Her hands tied, a long rope fastened about her, looping under her armpits, terminating around the trunk of the marula tree. She tested the cords that bound her, the realization that she'd fallen not registering with her. Before the idea reduced her to an unfamiliar brand of misery, the sound of feet shuffling on nearby stone drew her attention.

Up close, Harlaramu was taller but slender in a feminine way. With his delicate bearing—hips too rounded, eyelashes too long, and his voice too silvery from his toothy hideous grin—he should have been strangled at birth. Cowrie shells and copper scales decorated his sipuku. He leered at her breasts and legs. Dark eyes burned with intent to throttle her senseless if he couldn't bed her. Men like him bound women, capturing what they couldn't tame. They didn't know what to truly do with a woman other than own her.

'Lalyani. Once of the Mo-Ito. Outcast of the San tribe. Called to the Baluba, the Forgotten Ones.' His voice a low mumble, he started and stopped a few times, each time in a different tongue until he found her talk place.

'Harlaramu. Rabid dog in need of being put down.'

'You seem none the worse for wear after encountering the tokoloshe.'

'I dispatched that abomination for befouling my sight with its presence.'

'The great crone chose well in her guardian.' He leered at her bosom. 'You ... fascinate me.'

'Maybe your fascination could have your eyes meeting mine for a change.'

'A truce to your jokes, Clever One. Is that what the great crone taught you? Is cleverness the ultimate lesson of The Path? She asks a lot of you and what you have gained in return?

'You don't know what you believe and don't trust what you understand. I could help you, you know. I followed The Path for a while, but I saw it for what it was. I could have been many things to you. The father you never knew. The man that accepts you as you are without question. You could lead the Krys and together we could make this kingdom ours. Show The Path and its followers what it means to live outside their cages.'

Her face tilted, an almond oval in the gloom. Her unwavering gaze studied him. 'You are a creature of pain. You have known it in your time and have enjoyed dealing it to others. Your problem isn't that you no longer believe in The Path, but that you fear it might be right. That the reason your hopes and dreams have been dashed to dust isn't due to a failing of the faith, but a failing within you. So you seek to tear down any who might walk the ways of The

Path—any who might make a difference in this life—in a pathetic attempt to reveal them as being just as flawed as you. You are weak and a coward.'

'I ...' Harlaramu stepped back as if needing to catch his breath. Or not lose his composure. 'I don't think you understand the precariousness of your situation.' He nodded and three of the Krys stepped forward and hoisted her. She dangled over a donga in the forest, a clearing leading to a pit. Human bones bleached in the sun surrounding a cluster of six great anthills. Harlaramu tossed a piece of spoiled meat into the cluster. At first, only a few ants reared their heads. Then a wave of insects charged, pincers snapping, their barbed legs—each with a sharp claw—scurrying across the sand. Their poison sacs seemed swollen with anticipation. 'They are called "Warriors of Sunrise". They are the largest ants in existence. They can devour a man in long agonizing moments. You are so like them,' he said. 'Huge. Fierce. Strong.' Baleful eyes glared at her. 'I offer you what few women get: a choice.'

'I'd sooner plunge into the Zambezi. That is my choice.' She raised her leg to allow him a measure of a view and grinned with gleeful malice. He could grip himself in the night; she had better things to do than be a man-boy's plaything. Her clamorous voice and mocking tone drew a scowl from him. Little more than a beast, so easily roused to agitated frustration. He slapped her, first on one cheek, then the other, but she didn't cry out. He clutched her jaw, more in a vice than a caress and wrenched her toward him.

'Remove your hand or I'll have your heart,' Lalyani said.

'I believe you would.' He ran his hand along the top of her breast, but that, too, she didn't feel. No amount of abuse from men could deprive her of her pride and honor. Dignity was her own to claim. She withdrew into herself. She learned to face life's hardships without letting them turn her hard. Except when she needed to be.

With that, he kissed her. The kiss was passionless. He might as well have been kissing a corpse. It wasn't given nor was it his to take. She had never known true love, not that she was unfeeling, but a kiss was ...

◇

… *too personal, the only bit of love left in her. She stole back into the kraal one last time. She stood over Kaala until the weight of her presence stirred him awake. Though he was the reason she chose as she did, she didn't want hardness to be her legacy.*

'Goodbye, Lala.' His defiant eyes matched her own. Both were resolved to their fates.

'Sh, song of my heart.' She closed her pain-misted eyes and kissed him good night. A flicker of emotion, quick as a bird taking flight, caught her unaware, like a spear thrown by a hiding coward …

◇

… converging on her. Three of the Krys approached, carrying wide-tipped blades and clubs studded with crude nails. She thought about being broken. Possessed. She detested their leer of ownership as much as the idea of her loss of freedom.

Hers was a craft of subtlety. Her mind was as much a weapon as any spear, so she already out-matched the over-muscled lummoxes who thought only with their sword. Perhaps she hadn't left The Path as much as she protested.

Her lithe arms stretched taut, Lalyani kicked out to gain momentum. The Krys hacked at the ropes rather than go through the dance of torturously lowering her onto the ant mounds. The arc of Lalyani's swing landed her on the cusp of the donga as the knives cut through the cords. She entwined the legs of the nearest Krys and brought him to the ground. Still on her back, she eliminated as much space between their hips as possible and locked her feet tightly at the ankles so her thighs could squeeze his lower ribs. Lalyani shifted her hips to her left then fell towards her right, kicking his legs into the air and using him as a shield to deflect the blows of the second Krys. Heavy blades landed into her shield. The second Krys realized his error and spun off balance which allowed her left hand to under hook him at his shoulder. Her right over hooked at his biceps. She sat into him, straightening her right leg as if stretching to run. She rolled him over his head against her side, then drove her weight into his skull until she heard the terrible snap. She laid on his corpse to allow his blade to free her.

Palming his blade, she head-butted the approaching Krys before she scrambled away. Still weaponless, to all appearances, her eyes narrowed to grim slits. The last Krys gripped the hilt of his club with the fury of emotion. Trembling, the stink of fear rose from him. She met his charge with a fierce desperation, dodging his initial swipe and returning with a kick into his dangling bits. The man gasped and doubled over. Rage bubbled up in his eyes, another man easily led to distraction as he rained blows upon her without forethought or form, an ox yoked about. He disgusted her, little more than brute clubbing and she parried his clumsy strokes. A deadness in his eyes, his would not be a warrior's death, but an ending to misery. Before his body registered what happened, she slipped within his guard and slit his throat.

Harlaramu had returned to his obscene nursery, treating the wounds of the next tokoloshe. Chained spread-eagle on his table, flecks of blood dotted its face from its earlier wounds. Fatigue and fear characterized its face as it stared vacantly upward. A movement in the doorway focused its attention, causing Harlaramu to turn. His countenance was reduced to an ashy mask of terror, his wild eyes scanning for any exit other than the one Lalyani blocked. She leaned a little too heavily on her spear which had been planted just outside his hut as if awaiting her head to mount. Weary, wounds still bleeding, she took in ragged breaths. The image of her—not the picture of a woman about to pass out but rather one in the throes of barely restrained battle frenzy—was even more terrifying.

Lalyani grabbed him by his hair and forced his head back, setting her blade against his jugular. She pondered the type of death he deserved, but a slit throat was too quick. Her knotted muscles dragged him back to the lip of the donga. She shoved him over the edge. The ants swarmed. Hundreds up his legs. Harlaramu screamed as if he'd been plunged into boiling water. Blood ran down his legs and he sank into the quagmire of ants. Little more than ...

◇

... an abandoned flower in the dust. Lalyani chanced one last glance at the kraal she once called home, then took her first steps on the Journey to Asazi, the journey to We Know Not Where.

The Midnight Knight

Ed Greenwood

'My God! He'll *butcher* her! Hack her to bloody ribbons!'
Manuel Hartanueva was aghast, one hand crushing the balcony rail and the other fumbling for something to throw, or a gun, or *something* to—to—

The Lady Lauren's slender hand captured his, and stroked it soothingly.

'No,' she murmured, 'he won't. He'll not come close to managing anything of the sort. Easy, Manuel. Trust me.'

Manuel blinked at the richly gowned lady in disbelief, then stared back at the swordfight unfolding below.

A battle wherein one of the two combatants seemed doomed: the fighter who wore no armor at all—and was the most beautiful woman he'd ever seen in his life.

◇

The knight loomed tall and menacing at the stair-head, face hidden behind the impassive visor of his dark-crested helm. Candlelight gleamed off curved and polished plate armor as he swung his sword viciously.

It was a murderous slash, with all his weight and strength behind it—and it clove only empty air as his foe fell back.

As well she should, before such a long, heavy and gleaming-sharp blade.

Swing after swing he advanced, and his unarmored opponent retreated down the steps before those air-slicing slashes like a long, liquid black shadow.

She was a buxom woman with long, long legs, her delicious curves clear to any watching eye in her form-fitting black catsuit. Around her trim waist, a dark blue sash swirled as silkily as her long, unbound black hair. She wore soft-soled, piratical black boots and, below a harlequin's black half-mask, Manuel could see the white gleam of a calm, easy smile.

The long, slender sword in her hand was a real weapon, not a sport fencing toy—but was no thicker than a man's finger, and bent alarmingly as the two blades met in a brief clang that struck sparks.

The knight came on steadily, wielding his heavy blade with both hands now, swift slashes just above the banisters that swept from side to side with force enough to sever limbs—or heads.

The unprotected woman ducked and dodged, parrying deftly and often, in a smooth dance of singing steel and sparks that would have been sensuous if it had been slower, but was precise and blurred, as dazzlingly swift as leaping lightning.

They reached the bottom of the stair, the woman springing back as the knight barked out a 'Hah!' of triumph and crouched down, the restrictions of the banisters behind him now, to really put his shoulders into every blow.

His foe sank low, putting one hand to the floor to duck beneath his dipping blade, drawing back and away to turn her parry from something that would have shattered her blade in her face to something that merely *almost* broke it—

Which was when she slipped.

Manuel struggled to gasp and swear at the same time. He was still trying to choke out a warning shout, in the midst of the armored knight's eager rush, when it became apparent the 'slip' had been a ruse. Two shapely legs scissored armored ones into a helpless topple.

The knight's landing was hard, his helm coming blindingly half-off and one gauntlet whirling away—aided by the deft tip of a blade hooking at them as the falling warrior turned for a last vicious slash that would have lacerated unprotected flesh if it had landed.

It missed by inches.

Whereupon his foe's slender blade spanked the armored fingers of the knight's sword hand with a ringing clang, dashing his blade away.

A muffled, groaning curse came out of the helm, and the woman answered with a merry peal of laughter as she plucked it free to deliver a kiss to the sweating face beneath.

'Too overconfident, Colin. As always!'

And with those words, delivered with more fondness than triumph, she sprang free and rolled lightly to her feet, saluting him with her own blade ere running off lightly into the darkness at the end of the hall.

Manuel found his mouth hanging open as he watched her disappear. He closed it hastily, feeling the heat of his own blush, and dreaded to think what expression would be adorning Lauren's face.

Surprisingly, it was a broad grin.

'Drooling,' she said in mock anger. 'I *knew* it.'

Then, with a wink, the lady in medieval garb towed him along the balcony away from the battlefield, leaving Manuel wondering once more just what these Americanos were really like. Were they as gleefully mad as they all seemed?

Playacting or not, this Mednaiya Knight—an incredible beauty, beyond belief!—was unbelievable.

Almost as unbelievable as his own wild notion that beauty, agility, and piratical, swashbuckling swordsmanship might have some chance of saving his country from the machine-gun-toting army of Stonefletcher Global Logistics, with all their helicopters and their complete lack of hesitation to murder anyone who stood in their way.

◇

Mednaiya smiled. She *liked* what she'd seen of Mariacordoba so far.

It was every bit as sticky-hot and swarming with insects as she'd expected, but there was a delicious onshore breeze, and the taller, older buildings were, well, crumblingly enchanting. Lush green jungle across the river ... just the place for a jaunty little pirate movie.

Lauren had been *so* excited when she'd brought Mednaiya the invitation from a Manuel Hartanueva to bring the Merry Blades on tour here.

It sounded like a great vacation for her troupe, and a splendid chance to finally do a Blades promotional 'pirates in the jungle' film, rather than always falling back on the 'knights and ladies in Ye Olde Sherwoode Mit Crumbling Castle' bit.

Yet these were mere justifications. She really wanted to visit Mariacordoba because Stonefletcher Global Logistics seemed to be settling in there to stay—and after all these years, she very much wanted to see Maxwell Stonefletcher again.

Eyes of stormy grey, chest and shoulders of the dashingly handsome college quarterback he'd been ...

That fiery spirit, the strong arms holding her down ...

Dearest Max.

◇

'You are as beautiful as ever.' Max gave her that irresistible smile she remembered so well.

'So are you,' Mednaiya purred back, and meant it.

All it had taken was one glance, and the old, old feelings were stirring in her again.

In him, too, judging by Max's eagerness now, as he strode nearer, reaching for her ...

She knew he was ruthless in business, a user, was probably this instant thinking how to involve Knight Petroleum Enterprises in his affairs, to his advantage rather than hers ... and she had no doubt at all she'd be in his bed minutes from now.

It must be clear to the bodyguards standing discreetly around the walls how much he wanted that.

And by all knights and midnights, so did she.

◇

Manuel knew he was blushing.

Acutely aware of the cool amusement in those deep blue eyes—her presence was making him flush more and more deeply, and her friend Lauren was sitting on the sofa beside him, watching and *giggling*—Manuel struggled to make conversation.

He was in awe of the woman across the room, and a little afraid he'd invited a viper into his country. Until moments ago, he'd had no idea that Mednaiya Knight, leader of the Merry Blades, was head of Knight Petroleum Enterprises—and a onetime lover of Maxwell Stonefletcher.

Who, if he'd correctly read a maid's angry gestures as Stonefletcher's men escorted him here, was again Stonefletcher's lover *right now*. What could he—should he—say?

'Ah ... Mednaiya—how came you by a name like that?'

The tall, raven-haired beauty took pity on him, turning away to look out the window. One shapely shoulder lifted in an unhurried shrug. 'From my parents. Who are both too dead now to ask where they found it.'

'And you ... ah, like risking being sliced by men dressed like medieval knights? You find the danger ... exciting?'

'Yes,' she replied simply, 'and yes.'

Silence fell. Manuel took refuge in the excellent wine. The contents of his glass seemed to be rapidly disappearing. He was sinking into the leather sofa ... and was that a *real* tapestry of knights hunting a unicorn through a forest, freshly hung on the guest palace wall? Twenty feet long if it was an inch, and ...

'So where, in this day and age, does one find sword-swinging men in full armor, anyway?' he asked haltingly, increasingly afraid he would seem a lout and a boor and—well, whatever the current Americano term was for graceless foot-in-mouth-afflicted male idiots.

'Everywhere the Merry Blades perform. Two or three a year join my little club of fantasy-medieval re-enactors, to stay. Colin— you saw him sparring with me—is one of our best armorers.'

'Mednaiya founded the Blades, and sponsors them,' Lauren murmured. 'Very popular with lawyers, executives, and others too busy to spend summers doing Ren Faires.'

'So this is more a hobby for you than business?'

Mednaiya Knight turned to meet his eyes. Her sheer beauty made Manuel's throat go dry in an instant. Again.

'It's more than a hobby,' she said quietly. 'Having well-armed and adventuresome swashbucklers to call on can be useful. Particularly if they're knights or pirates with brains as well as swords—and know how to use both.'

'Yet ... so expensive,' he commented gently, trying not to let his leaping hope show.

Mednaiya shrugged again. 'I've never had any shortage of money.' The last word was uttered in the voice a fastidious matron might use to say 'sewage'.

Manuel nodded and looked down into his glass. It was empty now, and he gazed into it rather helplessly, wondering how best to phrase what he needed to say next.

While he was pondering, long and slender fingers plucked it deftly from his grasp, and refilled it.

'Lauren brought you here,' the tall, beautiful woman with the bottle told Manuel, 'because you have a problem she thinks I can help with. If she trusts you, so can I; there need be no secrets between us. So please, Manuel, set aside your unease, think of me as an old friend you can speak freely with, and tell me why you've come.'

'I ... uh ...' Manuel swallowed. Where to begin?

There was suddenly—with not a drop of wine spilled, though he abruptly found himself trembling like a young man first courting—a warm, sleek body beside him on the sofa, pressed against his leg. A long arm reached across him, gathering in Lauren.

'Let's sit and talk,' the beautiful hostess commanded softly. 'And you can tell me why the Midnight Knight needs to ride again.'

Even before Fernando pulled back the tarpaulin, Mednaiya knew what she'd see, thanks to the reek and the swarming flies.

More than a dozen local men—and women, too. Something with sharp teeth had been at most of the eyeballs, leaving empty sockets to blindly regard the Mariacordoban sky.

Manuel used a stick to turn and shift rotting flesh, and point out bullet holes. Lots of them.

'These tried to stop Stonefletcher's men. There are dozens more back in the jungle, or bulldozed into the Palace gardens. These were shot down in the market and left where they fell, as a warning to the rest of us.'

The Lady Lauren looked like she wanted to be sick.

Manuel waved at Fernando to let the tarp fall. 'I'm sorry to have shown you this, and hope you'll not be angry at my inviting you here, to try to lure you into a fight that is not yours—'

Mednaiya Knight waved away his words as graciously and firmly as if she'd been a queen. 'Righting grisly wrongs is what I do.'

Her voice was low, but hard with rage. Much rage. No fear.

Manuel looked from her to her friend Lauren. Both beautiful faces were white, eyes glimmering with unshed tears.

His gamble might—just might—have been the right thing to do.

'We'll need to film these,' she said curtly. 'Don't let anyone make them disappear. So, who's left in Mariacordoba who'll still dare to fight?'

Manuel and Fernando exchanged glances, then shrugs. 'Just the two of us, I think ...'

'The Palace servants; are they all Mariacordoban?'

'Si,' Manuel said slowly, mentally shuffling faces. 'All but two maids from Paloda.'

'There's your army,' she told him softly.

Manuel shook his head. 'They will help—and can work hard and keep silent, even under torture. If Stonefletcher kept inside the White Palace, and just took the oil, he could be King of Mariacordoba and welcome to it ... but he takes everything, commands everyone, and shoots all who disobey. The maids have been ... broken. By Stonefletcher's soldiers, who force them to bed. And stand guard over them in the kitchens, whenever they are near knives.'

'I see. Then we will be your army,' the Midnight Knight told him. 'Lauren and I and the rest of the Merry Blades.'

Suddenly, Manuel found himself fighting back tears of his own. And wondering if any of them would get out of this alive.

◇

'Say nothing yet,' Mednaiya told Lauren softly. 'I need to think this through, first. Colin, for one, might say something and wind up dead or warn Max that we know. Act carefree. They'll know something's wrong, but tell them to wait for my explanation.'

Lauren nodded and headed along the path to the guest palace, just inside the White Palace gates.

Mednaiya watched her put on jauntiness like a cloak, then turned the other way, into the little stand of trees around the pond. Without looking at them, she was aware of two armed SGL sentries watching her.

Her anger was deeper and darker now, the way she needed it to be. She had to think.

All important visitors were housed in the guest palace, closer to Stonefletcher than armed locals could get. The Merry Blades were the sort of diversion bored mercenaries might appreciate — until it was too late to evade the swung swords of laughing knights or pirates.

And we're Americans who'd be believed at the UN office in Paloda, to boot.

Stonefletcher Global Logistics was an expanding, thoroughly rapacious multinational that had distinguished itself in bold ruthlessness under Maxwell Stonefletcher's coldly precise guidance. Bold ruthlessness took one only so far on Wall Street, where some very large and wise old sharks cruised, savaging young challengers on general principles or for sport, but out here in South America, among a coastal row of tiny former Spanish colonies that were impoverished jungle backwaters but might — just might — have oil, bold ruthlessness could get you your very own country.

Naõporto, Paloda, and Mariacordoba together held no more than seventy miles of coast, their borders mere rock cairns beside cart-track jungle roads. There were ranches back in Arizona and Wyoming larger than Mariacordoba.

But Mariacordoba *did* have oil. And now, courtesy of a few hired assassins who'd killed the handful of politicians Stonefletcher couldn't buy, and more mercenaries to tighten his rule by providing Mariacordoba with the army it had never had, Maxwell Stonefletcher had Mariacordoba.

Oh, there was a President in the white-marbled, many-pillared White Palace, but every Mariacordoban knew Don Habro de Leon took his orders from the hated Stonefletcher. The men with guns at the gates were hard-eyed, tattooed Americanos — and in Mariacordoba, they *were* the law. If they shot down a dog, a boy, or a man on a whim or for not obeying their every ridiculous command, there the dog or boy or man lay rotting, and nothing was done.

Most Mariacordoban women had fled to Paloda, for there was no longer any safety in Mariacordoba for a good-looking woman. The palace maids would fight like panthers if they saw a good chance—but someone would have to hand them that clear hope.

Max would be seeking business partners with oil holdings to front for him, so he could ship oil from here stateside without alerting the wider world to what was happening in Mariacordoba.

The previous occupant of the White Palace, now resting forever at the bottom of a disused well at the far end of the vast gardens, had been adamantly opposed to oil development for religious reasons Manuel hadn't quite followed. She doubted Max had bothered to understand them, either, when a bullet through the head was so much faster and simpler.

No wonder dearest Maxwell had been so happy to see a surprise from his past. He gained both a bedpartner and an oil importer into the North American market. The former might last for months, or only for as long as it took to implicate her in his illegalities too deeply for her to betray him to American authorities. She'd have to act naïve or distracted or both, if he was this open about his tendency to do business at gunpoint.

Thus far, with satellite phones and uninvited tourists prohibited, and a lengthening series of unfortunate fatal 'accidents' befalling oil workers who talked or tried to leave, what happened in Mariacordoba very much stayed in Mariacordoba.

Being as bullets through the head weren't getting any more expensive.

◇

Lauren frowned. 'Of *course* she'll help. You heard her promise. You can trust anything Mednaiya says. *Anything*.'

Manuel sighed. 'I just don't see how one woman, no matter how skillful, with a few friends in costumes who run around waving swords, can do anything against Stonefletcher's hired guns. *Guns*, in the hands of hardened mercenaries! I dare to hope, si, but ... they've taken over our whole *country*, Lady Lauren.'

She sighed. '*Trust*, Manuel. Trust.'

'So when did she start this Midnight Knight nons—pardon, this unusual career?'

The lady in the medieval gown thought for a moment, then said softly, 'Mednaiya was always beautiful. And ... uninhibited. And rich. *Very* rich. She hid that, as much as she could; felt guilty about it. When some of us were down to eating canned peas with ketchup and raiding the Golden Mart dumpster, Mednaiya got the best city restaurants to deliver steaming steak and turkey dinners with all the trimmings to the rec hall, pretending it was some crazy old millionaire alumnus suddenly remembering his alma mater. She majored in pharma, working with the best in creating knockout drugs, and was in on early computers as they went from huge machines that filled rooms to things one person could lug around. Then her father died, leaving her alone in the world.'

'That shattered her?'

'*Oh*, yes. She found out the smiling father she'd loved and trusted had been one of the most dishonest, ruthless men on Wall Street. Howard Millingford Knight could've written the book on corporate deceit and exploitation. Done so slickly that the public—and the regulators—never knew.'

'So she became a shining crimefighter?'

'She ... changed. Put her wits, her acting and seducing, the pharmaceutical training and computer smarts, all of it, to work knocking down corrupt executives. Especially those who enriched themselves by drug-running. When she took down a mayor—he was *nasty*—we first heard the name "Midnight Knight".'

'But does she truly know what she's getting into? The name Maxwell Stonefletcher meant much to her, I saw, but—'

'Oh, she knows,' Lauren said curtly.

A long, long moment passed before she added, 'One of her father's closest business partners—partners in crime—was Burton Stonefletcher.'

'Maxwell's father?'

At her nod he added slowly, 'Yes, but surely the father was a successful man in a suit, the sort of criminal who never sees a jail, who never—'

'She knows, Manuel. I wasn't her only college roommate. Three of us shared the best rooms in the residence. Mednaiya, me—and Maxwell Stonefletcher.'

◇

'Surrender,' Max growled, holding her down amid the acre of twisted sheets.

'Force me,' Mednaiya whispered up at him, bucking under his iron-strong hands. 'You know I like it.'

He laughed. And came down on her with his full weight and strength.

He'd put ropes on the four ornately-carved bedposts, but disdained to use them, leaving her wrists and ankles free. Mednaiya devoted herself to giving him a good struggle, and it was a long and panting time before they lay idle in each other's arms, calm enough to talk.

'You still,' he said accusingly, 'like to bite.'

'Yet these days I draw no blood, and leave no lasting marks,' she replied archly.

He chuckled. 'Progress at last. You're well on your way to being tamed.'

'And you're well on your way to taming Mariacordoba, by the looks of things.' She smiled. 'So, did you always want your own little pet country?'

'Throne and crown and all. Right now it's much more fun being the power behind the throne.'

'Fun, or safer?'

'Bah, there's no fight left in the locals. We had to shoot a few just to show them we were serious, then wipe out the local ruling gang of thugs. Those left now are happy with what we'd done. What use is oil to them? Give them steady food, drugs when they feel sick, wristwatches and good shoes—they go ape over shoes, like little squealing kids at Christmas!—and they're happy. So I keep them that way, take the oil, and there's goodness enough to go all around.'

'Is there goodness enough in Maxwell Stonefletcher to go around with this lovelorn lass one more time?'

'C'mere, Lady Knight,' he chuckled, 'and I'll show you.'

And he did.

◇

Thank you, she wrote on the napkin with Max's best pen. Then reapplied her lipstick and kissed the paper below her words, to leave the crimson mark of her lips. *More, please*.

He was still snoring, of course.

Shoeless, she padded out of the room, smiled happily at the two hard-eyed SGL mercenaries outside the door, and obediently followed the one who gestured with his gun.

He did so only after they'd checked that their boss was sleeping, and not hurt. Then they searched her tiny purse to make sure she hadn't taken any Stonefletcher property out with her, before marching her back across the moonlit lawns to the guest palace, where more watchful sentries waited.

She got past them all, and inside the door they locked behind her, before she let out a long, shuddering sigh.

And thought about what might have been, if Maxwell Stonefletcher hadn't been such an utter monster.

He was worse than she remembered. A casual mass murderer, a vindictive tyrant.

She would have to destroy him.

◇

The first show had been a great success. The Mariacordobans hadn't seemed to mind having the wagons, handcarts, and stalls in the dusty central dockside market cleared away. They'd laughed and cheered a lot at the swashbuckling swordplay of the pirate-garbed Merry Blades, the playacting and the juggling.

Even the heavily-armed SGL sentries on the rooftops had guffawed, pointed, and shouted for more when Colin and Adam had flung the flirting and flouncing Lauren—that is, Black Bart and Old Scratch Skulltooth, tossing Red Nancy—back and forth. They'd roared down lewd encouragement when the eight pirates fencing with Lady Midnight had overcome her acrobatic leaps and swift sword to slash away her full-sleeved shirt and sash, to reveal a glittering mail corset beneath.

And they'd laughed themselves as whoopingly helpless as most Mariacordobans when Colin led a band of Blades in a stabbing chase across the square after rolling wild sweetmelons, bought from the stalls at twice the usual price, and 'slaughtered' for distribution to all.

A second show was scheduled for tomorrow morning, then a third two days hence, to end the tour.

But sufficient unto a day are the screw-ups thereof. The Blades had returned to the guest palace for lunch and a breather, and were now headed across the lawns to the White Palace for the 'afternoon of a little piratical filming in one wing' Mednaiya had cajoled Max into letting them do.

She and Lauren exchanged glances. Under their full gowns were no petticoats, just their topmost bustle-hoops, hung with wineskin after bulging wineskin—the leather belt skins that were part of every Merry Blade pirate costume. Skins that now held neither water nor wine, but slumbertime.

This was it. Their first strike against Stonefletcher. If any SGL man got suspicious, or tried to grope ...

Which was why they were right in the midst of a chatting, joking knot of excited men in pirate costume, carrying all manner of film gear.

◇

'For I am a pi-hi-rate king!' Colin bellowed, with more enthusiasm than polish, swinging on a rope across the vast marble ballroom with sword in hand, rakishly-tilted tricorn hat tied securely under his chin.

On a nearby balcony, a startled SGL mercenary lifted his gun. A blond-pigtailed but brown-bearded pirate in a pink satin shirt minced up, struck the weapon aside with a sweep of one florid hand, and said pettishly, 'No firing! You'll ruin the shot—*ruin* it, my dear!'

The pirate waved his other hand, bright with nail polish and bouncing gold bangles, to indicate a minicam a taller, fatter buccaneer was training on the pirates—three of them, now—who were swinging across the great open space between the chandeliers and the marble tiles far below.

'See? We're *filming*! Mister Stonefletcher gave his *personal* permission!'

'Yes, but—'

'No butts, my dear—it's not *that* sort of movie! Hahahahaha!'

The SGL man grimaced and recoiled, spewing choice and surly profanity—and a stream of ragtag Hollywood pirates, many with cutlasses clenched in their teeth, promptly swarmed past him, enthusiastically hacking at each other.

Blades clanged loudly, striking sparks, and men bellowed 'Avast ye, matey!' and 'Shiver me burrrrning timberrrrs!' and over-the-top worse. It was a roiling sea of tricorn hats, eyepatches, swashbuckling dirty shirts, and flopping seaboots. Two pirates were women in gowns, but the goggling SGL men caught no more than a few glimpses of them through all the merry mayhem being spread by the male Merry Blades.

This way and that the Stonefletcher triggernecks had to duck or relocate, to avoid hooting and roaring buccaneers happily swinging swords, while other pirates scurried around with minicams in hand, filming it all.

The SGL men were under orders not to be filmed, but the Blades knew that, and either waved mercenaries aside or turned their cameras away.

It was a good half hour before some Stonefletcher men began to suspect they were being herded—but by then, the pirates were winding down, gasping for breath over lowered swords and gathering wearily in one Palace hall.

In the happy heart of that ever-increasing knot, Mednaiya and Lauren exchanged winks and smiles.

They'd done it, thanks to the Blades' skill at coordinated distraction. Every last skin of slumbertime had been emptied into the water supply of the White Palace, and as many open bottles and decanters as they could find.

The SGL men who stuck to beer they'd just have to deal with the other way.

◇

Their breathing had barely slowed when Max rolled over to face her.

He gave her his familiar smile, but his eyes weren't smiling. 'You've been bad, Naya.'

'Indeed, but "bad" how, exactly?'

'The Blades, this afternoon. *Your* Blades, for whose conduct you are responsible. I gave you permission to film, but they spread general mayhem and tauntingly disobeyed my men—who were all armed, and operating under specific orders. Your Blades could very well have been killed.'

'But no one was hurt; I don't believe a single gun went off.'

'None did. That's not the point, my lovely Miss Knight.'

'I see. What is?'

Max reached behind himself. When his hand came back into view, there was a whip in it.

'The point, my dear, is that I am *not* to be disobeyed,' he said gently, hefting it.

Mednaiya Knight looked at it, then at him, and arched one shapely eyebrow. 'And if I ... like that?'

They stared into each other's eyes in a long, deepening silence before Maxwell Stonefletcher rolled out of bed and up to his feet in one abrupt lunge, tossing the whip aside as he strode out of the bedroom without a backward glance.

In his wake, tapestries parted along every wall, and stone-faced SGL mercenaries with ready assault rifles converged on the big four-poster.

One leaned forward to gravely inform the woman spread-eagled on the bed, 'Mister Stonefletcher has been called away on urgent business, and has asked us to escort you back to the guest palace. Without delay.'

Her response was a nod and a smile, before she rolled off the bed to calmly catch up her boots and clothes.

If Mednaiya Knight was discomfited at her unclad state, or at the thought that four heavily-armed men had witnessed the energetic romp she'd just enjoyed with their employer, she gave no hint of it.

'Stonefletcher Global Logistics has taken over the country of Mariacordoba at gunpoint! To get its oil, they gun down citizens in the *streets!*'

The astonished faces of the UN staffers changed, expressions sliding into disbelief. The two overweight security guards saw that, and started forward.

'Okay, lady,' one began, making shooing motions back toward the door. 'Spewing unfounded accusations against—'

'Unfounded?' the distraught and disheveled yet beautiful woman gasped. 'How do you explain *this?*'

She turned and aimed the gleamingly expensive camera in her hands at the wall beside the door, and projected a scene on it ... of swarming flies and dead faces, as a tarp was hauled back. The date and time stamp were clearly visible, even before a pale and grim American woman stepped into the frame, voice trembling, to tell the camera where these heaped bodies were, and how they'd been killed, pointing out bullet holes.

Dead silence fell across the Palodan United Nations development office, vapor wafting unregarded from a dozen suddenly-neglected coffee mugs.

Voice quavering on the edge of hysteria, Mednaiya Knight added, 'I had to flee from Stonefletcher's gunmen after we filmed this. I certainly didn't have time to invent or fake a pile of dead citizens riddled with bullets! These men—and women—and *children*—are dead. That company's private army has conquered Mariacordoba!'

She was hurling those words at the security guard, but really aiming them the staffers sitting behind him—the four who quietly reported to the oil industry, and the two who secretly passed information to North American intelligence agencies.

Not to mention the camera-festooned local stringers for global media, who'd arrived for their daily press release handouts, and were now gaping at a *real* story, dumped right in their laps.

The sudden burst of gunfire, right outside the front doors, was deafening.

Both security guards grabbed for their guns—but the knot of running men now crashing through those doors bellowed, '*Drop your guns!* Drop them or *die!*'

The intruders wore fatigues and combat boots, and waved gleaming assault rifles, some stitching warning bursts across the ceiling.

Staffers screamed, but as men slapped and kicked away the security guards' guns at gunpoint, their leader advanced, snarling, '*Nobody move!*'

Aside from swallowing, nobody did.

Yet they stared, seeing it all—the intruders' Stonefletcher Global Logistics badges included. Two of those gunmen had already seized Mednaiya Knight's arms, one trying to clap a hand over her mouth and the other wrestling her for the camera.

She flung it away, high and wild.

It hit the ceiling far down the office and fell somewhere among the cubicles. A gunman fired after it, spraying the ceiling again, but the SGL leader roared, '*Never mind that!* Grab her!'

In an instant, the woman was struggling vainly in the grip of eight burly gunmen.

'Help!' she shrieked desperately, as they dragged her out the doors. 'I'm an American citizen! I—help *meeeee!*'

But no one moved a muscle until long after silence had fallen, and all running men with guns had disappeared.

Then a siren rose in the distance—and nearby, the motor of a powerful boat burst into life and roared away at frantic speed, up the River Colobo toward Mariacordoba.

Inside the UN office, people started to scream and shout and swear.

◇

'It was *too* easy, Naya!' Colin shouted, to be heard over the outboard's roar as they raced back to Mariacordoba, the jungle a purple-green blur on either side.

'That, Colin,' the Midnight Knight replied, 'is exactly what I'm afraid of. Whenever things go very easily, they are unfolding *too* easily.'

All around, Merry Blades were peeling off stolen SGL fatigues and tossing them and the guns overboard. They'd made very convincing Stonefletcher mercenaries.

Her idea, of course. No reporter would be able to resist snapping a photo of a beautiful Americano woman struggling in the hands of brutish mercenaries, as they dragged her into the jungle.

None had.

It should make newscasts across America, all right—and the wider world. Whatever happened now, Stonefletcher Global Logistics had gained one very large black eye.

'Too easily,' Mednaiya repeated softly, shaking her head. And smiling.

She and her Blades would have to move like proverbial greased lightning to stay alive—and really do something about Max, while all the dithering began back home and at the UN—before Max learned what she'd done, and decided to *really* do something about her.

◇

'What do you mean they're all *asleep?* You're fucking *kidding* me!'

Maxwell Stonefletcher's usual coldly sneering manner deserted him for a moment. He glared at the three uneasy SGL men in his office then slammed a large hand down on his desk and spat, 'What do you *mean* you can't wake them? Are they snoring, or just lying there like they're dead?'

He didn't wait for an answer. 'Drugged, damn it! Who did this? Any intruders reported—or are the damned sentries asleep, too?'

'No, Mister Stonefletcher,' Gordon replied, a little sullenly. 'They're not, and saw no intrusions—nor attackers outside the walls.'

'Well, send up a chopper to look! Torture the maids! Find out who did this, and—'

'Certainly, Mister Stonefletcher, but we *do* have some intruders within our walls: our *guests*, the actor-pirates.'

Beside Gordon, the other two, Danran and London-Smith, nodded and muttered frowning agreement.

Stonefletcher simmered, glowering at them as he tried to think. 'Go get them—especially *her*. Now. Bring them here—no delays, no excuses, and *no* weapons, not so much as a toothpick. We'll put them somewhere secure and you'll stand guard, all of you. In shifts, three men at a time. So we'll need more triggernecks. Call Hamrelton, and hire another squad in.'

He strode restlessly away across the leopard-pelt rug—then froze as an idea struck.

'The boiler room; it has better doors than the Palace vaults. But bring Miss Knight here to me first. Go.'

His three commanders went.

◇

'What do you *mean* you can't find any of them?' His voice rose almost to a shriek during the half-incoherent string of profanity that followed. Snatching up his whiskey glass, he hurled it as hard as he could at the nearest wall.

Unsurprisingly, the wall won.

Maxwell Stonefletcher stood panting as the shards tinkled, staring at that wall and thinking fast.

His thoughts were not happy ones. He'd been a ruthlessly successful shark for a long time. He could sense when things were going very wrong—and he was sensing it now.

The mercenaries stepped back, their faces going carefully blank. Bowing their heads slightly against the verbal gale, they set themselves to weather the rant, then rush to obey.

No matter what he might order them to do.

They'd stopped their boat well short of where the White Palace lawns came down to the river and melted into the jungle—fake SGL mercenaries with one rich Americano woman in a dress.

Choppers had roared and clattered overhead all day, but no SGL men had come tramping through the jungle.

Mednaiya had smiled at that. Max must be having trouble awakening enough triggernecks to man his perimeter and search for the missing occupants of his guest palace, leaving futile jungle searches beyond him.

Soon it would grow dark. Time to light the dozens of fire-barrels along the riverbank, to foil SGL infrared nightscopes.

Then it would be time to stage a little coup. The traditional way.

As they reached the Palace pool change hut, Manuel leaned past Colin to give the Midnight Knight a bright grin—and Fernando appeared behind Manuel's shoulder to ask eagerly, 'So, Lady Knight, what's the plan?'

Mednaiya smiled. 'My Blades have been busy with some Stonefletcher rockblasting charges. In a minute we should—'

The rest of her words were lost forever in a blast that struck their ears like a flying fist, lit up the night blindingly, and flung tiles clattering off the roof of the White Palace—even before pieces of shattered SGL helicopters started to crash down out of the sky.

The Midnight Knight sprang at all three men, driving them in under the edge of the hut roof.

It rained chopper shards for a surprisingly long time, during which Mednaiya peered through her nightscope at the Palace.

'Damn,' she said calmly. 'Only two went off. Max still has a chopper to escape in.'

'To hunt us down in, more like,' Colin warned. 'Loaded full of mercs with their favorite guns, up high where they can look down on us, and ...'

'So we'll have to end this before sunrise,' she murmured.

Lights flared on all over the Palace, and there was much shouting. Men went running here, there, and pounding everywhere waving gleaming machine guns.

A fire was blazing on the lawn around two twisted and still-flaming heaps of ruin, but the third chopper was *whup-whup-whupping* into hasty life as men scrambled aboard.

As it lifted, someone was yelling order after order at them out of a Palace window with a loud-hailer. Maxwell Stonefletcher.

'Not waiting for daylight,' Colin snarled. 'I hope they don't shoot up the UN—'

The night erupted with the thunder of a big explosion down by the seafront.

Its echoes were still rolling back off the mountains when there was another blast, far to the east.

Manuel gave the Midnight Knight a frown.

Her smile was impish. 'I had to give Max a rebel army to hunt. Farewell to all vehicles parked at his guard posts at the docks and the airstrip. Palace gatehouse, next.'

Armored cars were roaring away from the Palace as she spoke, someone firing wildly into the night out of one as it picked up speed.

They should just about be at the gatehouse by—

A great *whump* rocked the world, and Colin winced.

Which is when he became aware that there was no longer a woman standing beside him.

Dark gown streaming, she was racing across the Palace lawn.

He, Manuel, and Fernando exchanged startled looks then sprinted after her.

◇

'You *are* going to leave Mariacordobans a little of their Palace to reclaim, aren't you?' Colin gasped, as they crouched in a dark Palace room, to catch their breath.

The Midnight Knight gave him her impish smile again. 'Why should boys be the only ones who get to blow things up?'

'Lady,' Fernando hissed urgently, 'we must get away from—'

A machine gun spat out of the darkness, and he toppled to the floor.

'It *was* you!' Maxwell Stonefletcher snarled from behind it. 'I thought so!'

Mednaiya kicked the door closed in his face.

'*Run*, Naya,' Colin panted, as he ran to put his shoulder to it. 'I'll—'

A heavy Palace statue toppled past him, crumpling the metal door into its frame with a metallic shriek. Stonefletcher's gun promptly started stitching holes in it.

Breathless from shoving the statue, the Midnight Knight panted, 'No, *you* go. The networks will land in Paloda, and we need those cameras here for the world to see. Stick to the plan. *Go*. You too, Manuel! Mariacordoba will need someone to lead it, when this is all over!'

'But—'

'I'll hold them off.'

'But Mednaiya ... dead is ...'

Those magnificent shoulders lifted in a smooth shrug. The glorious gaze meeting his was both dancingly excited, and calm.

'If no one takes chances, the brutes and bastards always win.'

Her long arms reached for Colin and gathered him in. He felt her lips brush his ear.

'Go,' she told him in the softest of whispers, and shoved him at an open doorway.

By the time he got his balance and whirled, she was gone, hair swirling in her wake.

Damn it, she could run faster than he could, too.

Empty.

Maxwell Stonefletcher flung the machine gun down, ran to his bedside table, and scooped out his little automatic.

There it was again. That faint sound. Bare feet, moving fast.

He grabbed up his flashlight—and saw who he'd expected he'd see.

'You bitch. You fucking bitch. *You* did this! Well, you made one little mistake: you didn't get me! Now, I'll—'

He fired.

Nothing happened.

Max pulled the trigger again, and again, but his gun produced only clicks, no matter how furiously or often he fired—or shook it disbelievingly.

It seemed someone had thoughtfully emptied it of ammunition.

The raven-haired beauty across his bedroom gave him a cold smile. 'I do my own dirty work, Max. It's finally time for you to do the same. If you can.'

Stonefletcher glared, flung down the gun, and sprinted across the glossy tiles at her, plucking down one of the crossed gold-hilted rapiers hanging on the bedroom wall.

The Midnight Knight's smile never wavered. From another pair of crossed swords she fetched a blade of her own.

'I'll slice you like a steak!' he snarled, hacking the air as he came. 'Cut you apart and feed you to my dogs!'

'Well, fangs a lot,' Mednaiya replied. 'I'd been wondering what to do with your carcass, being as you've been busily filling up the wells around here ...'

'Bitch! You're *dead!*' Stonefletcher spat, slashing at her wildly.

'Not quite yet,' she purred, dancing aside.

Max hacked at her again, teeth clenched.

Their swords met with a ringing clang that would have brought a dozen guards running if Mednaiya's slumbertime hadn't done its work.

Yet the two of them, it seemed, now had the White Palace all to themselves.

When Stonefletcher bellowed out names—presumably belonging to the men Mednaiya had left sprawled senseless across their Uzis outside the bedroom doors—no one came.

Max wasn't waiting for aid. He wanted the woman who'd dared betray him dead, swiftly and messily and right here at his feet.

Not that she seemed ready to oblige.

As their swords shrieked across each other and locked together, he tried to force Mednaiya over onto her back and down to the floor.

Trembling arms strained, metal screamed—and she stood her ground, braced strength matching his.

'You ... you ...' he ran out of insults, and spat at her instead.

'Me,' she agreed calmly, eyes going colder. 'And when I show up, Max, your luck has about run out.'

Suddenly she collapsed down to the floor, the sword set against his gone. Overbalanced, Maxwell Stonefletcher stumbled helplessly forward—which was when two fast and very hard feet came up into his crotch from below and hurled him onward, as he shrieked in agony—and stone pillars rushed up to greet him ...

The room swam above him.

He was on the floor, head ringing and nose streaming blood like a ketchup tap. When he tried to roll over there was a sickening pain in his crotch. He must have hit a pillar ...

Max fumbled for his satellite phone. One of only four allowed in Mariacordoba. The underlings who had the others could bring dozens of ruthless triggernecks down on this bitch as fast as a chopper could—

A hand like a striking snake dashed the phone from his fingers and slammed into his throat, as hard as any sword's edge ...

And Maxwell Stonefletcher's world went dark.

He was drifting in darkness ...

The voices seemed to come from far above him.

'What about ...?'

'Leave him. Don't kill him. I still have a use for him.'

Mednaiya, sounding almost gentle.

Still have a use for him ...

Trying to wonder about that, Max drifted deeper ...

The world swam blearily back to Maxwell Stonefletcher.

Cold hard steel handcuffs were around his wrists and ankles, attached to chains that rattled as he moved. Manacles.

Mednaiya's face was close above him. Behind her were some cold-faced men. Americans.

'You're coming with us, Mr. Stonefletcher. Stateside. To face quite a long list of charges.'

Some swaggering thug of a federal agent. Max ignored him, trying to focus on Mednaiya's face.

The bitch who'd betrayed him.

She wasn't smiling. Or sneering. She looked sad, but there was no pity in her eyes.

'Why, Naya?' he asked hoarsely. 'Why all this? You could've just killed me.'

'No, Max,' she replied, and there was an edge of hard steel in her firm voice. 'No, I could not.'

The Thirty-Ninth Labor
of Reb Palache

Richard Dansky

This is how Reb Palache decides, in matters of life and death. He does not decide who lives and who dies. It is given only unto the Lord of Hosts, the Author of Life to do so, and whither He sends His faceless angel who is Death, no man may know.

Reb Palache is many things, but he is not the Lord of Hosts, nor does he know His mind. He is a trader and a teacher, a sailor and a spy, a diplomat and a pirate of bloody intent, an exile and a man who has prospered in a new land.

And right now, he is a man who sees sails across the water. They are tiny, and they are distant, but they are neither so tiny nor so distant as they were an hour ago. He raises a brass spyglass and peers through it, reflexively muttering thanks unto Adonai for the keenness of eye that he still possesses, and sees more clearly what he had known all along he would: a fat merchant ship, wallowing through the seas heavier than she was designed for. Wind bellies her sails, but it is not enough, not enough. And above those bloated white sheets flies the flag he knows, the flag he hates, the flag that says unto him that this ship is prey.

Slowly, he casts his eye lower, along the decks. The crew is working furiously, he sees. Lines are hauled, more canvas unfurled. He can almost hear the shouted orders from the frantic captain, the crack of the whip against the bare back of a sailor whose work is not quite fast enough.

The ship is low in the water. He sees that, too. She is weighted down, perhaps with spoils from the New World, silver and emeralds or golden idols not yet melted down.

He looks away.

His own ship runs lean, a wolfhound leaping over the waves. His men need no lashes, no frenzied exhortations. They have done this before. They see the ship before them, and they are eager to close with it. Behind him, the snap of canvas suddenly pulled taut rings out, another sail unfurled in the name of the hunter's pursuit.

He hears them calling to each other, reminding each other of duties long known. They have sailed with him long, most of this crew. He has picked them, the flotsam that Spain cast out upon the waters. Strong men, the weakness burned out of them by sun and wave and battle until they are as beaten bronze, remorseless and dutiful and united in purpose. Some he found on the docks of Lisbon, or working merchant ships out of Malaga and hiding their heritage away from the relentless eyes of the Inquisition. Some he found in the streets of Rotterdam, sons of exile and of a new land that cared less what god a man worshipped and more what he might do.

And he has shaped them, and he has taught them, and he has given them blood and gold and vengeance.

They want this, he knows. They want to pursue the vessel that runs, that stumbles away from them. If they could, they would have their ship leap out of the water and down upon it, a falcon of the waves seizing its prey in strong talons of wood and rope and steel. And, failing that, they want to fall upon the men who sail that ship, who guard its treasure and tend its course, and take from them what the oceans have allowed them to possess thus far. There is no doubt among them, and no fear, and no thought that they might not be victorious. For do they not sail with Reb Palache, the man who consults with angels every night? Do they not bear good steel made in best Damascene fashion, and have they not always triumphed before? And this is just one ship, one lonely ship against which they will strike with a sword of wrath and fire.

This he knows. This is what he must decide.

He stares through the spyglass again. The gap between the ships has closed noticeably. There are men on deck pointing now, and urging the sailors to greater exertions. Others know it is hopeless, that the race is all but run and that only an act of the Divine can save them now. Fog, wind, rain, night—these might rescue them. Precious little else might.

And so a few men climb into the rigging with muskets and pistols, and long knives at their belts. Others struggle with the ropes, looking to find hidden speed that they might yet call upon. But the ship is low, and her prow is too square, and speed is not something her builders have blessed her with. The calculation seems simple. She is weak, she is rich, she is slow, she is poorly defended.

And yet there is something that is not right. He watches the sailors again, and then he has it. It is not that one man is too slow. It is that many of them are. These are not sailors, or at least not men who are sailors first. These men struggle too much with simple tasks, move too slowly on things that should be second nature.

They are soldiers, and this is a trap. No doubt there are more of them hidden below decks, guns primed and hearts pounding, waiting for the moment when they might leap forth and fire. Perhaps some of that weight is cannon, loaded and ready, hungry to tear the sides out of his beautiful ship. Perhaps the captain of the other ship, a wily old campaigner, looks back at Palache through his own spyglass, and slows his vessel so that the battle might begin sooner.

It is all very clever, clever and dangerous. Palache thinks for a moment—how did he hear of this vessel? A rumor in the coffeehouses, a whisper swirling round the docks, manifests and bargains and a dozen little things, all of which put him on the trail. They mean to kill him, he knows. A plot of this scale has power behind it, has the will of the throne and the Inquisition and the long shadowy machineries of state and Church. He has stung them too many times, bled their shipping white and come upon their colonies with righteous wrath.

The wise thing to do would be to sail away, to tell his men of the trap and seek a different end to the day. They are not fools; they would understand. Eager as they are for battle, they do not wish to die unnecessarily, nor to fight merely for the sake of fighting.

But they are his men, and they are superb. And surely, knowing that this is a trap, he can prepare them. He can spy out the vessel, cast the *gematria* and know how best to attack. He can ensnare the ambushers, draw them out too soon and then bloody them, and let it be known across Iberia that no matter how they might try, they will not have his head.

He looks up at the sun. It is just past its zenith. There is plenty of time for bloody work yet before nightfall.

'Men,' he says, and turns to face them, 'here is what we will do.'

◇

This is how Reb Palache prepares for battle.

He winds the phylacteries upon his arm, upon his brow, upon his chest.

He dresses himself in plain linen, and surmounts it with leather: vest and boots and gloves.

He does not remove the skullcap that he always wears, for one's head should not be bare when one stands before the Lord of Hosts. But he is a practical man, and a man who has fought many battles, and so he wears over it a cap of toughened leather, with flaps that hang down over his ears. His beard he binds, and tucks into his shirt, that it might not be seized by an enemy and used to pull him off balance, nor may it be fouled with the blood of those who stand against him.

Over his head he drapes amulets, each inscribed with skill and care and what those who do not understand the study of the Law might call magic. There are more amulets in his right hand, clay tablets imprinted with signs and powers and hung on leather thongs. Some bear the Hand of Miriam for protection. Others, the Tetragrammaton, or numbers of significance. They are black, these amulets, painted black over red clay, and the letters and numbers and signs upon them are bright gouges like unto sunlight piercing clouds.

He moves through his men, Palache does, and he bestows the amulets upon them. Most of them are here, all but the very few needed to do the ship's work. They are armed, and some are armored. There are sharpshooters here, and men bearing nothing but wicked swords, and one man who fights with a heavy hooked knife he swears came to him from the true Indies.

There is no rhyme or reason to those who receive the protections from him. He knows not himself why he chooses some and not others, save that once in a great while, there is an angel who whispers in his ear and guides him. These are potent amulets, he knows, strong enough to deflect a blow or staunch a wound. Theirs is not an obvious power, but it is enough, and more of his men are alive than would have been otherwise did he not gift them with these.

The angel whispers, and Palache drapes an amulet around the neck of a sallow, bearded man with a shaved head and a rich man's gut. What the angel has said is that he will need protection in the fight that is to come, and so Reb Palache offers what protections he might. He does not like to call upon the angel for this, prefers rather to debate with him about the nature of *Shekhinah* and the meaning of the Law, but there is no time for that now. There is merely time for the men, and a last prayer, and a fervent hope that not too many will fall.

The bald sailor nods his head and murmurs thanks. His mind is already on the battle ahead

Overhead, men begin to shout. They are close. Soon the first shots will be exchanged, the first blood will be shed. The sailors move to their stations. The ship groans and thunders as it shoulders through the last few waves separating it from its prey. Voices—Spanish voices—cry out.

And with a sound of thunder, it begins.

◇

This is how Reb Palache fights.

In his right hand, a sword, curved and edged on one side in the Moorish fashion. The blade is steel, but the hilt is simple brass, wrapped round with soft leather. On the blade is etched the letter *vav*, corresponding to the number six, which all good scholars of the Zohar know is the number corresponding to imperfection. For it is with this blade that he will mar God's creation and rend the flesh of those men who stand against him. Watch him now as he brings the blade up to parry a strike, then reverses and slashes across his opponent's throat. The man, a soldier, drops his sword and puts his hands to his neck, but he is already falling, falling, and Reb Palache has moved on, taking another man in the side as he stands over one of the Reb's crew to deliver a killing blow. The sailor—the pirate, for we must not mince words here—utters words of thanks, and then takes his fallen opponent's blade from stiffening fingers to dash off into the fray. Palache watches him for an instant, then runs to the rail and leaps the gap between his vessel and that of the accursed Spaniards. He bellows as he leaps, his voice cutting through the smoke and din of battle like the Great Tekiah, the blast from the shofar.

His men hear him and roar their approval, their voices echoing his. Quickly, they clear the last of the Spaniards from the decks of their vessel and then over they go, throwing themselves at the Spanish ship and at the men who still defend her. One man misjudges his leap, his foot slipping in a slick of blood at just the wrong moment, and over the side he goes. . He slams against the hull of the Spanish vessel and then falls, but there is no time to think of rescue, no time for one man who might be lost.

For just as Gideon roused his tiny band, so now Reb Palache exhorts his men. In the center of the deck, he meets the Spanish captain, and their blades dance. High, low, high, dart and thrust, parry and stab, they are evenly matched, and then the press of battle closes in and they are swept apart.

In Reb Palache's belt is a pistol, primed to fire one shot and one shot only. The stock is made from cedar brought from Lebanon, and it bears many dents and marks. When he draws it, his finger does not find the trigger, nor has it ever been fired. Instead, he uses the barrel to catch the blades of his foes, and to turn them aside. The stock, he uses as a bludgeon, striking a jaw here and a skull there as needed. Men fall, stunned or wounded, he cares not so long as they are out of the fight. He is everywhere, he is nowhere, and though the angel sings in his ear he ignores its voice, for this is a matter for men.

There is a shout behind him, and the whistle of air being sliced thin by steel. He does not turn. Rather, he brings the pistol up over his head and twists, and the sword that strikes it glances harmlessly away. With his other hand, he reverses his own blade and drives it back, under his arm. It finds flesh, the meat of the man who would have killed him, and it is a killing blow. The weight of the collapsing man pulls the sword downwards, and he draws it free before it can be wrenched from his fingers. Blood drips from it, smearing his shirt and leggings and painting rough round spatters on the deck. He does not notice; his mind is on other things.

He looks around.

There is the sound of metal on wood, and metal on metal, and the Spanish musketeers are fighting for their lives as Palache's men swarm upon them. They are swinging their muskets like clubs, or reaching for daggers, for they have not had time to reload after a volley that was fired too soon, and from too far away. His own men, Palache sees, are saving their pistols for close work, and deadly.

There is a clanging in the air now, a sound he knows well: more grappling hooks thrown from vessel to vessel, more iron teeth biting deep into wood to bind the two ships together. And, hot on its heels, the cacophony of running feet and men landing on the deck of a ship not their own. The battle is going his way. Were it not, it would be his ship feeling the tread of invaders' feet, and his men calling out to fall back, and his sailors' blood running out the scuppers into the ancient sea.

The Spaniards shout. An officer has rallied a band of them and they charge, blades out, at a knot of Palache's men who have just come aboard. The pirates hear them and turn to meet the charge, rushing forward pell-mell and hungry. These are his men, his sea-wolves, his spirits of vengeance clothed in flesh, and they shatter the Spanish charge as they meet it. There is screaming, and the thud of dead meat still warm hitting the reddened timbers, and then suddenly the Spanish officer is fighting alone. One man's thrust he parries, and then another, but a third of Palache's men has gotten behind him and brings a belaying pin down on his head with a broken-kettle crash. The Spaniard collapses, blood leaking from beneath his dented helm, and the pirates sweep onward, howling in triumph.

It is not a slaughter yet, but it will be soon.

'Enough!' he calls out, and his voice is as thunder. The angel in his ear falls silent. He is watching now, waiting to see what happens next. Perhaps the angel thinks that he is still in Canaan. Perhaps he wishes Palache were striding into battle with naught but the jawbone of an ass. But it is not his to decide what happens here, not any more.

All around Palache, men stop. Swings end, half-completed. Fingers freeze on triggers. Sparks gutter out too close to black powder. A hush falls over the entangled vessels. Even the creaking of spars and snap of canvas is muted.

And again, Reb Palache says, 'Enough.'

One by one, the swords fall. They hit wood with bright clangs and dull thuds, and the odd round sound of metal rolling away. Palache's men do not strike, nor do they drop their weapons. Instead, they herd their surviving foes to the rear of the ship, and set guard upon them. Belowdecks there is more of the same, shuffling feet slowing and the moans of the wounded replacing the cries of the freshly killed.

The Spanish captain is still standing, Palache sees. He alone has not dropped his sword, and he waits before the mainmast. The deck between them clears, and once again they stand face to face.

'So,' says Palache. 'Do you yield?'

The captain regards him. He is a proud man, Aragonese by blood, and his features are hawk-sharp. He wears leather gloves and fine clothes, and a hat with a long trailing plume. But his clothes are rent in a dozen places, and his hat has been notched, and there is dull dried blood on the silver of his blade. 'You are Palache,' he finally says, and raises his sword. 'I have been ordered to kill you.'

'I do not think you will,' says Palache, very softly. 'You should put down your blade, and we will make terms.'

The Spaniard's sword does not waver. 'I think not. I do not parley with a man who consorts with devils.'

'Devils?' Palache is shocked for a second. 'I do not consort with devils.' He thinks for a moment. 'I have fought a few, and a few more men who were like unto them, and I have conversed with angels. Is that enough to get you to lay down your sword?'

'I have been charged to cut out your heart, and preserve it in salt, and deliver it in a box made of cypress to my king. He will be most displeased with me if I return to him having failed.' The Spaniard stares at Palache, unblinking. The tip of his sword cuts tiny circles in the air.

Beware, the angel whispers.

Palache nods, and thinks. 'I do not think I can oblige your king, for he is no longer mine,' he says. Then, with shocking suddenness, he drives his sword into the deck of the ship. It holds fast there, quivering. 'But your king's words no longer hold sway on my vessel. For your ship is mine now, and you are a prisoner of war.'

'This is not war. It is piracy, and you are but a corsair. And this is my ship, and —'

'And you are my prisoner, and a fool.' There is a heaviness to Palache's words now, and a finality. He steps back and forth, ever conscious of the sword tip following him. He is out of range, or near to it. This is a risk, a calculated one even with the angel shrieking warnings in his ear. His pistol is in his belt. His sword remains where he has left it, impaled in the deck. He has angels and amulets, and he is utterly unarmed.

The Spaniard knows this, or thinks he does. For he may be a true son of the Church, but does not believe in angels, not in those who might perch on the shoulder of a man such as the one before him now. And amulets are devils' work, and not proof against the true steel of the faithful, and in any case the hand of protection he sees around Palache's neck is a Moorish thing and of little worth.

'I offer you your life,' Palache says. 'Your crew as prisoners, your ship as mine by right of salvage, and its cargo payment for my men. You will be put ashore by a prize crew when it is safe; you will not be treated badly.'

A sneer crosses the Spaniard's lip. 'And I am to believe this from the legendary Reb Palache? The spy who converses with the Devil and negotiates treaties good Christian kings must sign in blood? Who claims to study the word of God and yet sails the seas to commit bloody murder? Whose beard is shamed by his deeds, so that he dare not show it among decent and honorable men? What surety do I have, what surety can a man like you provide?'

He will try to make you kill him, the angel says. *Will you?*

Palache ignores its voice. 'What surety would you take? An oath? Blood? None would satisfy you. Instead, I give you this—those men who have thrown down their arms are still alive. Were I the beast you think I am, they would not be.'

'I do not think you are a beast,' the Spaniard says, and his blade is suddenly very, very still. 'I think you are a fool.'

And from the crowd a man rushes forth. He is screaming, and there is a hooked dagger in his left hand. Palache's men move to protect their captain, their teacher, but the would-be assassin is too quick. He dodges one, cuts the throat of a second, and then he is upon Palache.

Who has not moved.

And the killer swings, and the dagger comes down, and suddenly another man is there, the bald-headed Calatan who was given an amulet before the battle. His sword comes up but it is slow, too slow, and all who watch know where that dagger will end its stoke.

And Palache does not move, does not reach for his sword, does not reach for his pistol.

The dagger comes down. The tip tears at the fabric of the Catalan's shirt, cuts through it and continues, and then there is a sudden sound.

It is the sound of the blade upon the anvil, and the hammer upon the blade. It is the sound of a dagger shivering to fragments, and of clay cracking, and of a leather cord snapping. Pieces of the broken blade fall to the deck, and so does the amulet, sliced neatly in twain. And a moment later, so does the man who wielded the dagger, run through from behind by another of Palache's men.

'It's a miracle,' the Catalan breathes. 'Reb Palache works miracles.'

'Devil,' the Spanish captain says instead, but he reverses his sword and extends it to Palache. After a minute, the Reb takes it, and the killing is over.

This is how Reb Palache deals with the aftermath of the battle.

The dead are collected, and washed, and prepared for their final journey. The decks are washed clean of blood and offal. Kaddish is said for those whom would have wished it. With reverence, they are given to the sea.

The wounded of both sides are brought to him and to the other physicker who sails with him, for Reb Palache has studied medicine as well as Torah, and the hands that wield a sword in battle can also heal. With tinctures and amulets, scalpels and herbs and prayers, he tends to those who are suffering. The ones who will live receive all his skill and attention. Those who will not are dispatched swiftly, so that they might not suffer.

On this matter, the angel is conspicuously silent.

The prize crew for the Spanish vessel is assigned, trustworthy men and good sailors all, ones who will handle the broad-beamed craft well, and who can be relied on under any circumstance.

The prisoners have their wounds cleaned and bound. Their weapons are taken from them, and they are searched. Those who attempt to hide blades are treated roughly; those who attempt violence upon their captors are met with violence, swiftly. One or two inquire about joining Palache's crew. They are rebuffed, for they are fools to ask in front of their shipmates, and weak-willed to have their alliance so easily swayed. Others, later, will show more cunning in asking, and they will be listened to, and judged.

A trusted few men descend into the hold to see what plunder might be held there. Surely there must be something to make the ship ride so low in the water. The young and foolish among the crew ask about gold, or silver. The wiser wonder if there are cannon on board, their brass weighting the ship down until she wallows. But all are disappointed. The first man down below curses, and reports the bitter truth: Rocks. There is naught to be found but great heavy stones, packed into the hold to make the ship ride low. Had stormy seas come upon her, those rocks would assuredly have sent her to the bottom. Such was the gamble the Spaniards had taken, such was the risk they were willing to run to take Reb Palache. It was a compliment, after a fashion, but like most compliments, best not dwelt on. Disappointed, the men tell Palache what they have found. He thinks on it, and goes to see for himself, then issues his orders. Such men as can carry them heft stones overboard, so that the ship might ride better, and endure stronger seas. Below decks, the sound of the stones breaching the surface of the sea is like thunder.

A course is set: north and then east-northeast. The Reb and the man assigned to captain the Spanish ship confer, and agree. The sun is going down, and there are clouds in the distance, and night and weather may conspire to separate them. The prize crew captain knows his work, knows how to set the prisoners ashore far from any Spanish patrols, knows the name and address of Reb Palache's factor in Amsterdam. For even if the hold was filled with rocks, there are muskets and pistols and swords to sell, Spanish armor and the ship itself. Such is the way of the corsair; such is the necessity of the sea.

And finally, when all this is done, Reb Palache retires to his cabin and tends to his own wounds. He removes the garb of battle, and untucks his beard, and sees to where he has been cut, or burned, or battered. He pours himself a mug of wine, blesses it and drinks it, and thinks about food, and prayer, and about the sailor who fell to his death in the sea.

This is not yet ended, the angel says to him, and Palache nods. There is one thing left that he must do. Why the angel speaks to him, he does not know. He has studied the *Zohar* for some clue as to why, or how, or what it might mean, but there is no answer, or at least none that he has found. And in the meantime, when there is no hint of battle, he and the angel speak of *chochma*, and the number of plagues with which Egypt was smitten, and whether it might be possible to teach others among the crew to play chess.

'Send him in,' Reb Palache says, just loud enough to be heard outside, and the angel goes elsewhere. He can feel its absence now as once he felt its presence, and the thought worries him. The aspect of the Divine will not be with him now; perhaps it is for good reason.

But the door opens, and there is no more time for wondering.

The Spanish captain enters. He is clean-shaven, and his cuts have been tended to, and his hands are bound before him. His eyes roam around the cabin—across the small swinging lamp of the Ner Tamid and the small ark below it, the shelves of scrolls in their watertight casings, and the physician's tools and herbs. The bed is a straw pallet, the furnishings rough save for an elegant carpet that covers the floor of near the whole cabin. There is a chair, in which Reb Palache sits, and a stool, which is empty.

'Sit,' Palache says, and gestures to the stool.

The Spaniard sits. 'My quarters are much finer,' he says, 'and my ship better. You should move across. It would be more fitting, oh pirate king.'

Palache says, 'I like this well enough,' and pours his prisoner some wine. 'Here.'

'I will not drink your wine,' he says, and makes no move to take up the mug. After a moment, Palache shrugs, and set it aside in easy reach.

'What am I to do with you?' Palache asks. 'It would seem ignoble to kill you, yet foolish to allow such a...capable enemy to go free, and to try his fortune against me again some day.'

The man shrugs. 'Perhaps I have learned my lesson. I might not make such a bad pirate, now that I think on it.'

Palache snorts back laughter. 'You wish to join my crew? I think not.'

'No, no. Merely that I will not be well-received at court, even should you put me ashore safely. I might do better, and live longer, as a corsair.'

'Ah. I see.' A smile quirks at the corner of the rabbi's mouth. 'But you will need a ship, and money to hire men, and to outfit her. Where would you find such things?'

The Spaniard leans forward. There is hunger in his voice now, and Palache thinks on the angel's warning from before. 'There is treasure still on my ship. I know you did not find it. Come with me and I will show you. And you, perhaps, could leave me half, as an act of good faith, and I could swear on the holy Cross that never would we cross swords again.'

Palache nods, and scratches his beard thoughtfully. 'A generous offer, and you expect generosity as well.' His mouth opens as if he is going to counter-offer, or agree, but there is a sudden knock on the door. 'Yes?' Palache says to the door, and 'Pardon me,' to the Spaniard.

A sailor pokes his head inside. 'Reb, I just wanted to let you know, we have done as you ordered. The rocks have been removed from the other vessel.'

Palache looks at him for a moment, searching for something in his face. 'All the rocks? Impressive work.'

The sailor, who is young and somewhat callow and prone to believing every tale he has heard of Reb Palache, swallows visibly. 'Yes, Rebbe. Every last stone.' He pauses and swallows again. 'She rides high in the water now.'

'I will wager she does.' He waves a negligent hand. 'Thank you. You are dismissed.'

The sailor thanks Palache and the door closes.

'Does he know about your angel,' the Spaniard asks.

'Most do, in one fashion or another. A few even believe.'

'And should I?' The man's tone is mocking. 'My father's priest would find it hard to believe that an angel would talk to a lowly pirate.'

Palache stares at him for a moment. 'I am a pirate, as you say, but not a lowly one. And I have seen many things, I think, that your father's priest would not believe.' And Palache observes as he stares—the sudden nervous energy that courses through the man, the surreptitious glances toward the door.

'If we cannot speak of angels,' the Spaniard says, 'perhaps we can speak of emeralds. We should go now, before the sailors you have assigned to my ship find them.'

'Your ship? Mine, rather, and if they find them, they will bring the emeralds to me.'

'Nonetheless, we should hurry.' The Spaniard stood. 'We are at sea. Accidents happen. I would hate for your fortune and mine to be lost, or for the ships to become separated so that you might not find the treasure before putting me ashore.'

'It has waited this long,' says Palache, 'it can wait a while longer. Sit. Drink your wine.'

'I don't want the damn wine!' the Spaniard thunders, and kicks the stool. It spins away and crashes into the wall. 'I want to go back to my ship, and—'

There is a thunderous explosion, and the ship heels suddenly, sharply to starboard. Outside there is shouting, and the clatter of pieces of wood falling to the deck. A tendril of smoke curls under the door.

'No,' howls the Spaniard. 'No!'

'But yes,' says Palache. 'An ingenious trap, I must confess. Weight the ship down so that the infernal devices rigged to it are below the water line, and thus inert. And once the unnecessary ballast in the hold is removed, the ship rises, and they dry out, and then it is just a matter of time. No wonder she ran so slow—were the bombs on the outside of the hull? I think so.'

The Spaniard stares at him, wordlessly. His eyes are wide and full of hate. 'It was brave of you to attempt to lure me over there, I admit. Willing to sacrifice yourself, along with your crew. That is the stuff of the old aristocracy, not often seen these days.'

'You.' The Spaniard's jaw works against the air. Sounds occasionally emerge from it. 'You knew.'

'Yes.'

'But your men! And yet you sit there calmly!'

Palache permits himself a smile. 'My men? Why, they are my rocks, the strong bones I depend on. All were removed. You heard the man himself say such a thing.'

'So you left my men to die? Bastard!' And with that, the Spaniard flings himself on Palache. But his hands are tied, and Palache has been hardened by the sea. He dodges the blow, and strikes heavily at the Spaniard's face, ribs, and gut. The man falls, wheezing on the rug. He bleeds a little from the mouth where he has been struck. The blood and drool puddle on the rug, jarring against the pattern.

'My...my crew,' he manages to wheeze. 'You let them die.'

'You let them die,' Palache corrects him. 'You were ready to sacrifice all of them as well as yourself to kill me. It does not seem fair for you to judge me for what you yourself would do.'

'They were my men! Sworn to follow me, to death if necessary.' He stands and staggers to the cabin door, pounding upon it with bound fists. It does not give, does not open.

'You'd do better to lead men to life,' Palache says, and stands. He walks to the door and taps it once. It opens.

And the Spaniard sees his ship, still sitting low in the water. Perhaps she is a bit higher than before, perhaps it is for good reason. Near her is the wreckage of one of ship's boats, blown to flinders. Half a powder keg floats beside it. Small chunks of charred wood are on the deck, evidence of the meticulous nature of the deception. The air smells like burned pine.

And aboard Palache's ship, he sees his men being marched to the brig. They do not resist.

'Your men deserve a better captain,' Palache whispers. 'Perhaps they will find one.'

'Pah! What will you do with them?'

'What I have promised. You, however, will get what you desire.'

The Spaniard spins, suspicious. 'I do not like the sound of that.'

Palache does not smile, does not blink. 'No? But it is what you want, yes? Your ship back? I give her to you, with my compliments. I wish you joy of her, and her joy of her captain.'

'What!' The man's eyes bulge with rage. 'You cannot! You are a devil! I see that now! A devil!'

Two of Palache's sailors take the Spaniard and drag him, relentlessly, toward the edge of the deck. He is still shouting insults and curses as he goes, calling Palache a demon, a monster, a fiend. Palache merely watches him until he is safely aboard his own vessel, and his bonds are cut. Then he orders that the lines be cast off and the Spanish ship be set on its way, and that course be laid in for Rotterdam.

There is a whisper of wind that none feels but him, and the angel returns. *You are cruel,* the angel says.

'Less cruel than he,' Palache replies, as the Spanish ship begins to diminish. 'He has food, and water, and good sails. If he does not deplete his stores too fast, she will not rise much in the water before she is driven upon land.'

That is not what I mean, says the angel, unnamed and inscrutable. *You could have perhaps made more of him. There was greatness in him, had it been nurtured.*

'There was more murder, and long years of damage to be undone. And I am growing old. Let him find greatness elsewhere, if he survives.'

There is a pause, and then the angel tries one last tack. *You could have shown more mercy.*

'Ah,' says Reb Palache. 'But that was all I had.'

And he shuts the door, and turns to his shelf, and takes down a copy of the *Arba'ah Turim* that he might study. Later, he and the angel will debate on aspects of the *Hoshen Mishpat*, but that is later. For now, the Spanish ship can still be seen, and the lone man upon it, and the great hungry ocean beyond.

On Her Majesty's Deep Space Service

Jonny Nexus

New Chatham Spaceyards, Low Earth Orbit
29th December 1988

Three hundred miles below the departure lounge's windows, a blue-brown Africa floated.

Four years ago I'd volunteered for a tour in the Belt to escape the consequences of my then best-friend's unwise decision to leave his fiancée in my care while he underwent basic training. (Nice girl. Hope he found it in his heart to forgive her.)

Now I was about to embark on the final leg of my journey home to England, just as soon as the space-suited maintenance crew finished checking out the Supermarine shuttle that floated just feet away, connected to Chatham by an umbilical docking tube. A young man in a Royal Space Force Leading Spaceman's uniform floated up beside me and threw the slow, cautious salute that Newton's Third Law mandates whilst in zero-G.

'Space Lieutenant Stone?'

After four years in plain-clothes, half of that undercover on Soviet 'roids, it was strange to be back in uniform, and stranger still to be answering to a rank. I nodded.

'Message for you,' he announced cheerily, holding out a sealed envelope. There was a name tag on his uniform. Johnson. I noted the name, more from habit than anything else.

I ripped the envelope open.

'Going to any New Year's parties?' the young ranker asked.

I quickly read the message that had been inside the envelope. It didn't take long; there wasn't much.

LEAVE CANCELLED STOP PROCEED TO PORT TRANQUILITY STOP GO TO VICTORY BAR 0100 1ST JAN STOP CARSTAIRS

'Apparently not,' I told Johnson. 'Contact Control. I need my duffle taken off that shuttle.'

Johnson gave me a cheery smile. 'No problem sir. Going anywhere nice?'

'No.'

Approaching Port Tranquility, the Moon
Late evening, 31st December 1988

Two days of travel on an RSF intra-space tug later, I was dropping down to the Moon at what passed for terminal velocity at point one six gee, our downward progress interrupted only by occasional control jet bursts fired by the tug's cheery Glaswegian pilot.

'Be down in about five minutes, sir,' he promised.

Port Tranquility lay a few dozen miles downrange of us, a small settlement set inside an ancient crater with, as the old joke went, a big American dome, an efficient German dome, an elegant French dome... and a British dome.

A couple of hours and a few drinks in the officers' mess later, I slid into a chair at the Victory bar opposite the sour face of my boss. Carstairs didn't look best pleased to see me but, to be fair to him, I was thirty-five minutes late.

'Jack Daniel's, Coke, ice, no slice,' I told the waitress.

'Nice of you to turn up,' Carstairs drawled sarcastically.

'I wouldn't have done at all if you hadn't made it a direct order. I just arrived back after four years in the Belt and I'm owed six months leave.'

'You'll get your leave.'

'When?'

The waitress chose that moment to return with my drink. In the American dome I'd most likely have got a little umbrella and a smile. Here I got neither.

Carstairs screwed up his little piggy eyes in what he presumably intended as a commanding stare. 'I've got a job needs doing. You're not the right man for the job, but you're here and at least notionally qualified.'

'Thanks.'

'I need you to meet someone.' He waved in the direction of the shadows at the back of the bar. One of the shadows stood up and walked out of the gloom, becoming ever more recognisable with each spotlight that hit her. Princess Sophie, Queen Elizabeth II's eighteen-year-old eldest grand-daughter. The palace called her 'confident', the press called her 'headstrong', and the blokes in her protection squad allegedly called her 'trouble'. Word in the Force had it that this was one filly who needed breaking in, but whatever poor bastard took on that job would then be doomed to a lifetime walking one pace behind her.

She took a seat next to Carstairs and grinned at me.

'So you're the one who's going to protect me?'

'Apparently.'

Carstairs slid a sealed envelope across the table. 'Details are in there, but in summary, the transfer asteroid Liberty's heading through Earth space as we speak en-route to Mars, and the Royal Solar Yacht Club are commemorating the event with a race from Lunar orbit to Liberty and then back to Earth.'

'I do read the papers. What's that got to do with me? Or her?'

He nodded at Sophie. 'There's a British entry in the race whose pilot, for obvious security reasons, isn't being announced until just after launch.'

Sophie giggled. 'Officially, I'm just here to watch.'

'Right. But aren't solar yachts generally one-man craft?'

Carstairs glared at me. 'They are,' he growled, in a voice whose tone indicated a strong desire for me to not get any ideas. 'But the race doesn't launch until tomorrow and then there's a one day layover in Liberty. Your job is to protect the princess during those two periods.'

'Why me? I don't do protection.'

'Because you're available.'

Sophie grabbed hold of my arm and put on an undeniably appealing pout. 'Don't be grumpy, it'll be fun. Promise! Anyhow, let's go celebrate 1988 turning into 1989.'

I showed her my watch, which was showing a time of half-past one in the morning. 'It's already 1989. Shouldn't you be getting some sleep?'

She smiled. 'I don't do sleep. And it's only nine-thirty yesterday in the American dome. They're five hours behind.'

Cunard liner SS Queen Victoria, Lunar Orbit
Early afternoon, 1st January 1989

I'd finally dragged Sophie to her bed, screaming if not actually kicking, sometime after five in the morning British time, with the observation that while she might not feel the need to actually sleep, I did. Now, seven hours later, only three of which had been sleep, I was feeling a tad fragile. But I was at least within easy reach of a well-stocked bar, which was more than she'd be able to say, located as she currently was in a solar yacht control pod the size of a coffin.

The race fleet was a few miles below and behind the Victoria, catching up fast by virtue of its lower orbit, the yachts jockeying for positions that would allow them to intercept their boosting lasers and ride through the start just as race control sent out the starting signal.

A figure floated up beside me. I didn't take much notice; the Victoria's observation lounge was packed with support crew, friends, families, press, celebrities, and the general hangers-on that swirl across such events like flies on horse-shit.

'Quite a sight, isn't it?' the figure remarked.

I said nothing, and instead put my lips to my drink's teat, giving the bulb a long slow squeeze and me a few seconds with which to regard him.

'Giles,' he told me, extending a hand. 'Giles Townsend.'

The introduction had been superfluous; being the Queen's nephew does that.

He nodded towards the approaching fleet. 'Came here to watch my cousin. I understand you've been giving the unenviable job of looking after her at Liberty?'

I nodded. No point denying what he clearly already knew. And besides, while my involvement was still supposed to be secret, Sophie's taking part in the race had been announced to the press some half hour previously, an act that had sent them surging to the rear bank of phones like fish in a tank at feeding time.

A voice boomed from a dozen concealed speakers.

'Sixty seconds!'

The yachts were close behind now, brightly coloured sails miles across but only hundredths of an inch thick jostling for position as they hit the launching lasers that would boost them out of Lunar orbit. Sophie's giant Union Jack was moving fast; in fourth and challenging for third, which was actually second given that the joker at the front had clearly mistimed it and was going to have to go around.

'And the entry from MIT's gone through the line ahead of the starting gun and will have to go around.'

Told you.

'And... They're off!'

Cunard liner SS Queen Victoria, Cislunar Space
Evening, 1st January 1989

With the time aboard the Victoria my own, I indulged in a leisurely afternoon of gym, sauna and massage such that by the time dinner rolled round I'd pretty much sweated off the previous night and was ready for a spot of fine dining. The ship's dining room turned out to be sumptuous, if a little dated, but as long as the food was equally sumptuous but not as dated I frankly didn't care.

A couple of waiters floated by the entrance, wearing slightly absurd one-piece black and white jumpsuits. Imagine the bastard offspring you'd get if you threw a penguin in with a hippo and then kicked them hard until they agreed to give it a go, and you wouldn't be far wrong.

'Can I show you to your seat sir?' one of the two men asked, holding out a hand.

'No,' I told him, coming to a halt with a fancy back-turn and twist combo intended to show I knew my way round zero-G. 'But you can show me my seat. Stone. Pete Stone.'

'Certainly sir. It's the far table in the corner.'

The table already had occupants: Giles Townsend, and a dark-skinned Arabic-looking bloke who seemed familiar—in that nagging behind the eyeballs, where have I seen you, kind of way.

Giles smiled as I dropped into my seat.

'Lieutenant Stone. So glad you could join us. I don't think you've met my companion before?'

I shook my head. I might be convinced I'd seen the bloke somewhere, but if he'd forgotten me I didn't see any need to give him a reminder.

'This is Nigel Al Farooq. Nigel, this is Lieutenant Stone. He's the poor wretch who's been tasked with keeping tabs on Sophie during the layover at Liberty.'

Nigel, if that was really his name, smiled a tight, controlled smile and extended a hand which, when I took it, proved to be firm in grip and smooth in skin. A man's man, but not one who'd ever worked for a living. 'Lieutenant,' he said, in the smooth, cultured tones of an English public school.

More guests arrived: an equerry, a lady-in-waiting, a press officer, and a friend of Sophie's who on a different occasion I might have been up for a tumble with. Starters, fish, mains, cheese, and deserts came and went, followed by a round of coffees, each course spiced up by a constant torrent of bullshit from Giles. By seven-thirty we were all on the port and he was demanding that the waiter bring a bottle of some single malt or other. Given that he was already looking like a man about to float out of his seat, unconscious, I had to admire his spirit, if not his stamina.

But when it came to loud drunks, his friend Nigel was a notable non-contender, having restricted himself to the occasional tiny squirt of wine and the odd, guarded comment.

Where the hell had I seen him?

I was still pondering on that when the object of my pondering made his excuses and left, abruptly, with the air of a man who had a place to go to and a job to do when he got there. Which would have been fine if we hadn't been on a liner in the middle of space, and I hadn't been convinced that I'd seen him somewhere, quite possibly in a professional capacity.

I gave him a few seconds head-start and then yawned.

'Better get going myself. Long day, you know.'

I grabbed an unopened bulb of scotch from an approaching waiter and set off after Nigel.

Passenger quarters in the Victoria were in the bow, where the views were—so it seemed curious that Nigel had turned left out of the dining room and was headed towards the stern, gliding from point to point in the effortless manner of a man who'd spent time in zero-G.

Curious.

He paused briefly beside a door marked 'Crew Only' and, with only a slight backward glance, tapped in an access code to open it and passed through.

And curiouser.

I quickly glided over to the door, paused for a moment to listen, and then—hearing nothing—tapped my code into the control pad. The door slid open, revealing an empty corridor beyond. I'd got a crew-area access code by showing my RSF Special Investigation Bureau ID card to the First Officer.

How had Nigel done it?

An orange light was blinking a little way down the corridor, indicating that an airlock was currently being transited. Someone was going on a spacewalk, which wasn't something anyone in their right mind would be doing right now, given that the engines were currently booming every few minutes to boost the Victoria into a transfer orbit to Liberty.

Which meant pretty much no-one save Nigel.

And me.

I waited a few minutes until the light went green, then tapped the door open. Beyond was the airlock's tiny vestibule, and beyond that a door leading to the airlock proper, with a little glass window through which I could just make out a suited figure exiting to space. I grabbed a spacesuit that looked something like my size from the cupboard beside the door and quickly pulled it on, pausing only to grab my gun from its shoulder holster and shove it into the suit's belly pouch.

Two minutes later I was pulling myself hand-over-hand along the hull towards the bow in pursuit of the white-clad figure some way ahead of me. He was moving cautiously; he might have had his zero-G legs, but spacewalking was clearly something he'd only limited experience of.

I quickly closed in on him to within a dozen or so yards, but then kept that distance away. I didn't want to stop him; I wanted to find out where he was going. Now I was closer, I could clearly see a metal canister slung over his shoulder, floating a few inches clear of him on its strap. It must have been left in the airlock for him to pick up. What the hell was it?

Best way to find out was probably to wait and see what he did with it.

It was actually one of the easier tracking jobs I've had. It's pretty hard for someone to look over their shoulder in a spacesuit and you don't have to worry about the sound of you stepping on a twig.

After ten minutes of slow progress, Nigel reached the lifeboats, which on the Victoria were clustered in a ring around the bow passenger area. He moved in on one, took out a zero-G screwdriver, and started to unscrew a small access cover.

I edged closer, to see what it was he was doing, and be in a position to stop him if that proved necessary.

Of course, that was when my old friends Mister Fate and Captain Cockup chose to have Nigel fumble the screw he was currently taking out. It floated past him, he twisted to grab it— and saw me.

Through the faceplate I could see his eyes widen and his mouth go open in surprise. Then he launched himself at me. It was clumsy, and it was unskilled, but his lunge was on target and he had Newton on his side. The impact ripped my gloved hands from the handrail they'd been grabbing hold of and sent us spinning into space.

And then the engines fired, although I was a little too busy to notice that just then, given that Nigel was now trying to strangle me.

I'll say this for Nigel: he knew how to throttle a guy. His hands were like an iron ring around my neck, everything was starting to go a little fuzzy at the edges, and my repeated punching of his faceplate didn't appear to be distracting him. I summoned up whatever energy I had left and gave the faceplate a last hard punch. A small crack appeared, but the glass held. I punched again, and this time it gave way, with a shower of glass shrapnel that rattled off my own helmet and then a sharp rush of air that blasted him away from me. I had a momentary glimpse of his face beginning the unpleasant transformation a man's face experiences when he's killed by a vacuum, and then his body was spinning away.

My lungs were on fire, my vision grey, my brain barely there. I gave myself thirty seconds to let the shaking stop, then clicked on the radio. Nothing. Ah. I tried again, cycled through the channels, clicked it off and on, and finally banged my fists on every bit of spacesuit I could reach. Nothing. Dammit. Nigel's radio was probably fine, but given that it was currently floating about fifty yards away from me, and I had absolutely no means of propulsion whatsoever, it might as well have been fifty miles away.

Which, from the pinprick size of its exhaust flare, was about the distance that the Victoria was now away from us, a gap that would be widening by the second.

Bugger. That was me pretty much out of options, something which five minutes checking of spacesuit supplies and equipment only confirmed. Even the gun was useless—it was a recoilless zero-G model that fired rocket-powered slugs. The problem with the radio might just have been a loose connection, but the thing with spacesuits is that you do generally have to get out of them to repair them.

Damn.

Four years dodging Soviet agents in the Belt's cold reaches, only to bite the big one a few thousand miles out of Lunar orbit in—I checked the air supply reading on the suit's display panel— another forty three minutes. Forty three minutes? I really should have checked it before leaving the airlock, not that it would have made any difference. I wondered if Nigel was holding a place in the queue for me at the Pearly Gates. Oh well, there was one obvious way to pass the time while I waited to die. I clicked the suit's voice recorder on and began to speak.

'This is the last will and testament of Peter Nathaniel Stone, made this day, First January, nineteen eighty-nine. To my eleven-year-old red-headed nephew Godfrey, I leave my set of Forgan & Sons golf clubs. May he like the game more than I ever did. To my younger sister Alice...'

A half hour later, I'd rattled off the usual things—a small scholarship at my old school, a trust to fund an annual memorial dinner at the RSF club in Pall Mall, drinks for the lads at Chatham—and was ready to wind it up, and then, well, die.

'And finally, to my elder brother Geoffrey, whom I have always despised, I leave nothing save the observation that he will never amount to anything, and the revelation that when he was working so hard twelve years ago to make partner, his new bride was passing her time by knobbing his red-headed friend Roger. Thus ends the last will and testament of myself, Peter Nathaniel Stone.'

I clicked the recorder off and gazed out at the stars. They were magnificent, in a way they never are from Earth. Not a bad way to end it all. And then I realised what the canister still hanging from Nigel's shoulder was. It was unmarked, but the shape was that of a chaff canister, for loading into an RSF chaff dispenser. It was a long shot, but...

I pulled the gun out of the belly pouch, waited for Nigel's slow spin to bring the canister into sight, and squeezed the trigger. The canister exploded under the force of the pressurised gas within and the chaff—silver metallic strips—tumbled out in a cloud.

I waited.

Seven minutes later, the stars started blinking out as a shadow moved across them. A shadow that proved to be that of an Avro Liverpool-class patrol boat, with an RSF roundel on its side and a waving RSF Senior Space Officer in its nose.

Three minutes after that I was being hauled out of an airlock and into the cockpit and was having a bulb of hot, sweet tea thrust into my hands.

The Senior Space Officer made the introductions. 'I'm Butler. The two Space Officers here are my navigator Jones and my chief weapons officer MacDonald.' He pointed to a man across the compartment floating upside down. 'And that's our engineer, Space Sergeant Bruce. He's Australian, which we presume explains his habitually irregular orientation.'

Bruce's voice boomed across. 'G'Day!'

Butler gave me a suspicious look. 'Care to explain what you were doing out there?'

I reached into the spacesuit and pulled my ID card out from inside my jacket. 'Space Lieutenant Stone. SIB. I was on the Victoria. Took a walk. Got lost.'

Butler smiled. 'Understood sir, understood.'

'Thanks for picking me up. Lucky you were in the area.'

Butler looked a bit embarrassed. 'Yeah.'

I followed his awkward gaze and saw a big heap of sail material at the back of the cabin.

'We're members of an amateur solar-sailing club at Chatham,' Butler explained. 'Thought we'd loiter behind the fleet, pick up any discarded sails.'

'Faked an engine problem, then said you needed a test trip?'

'Erm... yeah. Sorry sir.'

'Relax. I'm not a man who shafts blokes who've just saved his life.'

That got thumbs ups and thanks all around.

I pointed through the cockpit windows at the tiny pin-prick of the Victoria's exhaust flare. 'Can you get me back onto the Victoria?'

'We've got five tons of Rolls-Royce's finest at our backs and the best damn navigator in the fleet. We can get you there.' Butler paused for a moment. 'There was a dead gentleman in a spacesuit floating next to you when we picked you up, sir. What do you want us to do with him?'

I shrugged. 'You can take him back to Chatham and mount him above the bar for all I care. Just get me on that ship.'

Liberty
Late morning, 3rd January 1989

When we arrived at Liberty, the place was in chaos. This was the 'roid's third Earth-Mars-Earth transit, and it would be carrying more emigrants to Mars than ever before. Some twenty thousand, if the newspaper reports were to be believed. All of them would be looking for somewhere to stay, half of them would be looking for jobs to pad out their seed money, and right now, they all seemed to be looking for somewhere to get a bite to eat and a drink.

The tabloid press would have you believe that Liberty's a twentieth-century Port Royal full of pirates and freebooters. It's not. This isn't the seventeenth century and deep space isn't the Caribbean. Liberty is, however, full of crooks, chancers, con-artists, and property developers, any one of whom will happily relieve an emigrant of his or her life-savings.

It was twenty minutes into this bedlam that Sophie, with only a giggle and a bit of misdirection, managed to give me the slip and head off with Giles.

Even on a crackling phone link, Carstairs clearly wasn't happy.

'You've lost her?'

'More she lost me.'

'Well you'd better find her then, hadn't you?'

Then he hung up. Man of few words my boss.

A fat cop shuffled past my borrowed desk. Of course, he wasn't strictly speaking a cop, just as this wasn't strictly speaking a police station. Legally, Liberty's not sovereign territory but a merchant ship, owned by a multinational consortium, and registered in Panama.

Tax, apparently.

So its police are actually corporate security guards, and this was just security central. When I'd reported Sophie missing their boss—an expensively suited Texan by the name of Marshall J. Peterson III—had declared she was just avoiding me and put only a minimal number of his guys onto the case. Way he figured it, he'd start worrying when, or if, she didn't turn up for the race tomorrow.

I put the phone down.

Sat across from me was Peterson's secretary, Silvie. She was smart, pretty, and had more class in her little finger than the rest of the wankers in that dump put together.

'Trouble?' she asked, one eyebrow raised.

'Let's just say my boss is attaching a higher degree of urgency to this case than yours is.'

'Guess you'd better find her then,' she said, smiling.

'Guess I better had.'

I grabbed my jacket and headed outside.

Liberty
Early morning, 4th January 1989

Truth told, I'd probably have agreed with Peterson if it wasn't for one thing: Nigel. He'd been just one link in the chain away from Sophie and up to something indisputably dodgy. But what was it he'd been doing, and did it have anything to do with Sophie?

I'd spent the rest of the previous day searching until finally crashing in my hotel suite for a couple of hours' kip before heading out again. Now I headed away from the hotel at random, floating up, down, this way and that along Liberty's maze of passageways and spaces, here in a rock-lined tunnel, there in a glass, domed crevice, here in a tunnel again.

Do it for long enough and you feel like a hamster, in one of those expandable hamster home sets.

If you're ever looking for somewhere to hold someone hostage, a place tunnelled out of rock in three dimensions is probably a pretty good one. Needle in a haystack didn't begin to cover it. If she and Giles weren't anywhere where they were supposed to be—and they weren't, Liberty's rent-a-cops had checked that much—then they could be anywhere.

I floated past a series of low-budget hostels and into a small mall area. To my left was a shop selling clothes, taking advantage of Liberty's not quite zero-G micro-gravity to pile them high and presumably sell them cheap.

(It costs a lot to lift goods out of Earth's gravity well—so emigrants are best off riding the shuttle with nothing but the clothes on their backs and then buying a new space-manufactured wardrobe when they get to Liberty).

I glanced idly across the shop's display. T-shirts. Socks. Underpants.

Underpants.

Nigel.

That was where I'd seen him. Two years ago, when I was lying in a cramped bunk in an American mining 'roid and flicking through a communal, and much thumbed, clothing and general goods catalogue.

Somewhere around page 567 had been Nigel, gazing a thousand yards into the distance while set into a heroic pose marred only by the fact that he was wearing nothing save a pair of blue and white striped Y-fronts and some matching socks.

I'd probably never have remembered him if he hadn't have looked so stupid.

But how the hell did a male underwear model end up floating dead in Cislunar space? Shame he'd never know that his demise was down to a pair of Y-fronts.

I floated through random passageways until I found a small phone booth.

Silvie — bless her — answered on the second ring.

'Central Security, Mister Peterson's office. How may I help you?'

'Hi Silvie, it's Pete. Can you check the files and see if there are any photo shoots or similar registered? Anything to do with models or things?'

'Yeah sure.' Sounds of tapping at a keyboard came down the line, followed by the sound of the handset being picked back up. 'No photo shoots, but there is short film being shot in an unfinished hotel complex up at the eastern end of the Equatorial Rift. Some English guy called Gerald Trent. You want the address?'

'Yeah. And anything else you've got on them.'

The Equatorial Rift was a deep irregular canyon that snaked its way around two thirds of Liberty's twenty-mile circumference. Most of the asteroid's development was clustered around the western and central sections of the rift, its sides now studded with windows some two dozen stories deep, and its expanse criss-crossed by a web of silvery metal and glass pedestrian float-tubes.

Had it been finished in time for this season's transfer, the Hotel Astropolis would have catered for the more discerning traveller; but being as it was an unfinished shell that was pressurised but not much else, it was currently catering for no-one but a British film crew apparently looking to make a series of 'experimental' films.

Right.

I'd taken some unfinished tunnels to within a mile of the hotel then space-hiked the rest of the way along the rift, breaking into an airlock with an override code I'd found while poking around Peterson's office. I probably should have called for reinforcements, but I didn't trust Liberty's 'finest' to do anything more than alert Sophie's kidnappers. I felt pretty naked without the gun I'd been forced to give up by Liberty's customs men, but then I've always found weapons a poor substitute for intelligence and quick thinking.

Not that I was necessarily using those at the moment.

Plan A had been to sneak as far as I could without being seen, but when the place turned out to be chockfull of people I switched to plan B: walk around like you're supposed to be there and hope that it's one of those outfits where half of them are strangers to the other half.

Turns out they weren't, strangers to each other that is, because the first guy I breezed past with a nod and a smile reacted with first a look of confusion and then a shout of, 'Hey, what? Who the—' and only stopped speaking because I'd punched him in the mouth. I gave him a second punch in the ribs and then a third cross to the temple that left him out cold.

I'd now have been on plan C, had I had one, but that dilemma was avoided by the swift arrival of another goon, who also didn't recognise me, but who unlike his earlier and now silent compatriot, had the benefit of entering the conversation holding a firearm. It was expensive looking model, American, designed to work in zero-G, and held by a man who looked like he knew which end was his friend.

I raised my hands slowly, and smiled a cautious smile. 'Is the hotel not open yet?'

Two other guys with guns had quickly arrived and together they'd pushed, prodded and dragged me to what would one day be some kind of lounge or bar, empty save for the array of hand-hold encrusted pillars that a large, high-ceilinged near zero-G space demands. I could have tried to escape, but getting away wasn't my objective; that was finding Sophie, and I'd figured that if these guys conformed to cliché, they were probably taking me to either her or Giles or both.

I was right.

Sophie was there, in a sleeper bag attached to a pillar, apparently sleeping, probably drugged. Giles was beside her, an arm wrapped lazily around the pillar.

'So,' he said. 'Space Lieutenant Peter Stone. How nice to meet again.'

I gave him no reply save a non-committal shrug, partly because I didn't really want to get drawn into conversation, but mainly because I'd just had a gag shoved into my mouth and was being tied to the pillar in front of Sophie's.

Giles floated, as theatrically as one can float, across the floor between us. The three goons took up positions either side of me and beside Sophie while Giles found himself a spot to pontificate from and began to talk.

And talk.

And talk.

It took him a full half hour of petty resentments, bitterly remembered slights, and hardcore Marxist-Leninist theory, before he finally made it out of his childhood and into his time at Oxford and his recruitment by a Soviet sleeper agent. As it happened, I'd managed to break the bonds securing my hands a full fifteen minutes before that point, but I was holding fire on escaping because I wanted to find out how the story ended.

Ten minutes later, Giles finally got onto the plan.

'It's simple,' he told me. 'Brilliant. Direct. As with all things Soviet. Someone dressed in Sophie's spacesuit will be boarding her ship—' he paused and looked at his watch '—about two hours ago actually. Nice thing about races is you get to avoid all the usual customs hassles if you just turn up that *little* bit late. Sophie's ship will set off, but a half hour in, or about ten minutes ago, its pilot will set it to explode and then bale out wearing a rather sophisticated stealthed spacesuit. As far as the world will be concerned, Sophie will be dead. Tragic young heroine. Never grow old. State funeral, commemorative coins, the works. Meanwhile—'

He paused for a moment, smiling, apparently needing a moment to consider his brilliance.

'—we'll still have Sophie, and we'll have her all to ourselves for another one hundred and forty-five days. When the time comes for her to walk past those customs men with dyed hair and a fake ID she'll be a loyal Soviet agent, and we'll have her entire education on film. On Mars we'll get to the Soviet colony, and they'll ship us home, ready for Sophie to be the figurehead of a people's revolution. We're going to create a new Britain. A classless society, in which the old order is just dust beneath our boots. I shall be first citizen, leading the workers into the new age!'

He smiled, and then added, with no trace of irony that I could detect, 'After all, I have the breeding for it. Which probably just leaves one question in your mind. What was Nigel doing?'

I shrugged, in half confirmation.

'That *was* annoying. The plan was for one of the Victoria's lifeboats to eject and home in on Sophie's replacement, screened by the chaff—with everyone watching thinking they'd seen some sort of malfunction, an ejection followed by an explosion. Of course, thanks to you the poor girl's now waiting for a rescue that will never come. But I'm sure she'll be glad to die for the glory of the revolution.'

I tried to say something past the gag. It might have been 'Nice!' but what it was didn't matter.

'You have something to say, Space Lieutenant?'

He pushed off from his pillar and floated over to mine, stopped himself, and bent down to lift the gag out of my mouth—just in time for me to hunch forward and bite down on his outstretched finger, hard. He screamed. I grabbed hold of him and slammed him into the goon who was floating to my left—something I was only able to do because my feet were tied to the pillar—and then swung an elbow into the face of the guy who was floating to my right.

That gave me the couple of seconds I needed to bend down and release my feet, then I was pushing down hard to send me cannoning up to the ceiling. I wasn't worried about Giles; he was still cart-wheeling slowly through the air waving his bitten finger while screaming like a girl. Professionals first, amateurs later.

And from the way they held themselves, moved, and stared, these guys were professionals. Three armed against one not was pretty poor odds for the not—except that from the slow and deliberate way they moved I was pretty sure they were new to zero-G.

They weren't clumsy; these weren't clumsy people. But I was gambling that their mental battle-space would still be resolutely two-dimensional. Look left. Scan right. Fail to notice the guy coming down from above. I twisted round in mid-air to hit the ceiling feet first and pushed hard to send me straight back down into the guy to Sophie's left. Nothing pretty, just his head into solid floor.

A gun boomed, but I was already heading up, and then back down. Goon number two went the same way. I made a grab for his gun, but the impact had sent it floating across the room. No time, up, across, down, slam.

'Impressive, Lieutenant Stone, very impressive. Are you sure you wouldn't like to join us?'

Giles. Who'd manage to stop screaming about his finger and grab the floating gun, and was now slowly drifting away from me towards the doorway, making damn sure to keep the gun pointed straight at me.

I shrugged. 'Don't think I'd get on with the management.'

'Shame.'

'Perhaps.'

I had to keep him talking just that little bit more.

'It's inevitable, you know.'

'Really?'

Bit further.

'You're a small man, Lieutenant Stone. Seeing the world only as it is, and not as it could be.

Just a little bit further.

'You think the Russians are going to leave you in charge?' I asked.

'They've promised!'

Almost there. If you can read body-language, if you can see a man's desires in the tightness of his smile, you can tell when a man with a gun is just about to shoot you. And Giles was just about to shoot me.

'When the time comes mate, you'll be off to the Gulag, and you'd just better hope they don't give you to the Siberians to play with on the way.' There. Just about in the doorway. Now. 'Still, probably nothing you didn't get at public school.'

I pushed off from the pillar just an instant before I heard the gun fire. The rocket powered slug tore inches past me and exploded against one of the huge plate windows, shattering it into a thousand pieces and leaving the room open to space.

I had just enough time for the thought to occur that the builders might not have completed the decompression safety systems. Then I felt the thud as heavy metal screens slammed down across each window.

And across each door.

I quickly floated across to Sophie. She was woozy, but a few gentle slaps got her awake.

'Stone? What? Where's Giles?'

I looked at the cloud of blood and body parts floating in front of the now very closed exit.

'He had a bit of a problem with the door.'

Liberty
Late afternoon, 4th January 1989

By time Sophie and I'd snuck our way out of the complex, space-hiked our way back to civilisation, called Peterson, explained what had happened, waited while his guys checked out the Astropolis and took all concerned into custody, and then explained to him that Her Majesty's government would be awfully grateful if none of this was mentioned, at all, ever, it was rapidly heading towards the end of the day.

Sophie came back from chatting to the British Consul just as I was finishing tapping out a somewhat abbreviated witness statement on a borrowed terminal. She wasn't crying. But from the look in her eyes she wanted to.

'It's such a mess. The press are telling everyone I'm dead. The authorities have let my family know I'm not, but aren't sure what to say publicly. Giles is the Queen's nephew and it would be just awful for it all to come out. And now I've just found out it's too late for us to get off Liberty. Apparently, we're too far past Earth and travelling too fast for anything to get off now and get back home. So I'm stuck on here heading for Mars. It's probably going to be a couple of years before I can get back to Earth, I'm going to miss university, parties, everything! What are we going to do?'

I put a finger to her lips, wondered over to the Consul, and showed him my badge. 'Stone, SIB. Say nothing to the press. Tell the authorities I'm handling it. Need to know and all that.'

I didn't wait for his reply, but returned to Sophie, grabbed her by the shoulder, and pointed her at the door. 'Come on.'

'Where are we going?'

'Home.'

'But they said there's no ship—'

'If you're civilians, and you're following the rules there's no ship. So it's a good job I know some guys with five tons of Rolls-Royce's finest at their backs and the best damn navigator in the fleet.'

Ten minutes of phone calls from a public call box later and it was all sorted. Butler and the boys were already into a hard burn that would put them on course to intercept Liberty in four hours. They'd pick us up and take us back to Chatham, where an announcement would be made that while on routine patrol they'd found a spacesuited Sophie drifting in space after bailing out of her exploding craft.

No mention of Giles, or of me—which is just how I like it.

Only thing that could bugger things up would be if someone spotted Sophie in the next four hours. We needed to hole up, fast. Across the passageway was a hotel that looked cheap but discrete, in a pay by the hour, reception desk behind a grill, kind of way. I nodded at the hotel. 'We should hide out over there. Make sure you don't get spotted.'

'But Space Lieutenant Stone,' Sophie said, a very naughty smile playing across her lips. 'What on Earth are we going to do to amuse ourselves in a cheap hotel room for four hours?'

I hooked my arm through hers. 'I'm sure we'll think of something, Your Highness.'

Cursebreaker: The Jikininki and the Japanese Jurist

Kyla Ward

'As often as I see it, I'm still amazed so many curses transform the victim into an uncontrollable monster. Don't you people ever *think*?'

'It wasn't me! The Abbot said Brother Manabumaru's sin deserved the most horrible degradation!'

'But you're the one who summoned the Cursebreaker, yes?'

'I, ah...'

'Come on; when I materialised, you didn't even blink.'

'You won't tell the Abbot, will you?'

'I suppose that's why you summoned me into the bath house.'

'No one comes down here anymore. The Abbot says it softens the flesh.'

'Oh, that it does. Can't remember the last time I had a real bath, let alone in a hot spring... oh, alright then, Brother—?'

'Shichiro, honourable lady of the spirits.'

'Please, just call me Mark. Especially if I'm in a monastery somewhere in Japan... I don't suppose you could give me some idea of *when*? I mean, Buddhism is pretty conservative. You could be wearing that robe whether this is the sixth century or the twenty-sixth. By the three, you're buff for a monk.'

'It is the fifth year of the Son of Heaven Ogimachi.'

'Who's the Shogun?'

'There's some dispute.'

'So we're probably talking the sixteenth century, age of the country at war. Now I'm surprised that a single corpse-eating maniac is causing such a fuss.'

'These are the sacred mountains of Dewa Sanzan. The war does not come here. But now the people say we have lost the grace of the mountain spirits and soldiers shall come, to plunder our treasures and their grain.'

'And in the meantime a jikininki is despoiling their graveyard.'

'He steals their sake, rapes the women and boys. No warrior can match him and when the exorcism failed—'

'I can see I'll need a word with this Abbot of yours. That's the second thing. Don't worry, Shichiro, I'll say I came according to the mandate of Heaven.'

'Many thanks, honourable lady. May I ask what is first? We can climb down to the village and see if they—'

'Some clothes. Tea would be nice. I suppose a massage is out of the question?'

In the ancient chronicle, *Things Unseen in the Middle Kingdom and Therefore Anywhere Else*, Shichiro had read of the Cursebreaker. When those afflicted by unbearable fates beseeched Heaven for aid in the right terms, a strange, pale-skinned woman might appear. A creature of some impossibly distant realm, she was bound herself by the most terrible of curses to aid the afflicted and would do so, although the book warned that the results might not be quite as the summoner expected. In the darkness of the Lesser Hour of the Hare he had resolved; the summoning was his only hope. But now, as he escorted the spirit incarnate back up the path, Shichiro wondered if his success might not validate everything the Abbot had said.

The decay the venerable Abbot, Tetsumonkai, spoke of was not physical. The moss about the path was as thick and glossy as that surrounding a mountain stream, the illusion assisted by the steam drawn up by the new sun's rays. As they climbed, the refectory rose before them, its cedar columns humble yet perfectly proportioned amidst the scarlet leaves. This was a mere prelude to the glory of the Golden Hall. The sight of the monastery rising from the forest held the same inexpressible sense of harmony that had comforted him on his arrival ten years ago, a small boy bemoaning what he had seen as exile. But Tetsumonkai was adamant: a rot had set into mankind and it must be scoured before the chance for Heaven's mercy was lost. Beyond the mountains, the entire country fell into ruin and madness: only they, through their most extreme efforts, could redeem it. I swore I would accept damnation, he reminded himself sternly, to redeem my brother. But then he looked at the creature picking along the path ahead of him and quite seriously considered his chances of throwing her off the cliff.

He was strong and quick; Tetsumonkai's training had seen to that. But the book stated conclusively that the Cursebreaker could not be harmed by any physical means. Besides, she was so tall; his head only reached her shoulder and the kimono he had found in the guest quarters barely covered her thighs, let alone her other feminine attributes, whose dimensions were likewise unnatural. Her dark hair was wild and straggly, and her eyes like holes poked in the pale dough of her face.

'Whoa! That's some serious bass!'

What did that mean? Although she pronounced the words flawlessly, like a courtier, Shichiro had no idea. Why was she addressing a horse? Why previously had she asked him to call her a target? It had to be part of her otherworldly nature. She shifted her bare feet on the stone, saying, 'The sound is everywhere! I can feel it, like it's coming up from the earth.'

That at least he understood. Newcomers to the monastery were always startled; dwelling here, one became used to the miracle.

'Ah! It's the chanting of the living Buddhas. Yes, their cells are quite close, beneath the Golden Hall.'

'Living Buddhas?' The idea seemed to perplex her.

'Those brothers who have transcended their fleshy limits.' If she didn't know that, then he had best explain before they penetrated any further, 'Brother Manabumaru was to commence the trials that would see him join their ranks. It was the very night before, when the Abbot cursed him.'

'And why did the Abbot do this, precisely?' Coming around the corner of the refectory, Shichiro saw the venerable Brother Heihachi. Brother Heihachi took one look at his companion, dropped the kettle he was carrying and fled.

'I do not know the truth of it,' he said, squaring his shoulders against the lie as much as the commotion. 'But some say that Manabumaru *refused*.'

'Look,' said the Cursebreaker, 'before you exorcise me, at least tell me if there's an escape clause. Can Manabumaru repent or something?'

When the Abbot entered the refectory—a place he seldom appeared—Shichiro had felt a twinge of remembered fear. It was the fear of a child confronted by a spectre, an impossible figure swathed in orange robes and a high peaked hat beneath which only the eyes could be seen. But Tetsumonkai had no attention to spare for him.

After three repetitions of the Treasure-Raining Sutra, the Cursebreaker extended her hand in a gesture almost friendly. 'You have to understand, I'm here now. The only way to get rid of me is to break the curse. Same with the jikininki: you can't exorcise a monster of your own creation.'

'That was no sorcery!' The Abbot flailed at her with a bundle of incense sticks, the priceless scent of amber coiling heavily about them. 'It was the law! The great and righteous law! I am but the agent of universal dharma!'

'Oh, you really shouldn't say that: she might hear. Now Sir, I'm not questioning your judgement; though as I said to Shichiro here, it might have been a little short-sighted—'

'The jikininki is the most debased of creatures. He barely retains a human form.' The Abbot's voice rang across the courtyard, through the columns and the equally still ranks of the brethren that had assembled for morning tea. They stood, a forest of bald heads and yellow robes. 'Forced to feed upon dead flesh and weltering in corruption, he loathes the foulness of his existence and hides from the world, repenting his sin and supplicating the mercy of the Buddhas.'

'Manabumaru seems not to have got that last bit,' said the Cursebreaker.

'He compounds error with error, even now. How grievous, that all my teaching should come to this!'

'So, you taught him,' said the Cursebreaker, her eyes ranging over the gathered monks. 'For how long, might I ask? How long does it take to bring a man to the threshold of living Buddahood?'

'Ten years, honourable lady,' Shichiro spoke up. 'He entered the monastery with me, on his twelfth birthday.'

'And he was a good student, a fine monk. He must have been, to approach such a dignity so young.' Shichiro risked a glance at Tetsumonkai. Impossibly, it seemed to him that the Abbot's fingers were shaking. 'Am I right?' No one responded and the Cursebreaker frowned. Then she dropped her voice confidentially.

'If he had doubts concerning his vocation, surely you of all people saw it coming?'

'Do not speak!' Actual emotion cracked the old man's voice. 'Do not speak of what a creature of the lower orders cannot understand. Ah, my son! My son!'

It seemed to Shichiro that the entire monastery held its breath; that even the subterranean chanting faltered.

Then the Abbot waved his cane. 'What are you gawking at? Are we peasants or women, to forget ourselves in the presence of an unruly spirit? Those plunging the waterfall shall leave without delay! Those climbing the three summits, drink your tea! The rest, into the Hall of Dharma and start those push-ups now!'

'Stay right there, Shichiro,' murmured the Cursebreaker. 'Going to need you.' To the Abbot she said, 'Honourable elder, how about we take a bowl into the garden and you tell me a little more about this place? Just how is it you serve the Buddhas through such... muscular endeavour?'

'In order to transcend our earthly incarnation we labour to perfect body and mind.' Once again, Shichiro answered when it became clear the Abbot wouldn't. 'By this in turn we may hope to purify the land.'

'Look,' said the Cursebreaker to Tetsumonkai, 'you clearly regret what you did. I'm sure that if you forgive Manabumaru, you will be on your way towards lifting the curse.'

'It can never be lifted. There is not forgiveness enough in the world for that,' said the Abbot. Then he struck the ground with his cane. 'Shichiro, since this thing dogs your steps, take it away and do not return until you are rid of it. Then we shall discuss your penance.' He strode away towards the Hall.

He must have realised, Shichiro thought with sinking heart, they're his books. I'll be lucky to escape with an overnight vigil in the snow. 'I'll take you down to the village,' he said. 'Perhaps we can find his lair.'

'Without breakfast? I don't think so. Anyway, it's plenty curious here.' The Cursebreaker crossed the courtyard to the table where the summit-climbers were sipping slowly from their bowls. As she sat down, the sipping became slurping, followed by a rapid clattering.

'From the generally robust nature of your order, I gather living Buddhahood is not a formality. What exactly is involved? Apart from not eating with everyone else.' She reached out to an abandoned bowl. The omnipresent rumble sent vibrations across the surface of the liquid.

'The enlightened never leave their cells. Their seclusion is complete.'

'What the Hell is wrong with this tea?'

'It's not really tea. Here we drink only the bitter infusion of the mulberry leaf.'

'Take me to the village. Now.'

'I can certainly see how the ideal of athletic monks might have evolved,' wheezed the Cursebreaker. 'This path's a killer!'

The sweet scent of the valley came to Shichiro's nose as he strode along the twisting defile known as the Dragon's Tail. Moss coated the slabs of weathered rock, starred with small orchids, but it was the fields he smelt and the smoke of the end of harvest. Behind him, the woman stumbled yet again and he turned his head to check he was in no danger of losing her down a crevasse.

'The monks of the Dewa Sanzan have always gone into the wilderness to meditate,' he said, 'just as the pilgrims come to purify themselves in the springs. But it is only since Tetsumonkai became the Abbot that we set out to climb to Heaven.'

Because he was looking backwards as he strode along, knowing the path so well, he was completely surprised when something hard impacted his solar plexus.

He saw the woman startle as all the air whooshed from his lungs. Stumbling, bending forward over the pain in his chest, his training brought his hand up to block the assailant's strike at his neck. He barely deflected the blow, feeling the warm iron of muscle as his attempts to breathe were thwarted by a sulphurous stench.

'Look, I don't know who you are,' said the Cursebreaker, 'but anyone who mugs a monk is either damned or stupid.'

'Oh, I'm damned,' came a cheerful voice, 'and you're—oh by Benten, look at *those!*'

Shichiro dropped on one arm, lashing out with a hook kick which his assailant jumped, all the while straining to get breath back into his lungs, all the while registering the voice, the fighting style—

The Cursebreaker coughed. 'I haven't smelt anything like you since Pompeii. Have you actually been rolling in sulphur?'

'What are you? A white goddess descended from the clouds, with breasts like blooming lotus!'

'Keep those hands to yourself, crusty!'

The scent beneath the stench! 'Manabumaru,' he screamed, 'don't, it's me!' Jumping back to his feet, readying hopelessly for another kick, he glimpsed the figure springing away up the side of the ravine. The discoloured, stinking, hairy body... 'Manabumaru,' he screamed again, and now the pain was all in his heart.

'He lairs in the cemetery?' The Cursebreaker addressed the village headman as he passed her a bowl of fine, green sencha. Inhaling the steam, she sighed with relief.

Clearly taken aback by their appearance at the door of his neat cottage, the headman nonetheless answered. 'We believe so. Where else could he wallow in such corruption?'

'Your cemetery lies on the lower slopes?'

'Of the monastery itself, yes. But he ranges far and wide,' said the headman. 'Wherever he may make trouble!'

'What precisely has he done?'

'Dykes in the rice fields are broken, sacks of grain stolen. Pilgrims have been attacked upon the road, and they are few enough already in these warlike times! Not to mention the indignity placed upon those of our community he has caught alone. In truth, the Abbot owes us recompense...'

'We too have suffered!' Shichiro interjected, 'I am not the first of the brethren to be attacked. Many have been found beaten senseless in the woods!'

The Cursebreaker glanced at him shrewdly, before returning her attention to the headman. 'Does he always look like that?'

'The appearance of a man wearing only his fundoshi, body stained and exuding worse odour than the lowest tanner or hauler of nightsoil. The Abbot must consider well his failure when selecting his portion of the harvest!'

'The Abbot has not failed!' Shichiro wondered at the heat in his own voice. 'Truly, all our sins must be great for Heaven to permit such calamity to befall us!'

'You are a monk who seeks Heaven amongst the peaks,' said the headman, 'but I have lived my whole life in this valley, as my father before me. Tales there were of Tetsumonkai, before he became Abbot. Perhaps the sin is his.'

Shichiro felt his jaw drop.

'Oh, do tell,' said the Cursebreaker, but at this both men shut their mouths and glanced aside, Shichiro at the noon light falling across the fields. 'Someone had better start talking around here,' he heard her mutter.

'If we are to examine the cemetery,' he said, 'we must do it soon.' He did not want to be caught in the Dragon's Tail by night.

The Cursebreaker sighed. 'Do you know the last place I got to sit down for an hour? To put my feet up and drink something hot? Well, it involved the Spanish Inquisition and that's why I shall now move onto the sake.' She held out the empty bowl. 'Then and only then shall we proceed to the cemetery.'

'Well, he's not lairing here.'

Shichiro eyed the grave markers, running up the slope until they disappeared beneath the drooping cypress. Even the afternoon's gilding could not cheer the place, which seemed to him to contain all too many potential ambushes.

'How can you be sure?'

'It's a Buddhist cemetery and as everyone should surely be aware, these are all cremains.' The Cursebreaker shuffled uncomfortably in the straw sandals she had pressured from their host. 'Unless a whole lot of pilgrims have vanished recently, I don't see how there *can* be any corpse-eating going on.'

'But... it's what jikininki do.'

'So says the legend. And the third rule of cursebreaking is seek out anomalies.'

Movement amongst the trees sent Shichiro into a fighting stance. But what emerged, picking her way between the slates, was a young woman in a plain brown kimono, holding a bundle of smoking incense. She peered at them in some agitation.

'Hello there!' The Cursebreaker smiled, such a display of white teeth as looked set to make her flee. Shichiro interposed himself.

'Although it is always seemly to make offering to your dead, in the present circumstances it is not prudent,' he told the girl.

'I don't suppose you've seen the jikininki?' asked the Cursebreaker.

'Yes! That is, no, not now.'

'But you've seen him here?'

'Well, he only comes when you're alone. And as I'm not alone, no!' The incense was heady, a rich blend of jasmine and sandalwood. It did not quite suffice to make Shichiro overlook the nonsense he was hearing.

'Is he here or not? If he is, we are all in danger!'

'Are you from the monastery?' The girl was still gazing past him at the Cursebreaker.

'Yes indeed,' the Cursebreaker answered.

'Oh, then he's definitely not here, but I was assaulted in a most grievous manner.'

'Oh yes, and when was this?' asked the Cursebreaker, as Shichiro glimpsed motion in the azaleas growing to the side of a large, stone moon lantern some way down the slope. He covered the distance in a flying kick, which he was forced to abort upon the emergence of a second woman, noticeably older and rounder, holding another bunch of incense.

'I haven't seen him either,' she flustered.

Behind him he heard the Cursebreaker eliciting details of just what had befallen the girl, several times in various discrete nooks around the village.

'But, honourable grandmother,' he struggled to concentrate on his own discovery, 'why conceal yourself? Were you afraid?'

'I wasn't concealing anything.' The old woman huffed. 'I was just waiting here.'

'For what?'

'For you to take that young hussy and go!' The scent of pine was making his eyes water, and he turned his head towards the moon lantern for relief.

'Leave me be,' came a voice from the lantern's depths. 'What I'm doing here is my business.'

'Yamamoto Saburo, you climb out of there!' cried the old woman, 'He only comes when you're alone!'

'But you were raped?' The Cursebreaker seemed to be labouring at this point.

'Well obviously!' The girl sounded indignant. 'I've a husband, you know!'

'For all the good it does him,' said the old woman. 'Now me, I'm a widow. No one cares what I do.'

Shichiro jolted as the meaning of her words hit him harder than Manabumaru's own kick. A woman, he thought, with a belly like a frog and gray in her hair. How *could* he? Suddenly unable to bear either the streams of incense or of talk, he jumped over the markers and ran upwards, seeking solitude in the trees.

'No, don't go up there!' screamed all three villagers.

It was the Cursebreaker who caught up with him, despite her tender feet. 'Steady on,' she said, 'I know it's hard, seeing your brother reduced to this.'

'Ten years we've been together,' he gasped, still striding blindly upwards. 'He was the kindest, the most seemly...'

'Yes, I'm sure he was.'

'The best at both training and study! The most devoted...'

'Let's just sit down for a moment, on this rock beside the path. This is a path, isn't it? Pretty well concealed. I guess he would have to use paths, despite degenerating into a beast.' Shichiro burst into tears.

They sat for a while, amongst the bamboo that had dug its way into the boulders on every side. Slowly, the familiar sounds of the mountain, the breeze and creaking stems reasserted themselves, enabling him to regain hold of himself. When he did, the Cursebreaker was waiting patiently with her legs crossed atop the stone.

'Shichiro: you summoned me,' she said. 'You did it on purpose, knowing what you were about.'

'Is there any other way?'

'Mostly people summon me by accident, which means I have to spend a lot of time explaining. But you didn't even ask me what the first and second rules were.'

'Ascertain parameters,' he gulped, quoting the book. 'And don't... don't make things worse.'

'No slouch at study yourself, are you? So you must also know that you don't need some kind of universal judgment to bring about a curse. It really can be just one individual. If you have the desire and access to any kind of power, be it magic, faith or just sheer bloody-mindedness, you have a curse.'

'Desire is the curse of the universe,' he answered. 'It condemns us to the misery of never-ending existence.'

'Well, I don't know about that, though if anyone could... anyway. What I mean is, not only might your Abbot be wrong in what he did, he may also have got it wrong. You're absolutely certain that he cursed Manabumaru to become a jikininki?'

'I was there in the Golden Hall — at least, I was close enough to hear him pronounce judgement, to hear Manabumaru scream!'

'Well, that's very strange. Because so far, all I've seen is an overzealous priest, a group of villagers taking advantage of the situation and a monster who's obviously not as monstrous as he's made out to be. The ladies didn't seem to have any complaints, or the boy in the lantern.'

Shichiro repressed another sob. 'So what? You're saying there's no curse?'

'Oh, there's a curse alright, else I wouldn't be here. I can be summoned by accident, but not on suspicion: it just doesn't work.'

'Please,' he said, 'I don't understand. Can you help him? Because if you can't—'

'All I'm saying is there's more going on here than meets the eye. Which brings us to our real problem.'

'Which is?'

'How are we going to pin down a combination marathon runner, rock-climber and martial artist for long enough to get some real answers?'

'We have to find him first.'

'This path is certainly leading us somewhere. And I have a hunch that it's going to be a sheltered cave. And I wouldn't be at all surprised if it contains a hot spring, the kind that monks and pilgrims just don't use.'

As Shichiro followed her up the slope, he wondered why she spoke of possessing a crooked spine.

The Cursebreaker had been right about the hot spring in the cave. But trapping Manabumaru in this net was never going to work. Nevertheless, Shichiro shouldered the heavy mass of rope and leather, and approached the crevasse. The sulphurous exhalation and sound of frenzied boiling would repel most explorers before they ever noticed how the space widened out below. Around the pool was a fair-sized cave, expanding into darkness. Lanterns had been judged necessary and acquired, with the net, from the monastery storehouse.

He climbed slowly down into the heat and steam. It was not a hard climb, but he took especial care that his feet were lodged securely on the wet rock before reaching for the next handhold. The net sagged, starting to unravel from its neat bundle. It was the means by which the brethren plunged over the waterfall known as the Dragon's Tongue, an exercise it had taken him long years to master. Perhaps he could manage to secure it across this vent, but even if this was the jikininki's lair, even if Manabumaru had been reduced to his basest instincts, not even an animal ran blindly into a snare. It had to be frightened or starving. Nothing frightened Manabumaru.

Only that was not true. Thinking back to this morning, Shichiro thought that Manabumaru had fled the Dragon's Tail the instant he recognised his opponent.

'Hurry up Shichiro, we're starting to lose the light,' called the Cursebreaker. She was standing up there, peering over the edge as his feet touched, then sank into the stinking morass at the bottom. Great bubbles burst from the spring, creating a ring of blackish deposits. But where his footsteps broke the crust, they showed yellow, red and a startling blue, as though here the earth rotted like a leper. Some of them he tentatively identified as the salts of alchemy, a practice which Tetsumonkai condemned as an evil sorcery. Truly, this was a place where one would only go who sought Hell.

His legs were itching and the hem of his robe befouled. He stared upwards, seeking a place where he might set the net, and fume and shadow disguise the ropes.

There seemed to be a deeper cleft in the darkest part of the cave. He could hide the net there, but to what purpose? Unless the darkness represented a further passage, perhaps to where the jikininki slept... by the mountain spirits, it really was a passage! His next step miscarried and he slipped, landing on hands and knees too close to that boiling pool. As he raised his hands they were already blackening: it looked like he had been beaten to the point of losing his nails. Once again, Shichiro remembered being a small boy crying in the dark, homesick and hurt but no longer alone. Then, as if summoned by his sheer longing, Manubumaru's voice fell to him from above.

'I knew it! A mountain goddess, come to assuage my hunger!'

'Goddess? No. Very much no.' The Cursebreaker sounded distinctly alarmed.

'Doesn't matter: I'm beyond all hope of redemption!' So this was indeed the jikininki's lair and here he knelt with the trap in his hands and the monster directly above. Any incautious move or sound louder than the roiling spring would surely draw his attention.

'You know Manabumaru, I doubt that,' said the Cursebreaker. 'Just so long as you stay on your side of the crevasse and I on mine.'

Perhaps the monster's preoccupation with the spirit woman would permit him to launch a surprise attack... Shichiro groaned silently, remembering how the same distractions had not prevented Manabumaru from overpowering him in the Dragon's Tail.

No. That was not the truth of it. His own distraction had been his undoing, just as it had been moments ago when he slipped. If Tetsumonkai had taught him anything, it was that no circumstance, no matter how dangerous or uncomfortable, justified the loss of control.

He inhaled the putrid steam, noticing for the first time the currents of air portending from the passage. He listened to the rhythm of the bubbles welling up in the water. To him it sounded almost like chanting, the constant repetition of Amida's blessed name, as matters worsened at the lip of the crevasse.

'I don't care what you are,' carolled Manabumaru, 'spirit or woman, peasant or Empress! Let me caress those heavenly orbs!'

'Look,' said the Cursebreaker, 'I'm not saying you're not... perfectly built, under all that shit. When was the last time you had a bath and a shave?'

'I had enough of that when I was human! Now I'm free! Oh, come and be free with me! What need do we have of baths, or clothes?'

'Now you just keep that on by—the—Fates: even if I was of a mind, your boyfriend would never forgive me.'

'What?'

'Well, I'm sorry; but it's pretty obvious.'

'Is he here?'

'Not exactly—oh wait, Manabumaru, don't go!'

'Just keep him away from me! I don't want him to see me like this.'

'Manabumaru, it's not that bad—'

'No!'

There was a scuffle and a startled gasp. Shichiro looked up in time to see the big, pale body in the kimono plunge towards the boiling pool.

He leapt up, dragging the net over his shoulder as another body flashed down through the fumes—

As a massive splash sent scalding droplets over his arms, his face and he threw the net out across the surface—

As he dragged the heavy weight through the muck to his feet, he did not see the pattern of the kimono. What he saw was reddened skin and shoulders, a man's shoulders. Again, he fell to his knees, hands grasping at the ropes, at the hot flesh and dripping hair.

'Oh Gods, I didn't mean to push her!' Manabumaru thrashed in the net. 'She's still in there, save her!'

'The important thing is that it worked,' said the Cursebreaker, wading out of the pool. Apart from being soaked, she seemed to have suffered no ill effect. 'And we're all down here together.'

Manabumaru had been lightly scalded on his right side but the most dramatic effect was the dissolving there of months of acquired dirt. Apart from his shoulder-length hair and the light beard and moustache, he looked exactly the same as ever and felt solid, so wonderfully solid in Shichiro's arms.

'He stays in the net,' said the Cursebreaker, 'until we've got a few things straight.' She squatted down, tugging futilely at her wet kimono. 'Manabumaru, I've got some bad news. You're not a jikininki.'

'Of course I am!' His eyes met Shichiro's with a flash of unease.

'No; you're a young man making a rather half-hearted attempt to behave like the myth says he should.'

'I know I haven't eaten any corpses yet, but there's bound to be some come Winter! And I steal food! I sleep in a hole! I get drunk and fuck in a cemetery!'

'And I've known places that would make you an undergraduate. Now, what did you do to piss off Tetsumonkai so very much?'

'I refused to undergo the ordeals.'

'To become a living Buddha. How does that work?'

Unmistakably, Shichiro felt Manabumaru tremble. 'You begin a great fast,' he said, hesitantly. 'Both of food and water. During that you perform feats of endurance for which our exercises are just the preparation. When I saw, I... I was afraid.'

'You weren't afraid,' said Shichiro. 'I was. I know Manabumaru, you refused him for me.'

A dark flush spread across the fuzzy cheeks. 'But I have to be cursed!'

'You obviously suffered a great shock,' said the Cursebreaker. 'People react to extreme situations in extreme ways.'

'But I couldn't possibly have stolen... I would never have gone with that... I wouldn't have enjoyed it!'

'For someone who spent his teens in a monastery, I'd call your behaviour perfectly natural.'

Shichiro felt his own face burning. 'But you said there had to be a curse!'

'It's around here somewhere.' She turned her face towards the passage, as though hearing something in the dark.

'It's alright,' Shichiro whispered, stroking his lover's hair. 'It will be alright, I promise.'

The Cursebreaker raised one finger. 'Have either of you ever seen a living Buddha?'

'Let me up!' Manabumaru flexed violently. 'I'll prove to you that I'm cursed, unable to enter sacred ground!'

'If this involves climbing back up to the monastery,' said the Cursebreaker, 'may I suggest we return instead to the village and wash?'

Shichiro felt Manabumaru relax. He peeled the netting from his head and down his chest before remembering that, in the martial arts, loosening the muscles did not necessarily preface inaction.

The force of his leap knocked Shichiro back against the wall. 'What are you doing?' he cried, 'Manabumaru, I don't care!' But he had already vanished into the darkness that was the guts of the mountain. 'Manabumaru!'

'Lantern,' said the Cursebreaker, handing him one.

This was the abode of spirits. Shichiro glimpsed inhuman faces in the fleeting light, felt the brush of stone-cold fingers as he followed the sound of Manabumaru's feet. Behind him the Cursebreaker scuffed and swore in terms he understood perfectly. He felt like using them himself, as the passage climbed and climbed.

Then he was no longer listening to the sound of feet. The sound he heard, the rhythm he followed without thinking, so familiar it was, came as chanting. The name of Amida, the promise of the Pure Land.

'The monastery!' he gasped. 'We must be *beneath* it!'

The next turn brought light and the next showed him Manabumaru, poised on the threshold of a roughly-worked chamber. One more burst of speed and Shichiro dug his fingers into his lover's shoulder.

'I can go no further.' Manabumaru sounded strangely content. 'The sanctity of the living Buddhas bars my way.'

'Sanctity...' panted the Cursebreaker, 'my... arse...'

'I cannot so much as look upon them,' said Manabumaru. 'Where I should see glory, I see only despair.'

The stench was appalling. A series of cavities had been scooped from the rock and inside at least five of these, he saw a withered corpse. The flesh had dried and shrunk, the skin tightening about the bones of crossed legs and hands retracted to the chest. Cheeks and noses collapsed into contours that nonetheless caused Shichiro shocks of recognition. But such things had no business speaking. No business shaking and twitching. Yet twitch they did and yet they chanted, an endless, meaningless drone like the boiling of water, the grinding of stones.

'Habitual dehydration,' muttered the Cursebreaker, 'a gradual restriction of calories... autohypnosis... by the kindly ones, it's *possible.*'

The sound that had accompanied Shichiro day and night for so long as he could remember was here unbearable. It worked into his ears and teeth. It was almost worse than seeing those eyes move, sunk in hollows so deep they seemed like parasites sheltering in skulls. Not a one of the living Buddhas turned towards him or showed any other sign they knew they were observed. That they knew they lived. He felt his stomach convulse and then he was hauling at Manabumaru, dragging him back down the passage that led to the spring. 'I am resigned to my doom, Shichiro,' he said, sounding positively happy.

'Tetsumonkai wanted you to become one of those? To do that to you? *He is a shit-eating demon from the seventh Hell!*' He clung to Manabumaru and stroked his face, knowing now what had snapped his mind and taken him so far from himself. He begged his forgiveness for not following him, for cringing from the sound of Tetsumonkai's fury as he now cringed from the chanting and the roiling stench of rotting flesh.

'This is the curse!' he cried, loud as he could. 'Oh merciful spirits, this is it!'

'I'm afraid not,' said the Cursebreaker.

'How can you say that?'

'Because,' she said, 'these poor souls are practically mummies. That stink isn't coming from them.'

'How DARE you intrude on this sacred place!' As Shichiro flinched from the Abbot's voice, Manabumaru's arms closed about him. The shadow of a peaked hat crept up the floor towards them, towards the Cursebreaker, who stood before the mummies without displaying the slightest tremor.

'Greetings venerable Abbot.' It was the calm in her voice that made Shichiro realise just what she was. How old and how terrible in her pale flesh.

'You are no spirit. A magician, then, come to oppose me?'

'Oh, I'm no magician either, though I've known a few. And witches. A saint, even. You're no saint, Tetsumonkai.'

'I have never claimed to be.'

'But you are a scholar; those were your books Shichiro read. So you know that any man can call down a curse. You also know that a man can curse himself.'

'Dharma. There is no way to avoid dharma.'

'I've seen far too much to be shocked at what a person can do to themselves and others in the name of faith. So how long has it been, Tetsumonkai? Since your faith condemned you?'

'In one day you have uncovered a truth I have hidden for forty years.' The Abbot's voice held an incredible weariness. 'I bathe in the spring that I forbid to others. I smother myself in robes and incense, and stay apart, always apart from my boys. I never touch one, save with my cane. Still, every day I expect they will smell me out.'

The shadow falling along the passage was of something bent, hooked and hairy.

'You feed off them, don't you,' said the Cursebreaker. 'The living corpses.'

'I can't help it.' His voice was a sigh now. 'But by helping them ascend, perhaps I may earn forgiveness.'

'The transformation is impressive, in its way. Only the very strongest could achieve it. But you understand, such a sacrifice can only be made by the self.'

'I know. I only wish to help them achieve what I could not.'

'Is that why you pretended to curse Manabumaru?'

'That was a warning! I tried, tried and failed once more.'

'I don't judge you, Tetsumonkai. I don't even care what it was that plagues your conscience so, that they still remember in the village.'

'She was only a woman, but my sin was the greater for that. Night after night I descended to meet her. She would have borne my child but all I could think of was the shame and penance I would endure if it became known. I blamed her and what I did to stop it, killed them both.'

'And so you cursed yourself.'

'And corruption entered men's hearts and the war began.'

'Well, you needn't imagine *that's* your fault. But this,' she waved at the niches, 'this isn't helping.'

'I help them avoid the trap that snared me!'

'You trapped yourself, Tetsumonkai.' The putridity in the air intensified and before the young monks' eyes the leftmost Buddha collapsed in upon itself, tongue stilling at last. 'But there is a way out.'

'I am so, so tired.'

'Accept you will never earn forgiveness. You can only ask and receive. Can you do that, Tetsumonkai? Can you forgive yourself?'

Through the thickening shadow, the human remnants and the ground itself a vibration ran, growing stronger, deeper and harder to distinguish from either mountain or flesh. The lanterns guttered and something that was not the light went out.

Then there was silence.

Chaos possessed the monastery. The cessation of the chanting had caught the attention of monks returning late from the summit and they had woken the others. The corpses below had been discovered and among them, the long-decayed remains of Tetsumonkai. Prayers and lamentations still resounded from the Golden Hall; while some roamed the complex weeping and others performed frantic star-jumps, a few had commenced plunging from the prayer gate on the grounds that the waterfall was too far away. Only here in this courtyard was there anything approaching calm. Brother Heihachi had been accosted by the Cursebreaker and persuaded to brew some genuine tea. Fears assuaged, he was cooking with increasing enthusiasm.

'Manabumaru won't stay.' Shichiro sat on the steps of the refectory, gazing at the lightening sky. 'He's asked me to leave with him.'

'It's a dangerous world out there.' The Cursebreaker swallowed a red bean dumpling. 'But I guess Manabumaru has discovered things in himself that can't be dealt with by climbing mountains.'

'Yes.'

'At least now he'll be properly dressed.' She speared another dumpling. 'And will you follow him?'

'No.'

How could he explain it, even to himself? The months without his lover had seen him desolate, plagued by guilt and fear. Only in the monastery and the mountains themselves had he found solace. Perhaps it was cowardice to stay, but it did not feel like cowardice. Not given what had happened here.

The columns cast shadows now, as a silvery luminescence grew in the sky. The guardian carvings patrolled the roof beams. Amongst the dark hills below, mist rose once more from the concealed paths and streams. All was as it had been before he performed the summoning, and the dawn before that; a thousand dawns. Someone should point that out to the wretches running around, behaving like monkeys.

'No matter what the rest of the world is like,' he said slowly, 'there must always be a peaceful valley here and mountaintops pointing towards Heaven. One day, maybe, Manabumaru will seek peace again.'

'Maybe so.' The Cursebreaker turned her face to the sunrise and put down her bowl. 'You're a good man, Shichiro. Perhaps one day you will become something more.'

At that, he had to speak the words that were hovering fearfully in his throat. 'The book I read said something of the origin of the

Cursebreaker. She was a scholar in a distant land and time, who challenged the great incarnation of Dharma.'

'I call her Fate. All three of her.'

'She was condemned to labour, unceasing, unending. There was... there was great wisdom in what you told Tetsumonkai. Could you not accept it yourself?'

'You mean, stop caring?'

'What I mean, is—'

'That is what you mean. For Fate to even consider releasing me, I would have to stop accusing her. But in each new place I appear, in each new curse, I discover more and worse. Such things as you can't, that you shouldn't imagine: a man unable to heal. A woman unable to love. I know you mean well, Shichiro. But *knowing*, how can I not care?'

The sun crested the triple summits and just as it was written, the Cursebreaker was gone.

Against the Air Pirates

Graeme Davis

Anyone who has been in the Pacific for a while will tell you that there are currents in more than just the water. Something about the ocean moves people as if they were driftwood, causing them to fetch up in certain places. For air bums and bush pilots, Louie's was one of those places.

The little island may have belonged to the Philippines or to Indonesia, and it may even have had a name. No one knew for sure, and no one much cared. Everyone just called it Louie's. Its position on the charts made it a useful refueling stop, the absence of colonial authorities made it a good place to do business, and Louie kept a good stock of the essentials: fuel, food and drink, and plenty of privacy.

At any time, a half-dozen floatplanes and small flying boats were moored round a small jetty anchored to the refueling barge in the island's sheltered lagoon. The jetty led to a cluster of bamboo and palm leaf shacks, the largest of which was Louie's Tiki Lounge.

On this particular evening, one of the more private tables was occupied by a tall, rangy American in grease-stained khakis and a smaller but equally lean Dutchman whose lightweight tropical suit was dark under the arms.

'Listen, Huysman,' said the American, 'I've got my professional reputation to think about. I can't have half the folks around here thinking I got bushwhacked and the other half thinking I was in on it. Besides, Doc Lacroix can't get morphine any other way. I imagine your rich friends have other options.'

Huysman sneered. 'I was told you were a businessman, Finnegan, not a Boy Scout.'

'Oh, I'm a businessman, all right, and your scheme is bad for business.'

'Then perhaps I should be more persuasive.' A gun appeared in the Dutchman's hand. Finnegan regarded it with mild interest, leaning back in his seat and running his fingers through his dark-brown hair.

'Put your hands on the table,' Huysman ordered. Finnegan complied.

'Now,' Huysman continued, 'you will stand up slowly and I will follow you to your plane. Together, we will deliver the cargo just as I have told you. What you tell people after that—if I let you live—is completely up to you. Move!'

Finnegan moved more quickly than the Dutchman expected. Glasses flew as he flipped the table into the air, knocking Huysman's gun hand up so his shot went harmlessly through the palm thatch. The tabletop slammed into Huysman's chest, driving the wind out of him. He could do nothing but gasp for breath as Finnegan took his gun.

'It's okay,' Finnegan called out amiably, 'just a little business negotiation.' The low buzz of conversation slowly resumed. Although they were not common, such distractions were not unknown at Louie's. The barman, a huge Polynesian called Mo whose real name was unpronounceable, hustled the Dutchman outside.

'You'll regret this, Finnegan!' he screamed over Mo's shoulder.

Finnegan laughed. 'That's what life is, Huysman, didn't they tell you? Nothing but piling up regrets.' He righted the table, shaking his head with a smile.

'What was that about?' Louie came over with a broom to sweep up the broken glasses.

Finnegan chuckled as he sat back down. 'He wanted me to help him steal my own cargo for one of his buyers.'

'Jesus,' Louis grunted. 'He can find Chicago on a map and he thinks he's Al Capone. I need a better class of customer.'

Louis finished cleaning up and Finnegan sat back down at the table. A minute later, a fresh beer arrived, with a daiquiri keeping it company. The woman holding the tray was definitely not one of Louie's staff.

'Are you Finnegan?' Her voice was like cigar smoke and fine brandy. 'Louie says you might give me a ride to Tamaling.'

◇

The *Lady Luck* had started life as a Supermarine Sea Eagle in British Malaya. Now, she was part Junkers, part Boeing, and part several other things. The other pilots joked that Finnegan had named her *Lady Luck* to help hold the various parts together, but she was a true-flying and reliable ship.

By the time Finnegan brought her two bags aboard, the girl was already strapped into the co-pilot's seat. She said her name was Eve Martin, from San Francisco.

'So what brings you way out here?' Finnegan asked as the *Lady Luck* taxied out onto the lagoon.

'The cool, crisp, mountain air,' she said with a straight face. 'I hear it's wonderful for the complexion.'

Finnegan laughed. 'Okay, miss,' he said. 'I know how to mind my own business.' He pushed the throttle forward and the *Lady Luck* accelerated. There was a slight buffet as her hull left the water, and she began a smooth climb.

'Well,' said Finnegan after they had leveled off, 'it's a couple of hours to Tamaling, and we have to talk about something. So how about those Yankees? Is it true Babe Ruth's sick?'

'So he says,' Eve replied. 'Some reporter called it the bellyache heard round the world. He reckons the Babe needs to lay off the hot dogs and soda pop. Other people say it's from cheap hooch or cheap women, though the papers don't mention that. But if you want to talk, tell me about Doctor Lacroix and this Tamaling mission. Do you know him well?'

Finnegan looked at her. 'Well enough,' he said. 'Seems strange that you'd be headed there without knowing anything about the place.'

Eve smiled. 'All I know is that he could use a nurse and I could use a job,' she said.

'So you're a nurse?' said Finnegan. 'What happened? Did you lose a patient? Or are you trying to lose one? I bet all your male patients fall madly in love.'

'Some do,' Eve laughed, 'but there's nothing like emptying bedpans to take the shine off a romance. So what about Lacroix?'

'Older gent,' said Finnegan. 'French. Runs the place by himself since his wife died. He just does what he can to keep the locals healthy.'

'Is he big on the religious side? Church socials were never my strong point.'

'No, he kind of lost his faith along with his wife. He couldn't figure out what was killing her, and just had to watch her die. He's never forgiven himself, or God. Her funeral was the last service he ever held.'

'That's rough.' Eve's face showed genuine sympathy. 'Will he be okay with a woman around again?'

'Hard to say. You tell me when you find out.'

Eve looked out the window for a while.

'There sure are a lot of these little islands,' she said after a while. 'How do you find your way around? They all look alike to me.'

'After a while you pick up on the differences,' said Finnegan, 'and with a map, a compass, and a good watch you can tell pretty much where you are most of the time. For example, this island down on the starboard side is'—his expression changed as he peered down—'curious.'

'Meaning we're lost?' asked Eve.

'Meaning it looks like a buddy of mine's having some trouble,' Finnegan replied. 'Do you mind a comfort break?'

'I could use one.'

Finnegan throttled back and trimmed the plane for landing.

Al Brooks had painted his Heinkel floatplane bright yellow because, he said, it would be easy to spot if he ever got into trouble. It certainly stood out against the palm-fringed lagoon, and as Finnegan taxied toward it he saw that it sat oddly in the water, with the tail too low and the nose too high. As he got closer, he could see that the Heinkel's engine was missing altogether. He leaned out of the cockpit and yelled for Brooks, but received no answer.

'That comfort break may need to wait a few minutes,' he told Eve. 'Sit tight while I check this out.' He moored the *Lady Luck* alongside and threw out the anchor.

Something was very wrong. There were bullet holes in the Heinkel's wings and tail. The hatch cover stood open, and the hold was empty. Brooks was nowhere to be seen, but there were traces of blood in the cockpit.

'I'm going ashore to look for the pilot,' he told Eve. 'It looks like he ran into some trouble.' He shook his head as Eve rose from her seat.

'This may be dangerous,' he said, holding up a hand.

'Don't worry about me.' She reached into her purse and pulled out a gun. It was pretty, a pearl-handled .22, but she held it as though she knew how to use it.

On the beach they found a single set of footprints interspersed with drops of congealed blood. At the end of the trail Brooks was slumped under a bush, his Webley .45 still in his hand. Dried blood crusted his shirt. Eve pressed two fingers to his neck, looked up at Finnegan, and shook her head.

'Who did this?' her voice was low but calm as her eyes scanned the bushes. It was clear she had been around violent death before.

'Whoever it was,' said Finnegan, 'they must have had tools and gear to lift the engine out. And at least one machine gun, judging by those holes.'

Finnegan buried Brooks on the island and dragged his plane onto the beach. He would spread the news when he got back to Louie's; maybe someone there could recover the plane. Bush pilots stuck together, but out here no one could afford to be sentimental about equipment. Maybe, too, someone would have heard of well-armed bandits operating in the area.

They spoke little on the way to Tamaling. The mission consisted of nothing more than a few huts around a clearing near a beach, where a small crowd of curious locals gathered as Finnegan beached the *Lady Luck* with a gentle bump and helped Eve from the cockpit. Doc Lacroix came over as Finnegan was setting her bags down on the sand.

'Ah, Finnegan,' he said, holding out a hand, 'you have my morphine, *oui?*' His eyes widened as he saw Eve. 'Or perhaps I have already taken it and I am dreaming? *Mademoiselle, je suis enchanté.*'

When Eve explained she was a nurse, the doctor's smile broadened and the flow of French gallantries increased. He carried her bags to the least ramshackle of the huts, promising it would be repaired *tout de suite*. Soon he was shouting at his cook in a mixture of pidgin French and the local island language. Finnegan guessed that the new arrival would be honored with a special meal.

With Eve unpacking and the mission's staff scurrying about on various food-related errands, Lacroix came over to Finnegan.

'You can still change these?' he asked, pulling out a wad of francs.

'One way or another,' said Finnegan, taking them with a smile.

'I told the *Société Missionaire* that dollars are more useful here, but they take no notice. I suppose I am lucky they send anything.'

'Don't worry about it. Everything been quiet here since my last visit?'

Lacroix raised his eyebrows slightly. 'Of course,' he said. 'Why would it not be?'

'Brooks is dead. I spotted his plane on the way here. It looks like bandits — very well-armed bandits.'

'I am sorry,' said the Frenchman. 'He was a good man, and I know he was your friend. I have heard nothing about these bandits, but I will ask. You know my spies.' His patients came from all over the surrounding area, and Doc Lacroix often got news before it even reached Louie's.

'Thanks, Doc,' said Finnegan, 'and watch out. I already had to fend off one eager buyer for your morphine.'

'Don't worry,' replied Lacroix. 'If anyone comes to steal it, I will be ready for them!'

◇

'You have got to be kidding.' Finnegan squinted at the shape in the distance. Even from three miles away, there was no mistaking it. Finnegan had seen a few zeppelins over France, and this was so big, so high, and so silver that it could not be anything else. He decided to take a closer look. The sun glinted off the airship's silver skin, but it was too far off to see any markings.

Germany had been forced to give up her zeppelins under the Treaty of Versailles, but other nations still flew them, most notably Britain and America. France and Italy had a few dirigibles each, but no colonies nearby. There was talk of commercial services across the Atlantic, faster than a liner but no less comfortable. Maybe this was a passenger ship.

He was a scant couple of miles away when the airship's belly opened and two small planes dropped from inside. They leveled out and made straight for him. With a curse, Finnegan pushed the throttles forward and banked sharply. British or American, it had to be military, and launching fighters was anything but a friendly sign. He had a hunch that Brooks had met with this zeppelin.

Even with the *Lady Luck* in a shallow dive at full throttle, the fighters gained steadily. The sea was coming up fast and Finnegan tried to think faster. Ahead of him a small, rocky island broke the flatness of the sea. Finnegan hoped the fighter pilots didn't know it as well as he did.

He ducked involuntarily as tracers flashed past. A glance over his shoulder told him that the two fighters were on his tail and matching his speed. Further away a third plane had joined the chase, and he smiled when he saw the floats slung beneath its wingtips. That must be the way they got their loot back to the airship. Launching it meant they wanted him — or the *Lady Luck*, at least — in one piece.

At that moment, the radio crackled into life.

'Attention, cargo aircraft!' The accent was German. 'You will land at the island ahead or we will shoot you down! Do you understand? Acknowledge!'

His best chance for now was to play dumb and wait for an opportunity. 'Who are you?' he replied, trying to sound panicked. 'What do you want? I am carrying no valuable cargo — repeat, no valuable cargo!' The only response was another stream of tracers, a little closer to his cockpit this time.

He rocked the stick left and right, waggling the *Lady Luck's* wings in the universal signal of non-aggression, and studied the fighters in the mirror. They were monoplanes with a parasol wing held above the fuselage on struts. Their landing gear had been removed, so they could only operate from their mother ship.

Keeping the island on his right, Finnegan throttled back and began what looked like a normal landing approach. As the *Lady Luck's* hull was about to kiss the sea the fighters banked away, planning to circle over their captive until the floatplane arrived with a boarding party. This was the moment Finnegan had been waiting for.

The *Lady Luck* lurched as he slammed the throttles forward, keeping one eye on the mirror. It would take the enemy pilots a few seconds to realize what he was doing, and several more to bring their planes back around and get a bead on him. He hoped that would be enough.

The shoreline flashed past on his right, pale sand fringed with palm trees. By the time the fighters had come around to chase him, the *Lady Luck* was about level with the rocky headland Finnegan had aimed for. Her starboard float almost touched the wave tops as he banked.

The fighters came up quickly, and the *Lady Luck* shuddered as bullets struck her tail. Finnegan held the turn until the headland blocked their line of sight, then pulled up hard as a stack of rock loomed ahead of him. The *Lady Luck* cleared the stack by no more than a foot.

The fighters were not so lucky. The first pilot clipped off half of his starboard wing against the rock and went pinwheeling into the shallow water. The second missed the rock but was hit by flying debris from the first plane. His propeller jerked to a sudden halt, fouled with wire and canvas. Finnegan saw the pilot fighting to keep control as his plane bellied down onto the sea in a welter of spray.

As Finnegan had hoped, the floatplane landed to assist the downed pilots. Keeping the island between himself and the zeppelin, he ran straight and level at maximum speed.

'A zeppelin, you say?' asked Gillibrand. 'That could explain a few things.' Louie put an open beer in front of the Australian.

'What kind of things?' asked Finnegan.

'I was just over at Puramaling and the locals were in a flap about something that flew over a few days back. Big and silver, they said, and very slow. Definitely not a plane. They thought it was a dragon.'

'The *Sally Anne*, too,' put in Cheng. 'My cousin works for Morton Shipping in Manado. Telegraph office. She sent out a mayday—attack by aircraft. Then nothing.'

'Makes sense,' said Finnegan. 'They can't exactly go into town for fuel and spares.'

'You said they were German?' Louie handed Finnegan another beer.

'I didn't see any markings, but they sounded German,' Finnegan said. 'And the fighters had that little round Fokker tail and wedge tailplane. D VIIIs if I had to guess. How they stayed in German hands after the war, I don't know. Did the Germans even have any colonies in the Pacific?'

'Bloody right they did,' said Gillibrand. 'Before the war they had part of New Guinea. Kaiser Wilhelm's Land, they called it. The Bismarck Archipelago was named after some other Hun bigwig, too. We had it all off the bastards in the first few months.'

Finnegan ran a hand through his hair. 'Well, how about that? So did they have any zeppelins out here back then?'

Gillibrand shook his head. 'Nah. They kept 'em all in the Mother Country so they could drop bombs on London and Paris. Too big, too expensive, and too hard to move all the way out here. No planes, either—or at least, nothing like a Fokker.'

Louie stopped polishing the bar. 'Here's what I'd like to know,' he said. 'Is anyone doing anything about these jokers? Britain, Holland, anyone?'

Gillibrand shrugged. 'I wouldn't rely on Britain,' he said. 'Even if we could drag some chinless Pommy wonder away from his pink gin long enough to tell him there's a German zeppelin running about, he'd laugh in our faces. The RAF's got next to nothing this side of Singapore. Holland has even less. The best either of 'em could do is send a cruiser or something, and that wouldn't be any use for hunting zeppelins.'

'Not much is,' said Finnegan. 'Nothing we had in France could get high enough to touch them once they were under way. All we could do was bomb their bases and try to catch them taking off or landing.'

'And nobody knows where these bastards hang their spiked little helmets,' said Gillibrand. 'Bloody marvelous. What about your lot, though? There's that U.S.S. Los Angeles. Set an airship to catch an airship?'

Finnegan shook his head. 'Unless she just happens to be on a fleet exercise in the Pacific, she'd take weeks to get here,' he said. 'Besides, I don't have a lot of credit with the U.S. Navy. It's a long story.'

'So it's just us, then?' Gillibrand took a long pull of his beer. 'Well, I don't know about you, mate, but I'm off to see a man about a Lewis gun. Those Fokkers'll have to watch out if they come near me.'

'I'm going back to Tamaling,' said Finnegan. 'The zeppelin must have passed close by there. Maybe the Doc can tell me where it was headed.'

◇

Finnegan spotted the column of smoke from twenty miles away. When he brought the *Lady Luck* down on the lagoon, the mission looked like a war zone. Two buildings were still burning, and the compound was deserted.

Everything was quiet when Finnegan stepped ashore. As he walked toward the compound, a small boy stepped out of the bush and waved urgently. Finnegan found a cluster of scared and wounded locals hiding at the edge of the compound, crouched around Lacroix. The old Frenchman lay in the shade with blood leaking out of three holes in his shirt. 'They came from the air,' he croaked. 'Took everything.' He coughed up a few flecks of blood.

'Eve?'

'Gone!' Lacroix grabbed Finnegan's arm. 'I tried to stop them!' Another fit of coughing racked his body. Blood dribbled onto his beard.

Finnegan held a canteen to the Frenchman's lips and he took a few swallows of water. Then his head sagged back and his eyes closed. The locals began a mournful wail.

Leaving them to bury Lacroix, Finnegan searched the ruined buildings. All the mission's medical supplies and equipment were gone, along with the kerosene for the generators.

Using a mixture of French, pidgin English, and the little he knew of the local language, Finnegan managed to get some idea of what had happened. The zeppelin appeared a couple of hours ago. It lowered some kind of cage containing a landing party of white men, who went from building to building gathering everything they could find. Eve wounded a couple of the raiders before they overpowered her. Lacroix was shot and left to die. They set fire to the buildings before being winched up with the looted supplies, and the zeppelin headed off northward. The attack took less than thirty minutes.

Finnegan set off to the north. With a map on his knee, he mentally plotted the zeppelin's course and the sites of the other attacks. The pirates needed a base. It had to be far enough away from anywhere inhabited that no one would see them coming and going, but big enough to accommodate mooring gear and everything else needed to maintain—and preferably hide—an airship over five hundred feet long. Eventually he found it: a small volcanic island named Kunatik. The crater was almost a half mile wide, and high enough to swallow the zeppelin completely.

The sun was low in the sky as Finnegan approached Kunatik from the west. 'Beware the Hun in the sun' was a hard-learned lesson from the Western Front, and he hoped the sunset would mask his approach from any lookouts. The raking light picked out every detail of the mountain. It looked almost pleated where wind and water had carved gullies down its flanks.

The western side of the crater was marked by a wide notch. According to a geologist Finnegan had once ferried around the islands, at some point the volcano had blown out its flank and erupted sideways, like Mount Pelée did in 1902. Silver glinted inside the notch, and about two miles out Finnegan could see the curve of the zeppelin's back nestled inside the volcano.

Below the mountain, the fringes of the island were covered in dense forest. Finnegan set the *Lady Luck* down in a small bay, running her onto the beach under the cover of overhanging palm trees. He slung a canteen of water over his shoulder and grabbed a machete. After some deliberation, he left his Colt behind. That zeppelin held a lot of inflammable hydrogen, and if Eve was in there he couldn't take the risk of setting it off with a spark from a ricochet. Besides, the pirates outnumbered him and gunshots would only give away his position.

The tropical sunset was a brief but spectacular affair. Night falls quickly at these latitudes, and the light gave out before Finnegan had gone more than a mile into the jungle. The clamor of bird calls gave way to the steady drone of insects as he made a makeshift camp.

At first light he set out again, climbing steadily upward and around the crater. By the time he arrived at the notch it was almost noon and his clothes were dark with sweat. Rock walls rose almost vertically on the other sides, enclosing a dormant crater and rubble floor.

A line of palm-thatched wooden shacks stood with their backs to the crater wall. The ground around them had been cleared of debris and flattened. The zeppelin hung over everything like a vast awning. It was moored to a mast with a small hut at its base—probably a winch-house for lowering the airship into the crater once its mooring lines were secure. A broad ramp led down from the belly of the ship onto the makeshift dock, where uniformed men moved about carrying crates and pieces of equipment.

Keeping low, Finnegan picked his way from boulder to boulder. There were no guards or lookouts that he could see, so the pirates must not have spotted the *Lady Luck* approaching the island. Soon he was within a few yards of the closest hut.

Finnegan had never seen a zeppelin at such close quarters. A control cabin jutted from the underside of the nose, with a secondary cabin about half-way back. Both were equipped with ladders giving access to the interior. Three pairs of engines hung from the exterior on latticework pylons. The men working on them looked like ants.

As huge as the zeppelin was, it was also fragile. Any flame— even a spark—could ignite the hydrogen gas that held it aloft, and if that happened it was doomed. Signs all around the base proclaimed *Rauchen Verboten*—Smoking Forbidden— in jagged German script. From what he could see there were at least twenty of the pirates, and there were probably more aboard the zeppelin repairing the damaged fighters.

Eve was probably aboard the zeppelin as well. Between the downed pilots and the raiders she had wounded, the pirates needed someone with medical skills. That might be the only thing keeping her alive. The base of the zeppelin's ramp was around fifty yards from where he crouched, and twenty from the nearest shed. Given the constant movement on the dock, he had almost no chance of boarding the ship without being spotted. He needed some kind of diversion.

No one seemed to be looking his way, so Finnegan risked a short run to the huts and worked his way cautiously behind them. He listened for footsteps, and when his ear told him no one was nearby he pulled out his lighter and set fire to the overhanging thatch on the hut furthest from the zeppelin. Then he moved to the opposite end of the row and waited as the fire took hold.

'*Feuer!*' The alarm was raised. The pirates on the dock grabbed buckets and ran toward the burning hut. More came running down the ramp from inside the zeppelin. When he was sure no one was left on board, Finnegan ran onto the huge craft.

◇

Even with the space taken up by its gas bags, the zeppelin's interior was larger than Finnegan had expected. Near the top of the ramp, a winch held the zeppelin's mooring line. Nearby, a kerosene-powered generator was connected to electric lights that hung from the metal latticework of the zeppelin's skeleton.

The floatplane and the two fighters hung from trapeze-like frames that could be lowered through the opening in the airship's belly. Benches had been set up beside the damaged planes, and Finnegan allowed himself a tight smile as he saw the evidence of their encounter with the rock. At the rearward end, metal steps led up to a walkway that connected several doors.

The zeppelin's sick bay was behind the fourth door he tried. Eve was tending an injured man in one of the two bunks, and looked up with a scowl as he entered. Finnegan grinned as her expression turned to one of surprise.

'How did you...?' she asked. Finnegan cast a warning glance at her patient, but she responded with a low chuckle. As she turned, he saw a livid bruise on her left cheek.

'Morphine makes for a co-operative patient,' she said. 'He won't be raising any alarms.'

'That's fine by me,' said Finnegan. 'What happened to your face?'

Eve grimaced. 'I told them I don't look after murderers,' she said. 'It didn't go down too well. This guy's their best pilot, apparently, but he had a disagreement with a rock while he was chasing down a plane that sounded a lot like yours. I'm glad you got away.'

'Plenty of others weren't so lucky,' said Finnegan. 'Are you ready to get out of here?'

'Am I ever!' She gave him a smile he could feel all the way to his boots. 'Lead on, *mein Kapitan.*'

They made their way back into the hangar, which was still empty. From the commotion outside, the pirates had not yet brought the fire under control. Finnegan led the way to the top of the ramp, using the docked aircraft and onboard machinery as cover.

'I'm making this up as I go,' said Finnegan, 'but if we—' He whirled around as Eve let out a sudden gasp. She was writhing in the grip of a tall man in an officer's uniform. Finnegan's machete was in his hand before he even thought about it.

'Lack of proper planning is a serious oversight,' he said in mock reproach. 'It has been the cause of many military blunders.'

The officer was as German as his accent. Beneath his cap his blond hair was cropped short. A monocle twinkled in one eye, and a red scar snaked down one side of his hawk-like nose. His left arm was wrapped tightly around Eve's throat, and his right held a long saber. Slowly but meaningfully, he raised the point of his sword until it dug into Eve's ribs. With an effort, Finnegan relaxed and took a step back.

'His business sense isn't much better, I'm afraid.' A smaller man stepped out from behind the officer, pointing a gun at Finnegan. The American groaned.

'Huysman,' he said. 'So I guess this is your buyer?'

The Dutchman's only reply was a greasy smile. The German pushed Eve toward Finnegan and clicked his heels sharply.

'Kapitan Freiherr Eberhardt von Falkenburg,' he said with an ironic bow. 'Late of the Kaiserliche Marine. Welcome aboard the *L66*. You must be Michael Finnegan, the American Boy Scout. Huysman here warned me about your misplaced sense of chivalry.'

Finnegan motioned Eve behind him and glared at the two Europeans. Huysman's face was full of malicious glee, while the German's showed nothing but arrogant humor.

'I suppose I should thank you, Mister Finnegan,' he continued. 'Since you declined Huysman's offer, I was able to obtain the morphine for free. Although I doubt that Huysman here shares my sentiment. He would have profited significantly from the transaction.'

'But of course, you have also caused me a great deal of trouble. Two aircraft seriously damaged, one pilot badly injured, and of course the two men shot by your lady friend here. She is quite the Calamity Jane, I think.'

'What do you plan to do about it, Fritz?' Finnegan growled. 'Talk us to death?'

'He's good at that,' Eve put in over Finnegan's shoulder. 'Been entertaining me with brandy and fancy dinners since they brought me here.'

'And I assure you,' von Falkenburg added smoothly, 'my intentions have been completely honorable. The fact is, Mister Finnegan, that we have—how do you put it?—time to kill. Once my men have dealt with that inconvenient fire—which you no doubt set as a distraction—I can kill you at my leisure, and in front of my crew. Since your little trick with the rock there has been too much talk about this American pilot with supernatural flying abilities, and it is very bad for morale. It will be good for the men to see that you are not also immortal.'

Finnegan spread his hands and gave a small bow of acknowledgement, stepping out from in front of Eve as he did so. He opened his mouth as if to speak, but instead he moved with blinding speed, pushing Eve to the ground and using the momentum to roll the other way so Huysman's bullet passed harmlessly between them. He struck at the winch with his machete, severing the mooring cable with a single blow. The zeppelin lurched slightly and began to rise.

Huysman raised his gun to fire again, then stopped. His eyes widened as he stared at the stump of his wrist where von Falkenburg's sword had passed through.

'*Dummkopf!*' screamed the German. 'You will kill us all!' The Dutchman crumpled to his knees in a widening pool of blood, whimpering as he clutched his maimed arm to his chest. Outside, a few of the pirates had heard the shot and seen the zeppelin start to ascend. They were running toward the ramp, but a glance told Finnegan they would not reach it in time.

'Sorry, Captain,' he said, hefting his machete, 'I'm not overly fond of crowds. Though time to kill sounds pretty good. Are you as brave without your men?'

Von Falkenburg raised his saber and one eyebrow simultaneously. 'A rash choice, Mister Finnegan,' he said. 'I was the captain of the student dueling society at the University of Königsberg. It was there that I received my scar.' He adopted a fencing stance and began to circle the American.

'That must be nice for you,' said Finnegan. 'Where I was raised, it's better to give than to receive.'

From the corner of his eye, Finnegan saw that Eve had recovered Huysman's gun from his severed hand and was pointing it at the German. He caught her eye and shook his head, directing her toward the suspended floatplane with a flick of his eyes.

Von Falkenburg leaped forward, aiming a savage cut at Finnegan's head. Instead of parrying or falling back the American twisted to his left, letting the sword miss his shoulder by a fraction of an inch. Carried forward by the momentum of the blow, von Falkenburg's chin was in exactly the right place to meet the butt of Finnegan's machete as he slammed it upward. The German staggered back a few paces, blood streaming from his lower lip.

'The thing about duels,' said Finnegan, 'is they're for gentlemen. Me, I prefer a good, old-fashioned knife fight.'

Wiping his chin on his cuff, von Falkenburg raised his sword. 'I shan't make that mistake again,' he said.

Using the superior reach of his sword the German beat Finnegan back, raining blow after numbing blow on the blade of the machete until the American's wrist ached. Finnegan kept blocking his attacks, moving counter-clockwise until he had his back to one of the work benches.

Thinking he saw an opening, von Falkenburg pressed his attack. Finnegan stepped aside, snatching up a heavy wrench in his left hand and crossing it with the machete just in time to prevent the German's cut from splitting his skull open. He caught the next slash on the shaft of the wrench and struck at von Falkenburg's midsection, gashing the German's sleeve but missing his skin.

Von Falkenburg replied with a slash across Finnegan's ribs that left him gasping, followed by a flurry of blows that forced him to his knees, the wrench and machete crossed defensively above his head. Finnegan's arms felt like lead, numbed by blow after blow, and it took all his strength to keep them raised. He felt the wrench jerk almost out of his hand as von Falkenburg's blade struck the open jaws.

Reacting rather than thinking, Finnegan twisted the wrench savagely, trying to jerk the sword out of his opponent's hand. Instead the blade snapped, the broken end ringing as it skidded across the deck. Von Falkenburg stared for a moment at the broken stump of a sword in his hand, and then threw himself on Finnegan with a guttural cry.

Finnegan dodged, tripping the German as he swept past. Von Falkenburg rolled and turned, bringing up his broken sword. Finnegan threw the wrench at him. It struck his left temple and hit the deck with a dull sound. Dropping what was left of his sword, the German fell back against the electrical generator, upsetting a can of kerosene.

He tried to stand, slipping in the liquid that pooled around him. His tattered sleeve caught in the generator's drive belt and pulled his arm round. He screamed as the unforgiving mechanical force dislocated his elbow. A grinding sound came from within the generator as it its engine labored to keep turning. Sparks lit up the inside of the casing and the kerosene ignited with a soft *whumph.*

Yelling to Eve to get into the floatplane, Finnegan turned and ran as quickly as his exhausted legs could go. Looking through the open hatch in the airship's floor, he could see that the zeppelin's altitude was a little over a thousand feet. He prayed it would be enough.

Ignoring the screaming pain in his arms, Finnegan clambered over the opening and along the suspension rail into the floatplane, gritting his teeth as he hauled himself into the cockpit. Eve was already in the back seat, unable to take her wide eyes off the spreading fire. The plane had no self-starter and there was no time to start the engine manually, so Finnegan pulled the release lever. The floatplane dropped away from the doomed zeppelin.

The wind hit Finnegan in the face like a blow. In an open cockpit with no goggles and a tiny windshield, he squeezed away tears and tried to decipher the German writing on the controls. The floatplane was nose down, and the ocean was coming up far too quickly.

Wires sang and the wood creaked as Finnegan forced the stick back, praying he could pull the plane out of its dive without tearing the wings off. A sudden burst of orange light reflected off the sea as the zeppelin burst into flames, but the wind drowned out the sound of the explosion.

Finnegan braced his feet against the rudder pedals and held the stick against his stomach as the sea got closer and closer. A wing strut failed with sharp crack, but the others held. A patch of fabric tore off the upper wing, flapping like a banner in a hurricane. Slowly, agonizingly, the plane approached the horizontal.

Spray exploded as the floatplane hit the water. For a moment Finnegan was afraid that the drag from the floats would either rip them off or pitch the plane's nose into the sea, but it righted itself and he kicked the rudder over, using the plane's momentum to steer it toward shore. Overhead the blazing zeppelin almost filled the sky.

From the shelter of the beach, they watched the zeppelin die. Its nose was a burning skeleton, drooping toward the sea as the gas from the forward bags burned off. The fire spread aft, peeling away the silver skin to reveal the metal framework beneath. Eve gasped as the zeppelin broke in two and both parts drifted down amid a welter of flame, the ironwork sagging in the intense heat. The pieces settled on the ocean for a few seconds and began to sink.

For a long time they said nothing. Then Finnegan put his hand gently on Eve's shoulder and said, 'Let's get out of here.' He turned and headed for the bay where the *Lady Luck* lay at anchor.

◇

'China?' Eve took a sip of her drink.

'That's what Louie says,' Finnegan told her. 'After the Armistice von Falkenburg and his crew didn't want to surrender. They must have taken that zeppelin all the way across Russia. Louie's buddy in Shanghai said they tried to set themselves up as warlords but the Kuomintang chased them out.'

'So they came here? Why?'

'Who knows? They probably figured they could make a living as pirates. Ships and planes vanish out here all the time. I wish the thing hadn't blown up, though. Do you know how much cargo a zeppelin can carry?'

Eve smiled. 'I don't see you as the airship type. Too slow. Landing that floatplane with no engine is more your style.'

Finnegan ran his fingers through his hair. 'Don't remind me,' he said. 'That wasn't the wind screaming on the way down, it was me.'

Eve chuckled, a low, rich sound. 'A big, tough pilot like you? I've been on scarier rides at Coney Island.'

Fangs and Formaldehyde

Monica Valentinelli

Between the skin shows and an endless supply of cocaine and hard liquor, the city of Las Vegas was perfect for any predator, mortal or otherwise. Usually, the mortal predators lurked in noisy casinos, preying on unsuspecting tourists. Vampires like Atlas, on the other hand, typically took to the streets to find their next meal.

'Wow. Is that a vintage Ducati? My dad had one of those,' a blonde girl shouted from a nearby crosswalk. Although she reeked of baby powder and cigarettes, her long legs and creamy skin reminded him of Constance, his missing wife.

Atlas walked his bike over to the curb and lifted up his visor. 'It's a 1959 Ducati Super Sport. Do you know anything about motorcycles?' The left mirror was the only part that wasn't genuine.

'Not any that old.' The blonde girl admitted. After a few moments, she said exactly what Atlas hoped to hear. 'I'd kill to ride one again.'

Atlas didn't believe in luck, but if he did—he'd be asking the Good Lady for help. 'Want a quick ride?'

Like most humans Atlas encountered recently, the girl hesitated. He wondered if she didn't like the way he looked. Even now, he was painfully aware of the deep battle scars crisscrossing his bronze face.

The girl shook her head and backed away. 'Sorry, but I'm with my parents.'

'Suit yourself.' Atlas shrugged her off and quickly wove back into traffic. Sure, he could have played with his food, but then he'd be late for his weekly poker game. He didn't like to be late. Not for anything. Poker taught him when to bluff, when to call and when to fold. The better the players, the more he picked up.

He was still learning.

A scream queen ringtone screeched in his ear. Even before he answered the call, he suspected it was Damian wondering where he was.

Atlas pressed a button on the side of his helmet. 'How's the buffet coming, Damian? I'm running a little late.' It was customary for that week's host to provide some warm blood before the cards were dealt. This week, their game was on the top floor of Bermuda Bay.

'No go, Mr. A. Gotta cancel.'

Atlas tapped his helmet. 'I don't think I heard you correctly.'

'No players? No game, Mr. A. I can't get a hold of Gramps. Him and Moira are gone.'

Even though Gramps resembled a ninety-year-old man, his vampiric age was about the same as Damian's. A professional saxophone player and former boxer, Gramps still performed on the Strip for an enthusiastic crowd filled with bloodstalkers and humans.

Moira was a tiny little thing who wore purple wigs and followed Gramps around. Unlike him, she wasn't much of a gossip, so no one knew how old she was or where she came from. Atlas admired his sparring partner. Moira was the only bloodstalker he knew that could keep up with him.

That's odd, Atlas thought. Neither Moira nor Gramps had ever missed a game.

'What about Carla? Can't she play?' The mortal was Damian's one weak spot and both of them knew it. A former singer, Carla devoted most of her time to masking her wrinkles with heavy makeup and cosmetic surgery. Although Atlas had no idea why, Damian enjoyed her high-pitched laughter and terrible dancing. Atlas cringed every time she opened her mouth.

'Look, Mr. A,' Damian lowered his voice to a whisper. 'She's sick.'

From the tone in his voice, Atlas knew something was wrong. Most bloodstalkers didn't scare easily, unless somebody new was breaking the rules. *Rule number one: a vampire must avoid strong emotions at all costs.* 'What do you mean?'

'Don't have time to explain. I'm leaving town. Tonight.'

Atlas sped up. It wasn't like Damian to jump ship. Whatever happened to Carla, it frightened one of the least paranoid vamps he knew. 'Okay.'

'That's it? You're not coming after me?'

Atlas growled into the receiver. Damian owed him money and information, but he wasn't the only one. 'I want to talk to Carla before you take off.'

'Then meet me in Room 672 at the Revenant.' Atlas could tell Damian was struggling to keep his voice down. 'You have thirty minutes, Mr. A. Then I'm history.'

'I'll be there in five.'

A few right turns later, Atlas pulled into the parking lot of the Revenant Hotel and waved a wad of hundred dollar bills in front of a valet's face. Not only did the valet park his bike underground, he also told him where the staff entrance was and which slots were scheduled to pay out. Atlas made up some excuse about stripping for a bachelorette party, but by that point the valet lost interest in him. As long as he tipped well, the locals didn't think twice about who he was or what he was doing.

On his way up to the sixth floor, Atlas accidentally ran into a hotel maid. Hungry, he pinned her face-first against the wall. The woman was too terrified to scream, but he threatened her anyway.

Tilting the maid's neck, Atlas sampled just enough blood to keep his hunger in check. Fortunately for both of them, the frightened woman fainted and collapsed to the ground. Since a corpse was a lot harder to cover up than a bloodstalker's bite, he tried not to kill his victims.

Flying up the rest of the stairs, Atlas reached Room 672 and tried the handle. The door burst open with a loud bang.

'Come on in, Mr. A.' Damian filled the doorway. His eyes were blood red and his veins pulsed with anticipation.

'You don't look so good, Damian. Don't you want to sit down?' The signs of Damian's intense emotions were all there: red eyes, bulging arteries, angry rashes all over his skin. If Damian didn't calm down, his blood would eventually burst through his brain and kill him. Atlas knew several mortals who would sacrifice their souls just to learn that little secret. Over the years, he had convinced several hunters that a combination of holy water, juniper and garlic were the tools of their trade. The truth was: vampires were their own worst enemies.

'You didn't answer my question. Don't you want to sit down?' Atlas carefully pushed him aside and locked the door with a decisive click.

'Not here to chat.'

Damian lifted a chair and hurled it at Atlas, who managed to roll out of the way. Circling the other bloodstalker, Atlas snarled, hoping he'd back down. His tactic failed. Damian leapt high into the air and pummeled Atlas with a flurry of sharp punches. The older vampire dropped to his knees and clutched his jaw, feigning an injury. This time, his ruse worked.

'Why'd you do it, Mr. A?' Damian leaned over him and traced one of his deep scars with a long fingernail. 'Can you tell me that?'

When he was close enough, Atlas grabbed Damian's arm and twisted it until he heard a sharp popping noise. Taken off-guard, Damian howled in anger and swung his other fist. Atlas caught it and squeezed.

'Are you finished?' Atlas asked him, wondering when he would take the hint. Even with his preternatural speed, Damian wasn't in the best condition to fight. 'You've got about five minutes before the convulsions set in. Then you're on your own.'

Damian pressed his lips together, forming a white line. Atlas squeezed harder and cracked his knuckles. For whatever reason, that seemed to do the trick. Damian's eyes turned pink then rapidly faded back to white.

'Guess we should have that talk now. Right, Mr. A?'

'Guess so.' Atlas released his grip on the younger bloodstalker and leaned against the wall. 'Now, you mind telling me what the hell is going on?'

'Only if you tell me what that awful stench is.' Damian collapsed into a chair and readjusted the bones in his arm. 'Doesn't that smell turn off your victims?'

Atlas licked his lips. It seemed the kid figured out something he didn't. Was that why he had a hard time feeding lately? 'It's catnip.'

Like every other bloodstalker before him, Damian froze. It was common knowledge among vampires that cats could detect their true nature. *Rule number two: a vampire should avoid cats at all costs.* Although he hated the little fuzzballs, Atlas kept a bag of catnip in his pocket. He figured that the best way to avoid being pegged as a bloodstalker was to pretend that rule didn't exist.

'So you're the one. Fire, too?'

'Yep.' If Damian wanted a show, he was prepared to give him one.

'Prove it.'

Atlas cocked his head and rolled his lighter across the bottom of his boot. Once lit, he slowly passed his hand back and forth through its bright yellow flame.

Damian sank deeper into the chair. 'Is the rest of it true then, Mr. A?'

'What part?' Atlas had heard a few rumors. That was the only downside to living in a city that never slept. There was always someone willing to spill your secrets—especially if you paid them enough.

'That you help other bloodstalkers.'

Atlas had heard that one before, but it always surprised him when someone else said it. As much as he hated to admit it, there were still a few remnants of his mortal identity left inside his rotting heart.

He carefully chose his next words. 'When it suits me.' If the other vamps in town thought he had gone soft, they'd gang up on him.

Damian spat at the floor. 'Then you did do it.'

'Do what?' Atlas grabbed a deck of cards out of his jacket and offered it to him. If he could get Damian to shuffle some cards, maybe they could have a quick game while they talked.

Damian eyed him suspiciously. It took him a few minutes before he finally blurted out his accusation. 'You made Carla sick.'

'Is that what you think?' Atlas shook his head. Nothing could have been further from the truth. He didn't give a damn about Carla. What was Damian thinking?

'Yeah, that's what I think. I see the way you and Moira look at each other. She probably told you to do it.'

'I got news for you, Damian. I have better things to do than go after Carla.'

'Like what? Helping some other vamp?'

Atlas growled. Damian wasn't thinking straight, but it was obvious he wanted his help. 'I do this, I do this my way.'

Damian chucked his cell phone at him. 'Press the little camera button.'

His large fingers made it difficult to press the tiny buttons, but eventually Atlas figured out where the photos were. Atlas tried not to smile. He'd spent a lot of time studying the latest gadgets and it was finally paying off. If a younger vampire like Damian was able to figure out how old he really was, he'd probably run away screaming. For good reason, he thought.

Ancient vampires were few and far between. The longer a vampire lived, the more enemies they made. The more foes they encountered, the more likely they were to lose control. Naturally, a lot of superstitions popped up about what it took for a bloodstalker to survive. He knew that some of them, like the benefits of bathing in a priest's blood, were true.

Still, Atlas was surprised that he wasn't already dead. He lost count of how many enemies he'd made over the years. The last time he was attacked, he was in Germany with his wife. Someone hit him from behind and knocked him out. When he woke up, Constance was gone. Panicked, he traveled for years hunting her down, but he never found anything but rumors. Hell, he wasn't sure she was still alive. If it wasn't for Moira and Gramps, he'd still be out there, searching for her.

From his travels, he learned he could substitute a body bag for a coffin, which was a hell of a lot cheaper and more portable. With the Mojave and Sonoran deserts at his disposal, his options for a decent haven were endless. For whatever reason, Las Vegas was starting to feel like home.

'You still with me, Mr. A?'

Atlas scanned through the pictures, snapping back to the present. It was clear from the gruesome images that Carla had been affected by something, but he wasn't sure what. Her skin was covered with purple bruises, her eyes were sallow and unfocused, and her mouth was slack. If Atlas didn't know any better, he'd think she had been turned into a zombie. Either someone had a sick sense of humor, or there was a new predator on the loose, one that knew a little necromancy.

'She still alive?' Atlas processed as many grisly details as he could from the tiny pictures, but he needed to inspect her in person. If necromancy was involved, he had other signs to look for.

Damian shook his head. A toxic blend of human emotions marred his boyish face. 'She wouldn't talk or eat or nothing for three days. I didn't want her to suffer any more than she had to, so I killed her. I had to.'

Atlas gave Damian a minute to feel something he shouldn't. Less than ten years old, Damian's vampire life wasn't that much different from his previous one. A former drug dealer, he still worked and played with several humans, which was dangerous for everyone involved. Atlas frowned. Was it possible the supernatural wasn't involved here? Some idiot mortal could be taking the saying '*Whatever happens in this city, stays in this city*' a little too far.

'Do you think this has anything to do with Gramps or Moira?'

Atlas leapt to their defense. 'Don't think either one of them cared that much about your pet. Where'd you dump the body?'

'In an alleyway. Cops blamed it on a gang.'

Even though that impressed him, Atlas suspected Damian was holding something else back. 'Any idea where she went before she got sick?'

Damian reached into his pocket and handed him a business card. Then he sighed, a worthless gesture since vampires didn't breathe. 'There's this new doctor in town, so I sent Gramps and Carla over there to check things out. I was going to buy her a facelift for her birthday.'

'Let me get this straight. You sent a human to check out a doctor accompanied by a *vampire*?' Atlas imagined his fist smashing into Damian's freckled face.

'What's wrong with that?' Damian threw his hands up. 'I trust Gramps more than I trust you.'

'You have a lot to learn,' Atlas warned him, remembering the third rule he had been taught. *Vampires don't trust other vampires.* Sooner or later, all bloodstalkers had to come to grips with the fact that they were all killers. Damian should have done his own dirty work. 'Where is this place anyway?'

'Doctor Sage's office? Right off of Fifteen.'

To keep up appearances, Atlas pretended to weigh his options. He already knew he was going to check the place out to look for Gramps. 'Unless you have anything else to tell me, I suggest you get lost.'

'No hard feelings, then?' Damian hopped up and nervously edged toward the door.

Atlas pointed a finger at him and cocked an invisible trigger. 'I'll be seeing you again, Damian Alfonso Scaglia.'

As soon as Atlas heard the door click, he lit a cigar and practiced pulling the smoke in and out of his lungs. Most vamps only smoked in public, but there was something about this exercise that helped him concentrate. What was the connection between a lover-turned-zombie and two missing bloodstalkers? Or were these events completely random?

A cold shiver crawled up his spine. *You're in danger,* his instincts hissed. Atlas told himself to shut up and get moving. Since he knew most of the locals, Atlas was confident that if a new player was in town, someone would squawk about it. If they weren't already, he thought. Too bad he didn't have time to head down to one of the vampire-run casinos to find out.

Before Atlas headed over to Dr. Sage's office, he stopped at a pawn shop to grab the good stuff: a handful of smoke bombs and a couple of explosives. Instead of paying the pawn shop owner, Atlas knocked the guy out and took his fair share of blood. Better safe than sorry, he thought as he strapped the grenades to his chest. He didn't want to investigate on an empty stomach.

The ride on Fifteen was slow and full of traffic. Atlas did what he could to maneuver through the crawling cars, but his mind was elsewhere. He remembered a joke: the only good necromancer was a decapitated one. Atlas prayed that Doctor Sage was not a necromancer. The thought of someone else controlling his body forced his survival instincts to kick in. They told him he should hide in the desert and let someone else look for Gramps and Moira.

Atlas pushed his fears aside and tried to focus. Why was he always rescuing other vampires? Weren't they supposed to be his competition?

He pulled off at the next exit and parked outside the building. A few of the windows were boarded up; the rest were covered with thick dust. The worn-out name on the front window—Las Vegas Cosmetic Center—confused him. Was this the right place? Atlas double-checked the address on the card and saw that it matched. Before he went inside, he scrutinized the building for occult symbols or signs of black magic but found nothing. For a split second, Atlas wondered if he should come back tomorrow. Unfortunately, a lot could happen in a single night.

'Well, this'll be fun.'

A small tornado of fur, teeth and claws bombarded him as soon as he stepped inside. The kittens weren't strong enough to knock him down, but they did their best to annoy him. One of the kittens managed to get caught in his long, flowing hair. Another one stuck its claws into his pants leg and hung on. Atlas wanted to fling the kittens halfway across the room and run away. They made his skin crawl just by looking at them, but not one of them hissed. The fur balls had no idea he was a vampire.

'You're so cute!' Atlas lied for the benefit of anyone who might have been listening. He was glad the catnip worked.

'Come on kittens, time to eat.' The kittens scampered toward a plain young woman holding several dishes of cat food. Atlas looked around for the other cat. Where there were kittens, the mama cat couldn't be far behind.

'I'll be with you in a minute,' the woman said to him.

'No problem.'

A black cat jumped off the reception desk, stretched out on the stained carpeting and headed for its food. Making a quick sign of the cross, Atlas was relieved that the cat avoided him altogether. The irony of his religious gesture was not lost on him. Black cats were the worst: Atlas lost a lot of friends during the Trials because they were used to target witches and warlocks. Even to this day, they still gave him the creeps.

'Hey, hope I'm not too late,' Atlas quipped, trying like hell to keep his voice light. 'I was just coming in for my appointment.' He pointed to the pink scars that decorated his face.

The woman wore a faded calico sundress that matched her stringy yellow hair. For a moment, Atlas wondered if she was a necromancer. She didn't look like she belonged in Las Vegas. Her hair wasn't curled and she didn't wear any jewelry.

'You're here for the free trial, right?' Her voice sounded rough and bitter.

'I guess so.'

'Follow me,' the woman said casually. She left the cat dishes by the door, forcing him to step over the hungry beasts. Walking briskly, they entered a modern room filled with shiny equipment and porcelain tiles. Although Atlas was a little apprehensive, he placed his faith in his reflexes and the explosives under his vest. If she so much as touched him, he'd have no problem detonating them.

'Redecorating?' he asked. He couldn't help but wonder where Dr. Sage got his money from.

The woman turned her back and wiped down a patient's chair. 'Don't worry. This will all be over soon.'

There was something about her that annoyed him, but Atlas couldn't put his finger on what it was.

'Well? You're here for the trial, right? I bet you're nervous.'

'Yes,' Atlas confessed. That was the most honest thing he had said all day.

Smiling, the woman scribbled on a broken clipboard and gestured for Atlas to lie down on the steel chair. The name on her tag—*Martha*—was as homely as her dress. 'Nothing to be concerned about, I just need to measure your scars,' she told him. Atlas knew he shouldn't be afraid of this mortal, but he was. Two, very capable bloodstalkers were missing. What if she was Doctor *Martha* Sage?

Martha placed a warm hand on his forehead and smirked. Then, Atlas felt something sharp poke him in the side of his neck. Immediately, his senses dulled and an unfamiliar feeling washed over him. Was he *drunk*?

'Well, at least you're not another vampire.' Atlas heard her say before he completely blacked out. 'Nosy family member, I'm guessing.'

A few hours later, Atlas woke up on a table in a room filled with shambling mortals. Frustrated, he yanked the nearest human over to him and lightly bit into her arm. Black, watery blood leaked out of the holes.

'Vampire blood,' Atlas murmured. 'Not good.'

Dr. Sage was experimenting on humans and vampires. Most likely, Carla's bruises blossomed after Martha injected vampire blood into her veins. What was Dr. Sage after, anyway? That wasn't the right way to turn a mortal into a bloodstalker. Atlas swallowed. He didn't want to think about which vampire Martha used to toy with, but he sure as hell hoped it wasn't someone he knew.

Grabbing a smoke bomb off his chest, Atlas bit the pin off and tossed it through the open doorway. The smoke camouflaged his movements as he snuck into the next room.

'Jackpot.'

Six or seven bloodstalkers, including Gramps and Moira, had been tied up. Thin tubes were sticking out of their necks and arms. A clear fluid dribbled into the hoses from a plastic bag. Atlas snapped his fingers, but none of them responded. Somehow, Dr. Sage had managed to immobilize a vampire without using necromancy.

'Worse than magic.' Atlas spotted a few blood samples sitting on the counter and mulled his options. Once he disconnected the tubes, the vampires would need that blood before they regained consciousness. After that? They were on their own. There was plenty of human blood in the adjoining room. Although it was tainted, it would still do the trick. The resulting chaos would be a good distraction, but that might tip off Dr. Sage. Once things got messy, someone might call the cops.

His other option was to leave the bloodstalkers alone.

The choice should have been simple. Any other bloodstalker would have pursued the doctor and gutted him where he stood.

Atlas was not like other vampires.

After tossing a couple of samples at Gramps and Moira, he cut the tubes. Curious, he tasted the spouting liquid: it was pure formaldehyde. 'Brought down by embalming fluid?' Atlas thought. 'I have to meet this guy.'

He cracked his knuckles and let his military training take over. 'No time to waste.'

To give himself some cover, Atlas ran toward the fuse box at the far end of the hall. Martha stood in front of it, her arms folded across her small chest. 'We have iron-clad proof vampires exist.'

'Do you now?' Atlas cracked her head against the wall and cut the power. He didn't need artificial light to see in the dark.

Sprinting back down the hallway, Atlas ignored a cacophony of screams and headed for the stairs.

'Atlas! Might I have a word?' Atlas spun around when he heard the familiar voice.

Gramps was covered in black blood and bile. 'You look terrible.'

'Son, you should really think about getting a divorce.' Gramps regarded him with fury, contempt and sadness.

'Why's that?'

'Your wife orchestrated this whole thing.'

'Constance?' Atlas folded his arms to stop himself from lifting Gramps up by his wrinkled throat. 'You're wrong.'

Gramps shrugged. 'If I'm right, will you kill her?'

'I've got plenty of firepower to send this place back to hell,' Atlas lied. He took more smoke bombs than anything else. 'Want to make sure Dr. Sage doesn't escape.'

'Sounds good to me. How can I help?'

Atlas flung Gramps the keys to his bike. 'Take good care of her.'

'That's not the lady I'd be worrying about right now,' Gramps warned him. 'Either you take care of her, or Moira and I will.'

'I work alone.'

'Not this time, Atlas.'

'Where is Moira, anyway?'

'Feeding.'

'Fine,' Atlas said. He didn't have time to argue and he knew Moira would want a little payback. 'I could use some back up. This might get ugly.'

'Consider it done.'

Blocking Constance's face from his mind, Atlas raced up the stairs. Hallway fixtures crackled to life, bathing his leather-clad body in a warm, amber light. 'Must be a backup generator,' he thought. Determined to find Dr. Sage, he moved from office to office, but the rooms had been stripped clean. Where was he?

He poked his head into the last office and immediately dropped to his knees. 'My Lady,' Atlas moaned when he recognized his missing wife.

Constance had been mounted to a wall. Metal restraints bound her wrists and ankles. Someone had carefully peeled the flesh away from her bones and pinned the pink flaps behind her. Orange tubes filled with liquid had been forced into her veins and arteries.

The blood boiled in his body. Atlas tasted his rage. To save her, he had to save himself. What was he supposed to do now? Wait for Gramps and Moira?

Since he couldn't take a deep breath, Atlas closed his eyes and counted to ten, but he couldn't get the image of his tortured wife out of his mind. Dr. Sage had even cracked open her chest. Her heart—that precious, rotten, aching *thing*—was on display for the entire world to see.

Shaking, he approached Constance to see if she'd recognize him. Did she miss him? The closer he got to her, the less he wanted to see. Ribbons of precision-cut flesh hung loosely on her face. Her beauty, her terrible and renowned beauty, was no more.

'No more!' Atlas wailed and smashed his fist through the wall. A wet dot formed in his eye. The blood tear trickled down his face and collected in a deep scar.

'I see you're admiring my work.'

Atlas wondered if he was slipping. He hadn't noticed anyone else walk into the room. Looking up, he saw a shock of purple hair through the heating vent. He was glad Moira was watching his back. Gramps must have known he'd get emotional.

'Vampire blood is such a precious commodity for those in my line of work. Wouldn't you agree?'

Atlas whirled around and roared at Dr. Sage. He felt his blood rising to the surface of his skin and knew he was moments away from convulsing, but Atlas didn't care. Not when it came to *her*.

'Might I remind you there are security cameras in every corner of this building? Evidence of your crimes against a prestigious plastic surgeon will no doubt be investigated. Isn't that right, Mr. Atlas?'

'How did you find her?' he whispered hoarsely. Atlas dug his fingernails deep into his palms and regained his composure. Dr. Sage may have gotten the better of several vampires and mortals, but he was only four foot nine and three hundred pounds of *human* flesh. In this battle, Atlas was the superior opponent. He had better start acting like it, especially since Moira was watching.

'Why, she was ravishing when we first met. It all started at the Palace when I asked her who did her nose...' Dr. Sage's words were charming, but Atlas wasn't listening. His eyes darted around the room, quickly assessing his surroundings. Ancient swords hung on the wall. Stone tablets were piled up on the floor. The windows had been covered in meaningless sigils. Other than the door Atlas came in, there was no way Dr. Sage could escape. Not with two, possibly three, pissed-off bloodstalkers in the room.

'Consider this a gift, Mr. Atlas,' the doctor intoned, pointing to his wife. 'She told me you've been apart for a long time.'

Atlas could not believe his ears. Who the hell was this guy? 'That's right. I haven't seen her in decades.'

Dr. Sage took a deep bow. 'Please, be my guest.'

'What's the catch?' For a split second, Atlas wondered if Dr. Sage was any good at playing poker. He was pretty calm and collected for an evil bastard.

'You will agree to turn me into a vampire at a time and place of my choosing.'

'Is that what all this is about? Injecting vampire blood and dissecting my wife?'

'Why, of course not! My immortality is only one part of my plan.'

Atlas feigned interest. 'Give me the short version.'

'Extract the cure for aging from a vampire's blood and become the richest man in the world.'

'That's all?' Atlas laughed bitterly. 'Inventive.'

'You could be the second richest vampire, Mr. Atlas. All you have to do is kill this creature.'

Plucking a broadsword off a display, Atlas pretended to test its sharpness by slicing his hand on the blade. Then, he touched Constance's heart with the bloody sword. 'We'll kill her together.'

Dr. Sage clapped his hands. 'Oh yes! Let's.'

'Like this?' Atlas slashed every tube connected to her body. Pungent liquid sprayed in all directions, covering them in formaldehyde. After slicing through her restraints, Atlas pivoted and faced Dr. Sage.

'I'm not alone, Dr. Sage.'

Beads of sweat formed on Dr. Sage's forehead. 'You're lying.'

'Is he now?' A familiar voice asked. Atlas turned around and laughed. Gramps had grabbed an IV stand and was brandishing it like a weapon.

'What is this all about? Vampires don't know the meaning of the word "teamwork". You're a selfish, blood-thirsty lot.'

'Did someone say "blood"?' a female voice purred. Her lusterless corpse had evaporated into a roiling fog. It blanketed Dr. Sage's body with ease.

Atlas kept his head level. He should have been the one to find her, not this asshole. To shield himself from his despair, Atlas whispered a few simple words. 'I live to serve, my Queen.'

Ignoring Atlas completely, Constance focused all her attention on Dr. Sage.

'I thought you could take care of yourself.' Atlas couldn't pinpoint his exact emotion, but he was relieved Gramps was here to meet her. Constance would never allow herself to be tortured just to trap other vampires. She had too much pride, a sign of her royal upbringing.

'Shall we dance?' Constance manifested into her human form and dropped Dr. Sage's body. Much to his surprise, she wore a black gown. She hated black. Or, at least she used to, he thought. He couldn't help but wonder what else about her had changed.

'Nice dress.'

She kicked Dr. Sage's bloodless corpse and laughed. 'He would have made a good vampire. I'm surprised you didn't turn him yourself.'

'I haven't turned anyone for a long time.' Atlas kept the conversation light. She always was a good listener.

'Too bad.' Constance bared her fangs, reminding him she was still dangerous.

Gramps broke the tension between them. 'Time to break up this reunion, Atlas.'

'What do you mean by that?' he asked, grabbing a pipe bomb out of his vest. There was no way he was going to kill his wife. Not now, not ever.

'Constance set this up. We overheard the whole thing.'

'Who? You and Moira?'

'No. Carla.'

Constance glided over to him and stared into his eyes with contempt. 'Just how many women do you have, Atlas?'

'Later.' Atlas bowed his head and lit the bomb's fuse. Something didn't feel right. If he didn't know any better, Dr. Sage was still holding all the cards.

'Ten seconds, everyone,' he bluffed, pointing to his watch. They had about a minute before the bomb really went off. 'Gramps, you had better get moving.'

'I'm not leaving until she does,' Gramps protested. 'I'm telling you, Atlas, she orchestrated everything.'

Atlas shook his head and pointed to his watch. 'Get going, Constance.'

Constance blew him a kiss and tossed her waist-length hair over her bare shoulder. The playful gesture threw him for a loop. Knowing her, she would be angry with him for her capture. She'd probably accuse him of letting down his guard and would threaten to expose his real name.

By the time Atlas forced himself back into the present, the woman was gone.

'Wait!' Atlas shouted. 'That's it. That wasn't Constance.'

'We've got your back,' Gramps said. 'Moira will catch her.'

Lurching forward, Atlas recovered the bomb, stuffed it down Dr. Sage's shirt and berated himself for his stupidity. What was wrong with him? After centuries together, he knew his wife inside and out. She would never dance with a corpse or pass up the opportunity to turn a willing mortal. That only meant one thing: Dr. Sage was after *him*.

Furious, Atlas grabbed the sword and beheaded the doctor in one, fluid motion. The impact of the sword sent the head flying; blood seeped from the wound. Shaking his head in disbelief, Atlas double-checked his watch.

Fifteen seconds.

'Damn.' Although he wanted to find out who the woman was, he dropped the sword and transformed his body into a fluttering mound of bats.

Seven seconds.

Escaping through the open window, Atlas half-hoped the bomb was a dud. He needed more time.

Three.

Was that man really Dr. Sage? If that wasn't Constance, who was it?

Two.

Atlas braced himself. No more time for questions.

One.

The bomb detonated with a loud bang, but it didn't go off in the office as Atlas had planned. The scent of gasoline and burnt paint drifted toward him. He traced the odors to a burning car parked down below. Atlas swore in earnest. Someone must have thrown the bomb. But who?

Once outside, he could sense dawn approaching. He wasn't ready to fold. He still had one more explosive.

Atlas glided back to the window and flew inside. A friendly face was there to greet him. 'Moira?' Atlas frowned.

She pressed something rubbery into his hand. It was a mask. 'It was all a trick.'

For the first time in a long time, Atlas was grateful he had put his faith into another bloodstalker. Then he asked the one question he already knew the answer to. 'Who did it? Who...'

'Martha.'

'Is she—'

Moira smirked. 'We'll keep her alive for you.'

He coughed uncomfortably. 'Guess we have a date.'

'Guess so.'

Atlas transformed one more time and sailed off into the failing moonlight. As he bolted toward his haven in the open desert, he burst with anticipation. It didn't matter what Dr. Sage had planned. All he could think about was that Martha's nightmares were about to come true.

Bad Beat for Aaron Burr

Kenneth Hite

Ray Cazador walked into the casino on Bedloe's Island like he was doing it a favor. Head tilted up, eyes cool, arms akimbo, feet pointed out and forward, just that much short of a swagger in the legs. He didn't mind all the faces turned to look at his—literally nobody in the world knew who he was. He wanted to see them, see who else they looked at, get some data to run a solution, to point him toward his target. Only Troutman might have guessed that someone like him might be there, might have looked for someone tonight, and Cazador didn't rate Troutman's guesswork very high. Cazador especially wanted Troutman to look, which was why he'd brought the girl.

She cost two thousand New Dollars a night, and even in this New York that was a lot of money. She was worth a look: tall and leggy, blonde and slightly imperious, with killer cheekbones and no tits. She wasn't Cazador's type. She was Troutman's type, if his browser history was anything to go by. Leggy, thin-waisted blondes and poker—mostly the virtual version of both—were apparently how Troutman killed the idle hour back on the Earth with an Internet.

Troutman's browser had been scrupulously clean of any searches or file dumps on the other Earths. Troutman had either been smart enough to do all his alt-historical research on a dump palmtop or stupid enough not to do any research, to take whatever the Bridgekeeper was selling under the table in a quick hop to any Earth with dentistry and air conditioning. Cazador thought it was most likely the former. Stealing your turbine designs from the company that owned them and hitting a Bridge was only profitable if you knew something about your new Earth's industrial capacity, and stupid people generally don't keep turbine designs in their heads. Then again, hydrodynamic engineering and being a cross-world fugitive were two very different skill sets.

For example, a key rule for cross-world fugitives is: 'Stay away from your past'. Not just your personal past—finding out what Mom is doing on this Earth is a great way to get rattled and get caught—but your Earth's past. For some reason, runners stop and gawk at places that aren't famous on their new Earth, wide spots in the Potomac marshes where the Lincoln Memorial should be, that kind of thing. On this Earth, France wouldn't give a statue to the whipped-dog United States when it could kiss up to the Empire that Aaron Burr had built in Mexico. So this New York had a casino in the old fort on Bedloe's Island, and Gustave Eiffel's Statue of Fraternity stood in Veracruz harbor. But Troutman wouldn't be in Veracruz, or anywhere else in El Imperio Mexicano. For one thing, Troutman didn't speak any Spanish. Troutman's politics probably ruled out the Confederacy, which was even poorer and more insular than this Earth's United States anyway. It wasn't impossible that Troutman had already gone north to Canada, cut a deal with the British. But not likely. In Troutman's place, Cazador would want the security of 'neutral ground' to negotiate any deal like that. And Troutman would need to get his legs under him in the new Earth. He'd be looking for something familiar and safe: poker.

All of this gave Cazador more than enough reason to bring the girl here to the Harbor Casino to flush his quarry. So he filled her slim hand with chips and sent her off to draw some attention:

Troutman's, ideally, but any attention would do. As heads predictably turned to watch the girl cross the casino floor, Cazador let his shoulders slump, shrugged his dinner jacket out of true, and turned his toes inward. He lowered his chin a fraction of an inch, ran disarranging fingers through his hair, and then let both hands drop like they were used to heavy burdens. By the time Cazador picked his diffident way to a corner, nobody bothered looking at him at all. If they did, they would never connect this slouching nonentity with the expensive blonde now laughing by the ten-dollar poker tables, drawing every male glance in the room.

Setting his point on the girl, Cazador watched her watchers. He watched the crowd form and re-form as she moved through the gamblers, the swells, the servants, and the sharks. Cazador read marriages creaking under the strain of her, read high rollers mentally figuring the number of her nights they could afford, read waiters reveling in the perks of working tonight and pit bosses taking the opportunity to switch dice. When he saw the snatch-and-grab men, he noticed them first by the off-green of their jackets. Casino guard jackets were darker, less olive. The snatchers didn't match the crowd, either. They weren't responding with their neighbors but to a signaler—there. And who was he looking for? Right, the swell who probably rode or swam and, on second look, carried himself like a fencer or even a kickboxer. Track back along the fencer's line of sight, then, past the girl to the man gripping his bright pink New Dollars too tightly, staring at the girl and gulping like he'd forgotten about oxygen. Cazador started to move, because the man was Troutman. Cazador was apparently not the only hunter at this particular watering hole.

The fencer's men had a better position, blocking the approaches around the poker table and moving toward Troutman careless of who they shouldered or what they spilled. Troutman was so gaffed by the sight of the girl that he didn't react until the second thug grabbed his other elbow. His reaction became a noiseless squeak when the strength of that grab showed itself. Cazador couldn't get there without vaulting a table or two, so he redirected toward the fencer, timing his arrival for the start of the snatchers' come-along. One casino guard, either not paid off or not remembering it, started moving about then. The fencer nodded his third man into action. At that moment, Cazador shoved a fortyish woman in the small of her back, sending her tilting past the fencer and spilling her drink on his right arm. Still looking like just another staring rube in the crowd, Cazador ducked around the fencer as he turned. He made the brush lift while the woman somehow protested and apologized simultaneously, her flat New England voice soon just part of a clattering wave of chaos expanding outward into the casino floor. Those disarrayed in the wake of the snatchers were gathering their own dudgeons and dignities now that the disturbing large men were moving safely away.

The snatchers moved away toward a set of doors Cazador had already scouted as leading back to a rear loading area. The fencer moved toward his lieutenant and the insufficiently bribed guard, a pink bill peeking out of his tanned fingers. Cazador knifed for the front doors, suddenly a man to defer to with his head slightly tilted and his right shoulder slightly forward; a hunting predator stance. Without knowing precisely why, people got out of Cazador's way. Cazador would have liked to try circling around and prying Troutman out of his predicament before the kidnappers could finish the snatch, but he reluctantly discarded the idea. The jackets and the loading doors showed at least some preparation on the fencer's part, likely including a boat and one or two more men waiting for their prize. But the jackets hadn't been close enough, when another day could have made them perfect. Cazador knew that, because he had a complete suit of Harbor Casino livery hanging in his closet back at the hotel. Which showed something else: the fencer was audacious and improvisational to the point of overconfidence.

Cazador could use that, but first he had to pin the fencer down a little more. In the water taxi on the way back to Manhattan, Cazador opened the fencer's wallet and read the name: Don Vicente Teodoro Garcia Estancia y Jackson. Mexican near-royalty, then. Then Cazador read the printing above the name: Ministeria Confidential de la Emperador. Don Vicente was near royalty in more ways than his blood: he worked for the Confidential Ministry of His Imperial Majesty Aaron IV Burr. And he was so sure he was untouchable he kidnapped people right off of casino floors in a foreign country. Audacious, indeed, although Cazador suspected there wasn't a lot these United States could do about it even if Troutman had been an American citizen on this Earth. But Don Vicente carried his ministerial credentials on his kidnapping jaunts. To the point of overconfidence, then — and perhaps a good way past it.

◇

Even, or perhaps especially, in this New York City, finding a store selling dodgy merchandise late at night was no problem. Cazador stopped at the second one he passed and bought a self-developing Eastman camera along with enough extra film packs to get him past any alter-tech stumbles. At an all-night dime store, Cazador picked up some cheap paper and envelopes, a fountain pen with its own ink reservoir, and a roll of quarters with James G. Blaine's head on them. The next stop was a phone booth with a good view of the street in both directions. Cazador laid out his coins and started calling hotels. It only took three calls to find out 'Mister Estancia' was registered at the Astoria: no low-profile safe houses for this not-very-secret agent.

Back in his room, he photographed Don Vicente's credentials until he had a print showing no part of the desk. He put that photograph into an envelope addressed to 'Don Vicente Estancia y Jackson, Hotel Astoria', along with one of Don Vicente's visiting-cards and the money from Don Vicente's wallet. Around that packet, he folded a note:

Your Excellency and I have inadvertently obtained one another's property. If you wish to discuss repatriation, I shall make myself available at the Harbor Casino tonight at eight o'clock.

Calling a bellboy and giving him a tenner to mail the envelope from Grand Central Station took only a few minutes. Cazador had cut the fellow out of the herd a week ago, marking his high intelligence and low scruples. Then he took off his shoes, his shirt studs, and his dinner jacket, and laid down for a few hours' sleep.

The next morning, Cazador shaved and dressed in his Harbor Casino guard's uniform and packed his dinner jacket, trousers, and dress shoes in a garment bag. Taking a tram down to the Battery, he stood with arms pointed in and shoulders back; he was a working stiff who neither needed nor desired any interaction. Lighting a cigarette and striding with bored disinterest, he walked into the casino and back into the guards' locker room uninterrupted. There he hung his garment bag in a vacant locker, put on a padlock of his own, and strolled out to begin his self-appointed rounds. After briefly inserting himself into his shift-mates' eye-line a few times, he put on a beleaguered expression, picked up a handy clipboard, and headed for the rear loading area the Imperial agents had used the night before.

It's not quite true that you can go anywhere on any Earth with only a clipboard as your credential. In Cazador's experience, you also needed a look of slow-burning exasperation, something which told the world you would rather be anywhere else and, if given half a chance, would expatiate on that theme for up to an hour. As it happened, nobody seemed willing to risk that hour of their time, so Cazador was able to stake out the rear loading dock. Boats, mostly loaded with food and drink, pulled up from Jersey and Manhattan and Brooklyn and unloaded cargo. Some dropped off more staff: janitors, clerks, and such. Some of them greeted the guard watching the boats unload, a short man with fat hands and an unattractive rill of hair on his collar. Most of them avoided him. Cazador watched all of this and, on his occasional stroll down to the pier with a smoke, listened. Once he bummed a cigarette from the guard, whose name was Emmett, and whose expression of meaningless injustice suffered in imperfect silence matched his own. Forty minutes and three cigarettes later, he had a very full picture of the casino's security and staff situation, albeit as seen through Emmett's jaundiced eye.

Half an hour before the afternoon shift change, Cazador walked back down to the pier.

'Why don't you knock off early, Emmett? That asshole Quintero is making me pull a double shift, but we don't both gotta suffer.' Emmett agreed with the general philosophy, and after a bare minimum of convincing, with the specific plan. Cazador readjusted his stance to match Emmett's bureaucratic self-righteousness and spent the next ten minutes rooting through the duty shack for a suitable set of forms for his clipboard. Then he took up the departed Emmett's mantle of boat greeter.

'You need to fill this out. Not all of it, just funnel number and your yard of origin.'

'Look, I know you. You know me. But Quintero don't care, and Levy really don't care.'

'Someone's been leaning on someone, someone didn't get their palm greased this month, so we gotta fill out bullshit forms now.'

'Funnel number, yard of origin. No, don't give me the cargo manifest. I don't need that hassle. Neither do you.'

When the next shift came on duty, Cazador explained the new dispensation. 'We need to get the funnel number and yard of origin for these boats now. I don't know, maybe just until the end of the month. Emmett? I ain't seen him — I got put on this shit job because he's too hung over to come in, is my guess. It's that way for me all week, swear to God…'

Rather than listen to any more of Cazador's extemporaneous workplace gripes, the new guard accepted the clipboard and the improvised data collection task. Cazador beat a retreat and stayed out of everyone's sight for the next few hours, slipping into the twilight time as the waiters and pit bosses and dealers began to flow in and the casino began to light up and come alive. Starting a little before seven, Cazador went back to staking out the loading dock, now watching the boats exclusively. Waiting for the familiar figure of Don Vicente or, more likely, his muscle and their straw boss. When they pulled up at 7:16, Cazador took the opportunity to watch their interplay and listen. The boat pilot and the two men in dark sweaters who stayed on board were all New York by their accents (more Irish-Italian-Breton than Jewish-Italian in this world), as were the two thugs in the too-olive jackets. The straw boss was tougher: Cuban? Guatemalan? Cazador didn't have enough data to be sure, but probably not a pure local. Probably a long-term Imperial Mexican asset, maybe even the local equivalent of the 'chief of station', an ambitious provincial frustrated at cooling his heels in a backwater like New York.

After they went into the casino, Cazador had to wait another ten minutes for the guard to put the clipboard back down. A few fast steps, a quick riffle, and an answer: the Ministeria Confidential moored its getaway boat at the 41st Street docks on the Hudson. Manhattan, then. And Cazador had another answer: nobody in his right mind would take that boat wallowing out of the harbor. Certainly nobody as image-conscious as Don Vicente Teodoro Garcia Estancia y Jackson. While a rendezvous with a Mexican ship or submarine couldn't be ruled out, Cazador didn't think either would be Don Vicente's style. He wouldn't want to share his glory with either a heroic sub captain or a pedestrian steamship officer. Extracting Troutman by train would take too long: hours to get to Colorado and the Imperial border. Hours in which anything could go wrong, including another border crossing into the nervous, touchy Columbian Union at Youngstown. A car or truck had the same problems, compounded by the grim prospect of an undignified road trip across a parochial, backward countryside full of people who sullenly resented Imperial Mexico. No, it would have to be an airplane. On a Mexican-flagged airline. That way Don Vicente could use his ministerial credentials to evict two businessmen from their cushy leather seats and fly his catch nonstop into Mexico City in first-class luxury and solo glory.

Cazador called the casino concierge from a house phone, and found out the last Aerolineas Imperial Skyliner would leave from J.P. Mitchel Airport at midnight, nonstop to Mexico City. Then he walked down to the employee cafeteria. He took his time over the meal, then went to his locker and changed into the trousers and shoes from his evening clothes. He carried his dinner jacket out over one arm, moving fast to prevent anyone from lingering past the uniform coat. In a briefly empty corridor, he switched jackets. He left the uniform one in a trash bin and backed out into the casino, hunching his back and tying his cravat with deliberately shaky hands as he did so. Anyone who looked would see someone perhaps a little under the weather, a little sick and hesitant. They would probably look away out of politeness or subconscious disease-fear, but there was an undeniable risk here.

The moment passed, though, and Cazador lengthened his stride, straightened his spine, and walked up to the bar as an only slightly disheveled, even rakish, swell. He curved his neck, shot his cuffs, and gathered in the nearest waitress with an eye roll. 'Here's a hundred. Whatever I order, you bring me ginger ale. Jake?' Out of the corner of his eye he saw Don Vicente sweep through the front doors, his stride proclaiming impatience.

Now all he had to do was find, or build, the right game. It took about forty minutes to find his seed crystal, a rich Texican cattleman at a high-dollar table with an empty seat. Definitely not a Tejano, not for this game. Cazador sat and made a friendly competitor with just the right man-to-man shrug at a freak flush. Then he began filling the rest of the table to his specifications. He played cards strong and close, cleaning out players he didn't need and losing to players he wanted to keep. The Texican, whose name was Marland, turned out to be in oil, not cattle. He stayed in mostly on his own strength; Cazador only needed to throw him one pot the whole time. He ordered rye whiskey and drank ginger ale and waited until 9:30 before sending a tequila over to where the increasingly agitated Imperial agent waited with his slightly-wrong thugs and his likely-resentful subordinate.

To his credit, when Don Vicente arrived at Cazador's table, taking advantage of the sudden departure of two local businessmen who had been winning slow and steady until just then, he was all gracious manners and suave introductions. He clapped the shoulder of the West Side real-estate developer. He murmured interestedly to the East Side furrier, and was positively courtly to the wife of the regional sales manager from Philadelphia who couldn't believe he was still holding his own in the game. He nodded remotely to the Texican oil baron, aristocrat to nouveau riche aristocrat. Only after taking his seat did he allow himself a flash of anger at Cazador across the table. His men ringed the table, almost but not quite blocking a quick retreat. Now the game could begin for real.

'So what brings you to New York, Mr. Hunter?' The question came from the real-estate man, who had been subtly encouraged in such curiosity for the past hour or so.

'I'm here to meet a friend of mine, an engineer. We're hoping to work on a project together. I saw him here yesterday, but I just missed him.' Cazador swept the eyes of all four Imperials, gratified to see the recognition bloom. 'But I'm not worried. I'll figure out where he got off to, and then we'll be back in business.' Four sets of eyes shifted or stared or squinted, and Cazador's eyes marked them.

Then the cards came around, and conversation ebbed for a bit aside from 'Draw two' and 'Forty to you, Mr. Welch' and 'Call'. Cazador had long since figured out the tells for his table mates, some of which could have been seen from a lighted stage. Now he looked for those little tics and gestures from Don Vicente, and from his watching men. The Cuban lieutenant tightened his lips at near-run plays by anyone at the table. One of the guards sneered whenever the Texican or the Jew played badly. The other seemed a little slow, but his eyes lit up when he saw something he recognized or there was a big win. And Don Vicente, as it happened, tilted his chin slightly to the left when he had good cards, and lowered one eyelid a millimeter at bad ones. Cazador kept the game hot enough, playing just a little wild and outside, feeding enough plays to unlikely winners, to get a whole range of reactions from the four of them. Every stimulus he played out drew four signals in return. For Cazador, it was like calibrating a four-way, card-driven polygraph.

'So is your ranch north of Houston, Mr. Marland?' Cazador asked it innocuously, but leaned a bit on *Hew*-ston. And the big guard sneered as only a New Yorker can when someone mispronounces Houston Street—pronounced *How*-ston, and named for Congressman William Houstoun in 1786 on both Earths.

For his part, Marland threw back his head and laughed: 'Nossir, I can't say as there's much north of Houston. My place is south of there, a good bit south.'

That was a gamble that paid off twice. First: young Sam Houston had thrown in his lot with Burr and eventually got something in Texas named after him on this Earth, too. Second: Don Vicente's chin tilted slightly to the left. A bluff?

'So pardon my ignorance, Mr. Marland, what exactly is north of *Hew*-ston?' Now the Cuban's lips tightened—he'd heard someone recently mispronounce the street, at a guess Don Vicente. And something *was* north of Houston Street.

'Just the river, Mr. Hunter. And a whole passel of Pawnee Indians.' The slow guard's eyes lit up—it couldn't have been Pawnee Indians—was it the river? A quick flurry of bets and some table talk on the last card of the next hand —'the river' in Mississippi gamblers' slang, also on both Earths—nailed it. But it couldn't be the Hudson to ping a native New Yorker… of course, River Street.

Now, it was the real-estate developer's turn to earn his place at Cazador's table. It took barely any time for him to start exalting various locations around the city, quite a few of them on the Lower West Side. And every so often, a street or a church or a park would get a hit on one or more of the four Imperials, and Cazador could narrow his aim even further. Cazador played the Philadelphia tourists on the furrier, since he'd already eliminated the East Side. Like all New Yorkers, 'the clever Mr. Dreyfus' was happy to explain how to get anywhere in the city on a streetcar or subway, and even happier to argue about his route with the other New Yorkers at the table. More streets, more locations, fed into the polygraph.

Cazador had to keep the cards fairly quiet to avoid washing out the signal. He started winning slow and early, calling bluffs before pots got too rich, and folding only when he was sure someone else had the hand under control. Don Vicente, meanwhile, began playing more and more aggressively, betting big and bluffing hard. And sometimes, Lady Luck likes the hard sell: Don Vicente's chin

Bad Beat for Aaron Burr

lifted on a very good turn. He and Marland were suddenly in play for a very big pot, with Cazador holding nothing. 'Hell, looks like someone found the key to the bank!' Marland said, throwing down another thousand New Dollars. That would eat up most of Cazador's remaining stake. It was worth it, however: a tic from the Cuban and lighted eyes from a guard put the Imperial safe house on Bank Street, north of Houston, near River. Cazador would bet everything on it.

He threw down his cards. 'I fold.'

Nothing wakes up a table like a steady winner who just lost big. Marland was too surprised to raise again, and Don Vicente cleaned up with Kings over Tens.

Now another gamble. Cazador stood, gathered up his diminished chips, bowed to Don Vicente, and turned slightly away. Don Vicente stood up in a rush: 'Señor Hunter. We have not yet finished our game.' A toss of the head; the guards began to move toward the casino entrance, blocking his retreat.

'You will excuse me, Don Vicente. It is after midnight'—the eyelid lowered more than one millimeter at this—'and I have an early day of looking for my friend tomorrow.' Cazador stepped around the table, on the opposite side from the Cuban.

'Stay here, play out the game, and I shall make sure you find him.' Don Vicente countered, blocking Cazador and coming closer.

'I cannot.' Cazador moved up, crowding into even Don Vicente's narrower Latin personal space.

'I insist.' Don Vicente's eyelid was really going now. Cazador judged he was all in, consumed with anger and frustration, with the spy's nightmare of Not Knowing.

Cazador lowered his voice. 'If you wish your subordinates and this arriviste blanco to know that I have your credentials, by all means keep me from leaving, Don Vicente.'

Before the other could react, Cazador pivoted. 'Or allow me to slip them to you as we walk outside, and word never needs to reach your enemies in Mexico City.' Louder: 'Perhaps a cigar, then, Don Vicente. If you insist.'

For a long second, the other man did nothing. Cazador waited—this had to be Don Vicente's move, or the fencer would riposte instinctively.

'A cigar. Excellent.'

Now was the time to weaken, to let Don Vicente think he'd won something. Cazador let his shoulders slouch, loosened his arms, lowered his chin. He did not slacken his stride toward the doors, but the Imperial kept up easily.

As the guards fell in behind them, Cazador turned to Don Vicente. Now was the time to damp that frustration, to give him what he wanted: an explanation. In a conversational tone, Cazador said 'Moscow'. France and Britain too easy to check, Japan too outré. The Russians seemed like the right touch.

A light of comprehension dawned. 'Your masters need to learn that this is our hemisphere.'

Cazador relaxed into his slouch, and raised his chin: beaten, but proud. 'They need to pay more, and provide better backup if they want to prove you wrong, Don Vicente.' Now, they were two professionals, exchanging shop talk.

Don Vicente's chin lifted in response. With an exaggerated roll of his eyes and a subtle roll of his head, he indicated the guards behind them. Cazador spread his hands: What could they do? They were both professionals, hampered by fools.

By the time they reached the door, Don Vicente actually gave Cazador a cigar and produced one for himself. Magnanimous in victory, he allowed Cazador to slip him his credentials under cover of clipping and lighting.

As he climbed aboard the water taxi, Cazador could still see the glow of Don Vicente's ash.

It had to be large enough for four or five men. It had to have sight lines down the street, and a rear entrance or yard. It was probably being watched—Don Vicente's shrug aside, Cazador was not about to underestimate Imperial Mexico's local talent. Not too many places on Bank Street fit that pattern, and Cazador found the safe house within half an hour. Then he settled in to wait.

It was almost two hours before the Cuban and his men returned—with Don Vicente. Apparently his generous mood had lasted, and he wanted to have one last moment of hands-on leadership before flying out the next day in triumph. The unexpected presence of His Excellency was more than enough distraction for Cazador. He slipped the lock on the back entrance while the guards were out front making sure Don Vicente hadn't been tailed.

Up or down? Cazador picked randomly and went upstairs. More arrogant to stash Troutman here, in sight of the street. The guard sitting in the hall didn't even get all the way out of his chair before Cazador's fingers speared into his throat. He went down, wheezing, and Cazador clipped him again.

A peek through the eyepiece in the door: Troutman, hunched up and lying on a bed. He would keep. Cazador rifled the guard's pockets, coming away with a thick key ring and a sap. It was better than nothing, but not much.

Voices on the stairs, coming up. Cazador jumped down the stairs, feet forward, slamming the guards and the Cuban backward, kept going at a run, using gravity and momentum and surprise until everyone was back on the ground floor. One more guard was down, and another nursed his wrist. The Cuban and one olive-jacketed thug were still up, though, as was Don Vicente.

'Take him.' The guard started forward, and Cazador backed up. The sap snapped forward, another wrist went numb and lifeless. Everyone stopped for a second. Cazador locked eyes with the Cuban, with Imperial Mexico's long-suffering, underpaid, unappreciated man in New York. 'If Don Vicente's mission ends in a fiasco,' he said in Havana-accented Spanish, 'you won't be seeing him back here again.'

With a wordless cry of outraged aristocratic pride, Don Vicente charged, blocking his men's approach for a crucial two seconds. This time, Cazador ducked and let the charge slam home, smashing both of them against the wall. He popped a leg lock around the fencer's calf and felt corded steel. Letting Don Vicente get out of this clinch would be very stupid, and very dangerous. But this Earth didn't have Krav Maga, dedicated close fighting invented by a Jewish wrestler who also believed letting enemies get away was stupid and dangerous. At the cost of another slam into the wall, Cazador got his arms around the other's neck in a head lock. A half twist and a squeeze, and Don Vicente was bent nearly double.

Cazador twisted again, and pulled them both down on the stairs. Don Vicente almost spun out of it—his reflexes were amazing— but the stairs came just a fraction of a second too soon, slamming his arm underneath two bodies. One last risk. Cazador released the head lock, reared back and the fencer came up straight, snapping his leg out of the other's hold. It was the obvious move for a man justly proud of his strength and angered beyond reason at having to wrestle like a peasant. The obvious move; Cazador knew just where to aim his elbow. Don Vicente's nose broke with a noisome crunch, and blood fountained. Now, Cazador whipped the sap around, breaking the fencer's collarbone. A stomp kick, and the Imperial's knee gave way. Again the sap; Don Vicente sagged to the stairs.

The Cuban and the two remaining Imperials looked up at Cazador. He looked down at them steadily. His arms hurt like hell, and his knee felt like it was going numb. He kept staring, evenly, unemotionally. The Cuban was the only one uninjured, and he probably had a gun. He had two ambulatory, if not precisely functional, guards. Cazador kept his gaze level, feeling Don Vicente's blood drying on his shirt.

'I'm taking Troutman. And I'm leaving. You'll never see him again, and you'll never have to face his turbines on an enemy sub.'

The Cuban's lips tightened. 'And why, Señor Hunter, do I not take him to Mexico City myself?'

'Because you're not authorized to leave this station. And truth be told, you don't really want to. Back in Mexico, you'd have to deal with him'—a gesture to the beaten aristocrat on the floor— 'and his friends, and people like him. Here, you run the show.

And you've run it well, until he'—another gesture—'showed up and ruined things.'

Cazador went all in. 'You can't commandeer a flight like he could. Like he still can. You'd have to spend a week or more getting clearance, then getting back. Don Vicente Teodoro Garcia Estancia y Jackson'—Cazador hit the names slow and hard, his Havana accent thick on the harsh J—'would spend that week taking credit for extracting Troutman. And he would spend that week trying to destroy you. Trying to destroy any man'—a quick flick of the eyes took in the other guards, trying not to look like they were listening—'who saw him beaten.'

'Dump him somewhere without his credentials. Clean this place out and go to another safe house—we both know you have one—and in the morning, report him missing to your normal channels in Mexico City. Tell them you were ambushed, tell them he got drunk, tell them he got involved with a whore, tell them whatever you think his enemies will believe. Stay here and serve your Emperor on your home ground, not back in the Palacio on his.'

The guards shuffled their feet uncertainly; one's eyes lit up. The Cuban's mouth relaxed. Just a bit, but enough. 'I will never see you again, either, Señor Hunter.'

Always leave them something on the table. Never make them understand how bad the beat was. 'Not me. I'm collecting my pay for Troutman and I'm going to France to see what the girls are like on the Riviera.' Now Cazador could relax, could open out his hands a bit, push his head forward. Now he was the mercenary, and the Cuban was the noble follower of a higher cause. It was even true, when you put it that way. The bounty on Troutman back across the Bridge on Earth wouldn't quite run to a four-star hotel on the Riviera, but there were plenty of other places Cazador could spend it.

He turned his back on the loyal servants of Emperor Aaron IV Burr and walked upstairs to get Troutman.

Charcuterie

Chuck Wendig

Mookie's hands are rusty with dry blood. Under his fingernails is a rime of blue dust. He gently sets the plate down in front of Werth—Werth the old goat, Werth with those wiry chin-hairs, Werth with the one dead tooth and the one dead eye.

'What's this?' Werth asks. The gaze from that one good eye roams over the plate.

'I fixed you a plate,' Mookie says, still standing. 'While we talk shop.'

'Fuck is it, though?'

'It's meat.'

'Doesn't look like meat.' Werth holds up the plate, smells it. Licks at his gray incisor. He glances around the bar to see if anybody else is watching; they aren't, because nobody else is here. 'Are they sausages? They almost look like sausages, if, say, you first took those sausages and ran them through the bowels of a dead guy.'

Mookie stabs the plate with a finger as thick as a bull's nose. 'This here is bresaola. That's a culatello over melon and next to it, a cocoa nib salami. This is duck galantine at the edge, here.'

'It got flies in it?' Werth picks up the neat circular slice of duckmeat, waves it around, *flap flap flap*.

'Currants. Dried blackcurrants.'

'And this?' Werth looks at a strip of white fat.

'Lardo.'

'I used to call my brother Lardo. Or Lard-ass. Or fuckface. Mostly fuckface.'

Mookie doesn't say anything. He just growls and grinds his teeth.

Werth finally rolls his one eye, eases the duck galantine into his mouth with all the excitement and technique of someone forced to eat a dead butterfly. He closes his mouth around it and chews slowly, gently, methodically, as Mookie watches.

'It's good,' Werth lies.

'You don't like it.'

'Listen, if we're going to do this thing, can't you just make me a goddamn sandwich instead of these fucking fantasy meats? Fry me an egg or something instead of pegasus *paté*?'

This doesn't sit well with Mookie. He worked hard on these. Hanging the meat. Cutting off the mold. Curing the flesh. Emulsifying the forcemeats. All that chopping and cutting and tasting. Werth doesn't know what a pain in the ass it is to get saltpeter. Harder to get than meth by a country mile—almost as hard to get as the Blue Blazes. Werth doesn't like this side of him. The old goat likes Mookie as a single-serving tool: a hammer. A skull-crushing, ball-smashing, drive-a-fence-post-through-some-mean-fucker's-heart hammer. Besides, weren't old goats supposed to eat everything? Rusty cans, rubber tires?

'No sandwich,' he growls, then finally takes a sit. He tugs the plate to his chest and begins to eat. The flavor—*the fat*—explodes in his mouth and for a moment he feels centered.

Werth leans in. 'You did good down at the docks today.'

'Mmn.'

'Those gobbos didn't know what hit 'em.'

Mookie pauses, looks at the dry blood on his hands before popping a strip of Lardo—cured pork fatback—into his mouth. It melts.

Werth watches him eat, disgusted. Look on his face like he's watching a snake eat a baby. He shakes his head, slides across an envelope fat with twenties. A small metal tin — like one that might hold lip balm or some strange unguent — joins it.

'There you go. A bit extra in the envelope since, ahh, the situation was *worse* than we figured. And the tin, well. You know what you need. A little Smurf Blood, make it all better.'

Mookie twisted the cap off the tin. Inside, a cerulean powder, blue as a peacock.

'You know,' Werth says, picking up a paper-thin cut of bresaola with his spidery fingers before smelling it, 'you should really quit this *out-of-the-way* shit. Close this place up. I mean, Christ, Mook, you're in the exact epicenter of nowhere. No customers. No traffic.'

'It's how I like it.'

'You come back to the city, you might actually climb the ranks. Get a crew of your own instead of doing this mercenary shit. What? You allergic to work?'

'Just tell me about the next job.'

'I'm just saying, Mook —'

'The next job.'

Werth knows that tone. He nods, then starts talking.

This is Mookie Pearl.

Mookie the Meatman. Mookie the Monster. Mookie the Merc. Mookie the, well, *Mook*.

Some people pronounce it *Moo-key*. Others say, *Muck-ey*.

Some people, like that old goat Werth, just call him 'Mook'.

Because that's what he is. A fucking mook. Least, that's what they say.

He's built like a brick shithouse whose bricks are themselves brick shithouses. He's got hands so big, each finger is like a baby's fist. Chest like a tomb, forehead like a marble slab, bald head like the skull of a king gorilla. An underbite so bad some of his white pebble teeth press on his upper lip, giving him a perpetual sneer.

Mookie makes money by helping bad people get rid of worse monsters.

Example: Mookie spent this morning down at the docks putting fist-to-face in order to stop a cabal of goblins from pilfering a shipping container full of Filipino immigrants. Mookie's bosses wanted to put the Filipinos to work: sex, muscle, whatever. The gobbos wanted to cook the poor bastards over a barrel fire. Easy choice. The night before that? Mookie cleared out a meth lab that a bunch of gray-skins set up in a pigeon coop. Amazing how many of those goddamn uglies they were able to cram into that tiny space (with pigeons still present, cooing and shitting down tarps pulled taut over windows.) One week ago? More goblins. Making weapons down in the warehouses. *Strange* weapons. Things that could turn a human inside out.

These days, it's *all goblins, all the time.* They've risen up. They're everywhere. Like a plague. A plague that needs to be stepped on, choked out, curb-stomped. The money that Mookie makes goes two places, and two places only. Some of the money he spends on his bar, a bar whose only name is 'Bar', a bar that sits so far off the beaten path that the only people who find it are the ones who know where to look. In this bar is a small kitchen and a big freezer, and Mookie keeps the freezer turned off—it's where he hangs meat: pigs, mostly. Good breeds, too, not those garbage eaters you find in the grocery store. Duroc, Hampshire, and his favorite, the Berkshire. He's even got a Mangalitsa and an Iberian Black back there, each growing green-gray fuzz right now, each an animal closer to the *boar* than the modern *pig*—each a snarling brute, dark and bristled, meaner than a bee-stung rattlesnake. In that way, those animals are just like Mookie.

As to where the rest of his money goes…
Well.

The front door squeaks open. Werth jerks his head to see as Mookie stands fast, hand moving to the wooden chair, ready to shatter it into pieces and use any part as a bludgeoning device.

It's a girl. A teen girl, actually—black sweater pulled tight, tartan skirt over pine leggings. Plain hair draped over slumping shoulders.

Bathed in the light of the neon beer signs, one might wonder if she has been crying.

'Dad?' comes a small voice, a mouse's voice, a voice that has drawn his heart time and again like a butterfly toward a bug zapper, and Mookie grabs Werth by the top of the head and twists the man's gaze 'round to him once more.

'You gotta go,' Mookie says to Werth.

'We ain't done talking about business. I got a gig for you.'

'Give it to somebody else.'

'But there's someone new moving in downtown, we need your—'

'You gotta go.'

Mookie has That Voice. He says something in That Voice, you know he means business. You know that you don't do what he says he'll twist your head off the neck and take a big bite of it like it was an onion or an apple. Werth knows the score.

Werth knows the score. He scowls, skirts past the girl like she's uranium on two legs, then disappears.

Mookie doesn't cross the distance.

The girl doesn't, either.

'Sit,' he says, finally, pointing to a table. 'I'll fix us a plate.'

It's the culatello on melon she eats first. 'It's good,' she says. He thinks she's telling the truth but he's never sure. She knows how to play him, drag him along like a suckling pig on a string. Still. The look on her face: Mookie thinks her pleasure is sincere because before she says anything, she's lost in a moment. An unconsidered instant of pleasure.

Mookie knows that look. It's the only way he gets enjoyment.

'How's things?' he asks, feeling himself slipping into that same rigmarole, the *routine* of expected questions. He's nervous. He never gets nervous.

'I dunno.'

'How's your mother?'

'I guess okay.'

'The car? The car working?'

'It got me here.'

'What about school? You gonna be in the school play or whatever? They do one every year, yeah? You like that acting thing.'

'I wasn't good at acting. I mostly did set design.' Even Mookie gets the irony, there. She stares down at the plate of charcuterie. 'Besides, I graduated last year.'

'You graduated?'

She nods.

'Shit. *Shit.* Hold on.' He stands fast, almost knocks the chair across the room, then hurries to retrieve the envelope Werth gave him. Mookie presses it into her hands. It's how it always is: him racing to do for her without a hair's breadth of hesitation. She doesn't have to tell him to jump to get him to ask how high. She just needs to pout, or sigh in just such a way, to have him hopping about like a clumsy Lord-a-Leaping. 'This is for you. Graduation present. Take it.'

'I don't want it.' She's lying. She always wants it.

'I said take it.'

'That's not why I'm here—'

'I said take the goddamn fucking money, Nora.'

That did it. The words came out his mouth, a tumble of boulders, a verbal truncheon, and he sees her suck in a scared breath and pull the envelope into her lap and stare straight ahead—not at him, but at any point around his prodigious bulk. He knows the look. The pout. The watery eyes. The tender hands pulling back and hiding under her armpits. Is it real? Or just a show? He feels guilty just for thinking that. Shame rises in his gut and sucks at his heart but it is what it is and this is what he is.

He sits back down, fumbles another piece of Lardo into his mouth.

'It's my boyfriend,' Nora finally says, still watching the margins of her father.

'You have a boyfriend?'

'He's sick. No. Not sick. But in the hospital. Someone… did something to him…'

She goes to brush a stray hair out of her eye, and that's when he sees it.

Her fingertips: stained slightly blue.

As she moves the hair, he sees that her temple has a similar azure smear, like a fingerprint of faded library ink.

The moisture goes out of his mouth. Feels like he's sucking on a stone. He bites down on his own teeth so hard he's afraid they'll crack.

He grabs her hand, tilts them up under the light above the bar table.

'Nora,' he says, his voice a rising growl.

'Don't be mad.'

'The Blue Blazes,' he whispers—more for himself than for any edification he could give her. An image, then: him, sitting on the living room floor, a bent needle of a Christmas tree in the corner coiled too-tight with pretty lights, her mother crying on the couch, little Nora in two blonde pigtails like the McDonald's arches (her hair would eventually change to a dark chestnut), and him leaning up against an old bunker of a television, dipping each index finger into a little makeup kit of blue powder— 'I got work to do,' he says before massaging the stuff into his temples, his eyes rolling back in his head…

In retrospect, he probably should've seen this coming.

Shit.

She's really crying this time. She's wounded. Someone did something to his baby girl. Whoever hurts her *gets* hurt. That's how it's always been.

'Hospital,' he says. 'Name. Now.'

The stink of antiseptic completely overwhelms the odor of disease, but Mookie thinks he'd rather just smell the sickness. Sickness is natural in its own way. Putrefaction and decay, fermentation and chemical entropy—it's all as it should be. And just the thought of it is making his stomach growl.

The kid—Bentley, what a fucking name, *Bentley*—lays there comatose on the bed, pale like a grub under a sweat-soaked sheet. Big black staples hold closed a monster-sized gash on his head. Mookie picks up the chart like he knows anything about anything, reads the words 'brain' and 'bleeding' near enough to one another to tell him what's up.

He throws back the covers, sees one of the kid's hands there, fingers curled up like the legs of a dead, sun-baked crab. The fingertips, blue. Blue like the blue on a crab's claw, too.

Mookie looks to Nora, his daughter. Wonders how she got the boyfriend into this mess. What did she tell him? What promises did she make? She quickly wipes tears away, then taps at her head at the same spot Bentley's gash sits.

'Shit,' he says, pulling out the little tin of blue powder. Smurf Blood, Smurf Jizz, Blue Raspberry, the Blue Blazes, a hundred names for the same shit. He holds it up, uses it to gesture at his daughter in the same way a father might gesture with a pack of condoms or a pack of cigarettes. 'You're done with this stuff.'

'I know.'

'Just because I use it doesn't mean you use it.'

'Okay.'

'What I do isn't what *you* do. You're better than me. You have to be.'

To this, she says nothing. Nora merely trembles in the doorway.

'Fuck it,' he says, and rubs some of the blue powder between callused thumb-and-forefinger. He massages it into his temples. His knees almost buckle. He almost goes down like a stack of crates. He smells lilies. Feels ants on his skin. The world goes sideways. It shifts, tilts, then snaps back. The edges of his vision are electric blue. The clouds are gone. The veil is pierced. He feels hot, alive, aware.

The gash on Bentley's head isn't just a straight line anymore. It's a fat knobby knot split both ways by a plus-sign cut. Clinging to his head is a foul, grey-skinned creature—like some unnatural conglomeration of *monkey* and *worm*—and from the thing's rubbery translucent lips slips a tongue like the tongue of a hummingbird, darting out and sucking at the pus and blood like it's sweet nectar. The fiend's eyes roll around in its head.

Mookie grabs it with one hand. It barely has time to thrash and scream before Mookie pops its head like a zit. Black brains like pomegranate slurry ooze to the floor.

Bentley shudders. He doesn't awaken from the coma. Not yet.

'Wh… what did you do?' Nora asks. She can't see. Because she's not on the stuff.

'He had a… friend,' is all Mookie says. A *gobbo*—goblin—larva. Goblins are forever the kings of mad misery, their weapons deliver effects far beyond those of mere physical damage. Bentley's injury looked to be from a slug cudgel: a star-headed beat-down stick that, if it tastes blood, plants a little egg—like a frog egg, gelatinous and ocular—in the wound. Not long after, it grows another baby gobbo who crawls free from the wound and sups on the suffering like a kid with a milkshake. Until the victim dies. Easy to get rid of if you know what to look for or who to call. But so few do. 'I took care of it. He'll get better soon enough.'

'Now what?' Nora asks.

Mookie stands there, scowling. 'Now you get the hell out of my way.'

She does like he says.

'What are you going to do?' she asks.

'Break bones till someone tells me who sold you that poison.'

'Here,' she says, pressing a slip of paper into Mookie's hand. The paper is no bigger than the fortune from a fortune cookie. It has one word on it. A name.

'This is where you bought your stuff?'

She bites her lip, nods. The dominoes fell in a straight line: Mookie was a user and, eventually, his daughter became one,

too. But the Blue Blazes wasn't easy to come by. Few people'd
ever heard of the stuff. Even fewer had managed to get a hold
of it and use it to rip the scales from their eyes and see the truth
about the world around them — the really old blazeheads called
a Blue Blazes trip a *katabasis*, a 'journey to the Underworld'.
Nora dove in, went deep, got caught with the wrong people to
get a hold of the stuff — people that weren't people at all. Those
goddamn cannibalistic in-bred goblins. Gobbos, grubs, worms.

Monsters.

'I'll be back,' he says. 'I know where to go. Who to see.'

'Thank you, Daddy.'

There it is. The kicker. He lives for that. *Thank you, Daddy*.
As satisfying to him as the taste of cold-smoked Speck ham. Both
enlivening and enervating. Fills him with life and takes the air
from his lungs. Mookie wants her to say it again.

But he won't push his luck. Instead he wonders if maybe
he should kiss her on the forehead or hug her, but he knows
if he hugs her he'll probably collapse one of her lungs. The
Blazes drug makes it hard for some to know their own strength
sometimes. The most affection he can clumsily muster is to poke
her in the breastbone with one of his big fingers and say, 'Don't
go anywhere. Don't leave this room. You leave this room and
I will hunt you down and tie you up and duct tape you to the
ceiling so you don't run off and do more stupid shit.'

She nods. She plays scared. But is she?

Mookie shoves past her, only for a moment pausing to
consider that his affection is as blunt and crushing as his massive
hamhock hands.

The city is where Mookie belongs. It's why he doesn't come here.
He doesn't like belonging to this place. Tall shadows ever-swaying.
Grease and blood in the storm drains. A smell in the air like death
and rotten food (garlic, curry, fish sauce).

He walks the streets, though, and the city knows to fear him.

A snake with a human face coils around a lamppost, tries not to be seen.

A pair of knockers hunker down next to an ATM. One taps on it with a small ballpeen hammer. Another listens to it with a stethoscope, looking for its heartbeat. The one with the hammer sees Mookie coming, screams, and bolts.

In the gutter lurks a nixie, sagging breasts resting on the cracked curb—occasionally she bows head to drink the foul water run-off. When she sees Mookie, she holds out her hands and whispers: 'You've come to kill me.' A statement, not a question. And wrong all the way. Mookie waves her off, keeps moving.

He knows his destination. It's written on the little piece of paper Nora gave him.

Sgradevole's.

The restaurant is packed. It always is. Lot of humans, humans who think this is *haute cuisine* but damn sure don't know any better. That guy there, he thinks he's eating an amuse-bouche of beef tartare with carmelized fennel, but what he's really getting is a Ritz cracker slathered with goblin vomit. The guy's date, the blonde with the shiny hoop earrings? She's eating a bile-soaked shoelace, thinks it's calamari ceviche. Sucking it into her mouth like that dog from that movie. Lot of these people will end up with stomach problems. Parasites, too. A few might get fat. Others might get dead. You never know at Sgradevole's. Tastes good going down. But it always comes back to getcha.

Mookie doesn't have long to think about all this. The maître-de—a sallow-faced jowly goblin stuffed in an ill-fitting tux, his teeth red with old blood—sees him, knows him (because they *all* know him) and sounds the alarm: an ululating scream.

He shouldn't have come.

But he had to. His anger knows no margins. It is boundless. These creatures hurt his daughter. And now he has to hurt them. The equation, and what it adds up to, are alarmingly simple. With Mookie, it's always simple. Even when it's not.

Three blow-darts stick in the meat of his arm. *Thwip-thwip-thwip*. Each tasseled not with feathers but with the seaweed-like underarm hair of goblin assailants.

The darts are probably tipped with poison. Mookie doesn't give a shit. Won't work on him; he's too big, and the Blazes have him jacked up hard.

The maître-de tries to run. Mookie grabs a chair and throws it overhand. It hits the fleeing gobbo dead-center of his bulging tuxedo back. Mookie hears bones break.

They're coming from everywhere, now. Gobbos at all corners. Out from under tables. Swinging and shrieking on a chandelier. Rolling forth on food carts and dessert trays. One comes at him with a hatchet: Mookie grabs the creature's arm, snaps it like he's breaking a goose's neck. Another fires wantonly with a rusty revolver. Mookie takes three to the back, but doesn't care. He's still got a grip on the hatchet goblin, so he uses the shrieking freak like a weapon—the thing's filthy razor teeth bite into the flesh of his wretched cohorts. He takes out the gun-toting fucker first.

The humans here—well, they react like any human confronting the madness of the monstrous reality. They pass out. Face first into soups, desserts, filets. After which most are dragged away by enterprising goblins (soon becoming victims for the goblin breeding tents, the work camps, or the kitchens of this very restaurant.)

Mookie wades through the fray. He feels the blood pooling at his lower back, above the hem of his pants. A piece of glass bites into his thigh. He crushes his attacker's rotten melon head between forearm and bicep: one squeeze, *pop*. Skull goo like forcemeats.

The goblins scream. They keep coming. He keeps dispatching them. With each a new cut, a new hole, a new bite mark on his brutish body. His fat head's too slow to duck the crude gobbo tomahawk coming his way, so instead he just offers it his forehead and stops it dead in the air.

He still doesn't see who he needs to see.

The table in the back, that's where he should be. But the table—a round table for eight ill-concealed behind a dark screen woven of bird bones and cat-gut—is empty.

The boss isn't here.

The rest of the goblins are all over him. Like cats on a beached whale.

He sees the maître-de crawling away—the gobbo's back legs don't work anymore since his spine met a flung chair. Wearing a coat of biting, clawing, hacking goblins (with blood now streaking his legs and pattering against the floor), Mookie reaches down and rescues the maître-de in a meaty grip, and holds the monster's face close to his own. He smells the rank breath, breath born of old blood and rotting skin. It makes him want to throw up.

But he chokes it back down.

'The boss,' Mookie says. A goblin bites off the bottom of his ear. He shakes his head like a dog with an infection and flings the goblin skyward. The maître-de squeals and belches and tries to wriggle free, but then Mookie uses *that* voice: '*Where is the boss?*'

The goblin doesn't answer him, but doesn't have to. Its wide, round eyes—eyes ill-contained by their mushy sockets—dart for half-a-second toward the kitchen.

That's where they're hiding him.

That's where Mookie will find the boss.

He headbutts the maître-de into a putrescent pulp. Then Mookie ducks low, doing a squat thrust that grinds his bones against one another—when he rises again, he does so with great speed like a great white shark breeching, and he pivots hard, casting the carpet of goblins crawling all over him to the far shadows of the restaurant.

Then, with heavy boots and a hateful heart, he stomps toward the kitchen.

The boss is bigger than all the others. The gobbo bosses always are — they're more than bosses. They're fathers. (*Like you*, Mookie tells himself. *Ugly monster poppas, don't know how to keep track of their goddamn kids. Do their kids push them around, too? Like the old TV show asks: 'Who's the boss?'*) Fat bellies pregnant with egg sacs and sulfur-stink placentas — this belly in particular stuffed into an faded green smoking jacket, the fabric eaten by moths. Like a tumor swaddled in patchy moss.

The boss gurgles around Mookie's fist: 'Why?'

'Because you hurt my daughter.'

'I did no such thing!' The monster's words punctuated by burps and blorps.

'One of you sold her poison.'

'But not me!'

'You're all a tribe. You're a pox. And you're done in this city.'

The thing's noodle-tongue flails out of its mouth, licks the air. Mookie pulls his head away — that thing finds purchase, it'll hurt. Could suck the eye right out of his head.

'We'll be back,' the thing croons.

'And I'll be here,' he says, not really sure if that's true. He thinks the bullets stuck in his back might've hit something important. And he's losing a lot of blood (though he has a lot of blood to lose, so that's good.)

He grabs the goblin boss's whipping tongue, then pulls it taut. Mookie wraps it tight around the creature's bulging throat and yanks hard.

The creature's gray skin goes blue, then purple.

Its eyes go dead, then turn dry in their sockets. Like grapes off the vine, in the sun.

◇

By now, Mookie's got that low-blood-sugar feeling — the Blue Blazes haven't worn off, not yet, but they will in a couple hours. He's on the tail-end of this thing. He's also got that low-blood feeling, probably because a lot of it has leaked out.

The nurses here in the hospital all look at him in his blood-streaked horror. Like they want to say something, like they want to get him into a bed, but are too afraid.

He stomps past them, doesn't give 'em a chance.

In the hospital room, Bentley sleeps. Nora's nowhere to be found. Mookie has a sinking feeling. He snaps his sausage fingers right by Bentley's ear: it sounds like a stick breaking over someone's knee. The kid's eyelids flutter and shoot open.

'Nora,' Mookie says. 'Where is she?'

The kid tries to speak, but only croaks out a dry crackle.

Mookie grabs a glass of water and shoves it against the kid's mouth and dumps some into his foodhole. Bentley coughs, tries not to drown, spits some of it out.

'Jesus!' the kid cries.

'Good. You can talk. Nora. *Nora.* I want to know where Nora is.'

Bentley's eyes go wide. Pupils telescope to tiny inkspots. He's scared.

'Nora,' Bentley whispers.

'What about her?'

Then he says something that chills Mookie's bones. Something Mookie doesn't understand. Not yet.

'Keep her away from me!' the kid says, almost gibbering. 'She's not here, is she? Oh, god. *Oh, god.* Don't tell her where I am.'

Mookie staggers away from the bed. He feels thunderstruck but still doesn't know why. He can't put it together.

Bentley feels at his head, feels the fresh bandage there.

'She did this!' he cries. 'She did this to me! Oh, God, I loved her…'

Back at the bar.

Mookie wants a drink, and he wants some meat. He thinks — shot of Tito's vodka, some slices of Prosciutto de Parma, then maybe back into the freezer to hack some of the mold off some pig flesh. Just to clear his head. Just to think this through.

But someone's already inside.

Werth. Sitting at the same table they were earlier.

'Goddamnit,' Mookie says, storming over. 'I didn't give you keys which means you broke in, which means I'm going to have to break *you*—'

'I didn't break in,' Werth says, turning a slow head toward the rampaging bull, and as Mookie reaches in to grab Werth by the face, he sees—

The old goat—literally, he's an old goat, a chin-whiskered satyr with that milky cataract and the gray tooth, but that's not the surprising part as Mookie has long known who Werth was—has been gut-shot. His lap is soaked with blood. His hands weakly hold onto the table's edge as if, were he to let go, he might spiral off into death's hungry maw.

'Werth. Christ.'

'I told you somebody new was in town,' Werth says with a dry chuckle. He taps a goat's hoof against the concrete floor. 'I just didn't know it was her.'

'Her,' Mookie says, still not getting it until she comes out of the kitchen, into the bar.

Nora.

No.

No.

'No,' he says.

She shrugs, then says, 'Yes, actually. Me.' Her voice isn't her own—except, truthfully, Mookie realizes it *is* her own. The voice before, the mouse squeak, the bird's peep, *that* was the lie. He remembers something said about a school play. *I wasn't good at acting.* Itself an act. No. A lie. She played him. Again.

Nora points the gun—a .38 snubnose—and cocks the hammer.

'You're a loser,' Nora says. 'Always were, dear old Daddy.'

He shrugs. 'Can't argue with you there. So shoot me.'

'You're like this... this meat,' she says, ignoring his command and instead gesturing toward an old cutting board of left-out sausages. 'You are truly an acquired taste. Did you know that?'

'Thought you loved me.'

'You left us. And you were never nice.'

'Not nice. But I was good to you. And you didn't care.'

She laughs. A sound without mirth. 'Is that what you call it? I do what I have to do to survive. Like you. I just happen to be a lot smarter is all.'

'I love you, Nora.'

'And I love you, too.' A long sigh. 'It's why I'm not going to kill you.'

He puffs out his prodigious chest. He slaps at it: it sounds like he's punching a side of beef. 'Shoot me. Just do it. I deserve it, probably.'

'Probably. Still, no. You did me a solid today. You're like this gun. I pointed you toward my enemies and you wiped them clean: one brutish arm across the table and suddenly the path is clear. See, I'm in the business. I'm the new girl in town. I got a supply of Blue Blazes and I'm ready to sell. The gobbos had risen up of late. Increased numbers. The gray-skins were in my way. They and your old masters had the market share. I knew Daddy would do anything for his baby's love and so… here we are.' She shrugs, then assures him: 'You did a good thing. Ended their uprising. And now the goblins know my strength. Sure, they'll be back. Except this time, they'll work for me.'

'I can't let that happen.'

'You will. This is an old pattern, Daddy Dearest. You're my dancing bear.'

He snarled. 'I'll kill every last gobbo that does your bidding.'

'I know. And I don't care because you won't kill me and the world will always make more monsters.' She emerges from behind the bar. 'All you do is destroy.'

'Not true. I cook.'

Snort. 'I'd rather eat at Sgradevole's, thanks.'

This hurts him most of all.

Nora looks her father over. 'You should really go to a doctor. I assume you have one. I know this isn't the first time you've been worked over like this.'

'No. But this is pretty bad.' He feels sad. Confused. 'But I got a guy. Yeah.'

'I'll see you later, Daddy. You know, you could work for me. Forget the Old Goat—I don't even think he's going to survive. I'll pay. Even better than whatever that old goat was giving you.'

His hands curl into fists. 'I could punch the head off your shoulders, you know.'

'I know,' she says. Smiling sweetly. 'But you won't. Because I'm your little girl and because inside that scarred-up crater-marked fat-and-gristle chest of yours is a heart as sweet and tart as a cranberry. I am me and you are you and nothing changes.'

She reaches up on her tippy-toes and kisses his chin (she cannot manage to stand any taller than that without a step ladder.)

With that, she leaves. Disappearing into darkness. Door closing gently behind.

Mookie staggers over to the bar, sits down. He pours himself a vodka and eats some old meat. The Blazes fade, now. The electric fire at the edges of his eyes gutters and goes out. He feels deflated. He sucks down the vodka and keeps him going: fire for the furnace.

Werth groans. 'You gonna call me a doctor?'

'In a minute.'

'I'm fucking bleeding like a twice-stuck pig over here.'

'So am I.' Blood is wet on the floor. 'You're a tough old goat.'

For a little while, Werth is quiet. Except for the gurgling wheezes. And the occasional sniffle as he sucks a blood bubble back up his nose. 'So you gonna do it, then? Go work for her?'

'Nope.' He doesn't have to think about it.

'But she's your daughter.'

'And you're my boss. I got gobbos, and God only knows what else, to kill. No matter who they work for.'

Werth coughs. It's wet. Rattling. 'So. The same ol', same ol', then.'

'Mm,' Mookie says, and pulls the cutting board closer.

Sundown in Sorrow's Hollow

Monte Cook

Duncan's ears perked up. He growled at the sorcerer. A good length of Eradian rope bound Nihilan's hands, ensuring that he could work none of his necromancy, but that did not keep the stalwart canine from watching the prisoner with a suspicious eye.

'Easy, boy,' Iona said. 'He won't cause any more trouble. Isn't that right?' The last remark was aimed at Nihilan, but she of course expected no answer, due to the gag in his mouth.

You can never be too careful with his kind, thought Iona.

Iona sat astride her roan, Lotus, with Nihilan's rope lashed to the saddle. She pushed her brimmed hat back so that it dangled behind her neck by its leather cord. Long, reddish brown tresses spilled from her head. She heard Duncan through the psilence, but didn't bother to answer him directly. Instead she just smiled. A normal dog wouldn't be able to interpret such a gesture, but Duncan was a soulbound companion, far from a normal animal.

And as a Soulbound Knight, Iona was no ordinary woman.

Iona and Duncan escorted Nihilan to the nearby city of Duralo. The Imperial Marshals there could put the criminal sorcerer on an airship for his trial in the capital for demon trafficking. Their destination was still days away. Already the man had tried to escape twice.

Nihilan was fair skinned, but he dyed his hair and beard as black as the depths of the vast glacial lake they now circumvented. His clothes were tattered and dusty from the road, but once were black as well. Inappropriate silks and thick velvets that Iona knew must have been warm and uncomfortable as he walked behind her horse.

She didn't smile at the thought, but she almost did.

Nihilan's people, the Uquanath, might show up at any time to stage a rescue, so Iona knew they had to keep a steady pace. With Duncan watching over their charge, she pressed onward.

The thick deciduous woods around the glassy lake grew dark as the sun settled behind the western mountains. With only its pale glow showing over the peaks, Iona figured they had about an hour of usable light left, maybe a little less. She wanted to get at least three miles behind them, and the road was rough.

Their path took them away from the lake's edge and down into a shallow ravine. A weathered signpost read 'Sorrow's Hollow'. She'd never heard of it, and didn't remember seeing it on the map. Little towns out here on the frontier were like seeds blowing in the wind: some survived, and some disappeared without anyone's knowledge. Sorrow's Hollow, if it was a settlement at all, was as likely as not a small collection of long-abandoned buildings filled with nothing more than cobwebs and nesting birds. She'd seen such places before.

The ill-used path down into the vale confirmed her suspicions. No one had come this way in quite some time. Nihilan mumbled something behind his gag. She ignored him.

Duncan growled. He perked his ears and the light brown fur on the back of his neck rose.

Eventually, she could see a few buildings ahead in the fading light. To her surprise, a few people milled about as well, finishing the day's tasks and heading for their homes.

Sorrow's Hollow still lived.

Iona rode straight into town with the confidence befitting her station. The men and women within sight stopped where they stood and stared. A young boy ran off into one of the houses.

Like so many frontier towns, Sorrow's Hollow appeared to be centered about a large wooden church. Atypically, however, it appeared to be the building in town in the state of least repair.

Iona dismounted and shot Nilihan a warning look. The man said nothing. He barely moved. But his stare conveyed a lifetime's worth of contempt.

Watch him, Iona told Duncan.

I will.

None of the folk of Sorrow's Hollow made any attempt at a greeting. Iona didn't hesitate, however. 'My name is Iona. I belong to the Order of Soulbound Knights. I need to speak with the local reeve.'

No one stirred.

'Please don't make me repeat myself,' she said, wondering if maybe these were settlers of some ethnic group who didn't speak Navarene. It was rare, but it happened. It might even explain the town's isolation.

Finally, a woman in a work dress faded into gray and a floppy brown hat took a few steps forward. 'Ain't got no reeve. Ain't needed one.'

Iona nodded. 'All right, then. Who's in charge here?'

The woman shook her head. 'Ain't got no mayor or headman here, neither. Ain't to our liking. When decidin' what need be done, we all take an equal hand.'

'All right then,' Iona repeated. 'Then all of you that can hear, listen to me. This man is a dangerous criminal. I need a place to tie him down. I need food for my horse and a place to sleep. I won't ask you for anything else. But I do and truly need your aid in this, in the name of the Twelve Immortal Navarene Emperors.'

Now a man stepped forward. He wore denim and flannel. His veinous nose dominated his worn face. 'Don't have many come here and toss around names and such. Not for many a year. We ain't strangers to hospitality, I suppose, but what kind of man have you brung into our midst?'

'Don't concern yourselves with that,' Iona replied. 'I'll see to him. So will Duncan.' She nodded toward the hound. 'Can I assume that you've heard of soulbound companions out here?'

Many of those listening to her looked to the dog, and then back to her. A smattering of them nodded, a few with a touch of respect in their eyes. Even in the most remote corners of the frontier, most had heard of the Soulbound Knights, their prowess, and the capabilities and intelligence of their psychically linked canine companions.

The woman said, 'We'll find you a place, some food, and some water. Can't offer you much more.'

Iona nodded. 'I'm grateful. What's your name?'

'I'm called Claris.'

The man added, 'You'll be leaving in morn's light, though?'

'I will.'

The folk of Sorrow's Hollow provided Iona, Duncan, and their charge a shed of gray boards half-filled with grain. Lotus remained outside. Duncan told the horse not to stray far and, like all normal animals, it understood his psilent speech and did as it was told.

Iona tethered Nihilan to a post in the middle of the shack. After gulping down some of the bread, cheese, and sliced pork they'd been provided, Duncan volunteered to take first shift keeping watch over the captive. Iona didn't bother with her bedroll. She instead just made a surprisingly comfortable bed in the grain.

She kicked off her boots, placed her gunbelt next to her and waited for sleep. Iona mused to herself what Justan, her mentor, would have said about the importance of her pistols as opposed to say, her boots. *You are a knight, Iona,* he would say. *Your weapon is a sword, no matter what shape it appears to have. A holy blade, always pointing to the future.*

Iona awoke to the sound of Duncan's barks. Even as she briefly passed through that region between sleep and wakefulness, she realized that the barking was coming from far too far away.

White moonlight filtered in between the boards in the roof and walls. Nihilan wasn't there. She leapt instantly out of her makeshift bed. The door to the shed hung open, and she ran out without even putting on her boots or belt. Both of her Karrath-Ultcher pistols were in her hands, however. The silver of their long barrels glinted in the light.

Duncan! Where are you? Where's Nihilan?

Here!

Iona heard Duncan bark again from somewhere out in the night. She ran toward the sound. Rocks and twigs tore at her stocking-clad feet, causing her stumble.

Finally, in moonlight filtered by the clawed hands of trees, she saw Nihilan standing among the rocks at the bank of a small stream.

Duncan?

Don't worry about me. Stop him!

Iona held both weapons ahead of her as she crossed the distance toward the sorcerer. She took a practiced Pranic Pistolry stance as she moved, with one weapon held straight out, and the other behind her, straight up, like a scorpion's tail, ready to strike.

Nihilan did not move.

Closer, Iona heard the man chanting softly. She saw that his eyes were closed. He didn't even seem to know that she approached. With a swift motion, she flipped a massive pistol around in her hand and brought the handle down upon Nihilan's head. He crashed wordlessly to the ground, his face colliding messily with a large, wet stone.

Iona took a moment to see that he was unconscious, not pretending nor, in fact, dead. Then she looked around for Duncan.

As if in response, he barked. She followed the sound again through the dark. Finally, she saw the dog with his leg trapped between two large stones.

Did it with a spell, Duncan said psilently.

'Hang on,' Iona said aloud. She gingerly stepped toward him, getting her feet wet in the shallow stream. Once she got herself into a good position, she was able to move one of the rocks enough that Duncan could pull himself free.

He licked her face, and then his paw.

'You're welcome,' Iona said with a smile.

Despite Iona's assurance that Nihilan was down, Duncan still went to check for himself.

What happened? Iona asked her companion.

He used some kind of spell on me. Before I knew it, he was free and out here chanting. When I tried to stop him, the rocks grabbed at me.

'Sounds like he had this well planned,' she replied aloud. 'Except he wasn't ready for me at all. I wonder why.'

Maybe he did what he needed to do by the time you got here.

What does that mean?

Duncan made a noise somewhere between a growl and a whine and shook his head violently. Iona knew the gesture to be the equivalent of a shrug.

'Maybe when — if — he comes to, we can ask him.'

Nihilan didn't return to consciousness until many hours after sunrise. Iona had seen to his head wound, but had already determined that his fall would result in a terrible scar that would mar his face for the rest of his life. Of course, once he got to trial, his life would likely end soon thereafter. Trafficking with demons was punishable by death under Imperial law, and Iona had no argument with that.

Nihilan was bound to the wooden post as he was before, but this time Iona had hobbled his legs and bound not just his wrists, but had used leather cords to bind his fingers. Mostly, though, she imagined that his wound would keep him from using a spell. Because of this, she took the small risk of keeping his mouth free so that he could talk.

She squatted next to where he sat on the dirt floor. 'What in all the hells were you doing out there last night?'

After she asked him the same question three times, he finally answered, 'You'll find out soon enough.'

'That's no answer.'

He spat clotted blood. 'The Uquanath have many ancient pacts. There are things out here of which you know nothing, from ages undreamt by your kind.'

Nihilan grinned widely, despite the fact that it likely pained him greatly. 'Soon, however, soon you will know these things all too well.'

Duncan barked outside. Iona turned toward the open door. *Duncan?*

Come out here, Iona.

Iona gagged the sorcerer again, rechecked his bonds, and went to the door. She saw Duncan standing vigil. Lotus was nearby as well, but nothing or no one else.

What's wrong?

The people. They're all gone.

Iona looked about again. The scattered wooden buildings—and, more telling, the open spaces between them—stood in silence.

'Where did they go?'

Duncan shook his whole body. *Don't know.*

'Did you see them leave?'

Duncan sniffed at the ground. He took his time examining the area around them before answering. *Saw a few early this morning, then no one. No one's been nearby here since then.*

Iona realized that Duncan likely had not slept.

'Hey,' she said. 'Why don't you go inside and rest for a while. You can keep an eye on him in there as well.'

Duncan paused, took a long look at Iona, before bounding into the shed.

Convinced that Nihilan's injury would keep him in place better even than his bonds or the suspicious dog sleeping next to him, Iona walked to the nearest house. She knocked on the door, calling out a greeting.

No response came.

She went to the next house and knocked on that door. Again, no one answered. Iona did not hear anyone inside. She tried a few more homes, with similar results.

Iona went to the church in the center of Sorrow's Hollow. She knocked on the door, but then just tried to open it. It was, after all, a church. The door opened only slightly—a chain latched on the inside kept it from opening further.

'Hello?'

No response came, although logically someone had to be inside, because the chain had been latched from within. Iona peered into the unlit interior, and saw a fairly typical looking interior with pews and a lectern. Only the altar appeared strange. Topped with a yellow and blue cloth, the altar held a strange silver shotgun adornment atop it, held aloft on arms of silver. Iona wasn't certain if the weapon was real or simply an object of... veneration? She had never seen the like.

'Ain't no one talkin'?'

Iona turned to her left to see a man standing just five strides away from her. Her surprise at having someone sneak so close to her ended when she saw the intricate blue tattoos on his face and hands. These marked him as a Mamoui, one of an infamous organization of thieves and sometimes assassins Iona and Duncan had faced before. They had barely survived the experience.

Her hand was already on one of the leather covered grips of her pistols, but she didn't draw. The man appeared unarmed. He wore a cloth and leather jacket too small to conceal any serious weapons.

'What's your business here?' Iona asked.

The Mamoui smiled. 'I keep m'self here in Sorrow's Hollow from time to time. Marshalls and... Soulbound Knights don't come 'round here too often. And the folks here are all right.'

Iona nodded. That made sense for a thief. This was an excellent hideout. 'Where is everyone?'

'Hidin', I'd say. You most likely won't find 'em.'

'Why?'

'Search me. You do somethin' to spook 'em?'

Iona didn't answer him, but she thought for a moment that the villagers might have heard Nihilan's chants the night before. That was certainly the kind of thing that might spook a simple settler.

'Name's Jarisus. You?'

'Iona.'

'Who's that'n up there with you in the shed, Iona?'

'My companion, Duncan.'

'No, I mean the dude wit' the busted face.'

He'd obviously been spying on them for some time. And he was good. She kept her hand on her weapon. 'A criminal I'm taking to trial. You have a problem with that, Jarisus?'

'Nope. Can't abide no criminals, m'self,' he replied with a smile and even—in Iona's opinion—an audacious wink. Jarisus had a charisma about him that probably helped him in his chosen profession. She could imagine him talking his way out of a lot of tense situations. He was easily twenty years her senior, but even with the thick tattoos she could see that he had a clean, well-shaped jaw, a small nose, and bright eyes. He showed straight white teeth when he smiled, with a slight gap in between the two in front.

Iona couldn't find it in her to trust him. It would not be out of the question to think that Nihilan's people, the Uquanath, would hire a Mamoui spy to try to free him. In fact, Jarisus might not be working alone. She immediately headed back to the shed.

Duncan?

When no reply came, she sent the psilent message again. *Duncan?*

Duncan's eventual response indicated that he'd been asleep. He said that everything was fine, however. Iona arrived at the shed. Nihilan had not moved. She searched the perimeter and satisfied herself that no immediate threats presented themselves.

Duncan awoke when she came back into the grain storage shed.

'It's time to get moving, Duncan. Nihilan needs to be in Duralo in four days.'

Duncan barked in agreement.

Iona bent down to free Nihilan after gathering up her gear. Despite the fact that she untied him from the post, he did not awaken. Even when she became more forceful in her attempts to wake him, he did not stir.

Undeterred, Iona carried him out to her horse and indecorously tied him to the saddle. Looking around carefully for Jarisus but not seeing him, Iona led the horse away from the shed. Duncan guarded the rear.

They hadn't traveled a mile before Lotus began to make pained noises. Iona stopped her.

'Duncan, what's wrong with Lotus?'

Duncan paused for a moment, mentally speaking with the horse.

She's weak, Iona. Something's wrong. She's unsure if she can support his weight.

She's sick?

Maybe. Duncan sniffed at the horse's hooves. *Or maybe someone's done something to her.*

'Dammit.' *Ask her if anyone came anywhere near her or her feed during the night.*

Iona looked around as she patted Lotus's side lovingly and made a cooing sound. The dense crowd of trees obscured the sun with a menacing darkness. The babbling of the unseen creek was the only sound—no animals stirred in the woods.

Something was very, very wrong.

She doesn't know, Iona. It seems likely, however.

Iona knew Duncan to be more than a bit paranoid, but Iona thought it seemed likely as well. She was still worried that Jarisus might be involved.

With Lotus ailing, however, she was going to have to either go back to the settlement or find a nearby place to hole up. She couldn't move the unconscious sorcerer very far under her own power.

Do we go back or stay out here, Duncan?

I didn't like that town, Iona. Those people were strange.

Iona nodded. 'I agree. Let's find someplace safe and hope that Lotus works this out of her system.'

The best place they could find before Lotus threatened collapse lay at the top of a small rise with thick brush on one side. Both Iona and Duncan could feel something amiss in the woods.

Lotus's condition improved slightly once her load and saddle were removed, but that blessing didn't last. Iona kept a few herbs and remedies in one saddlebag. She gave them to the horse reluctantly, because while they might help her condition, they would almost certainly put her in a deep sleep for many hours.

By the time the obscured sunlight faded entirely, Lotus was lying down in a bed of heather and lupine. Iona lit a lantern but kept the flame very low. Duncan padded around in a tight perimeter. Iona crouched next to Nihilan's still unconscious form, a hand resting on one weapon.

That weapon was in her hand half a heartbeat after she first heard movement in the distance. A moment later, she drew its companion with smooth clarity as a second sound confirmed the first. Something approached.

Iona.

I heard.

Smells bad. Smells like old death.

Iona could hear Duncan began to growl.

Let's keep quiet. Maybe it will pass.

It's coming right for us. And it's not alone.

Duncan's nose and ears were uncanny, but Iona relied mainly on her eyes. She didn't act until she saw the thing worming its way through the trees. Despite its man-like shape there was no mistaking it for a human. The thing scuttled with a palsy that made it somehow more like a segmented insect than a person or even some woodland beast. Its hairless, gray skin showed a striated pattern the color of a bruise, just beneath its surface. Long fingers writhed at the end of spindly arms like newly hatched serpents. The thing's worst features, Iona thought, were its eyes, yellow like dried pus and as lifeless as gravestones.

When it got close enough for Iona to see that another such thing followed behind, it hissed like an angry animal. Iona could smell it, and Duncan was right. It stank of rot and death.

That was all Iona needed. With an aim so well-practiced that it required no effort or thought, she shot the closest thing in its sunken chest. It staggered backward, but did not fall. With a smooth motion, she brought the other pistol up and fired again, this time striking the horrific thing where its clavicle would be, were it human. Again, it took a step backward, then pressed forward, hissing in anger. Its wounds produced no blood, just a thin, oily bile the color of rotten teeth.

Closer now, Iona saw that its mouth swarmed with jagged teeth surrounding a black tongue. She shot it again, this time in its hideous face. Normally, at this range, a hit from her Karrath-Ultcher six-shooter would all but remove a foe's head, but in this case it drilled a hole through the thing's right eye that extended to the back of its skull. It was like shooting into iron rather than flesh and bone.

And still the thing did not fall. Instead, it screamed shrilly, turned and ran off into the darkness. It might be impossible to kill them, but at least she could drive them away.

The other creature moved in to take the place of the first. At least two others writhed their way through out of the deep wood.

Calling upon her Pranic training, Iona began firing both heavy pistols in a complex rhythm of violence. She became a thing of grace and beauty in the eye of a gore-filled storm of brutality. Her movements were both fluid and precise, making each shot count.

No matter how exacting the punishment she dished out, however, it took at least three hits to drive one of the creatures back into the woods. And they kept coming. Iona could hear Duncan's angry growls. She knew that her companion was fighting off more foes behind her.

Iona calmly reloaded. Her practiced motions might have appeared to be the arcane gestures required in casting a spell. Then her weapons fired their careful barrage once again, each step and gesture a honed movement like that of a dancer.

Suddenly, one of the creatures loomed large, almost upon her. Its breath stank of putrescence. She could see the bloodlust welling up in its flat eyes. These things were blood-drinkers.

She thrust the barrel of her weapon directly into its mouth. She fired even as it reflexively bit down. The blast removed the back of its head and it fell to the ground. Without hesitation, it scrambled backward like an insect, leaving a wide trail of black bile behind it.

Duncan! Are you all right?

Bite them hard enough and they run, but it's not easy. I have to all but chew an arm off.

Hang in there.

In the shadows beyond her lamplight, she heard gunfire not her own. She sent the only remaining blood-drinker in sight screaming off into the night and then looked toward the shots.

A man — not one of the things — stepped into view.

'Don't shoot, Iona.' It was Jarisus. He held a red-handled six-shooter in his hand.

'What in all the deep places are you doing here?'

'Giving you a hand with the hemovores.'

Hemovores. That made sense.

Duncan came out of the brush with a vicious snarl. His coat was aflame with bloody wounds.

Hold up, Duncan. He might actually be on our side.

Those things got to Lotus, Iona.

Iona looked to her horse. In the midst of the fight, she hadn't seen or even heard the things attack Lotus, but in a short amount of time they'd torn the poor animal into pieces.

Dammit! I'm so sorry,. Lotus, Iona thought. *You deserved much better than that, my friend.*

She faced Jarisus, unable to keep the anger and loss from her voice. 'Why would you come out here to help us? How did you know where we were?'

Jarisus' reply was as calm as ever. 'Well, to answer the second first, I just followed the stream of the beasties. They were drawn to you and your dog like bees to nectar.'

Or to the sorcerer, Duncan said psilently.

'And as to why, well, I figure with all these hellborn freaks up and about, I'm safer with you still kickin' than without you.'

'Where did they come from?'

'Beats me. I first saw them down by the river.'

Where the sorcerer was spouting his magic, Duncan told Iona.

Yeah, I'm with you, partner. I think it's pretty clear now what he did.

'Didn't see them until after sundown,' Jarisus said. 'Don't think they like the sun. But there's a mess of hours before sunrise.'

'You've heard of these things before?'

'Yeah. Drallis in town told me about them once when we shared a bottle of black ice whiskey. Came up and about around here when he was a youngun'.'

'What are they?'

'Dead things. Ancient things that lived here long before our kind settled the frontier.'

'Is there some way to kill them?'

'Not sure "kill" is the right word. As you saw, you can blow 'em apart, but that don't kill 'em. Worse, they'll heal those holes we blasted into them real fast. They'll be back Iona.'

'Well, shit,' Iona whispered.

'But he did mention something real interesting. Maybe something of use.'

'What?'

'Well, he was drunk as a brickbug, remember... but he said that the town had a weapon. A shotgun crafted by an angel back in the old days. It kills the hemovores.'

Iona scowled. She had seen many things in her time, but an angelic shotgun would be something new. There was, however, that strange altar in the church.

'I saw a shotgun on the altar in the church.'

'I ain't seen no one go in or out of that place in all my visits here. These folk ain't religious, Iona, but they got themselves a big old church just the same.

'For some reason,' he added.

'We could use that right now.'

'I don't know why we're still jawin'.'

Iona saw to Duncan's wounds. None were serious—the dog knew how to protect himself in a fight. He wouldn't let her spend much time fussing over him.

With Jarisus' help, Iona carried Nihilan back to town. She promised herself she'd come back and inter Lotus when she could. Duncan, as always, watched her back. Despite the time it took to cross that single mile, they neither saw, heard, nor smelled sign of the hemovores.

With no better place, they put the sorcerer back in the shed, and tied him back to the post.

Watch over him, Duncan. We're going to see about this so-called angelic shotgun.

This new fellow, Iona. He smells... all right. For what it's worth.

That's worth a lot to me, Duncan.

Iona and Jarisus crept toward the dilapidated church at the center of Sorrow's Hollow. Both had a weapon in hand.

Jarisus told Iona that he would look around back. Iona moved to the front of the structure.

She found the main door of the church open, this time. Dim light filled the interior of the one-room building. Claris, the woman Iona had spoken to when she arrived, stood there, holding an old but clearly functional rifle.

'You can't come in here,' Claris said. 'This ain't yours.'

'I've come for the shotgun.'

'Ain't yours.'

'We need it. The hemovores are swarming out there. They'll kill us all.'

'Nope. Just you. That sorcerer you brought into our midst called them up. This time they ain't our never-mind. Shotgun's ours. We'll use it if they ever threaten us. But not this time.'

While Claris talked, Iona saw Jarisus creep in behind her. She could not imagine where he had slipped in, or how he was moving so quietly now, but Claris gave no sign that she was aware. Was Jarisus going to take the woman out from behind?

Jarisus did not approach, but instead slunk like a weasel toward the old church altar and the silver shotgun atop it. He looked up once toward Iona, motioned toward his mouth and then toward Claris.

Keep her talking was the message Iona took from that. 'What if you're wrong,' she asked her. 'What if they do come after you and your families once they're done with us?'

'Don't believe it,' she replied. 'But if they do, then we'll use our weapon. Not before.'

Jarisus' hands moved across the altar like a lover. He appeared to find some hidden latch and smiled.

'Where'd you get the shotgun?'

'Ain't your business.'

'Did you folks actually get it from an angel?'

'More complicated than that. But it ain't your business.'

Jarisus lifted the weapon gingerly from the arms holding it. He stood, the shotgun with its twin barrels gleaming like silver held lightly in his hands. Strange writing ran the length of each barrel. Then, with a wink, Jarisus disappeared into the shadows with his prize.

'Well,' Iona said, 'I'll leave then. But I'll remember your unwillingness to cooperate.' She'd never been very good at deception, but figured it didn't really matter what she said at this point.

She met up with Jarisus near the shed. He handed her the shotgun.

'You're likely a mite better with somethin' like this than me.'

She took it, and marveled at its warmth. It felt good in her hands. She reflexively checked and saw that it was loaded with a golden slug in each barrel. 'Thanks,' she said. Then, 'You don't have to stay, you know. You've already endangered yourself enough.'

Jarisus smiled, then nodded. 'Maybe I'm lookin' for a little redemption. Figured you were the only one 'round here handin' it out.'

Iona did not know exactly what to make of that comment. She wanted to ask what he needed to atone for, but thought better of it. It didn't really matter. And besides, she didn't know anything about redemption.

Before she could say anything, however, Duncan's barking alerted them both. Iona heard the sound of breaking wood. The hemovores were tearing their way into the back of the shed. She started to move around the small building to the left when she saw three of the hideous things rounding it toward her, teeth bared and hands reaching for her.

Without hesitation, she raised the shotgun to her shoulder and fired. It packed a tremendous kick, and it forced her back a step. There was a bright flash of golden light which caused all three hemovores to recoil. The lead creature looked down to see a large hole in its chest, from which the glow continued. And spread. The hole widened, as if the light from the wound was consuming the creature.

Which, in a manner of seconds, it did. Every bit of the hemovore disappeared as it disintegrated from the inside out, leaving a momentary image of fading light in its shape behind before even that vanished.

'Sunlight,' Iona whispered.

The remaining two creatures screamed and charged toward her frantically. She fired the other barrel and blasted the head off another. It, too, was devoured by the light. The third reached her. It grabbed her by the arm, pulling her in toward its gaping maw. Its stench, which seemed to come from deep within that horrible dark mouth, almost made her gag. She swung the shotgun around like a club, striking the hemovore in the neck with the butt. To her surprise, it staggered back and then began to glow brightly like the others.

Even the merest touch of the shotgun spelled the end of these things.

Iona cracked the shotgun's break action. It was still loaded with two slugs. Nothing about this weapon was natural. She ran around to the back and rained death upon the hemovores there which had torn the back from the shed. She fired and fired, never needing to reload.

When she had cleared them away, she saw Duncan tearing the throat out of one of the things tugging at Nihilan's still unconscious body. They *were* acting on the sorcerer's behalf. Trying to free him.

When the horribly wounded hemovore attempted to run, Iona blocked his way and finished him off with a shove from the shotgun.

Wow, Duncan said psilently.

It's handy, Iona replied.

She heard more of the creatures outside the shed. She exited through the door in time to see two of them covered in fresh blood. She blasted them into glowing oblivion before they could even react to her.

Behind where they stood, another knelt over something in the darkness. She approached, and then bashed the blood-covered thing with the shotgun's butt.

Jarisus lay on the ground, multiple bite wounds having removed a great deal of his flesh. He looked up at her with pained eyes, but still managed one of his charismatic smiles.

'Jarisus,' Iona whispered, kneeling.

He tried to respond, but only blood came.

'Shhh,' she told him, touching his forehead. She couldn't bring herself to tell him he would be all right. He wouldn't.

'Thank you,' she told him. 'Whatever you've done in the past, you got your redemption, as far as I'm concerned.'

Iona didn't know if he heard her.

She stood over Jarisus' body and looked around. If there were more hemovores, they had fled. Dawn wasn't far off.

Looking down at the marvelous weapon in her hands, she contemplated keeping it. She knew, however, that she would have to give it back to the folk of Sorrow's Hollow. They needed it. For its return, she'd ask for a pair of horses—Nihilan's sorcery surely affected only Lotus.

Back at the shed, the sorcerer was finally conscious. He grinned through the debris of his face, but as he met Iona's gaze, his smile faded into the realization that his plan had failed. Iona had nothing to say to the man. He would meet a fate beyond words of recrimination soon enough. She was certain of that. She walked back out to watch the sun rise. Duncan at her side, Iona mused over all she'd lost in Sorrow's Hollow. It was aptly named. She knew she'd never come back.

A Man of Vice

Alexandra & Peter Freeman

I well recall my first encounter with Violet Meeks, although I did not know her name at the time. She stood among the tombs, as quiet and pensive as if she were a stone angel. Only her eyes betrayed her vitality, watching me as I passed between the lichgate and the rectory. I recall that she was barefoot, her dress no more than a limp rag of black cotton, as if she was some vagrant child. Dark hair hung straight and unkempt to the level of her knees, and her stare made me wonder if she was entirely sane. When I emerged from the rectory, just minutes later, she was gone.

That was at the Church of the Blessed Heart, during those events which culminated in the death of the Rector, the Reverend Piers Myton, by suicide as I believed. It was the first such event of my career, and while my training had to some extent prepared me for such tragedies, it was nevertheless a considerable shock. Perhaps I should explain. I am, by profession, a lay brother in the Church, a Quæstor. It is my specific responsibility to ensure that those funds distributed to the parishes are put to their proper use and, when necessary, to bring to the attention of the authorities any peculation or other financial misdemeanour.

As you can no doubt imagine, it is a vocation which meets with little gratitude and not infrequent hostility. I invariably find myself junior in both age and dignity to those I am duty bound to investigate, and if my status as a Quæstor of the Church ensures co-operation, it does not ensure a warm welcome, rather the opposite. In the case of Rector Piers Myton he had done everything in his power to obstruct me, up to and including the destruction of those ledgers on which any case I might have brought would necessarily have rested. What he hoped to achieve by this I was uncertain, and only later realised that it was an act of desperation. He would have been doomed in any case, having relied on the isolation of the parish and his high dignity, making little effort to conceal his redirection of funds towards what proved such horrible vices. Once my attention had been drawn to him exposure was inevitable, and yet I was still surprised that he took his own life, choosing eternal damnation in the next world over disgrace in this. Only when I later came to examine the crypt beneath his church did I realise that he had already assured himself of a place far deeper in the pit than that reserved for those who take their own life.

It was some months later, in the fall of my third year as a Quæstor, that I was sent to Saint Petroc's in the Diocese of Bodmin. The parish had for many years been under the care of the Reverend Stephen Harland, but he had at length gone to receive his reward. His replacement, the Reverend Saul Bulmer, had been in residence less than a year. When a long established and popular incumbent dies it is the rule rather than the exception that a few complaints are made, generally by those who had grown comfortable with established ritual and enjoyed the patronage of the departed.

Normally such matters would be handled within the Diocese, but in this case a specific accusation of personal indulgence with Church funds had been levelled at the Reverend Bulmer and so at length it fell on my desk. I in turn would have smoothed the matter over with a suitably worded missive, but important feathers had been ruffled and influence was duly brought to bear. Even then I might have passed the matter on, but my superiors felt that

I would benefit from the experience of having to apply tact rather than pure arithmetic.

I was duly dispatched to Cornwall, and as I travelled down my spirits were high. Michaelmas had passed, bringing an abundant harvest and leaving the red soil of the Devon fields in plough. I was obliged to change trains at Exeter, and again at Okehampton before my arrival at Bude, allowing me to enjoy the fresh air and the sight of the great green locomotives at their work. From Bude I engaged a vehicle to travel north along the coast, an engine wagonet painted in the smart black and gold livery of the county. The driver already had the steam at good pressure and we set off immediately, through bright sunshine that lit the sea and lent such beauty to the scenery of harsh cliffs and verdant fields that I found my voice lifted in song. With the glory of the Lord's creation all around me it was hard to image the existence of malice or vice at all, until I once more recalled events at the Church of the Blessed Heart.

The Reverend Saul Bulmer proved a large man, round of face and round of body, his expression beneficent and his manner avuncular. He greeted me cordially, calling for cider and cakes as I entered the Vicarage, a reception quite different to what I had come to expect. I could see no reason to refuse his hospitality, so long as his offers remained within the bounds of propriety, and so accepted with pleasure. His was an old residence, the main part a long, low house built into a hollow in the ground to protect early incumbents from the Atlantic weather. This had been a wise choice, as a space of but two fields separated church and living from Youlstone Cliffs, a great grey-brown buttress of rock rising three hundred feet from the sea. Since that time additions had made as man's demand for comfort and space grew over the centuries, and what had once been the entire house was now a single room, furnished with comfort but never extravagance in tones of rich brown, red, and old gold. A great table ran the full length of the room, set with ornaments, books, papers and two vases, each containing a neat arrangement of autumn anemone and black roses, which I thought in peculiar contrast to both the

Reverend Saul Bulmer and the rest of the room. He noticed the quality of my attention as he indicated a chair.

'My housemaid has somewhat individual tastes, but she's a good worker. Do make yourself comfortable.'

As I sat down, the girl herself entered the room. I did not recognise her immediately, as she was now dressed in a prim black and white uniform, while her long, dark hair was coiled onto her head and confined within a well starched cap. She was also heavily laden, supporting a tray on which stood two ample flagons of rich gold cider and a plate of honey cakes. Only when she glanced at me did I recognise her as the girl from the tombyard at the Church of the Blessed Heart, that pensive stare unmistakable, although I had not realised that her eyes were deep violet in colour, something I had never seen before. She placed the tray on the table and left the room without a word, her slender hips barely stirring the material of her long black skirt as she moved. Again the Reverend Saul Bulmer noticed my attention.

'Toothsome little thing, isn't she? If you like 'em skinny that is.'

It was an extraordinary remark, coming from a man of the cloth, and I felt myself colour a trifle before finding an answer.

'I was struck by the colour of her eyes.'

'Ah, yes. Remarkable. That's why we call her Violet. It may even be her real name.'

'She has references, I would suppose?'

'Nothing of the kind. Mrs Penreith, who used to do for old Harland, was far too set in her ways, and a bit of an eyesore, so I gave her the push. Violet answered my advertisement. She's pretty and she does as she's told, so I took her on.'

As he finished speaking he emitted what honesty forces me to describe as a lewd chuckle, again making me wonder as to his suitability for the church. He had also touched on one of the various complaints which had brought me to Saint Petroc's, allowing me to broach the subject without seeming unduly impolite.

'Ah, yes, Mrs Penreith. I regret to say that her dismissal has caused a complaint to be raised against you, one of four.'

Most of my accused, whether innocent or otherwise, would have bridled at such a remark. Not so the Reverend Saul Bulmer. He shook his head, smiling in wry amusement, took a swallow of cider that drained half the pot and helped himself to a honey cake before he troubled to reply.

'That'll be Lady Morwenstow, eh?'

'I fear I am not at liberty to divulge the sources of complaints.'

'Of course you're not, but it'll be Lady Morwenstow none the less. She's not sister to a bishop for nothing. Who else in these parts has the influence to have a mighty Quæstor sent all the way from Canterbury just because a rural vicar enjoys the odd glass or two? Daft old baggage. She used to employ Mrs Penreith, you see, and that's really the width and breadth of the thing.'

'You also stand accused of peculation.'

'I had gathered as much from your presence.'

He spoke without rancour, and as he did so he reached out to take up a set of ledgers, their black leather binding and discreet symbol unmistakable. These he pushed towards me, his manner so casual that I immediately wondered if he had not taken the precaution of falsifying his records. Certainly his bonhomous manner hid considerable intelligence, while he had already shown himself remarkably perceptive. Yet to the trained eye the misappropriation of funds leaves certain distinctive patterns, and it was these I sought as I began to examine the first and most recent of the ledgers. He watched me, his rubicund face showing no trace of concern, nor irritation, but only amusement. I had turned to the third page and he had consumed a second honey cake before he spoke once more.

'You won't find anything amiss, you know. In fact, I've scarcely had time to indulge myself in the way the foolish old witch implies. Most of that is from old Harland's time, by the way.'

So far as I could tell, at least from the figures before me, he was being entirely truthful. An ascetic would no doubt have judged him guilty of gluttony, and perhaps also sloth and lust, but these were matters between him and his Bishop, and, ultimately, the Lord. His dismissal of Mrs Penreith also seemed somewhat uncharitable, but it was not illegal under the law of the Church and certainly not a matter for my attention. Nevertheless, I was bound to make a full investigation, and told him as much.

'I shall need to study these, and to compile a complete report in answer to the accusations made against you.'

'Naturally, you are very welcome to examine whatever you please, and you can be assured of my full co-operation. The innocent need not fear justice, as the Blessed Augusta remarked, but let me tell you a little about myself in order to facilitate your investigation. More cider?'

'Thank you, no. I rarely drink before eventide.'

'As you please. Violet, more cider. Stir that rump, girl!'

Violet appeared, so promptly that she must have been anticipating his demand, although that hardly required clairvoyance. She set a fresh flagon of cider in front of him, removed the old and left. Again she made no remark, leading me to wonder if she was mute, or lacked her full wits.

'Is she...'

'Dull? No, far from it, merely shy, I would suppose. Now, where was I? Ah, yes, my career. I imagine you're thinking that I'm an earthy sort of fellow as priests go, and you are right. We Bulmers are an old county family, with old county traditions. The eldest son inherits and any spares have a choice between the Church and the army. I have no desire to be shot at by foreigners, and so chose the Church. I became a catechumen a year early and studied theology at Corpus, where I secured a first. Nevertheless, whatever my faults, vainglory is not among them and I do not intend to climb the greasy pole of Church hierarchy. I was a first curate at Wolsey House, still in Oxford, and a senior curate at Saint Edgar's Blackingstone, under old Truscott, who you will find gave me excellent references. Here then you have me, a rural vicar content with his lot. Are you sure I can't tempt you to some more of this cider? It really is excellent. The apple is Royal Wilding, from my own orchard.'

'No, really.'

So began my investigation of the Reverend Saul Bulmer. I confess that almost from the first I regarded the matter not so much as a piece of work but a holiday. The Reverend Bulmer himself proved the quintessence of hospitality, for all that his bluff manner frequently verged on the ungodly, while it was impossible not to be charmed by the presence of Violet Meeks, for all her exaggeratedly shy manner. By contrast, Lady Morwenstow proved impossible to like and difficult to view with the detachment that is essential to my vocation. Only by the utmost exercise of my will was I able to retain my composure in the face of her arrogant and hectoring manner, while it became increasing hard not to sympathise with the Reverend Bulmer's open distaste, and indeed, not to smile at the increasingly unkind remarks he made at her expense.

The parish accounts proved both honest and carefully recorded, each entry in the thick black ledger correct to the last farthing. Funds had arrived and been disbursed with no hint of misappropriation or even extravagance. That amount set aside for household expenses was in fact rather lower than it had been during the previous tenure, largely owing to the savings made on the medicinal preparations that both the Reverend Stephen Harland and Mrs Penreith had considered essential to their health. It was true that certain changes had been made in terms of which of the local charitable causes benefitted and to what extent, but if anything these alterations reflected credit on the Reverend Bulmer. He had, for example, increased the amount set aside for the upbringing of children conceived in sin and born out of wedlock—a cause of which Lady Morwenstow strongly disapproved—but altogether halted payments to the Guild of Gentlewomen—a society at which she took the chair. Clemency to those who have strayed is a virtue too seldom encountered, as is compassion towards the innocent progeny of wantons. For all the Reverend Saul Bulmer's rude manner he was clearly an exponent of both.

Never before in the course of my investigations had matters gone so smoothly, nor a host been so considerate. The Reverend

Bulmer kept a good table, if not an extravagant one, and I even allowed him to tempt me down to the local hostelry. Violet also was invited, again demonstrating on the one hand his unsuitable familiarity towards women and on the other his worthy indifference to social distinctions. She drank mead, which I thought unusual, and demonstrated extraordinary proficiency at the game of darts, beating both myself and the local champion. That same evening I had occasion to criticise the Reverend Bulmer for his over familiarity, when he made a jocular threat to spank her for not troubling to make the sign as we passed the church. He accepted my reprimand with good grace, allowing me to hope that I might be bringing a good influence to bear on his character.

Had it not been for the persistence of Lady Morwenstow I would have concluded my investigation at the end of the second week. My report would have stated that the Reverend Saul Bulmer was an honest man of robust character, well suited to the rustic living to which he had been appointed, although unsuitable for high office. How wrong I would have been, and so it must be admitted that I, and many others, owe Lady Morwenstow a debt of gratitude, for all that her actions were unintentional. That said, I myself cannot lay claim to any real credit for subsequent events.

I had in fact begun to write my exoneration of the Reverend Saul Bulmer when the missive arrived from my superiors at Canterbury. The wording was most precise, remarking on my excellent record but stating that influential parties felt that I was being insufficiently thorough, the implication being that I had allowed myself to be gulled into complacency, or even corrupted. The signature was that of Archdeacon Hulme, who I knew to be a close friend of Bishop Tremain of Silbury, Lady Morwenstow's brother. Thus it became plain that in order to maintain my standing my investigation would have to be comprehensive.

It was with some irritation that I made out a careful list of those avenues requiring exploration. At the head was Saint Edgar's Blackingstone, where the Reverend Saul Bulmer had spent the latter part of his curacy. The parish lay on the borders of Dartmoor, in country wilder even than Saint Petroc's, if less remote. The church stood below that great rock from the top of which the name saint of the parish had denounced the Horned God as an incarnation of Satan thirteen centuries before. It was therefore a place of pilgrimage, to which worshippers would travel, walking barefoot from Exeter Cathedral in order to supplicate the saint in his aspect as patron of those as yet unblessed with children, and perhaps to light a candle at that shrine built on the spot where Edgar's body had lain broken and bleeding after he had been thrown from the summit by the worshippers of the demon Herne.

The incumbent was the Reverend Alfred Truscott, who had held the living for forty-three years and was now in his middle eighties. He greeted me with a courtesy that almost succeeded in concealing his underlying dismay, although as he escorted me from my hired wagonet to where the vicarage lay surrounded by great oaks at the rear of the church he tried to make light of the circumstances.

'It's my weakness for elderberry wine, isn't it? I knew you would catch up with me in the end.'

Sympathetic to his embarrassment, I assayed a reassuring laugh before I replied.

'Not the elderberry wine, no, Reverend. The matter concerns the Reverend Saul Bulmer, who was curate here for some time.'

'Nine years, yes. Has his conduct been called into question? How sad.'

'You are not altogether surprised?'

'No, no, just the opposite. He is a merry fellow, perhaps lacking something of the dignity one might hope for in a man of the cloth, but he was a most able assistant, and quite untiring, a great help to a man of my advanced years, as you may well imagine.'

'What were his duties? Was he responsible for the disbursement of funds, for example?'

'No, no. That I keep to myself. It is a sedentary task, and one at which I have a great deal of experience, so better suited to my own capabilities. No, no, Saul made it his special responsibility to deal with the pilgrims, both in mundane matters such as accommodation and sustenance, and in spiritual matters, counselling, confession and so forth.'

We had reached the vicarage, a structure of old oak, granite, black iron and slate that seemed to meld with its surroundings. The Reverend Truscott paused in his narration as he ushered me within, offering me tea with the assurance of scones, clotted cream and blackberry jam. I accepted with gratitude, but his call for his housemaid went unanswered and I was left in the hall as he went to find her.

My eye was immediately drawn to the photographs that lined the walls, of celebrations and friends from across the vicar's tenure and before. The Reverend Saul Bulmer was easy to spot, his large frame and ruddy face unmistakable across the years. He was present in four of the photographs, three among groups who were presumably pilgrims, and in every one he appeared the benevolent, smiling patriarch, supporting what I had already learned. Indeed, it was hard to imagine a man more thoroughly pleased with himself and his place in the world. The word 'smug' even came to mind, although I quickly put it aside as an unworthy thought.

The Reverend Truscott presently returned, himself bearing the tea tray on which all the promised bounties had been laid out on a set of china painted with tiny, delicate flowers. The door to his living room was open and I followed him inside, taking a seat as he began to fuss with the cups and saucers, plates and knives. I waited, wondering what question I should frame, but he himself returned to the subject of the Saul Bulmer.

'Do you take sugar? No? I'm afraid it is one of my little indulgences. Now, where were we? Ah, yes, we were speaking of Saul. I must say that I was most surprised to learn that he has come to your attention. As you may know, he was not called to the Church, but I cannot fault his zeal, no more his care with financial matters, lest it be his dedication to charitable giving. He is one of those who would take the weight of all the sins of the world on his shoulders, where he able.'

'Just so. A note of his compassionate attitude towards sinners will be included in my report, for all that it is not strictly relevant. Indeed, I think I can fairly say that in visiting you here I am simply placing a seal on an investigation already complete, and which exonerates one who I take to have been your friend as well as your subordinate?'

'Oh indeed. Saul was a cheerful companion, always, and often as great a comfort to me as he was to our flock.'

'I can well imagine. Nevertheless, I am sure you will appreciate that I will need to inspect your ledgers as they pertain to his activities.'

He agreed, as he was bound to, and once we were done with tea became positively eager to assist. It was not until he left in order to prepare for evensong that I was able to study the ledgers in full detail. What quickly became evident was that while the Reverend Truscott might have been in charge of financial matters, and indeed his neat signature appeared at the foot of every page, his senior curate had enjoyed considerable influence over decisions on expenditure. As at Saint Petroc's, a proportion of charitable expense went towards the support of unmarried mothers and their offspring.

Seven women of the parish appeared to have been receiving alms in this cause, a high number in an area so thinly populated. This led me to wonder if they existed at all, payments to imaginary or deceased persons being a common, if clumsy, way of diverting funds to a personal account. A brief examination of the local census proved that they did indeed exist, which in turn led me to speculate that the women of the parish might have been the victims of a lothario. If so, he was evidently as skilled in the black art of seduction as he was wicked, for one of the women, a Miss Emilia Turner, had conceived and born four children, while two among the others had a second child.

Puzzled, I rose from my chair to pace the room and once more found myself in contemplation of the Reverend Truscott's memorial photographs. The second of the pictures over which I chose to run an eye was of a group standing in front of a charabanc, and the Lord must have guided my steps, for among them, looking out with her sullen, knowing stare, was Violet Meeks. Beside her was another young woman, as plump and rosy as an apple, all too evidently expecting a child, and she in turn stood next to the Revered Saul Bulmer.

He had lied to me in stating that Violet had answered his advertisement for employment at Saint Petroc's. The date on the photograph revealed that he had known her for eight years at the least. Possibly she was fallen, and he had sought to shelter her from further shame, but that in itself raised what seemed to be a paradox and one further compounded by her appearance. On the first occasion I had seen her, at the Church of the Blessed Heart some months before, I had imagined her as little more than a girl. On discovering her to be employed as the maid at Saint Petroc's I had revised my opinion, supposing her to be perhaps eighteen years of age. In the photograph, taken seven years before, she looked no younger.

I put the thought aside, concluding that she was simply one of those fortunate few blessed with the appearance of youth. After all, if she was eighteen in the photograph she would only have reached the age of twenty-five, which while unlikely for one so fresh and slender was by no means impossible. If so, and if she was a fallen woman, then the Reverend Bulmer had clearly taken her into his employ in order to save her from a further fall from grace, a highly charitable act, while I could understand full well why he would wish to keep the fact hidden. Lady Morwenstow would have made much of it, while the Church could not help but look poorly on a man who had dismissed a righteous woman from his service in favour of one disgraced. I was bound to report the circumstances, although it would be a task in which I took no pleasure.

Hoping that my reasoning was incorrect, I put a question to the Reverend Truscott as he returned to the room, now robed for evensong.

'Reverend, a moment, if you please. Would you be so kind as to identify the people in this photograph?'

He peered close.

'Yes, yes, certainly. Saul you know, and with him are er... certain young women who had fallen victim to temptation. They are pictured on an outing to Paignton. I remember the occasion well.'

'And this young lady?'

'That is Emilia Turner. Poor Emilia. She is, let us say, far too charitable for her own good.'

'No, beside her, the dark haired girl.'

'Ah, I see. Yes, yes, I recognise her. She first came here as a pilgrim, seeking intercession if I remember rightly. Saul, I remember, was most solicitous towards her, providing both comfort and advice. No doubt he invited her on the outing in order to raise her spirits. Curiously, Emilia also came to the parish as a pilgrim, also barren and seeking intercession, but her prayers were answered, although with tragic consequences. She proved to be with child, and all the time she had been here her husband had been at sea.'

With that it came to me, with such force and such clarity that it can only have been divine elucidation. There was indeed a lothario at work, the Reverend Bulmer himself. That he had a weakness for the fair sex I already knew, from his attitude towards Violet and others. Evidently, finding himself in the role of confessor and friend to so many nubile but barren young wives he had been unable to resist temptation.

No doubt he had set out with the intention of seducing only those who were unable to bear children in any event, thus allowing himself full scope for his depravity. In the case of Emilia, however, it had presumably been her husband who was barren and not she. After one such error, and with his need rising, as it invariably does with those who fall into the sin of incontinent lust, he had abandoned all restraint.

The web of logic contained but a single fault. Why, over the course of nine years, had no complaint been raised against him? In the case of Emilia Turner there was no surprise. Divorced for her adultery and thrown on the charity of the Church, she would have had no choice but to comply with his wishes, while to expose him would have been to risk a ruin yet deeper than that into which she had fallen. Yet what of the others, a further six women of the parish and the Lord alone knew how many hapless pilgrims? A moment's thought and I had found a possible answer, although I hoped I was incorrect, as if not then the Reverend Saul Bulmer was not only a lothario but a true monster.

It seemed likely that the solution was within my grasp, and I once more addressed the Reverend Truscott.

'Would it be possible to speak with Miss Turner?'

'By all means. She will be at evensong. Behind the lapse screen necessarily.'

In the minutes remaining before evensong I threw myself into the investigation with full zeal. As I had expected, in the nine years prior to the arrival of Saul Bulmer at Saint Edgar's few women of the parish had fallen, indeed, none. During evensong I was barely able to concentrate on my responses, although you may be sure that my prayers were fervent indeed, and once the Reverend Truscott had concluded the service I lost no time in seeking out Miss Emilia Turner. She was easily recognisable, her head hung in shame as she stood behind the lapse screen with her companions in misadventure, waiting for the more worthy parishioners to file out. I had no wish to further compound her misery and spoke gently as I approached her, asking for a moment of time alone before announcing myself. Her eyes grew wide at the realisation of my profession and I quickly sought to calm her, but also to cut directly to the core of my suspicions.

'Tell the whole of the truth and you have nothing to fear from me. What was the secret with which you came to the Reverend Saul Bulmer at confession?'

Her eyes misted with tears and she fell to her knees, her fingers clutching at the hem of my robe. I sank down beside her, twice more reassuring her that her private sins were not my concern before she at least began to speak.

'I... I came to confession, and... and I told how I had lain with a man other than my husband in the hope of getting a child. Instead of absolving me, the Reverend Bulmer demanded that I too lie with him, otherwise he would tell my husband what I had done! I had no choice, Brother, and I could not know that the Lord had already answered my prayer...'

There was more, and I let her speak, but I already knew the full, dreadful truth. The Reverend Saul Bulmer was a monster indeed, a seducer guilty of coercion, holding out the fruit of bribery while simultaneously wielding the flail of blackmail in order to achieve his wicked ends.

My one thought as I drove back towards Exeter was to confront Bulmer without delay, but it was as if Satan himself sought to work against me. At first the fire would not take on the wagonet I had hired, and when it did the steam seemed to require an age to reach adequate pressure. Having finally reached Exeter I discovered that a westbound locomotive had just left, obliging me to wait a further hour. I arrived in Bude so late that I had to pay double in order to convince a driver to take me out of town, and it was approaching midnight before I finally alighted at Saint Petroc's.

The lights of the vicarage were still on, and at the sight of Saul Bulmer reclining easily in his study chair with a mug of cider in one hand my fury redoubled. He looked up in surprise, but although I had rehearsed my denunciation a hundred times during my journey I now found myself unable to bring words to my lips, nor to act. Not so Saul Bulmer. One glance must have been sufficient to tell him that I knew his crimes and in an instant he was upon me. I threw up an arm to guard my face from his blow, realising too late that it was a feint. The heavy pewter flagon from which he had been drinking cracked onto my skull, once, twice, and I knew no more.

When I regained my wits it was to find myself securely bound into his heavy lectern chair, also gagged, with a wad of sour chamois leather packed into my mouth and tied off. My head was cut, the hair on one side caked with blood, and the room seemed to swim before my vision. It was moments before the full horror of my situation sank in. Saul Bulmer sat opposite me, drinking from the same flagon with which he had rendered me insensible, the side still smeared with my blood. His eyes were full of malevolence, and as he saw that I was conscious he spoke.

'You know, don't you? Why couldn't you leave well enough alone, damn you? Now I find myself forced to dispose of you, but how? An accident, perhaps, struck by a passing vehicle? Hard to arrange.'

I shook my head in urgent remonstration, but he ignored me and continued his horrifying deliberations.

'Down the shaft of an old mine, perhaps? Easy enough, but there would be questions. A Quæstor does not disappear without them, damn you. No, it must seem a justifiable accident. Off the cliff perhaps, the victim of a foolhardy walk in the moonlight, or drowned while taking a morning swim in ignorance of the rip tide? Both ideas have merit...'

He trailed off, rubbing his chin as he pondered. It is an ill thing to be helpless and faced by a man bent on your murder, your death postponed only until he decides how best to escape the wrath of the authorities. In those first few moments I came close to losing my mind as fear and despair crowded in, and it may well be that I sat bound to that chair for far longer than it seemed. Nor do I remember how Violet Meeks came to be in the room, only that suddenly she was standing there, perfectly still beside the study table. Even at that awful moment I felt pity for her, as there could be no question that having come in on us she would share my fate, or so I thought. He saw her and turned, surprised, then angry.

Her movement was a blur, so fast and so brief that I did not even realise what she had done until Saul Bulmer toppled from his chair to the floor. I did not realise she had caught up the ornate paperknife he used for his correspondence, nor thrown it, but there he lay, on his back, the knife sunk to the hilt in one eye so that the carving of the Blessed Ignatius that formed the handle seemed to stand in obscene juxtaposition from the socket. He never uttered a sound.

I turned to Violet, relief welling in my breast as I struggled to express my gratitude for my salvation. She took no notice, at first, a soft smile playing on her lips as she looked down on her handiwork. Her expression grew grave once more as she spoke, her voice calm and soft.

'It is done, if I did not mean it to be this way.'

She stepped forward, to draw the knife from the corpse's face with no more concern than had she been tying her shoe lace. The blade she wiped on a tissue, before cutting the cord that held the gag into my mouth. Even as I spat the foul tasting piece of leather from my lips I was babbling my thanks.

'Bless you... the Lord bless you, Violet.'

To my surprise her face flushed, and her words were rich with anger as she answered me, the first time I had ever heard her speak with emotion.

'Your Lord is not my God.'

New fear hit me as I realised the implications of her words, for as she had spoken she had raised two fingers of her forehead in the sign of the horns. I was helpless, in the presence of a Satanist, a worshipper of the demon Herne, Master of the Wild Hunt, one who had just killed a man with a single strike. Yet as she moved the knife once more it was not to plunge it into my chest, but merely to cut the bonds that held my body to the chair. I relaxed a little, still cautious as she worked to free me, allowing her to speak without answering.

'You may give me up, if you wish. I ask only an hour's grace, surely a small price for your life? That, or you may help me dispose of this carcass and support me in my testimony, which will be simple. He left the house late, to walk in the moonlight. I went to bed, and in the morning he had not returned. His body will be found on the rocks beneath Youlstone Cliffs, the head terribly crushed. Which is it to be?'

She had cut the final tie, freeing my legs. A dozen questions crowded my head, not least a demand to know how she could remain so terribly calm with Saul Bulmer's body cooling on the floor beside us. Rather than answer her, I babbled something about my report and the questions my superiors would inevitably raise should such a supposed accident occur on the same night I had returned to make my accusation. She answered promptly.

'Does anybody else know?'

'That I have returned? Yes, the wagonet driver for one, but of my findings, no, save for Emilia Turner.'

'Emilia will be glad he is dead. She will say nothing. He ruined her.'

'I know, and others too, by exaction, seduction...'

'Thirteen in all. I should have taken him long before, but let justice be mine.'

Saul Bulmer was beyond the reach of Church law and no doubt already in torment for his many sins. I, meanwhile, had a choice, to betray Violet, or to betray my vows. It was a choice I had already made.

'Justice is yours. You have my word.'

We set about our grisly task. Saul Bulmer had been a large, corpulent man, but I was taken aback by the ease with which Violet lifted him, taking his upper body while I held his legs. Just three times we were obliged to rest as we crossed the moonlit field behind the vicarage, keeping to the shadow of the hedge, my heart in my mouth with every step and every sound. At the cliff's edge we stopped. I began a prayer for the dead man's soul, for all that my words felt hollow, but Violet responded with a hiss of impatience.

'He is bound for your Hell, and eternal torment. Spare your prayers.'

'Yet still...'

I broke off as she slipped her arms under the corpse, lifting his full weight to hurl him from the edge, and as she did so she gave a sharp cry, perhaps merely for her exertion, perhaps of exultation. I stepped close to the edge, allowing myself a measure of appreciation for the irony of his fate when it might have been the very one he chose to inflict on me. The moon lit both cliff and sea, but Saul Bulmer's body had vanished into the gloom and no sound came back to us save the crash of the Atlantic breakers far below. For a space we stood together at the edge of the cliff, Violet Meeks and I, surely as strange a pair as ever had come together in that place, and on as strange a mission. At length I ventured a question.

'You said that you had not meant it to be this way. Am I to suppose...'

'You are. He would have walked out one evening and never come back, as indeed will be the tale.'

'You are confident in your strength.'

'He was nothing. A braggart, a bully. He was also slow and clumsy.'

'Against you, I have no doubt of it. Where did you learn to throw with such precision?'

'It is a gift from my God, as is my strength.'

'And your youth, if the question is not impertinent?'

'It is. One task yet remains.'

With that she slipped over the edge of the cliff and began to make her way down to where a mangled corpse lay somewhere among the shadows.

Thus I became complicit in the death of the Reverend Saul Bulmer, I will not call it murder, and in the life of Violet Meeks. That night, and over the succeeding days, I learnt much. Bulmer was not the first. There was Piers Myton, as I had guessed, his death no suicide but the result of her careful machinations. Having visited his crypt I could feel no sympathy for him, only a certain awe for her calculated lethality and indifference to what might have happened to her had she become his victim rather than the reverse. It seemed likely there were others, but she was reticent as to the details, as she was to her age, admitting only that she had dedicated her time in this world to the destruction of those priests who abused their power and privilege.

I also learnt that I had been mistaken in assuming that her avowed worship of the demon Herne had made her a threat. While I could not accept Herne the Hunter as other than an aspect of Satan, as such in opposition to the Lord and therefore inherently evil, she believed the reverse. One night, as we sat together in the vicarage, I attempted a theological disputation in order to show her the error of her ways. She proved as fervent in her belief and as clear in her logic as I, so we chose to let the matter rest. Nor could I bring myself to criticise her for her lack of moral scruple, given that I owed my life to her flexible attitude towards the Prime Commandment.

When I eventually submitted my report it stated simply that the Reverend Saul Bulmer had not been responsible for any financial misdemeanours, which was true save for the distinction between a bribe and a charitable donation and that was not apparent in any ledger. By then his death had been accepted as a tragic accident, to my profound relief, although the memory of hauling his corpse to the cliff edge at dead of night will haunt me to my grave, and beyond, while I prefer not to know precisely what Violet did down on the rocks to ensure that no suspicion would attach to the manner of his demise.

I myself spoke at his memorial service, as did Lady Morwenstow, although with the coming of judgement we will both no doubt be called to account for the words we spoke in false eulogy. Violet showed greater honesty and declined to attend the service, or perhaps it was that as a worshipper of the Horned God she preferred not to enter the church. When I came out she was gone.

The Captain

Adam Marek

Greg heard the beep of the dump truck's reverse alert and was instantly awake. He charged down the stairs, caught his fingertips sliding across one of the many bolts on the door. 'Stop!' he yelled, but his voice was lost in the sound of the truck's wheels crunching gravel and the hissing of its hydraulics.

The two men in the truck paid no notice to his shouting and arm waving when he burst out from his front door in his pants and t-shirt, walking in the way that one must on gravel in bare feet. The truck was as tall as his house and it was yellow. Already the dumper was inclining, the arms telescoping out, blotting out the low morning sun, and scaring off a gutter-full of house sparrows.

'Stop!' Greg called again. 'Not there you idiots!' He ran round the side of the truck, climbed up onto the driver's step and banged on the glass with the bottom of his fist. The man in the driver's seat turned his head to look at Greg in a bored way, raising his eyebrows. He pushed the red button on the dash. Greg's expletives came out in an eloquent flurry, flecks of his spit spattering the glass. The tailgate dropped. The dumper continued its incline, until gravity broke the inertia of the bodies inside, and it spilled them in a great heap before Greg's front door.

Arms and legs wrestled against each other as they fell. Heads banged against heads and against his doorstep. Pale ankles bashed on bootscrapers.

'Not there!' Greg yelled one more time.

The truck's hydraulics chugged four times, repeatedly driving the dumper trailer up a few degrees, pushing out the remaining bodies, the ones that were stuck. These last few dived out, eyes still open, mouths agape, surprised refugees emerging into freedom after days in the dark.

Still in bed upstairs, Amanda wrapped her arms around her head, a soft helmet that covered her ears against her husband's shouting, his kicking of the front door. Cruelly, the clock showed just two minutes until it was time to get up. She did not feel that she'd slept at all, but she must have done, and with her mouth open, because her throat was sore, and her front teeth were dry and sticky. The minute went quickly, and she felt she'd wasted it worrying through the list of things that needed to be packed for today's party.

In the kitchen, Greg had left the door flung open. Barely a sliver of sky and hedge was visible round the steep slope of corpses.

'Every damn time!' he said. 'The two minutes it would take them to open the gate and drive down into the field costs me a whole bloody day!'

Amanda shut the door against the smell from outside and moved around the kitchen like he wasn't there, pouring the last of the orange juice from the box into a cup, eating a piece of buttered toast which she'd folded in half for speed. There were three plastic crates on the dining room table, and into these she put boxes of eggs, bags of flour, cocoa and packs of butter, and then, as a protective layer over the top, two-dozen freshly washed children's aprons.

'I'm going to have to pay Wilkie and James to come help me again,' Greg continued. 'I'm going to call the council about it. I've had it this time.'

'Don't,' Amanda said. 'You'll make things much worse.'

'I'm losing money doing something they forced on me,' he said. 'It's not...'

'Fair?' Amanda said. 'Show me one person who can say they're getting a fair deal.'

'I was going to say efficient,' he said. 'If their drivers were just two percent more helpful, I could have my day back.'

'At least they let us keep the place,' Amanda said. 'We have to be grateful for what we've got.'

'You always say that.'

'Other people are much worse off.'

'I have to call them. I have to. This is driving me crazy.'

'You've got more than yourself to think about now,' Amanda said, her fingers spread wide over her bulging stomach.

'Just two minutes,' Greg said. 'Two minutes and who knows, maybe I could actually grow something.'

Amanda put one crate on top of another and hefted it up on top of her stomach.

'Good god woman,' Greg said, 'put that down. Let me do it.'

'I'm going to have to do it myself at the hall,' she said.

'Get Melissa to help you.'

'Melissa is never on time.'

Greg took the two crates from Amanda and she picked up the remaining one. Together they side-stepped out of the door, round the heap, being careful not to tread on fingers, trying to ignore the faces.

A big black limousine with the two little red flags mounted on its bonnet was parked up outside the town hall. Either side of the car were two military trucks. One of the many soldiers gathered around the trucks walked out into the road in front of Amanda's little Ford van and raised his hand.

Amanda wound down her window and smiled at the soldier. 'Good morning sir,' she said. 'I'm here for Governor Franco-Basoni's party.' She inflected her voice at the end making it sound like a question.

The soldier called over one of his colleagues who was carrying a clipboard.'

'Your name?' he said.

'Amanda Melman,' she said, 'from Cele-bake-tion.' She gestured to the side of the van, where the name of the company was printed.

'ID?'

'It hasn't arrived yet,' Amanda said. 'I have this problem every time. They misprinted my name. I sent it back three months ago. I'm just waiting for the new one. I keep chasing them.' Amanda took her bag from the passenger seat and pulled out a handful of envelopes. 'I have utility bills,' she said. 'And as you'll see, I've got cake-making stuff in the back. I'm not a terrorist, I promise.' Amanda made a big smile. It was not returned.

The soldier with the clipboard took the envelopes from her, opened up a couple and scanned through the bills. The other soldier walked around her truck, crouching down to examine the wheels, kneeling on the road to peer under the chassis.

'Okay,' the clipboard soldier said. He scored a line through her name on his sheet. 'Park around the back.'

'Thanks,' Amanda said. 'My friend who works with me will be arriving in a few minutes too. Her name's Melissa Hale. Just so you know.'

The soldier stared at her in a way that caused Amanda's cheeks to flush red. She wondered whether maybe she had breached some line of formality, and replayed what she'd said, in case there was an ambiguity that the soldier may have misinterpreted.

He waited the longest time before saying again, 'Park round the back.'

'Thank you,' she said. 'Have a lovely day.'

Her hand went to the window handle to close it, but she stopped and put her hands back on the steering wheel. The first soldier kicked her tyres as she drove away. She watched them watching her in her rear view mirror all the way to the car park.

Wilkie arrived with James in James's truck. The three men stood at the foot of the stinking mound of people, which was already attracting a noisy cloud of flies.

'Jeez,' Wilkie said. 'What a thing to wake up to.'

'You know what scares me?' Greg said. 'That one day this will become so normal I won't think about it.'

Wilkie put both hands flat on top of his head and gazed up the edifice of limbs. Many of the bodies were wearing suits. Smart shoes stuck out here and there, still laced. Women's bare feet with painted toenails. Wrists with watches that were still ticking. 'You should be more scared that you'll run out of land and they'll stop your subsidy,' Wilkie laughed. 'Then you'd be really screwed.'

'You can always dig deeper,' James said.

'Very profound,' Wilkie said. 'Come on Stephen Hawking, let's get this shifted before the sun gets hot.'

Melissa arrived in a cloud of perfume, clutching a stack of plastic boxes to her chest. Amanda was sweating in the heat, working fast to set out equal amounts of the cake ingredients on each of the twelve tables.

'Where have you been?' Amanda said.

'The soldiers,' Melissa said. 'They wanted to search me before I came in. They were very thorough.'

'What is that perfume you're wearing?'

'I dropped the bottle in my lap in the car. I didn't have time to change.'

'Come on, they start arriving in half an hour.'

Four soldiers stood at the entrance to the hall, rifles on their backs, arms folded across their chests, watching Melissa and Amanda laying a stack of four aprons on each of the tables. Amanda patted down each stack to make it neat and flat. She put a wooden spoon into the mixing bowls, always at the five o'clock angle. Melissa opened up the plastic boxes and in individual ceramic bowls shared out crystallised fruits, Smarties, hundreds-and-thousands, and marshmallows.

One of the soldiers, a man with a big ginger beard, came and grabbed a handful of Smarties and clamped his hand over his mouth as he chucked them in. Melissa moved to replenish the bowl, but with a subtle move, no more than placing her fingertips on Melissa's forearm, Amanda stopped her. Together, the two women watched the man grin at them while he chewed. Amanda reciprocated his smile, but pulled it back when it encouraged the soldier's grin to widen enough to show a blue Smartie clamped between his teeth.

Greg reversed his truck close to the heap of bodies. Wilkie plucked an earring from the ear of a big dead woman at his feet. Her taupe skirt was torn all the way from her knee to her waist, and her enormous thigh spilled out, streaked with cellulite. Wilkie tossed the earring into a plastic washing up bowl on the doorstep.

James stood at her feet, bent forwards, hands on his knees, looking up and down her. He puffed out. 'How are we going to handle this one,' he said.

Wilkie grabbed her wrists. James grabbed her ankles. Wilkie said, 'One, two, three, lift.' They raised the woman from the ground. With her arms pulled taught above her head, her chin was forced forwards onto her chest, closing her mouth and rolling out a cushion of fat on which her frowning face rested.

'Lift man!' Wilkie said.

'I can't get a grip,' James said. The woman's wide ankles slipped through his fingers, and her bottom dropped to the ground.

'Your fingers are too small,' Wilkie said. 'They've still got some growing to do.'

'Up yours,' James said.

Greg jumped out of the cab, leaving the door open. 'Swap ends,' he said, and then to James, 'Take an armpit'.

Greg and James each hooked their forearms under the woman's armpits. Wilkie, the biggest of the three, gripped her ankles and counted again. The three of them lifted her together.

Wilkie's face wrinkled with the effort, the bristles around his mouth rolling together into dark creases. The woman's ankles were slipping through his fingers. He hefted her up into the air a little, slid his grip up under her knees so he could lift her higher. The body sagged between them.

Wilkie began to count again, swinging her like he might a sack of potatoes. But James said, 'Don't. Not like that.'

'Oh give me a break,' Wilkie said. 'She not going to feel it. I want to get home before dark.'

James looked to Greg.

'Let's just get her up before my back gives,' Greg said.

Wilkie began to count again, and this time, they swung together.

◇

In the town hall kitchen, Amanda opened the oven and found it to be full of oily lumps of blackened crumbs and a shrivelled half-tomato. Melissa unpacked rubber gloves and fresh J-Cloths from her bag, filled a bowl with soap and hot water, and together they stuck their arms into the oven and began to scrub.

Kneeling like this, their heads close together, they filled the oven with whispers.

'I'm worried about Greg,' Amanda said. 'I'm worried he's going to do something stupid.'

'Like what?' Melissa said.

'I don't know. He gets crazier every morning when the truck arrives. He keeps talking about calling them up and complaining.'

'Well, what if he did?' Melissa said.

Amanda stopped to look at Melissa, frowning deeply.

'Are you serious?'

'He's got principles.'

'He can't afford to have principles,' Amanda said. 'He's going to be a dad. He's got more important things to think about.'

'I think I'd be proud of my husband if he stood up for himself.'

'You wouldn't say that if you had one.'

Melissa did not reply, but scraped a big blob of black foam from the back of her glove and flicked it into the bowl.

'I'm sorry,' Amanda said. 'I didn't mean that.' And then, 'Your perfume really is giving me a headache.'

The back of Greg's truck was filled, the peak of the bodies rising higher than the cab, held in place by weight and the interlocking of limbs. All three men heaved against the tailgate, pushing against the bodies, until the locking mechanism clicked into place. It had taken them an hour and a half to get a quarter of the heap onto the truck. Now the sun was higher and the flies more numerous. James went through the cleared space on the gravel, throwing stray shoes high up onto the truck and picking up lost watches and coins from among the bloodied stones and throwing them into the washing up bowl, which was now filling up.

'Can we have a cuppa before we set off?' James asked.

Greg looked to Wilkie. 'We should pace ourselves,' Wilkie said.

'I want to get this done before it gets too hot,' Greg said. 'Let's stop for tea after we've unloaded this one.'

James wiped his hands on his jeans, and where he did, the denim was dark with dirt and other people's blood. Greg and Wilkie got in the cab.

'I'll ride on the outside,' James said, and he climbed up onto the driver's step, clinging to the mount of the wing mirror.

'You know I can't concentrate with your face peering in at me,' Greg said.

'Yeah,' Wilkie laughed. 'Why don't you just ride in the back.'

Greg set off down the track, his truck groaning and shuddering with every dip in the road. Thirst made the men quiet, and in this silence they could hear bodies slipping down the pile, things bumping into the painted steel sides, knuckles, shoes, foreheads, zippers, knees.

◇

The children arrived dressed in various versions of the Captain outfits. Some of them had the official merchandise, produced in red polyester with foam padding to replicate his muscles on their scrawny chests. Others were home-made affairs, red t-shirts with a five-pointed star cut from yellow fabric and stitched on, the black fist at the centre of this logo drawn onto it with marker pens. Boys and girls wore the same costumes. As each new one arrived, they joined the dog-fight round the tables, chasing each other, both hands held out flat in front of them in the Captain's flying position. Every few seconds one would stop, spread his or her fingers, and then mimic with varying levels of success, the sound of the Captain's death ray, a sound most effectively rendered by screwing up the corner of the mouth, enough to twist the nose out of shape, biting the front teeth together and forcing out air in a slow, bubbly, hiss. Whereupon, the others would clutch their hearts and drop to the parquet floor, to lay for a few seconds before getting up and awaiting their turn to kill everyone.

'This is mental,' Melissa said. 'What's wrong with their parents?'

'Stop,' Amanda said. She tied a small knot in the strings of her apron at the zenith of her belly. Within a couple of weeks she would have to tie it round the back instead.

The birthday girl arrived, Sasha, her strut making her thick black hair swing from side to side behind her. Her mother, Governor Franco-Basoni, followed after, flanked by four soldiers. She looked around the room at each of the people present. When her gaze reached Amanda and Melissa, the two women nodded with respect, but this gesture received nothing in return but an indifferent pout.

The soldier with the clipboard who had stopped Amanda earlier, came over and told the women that everyone had now arrived and they could begin.

A boy with his red face-paint already smudged around his mouth ran into the legs of the soldier, gripped the man's jacket and tugged at it with both hands. 'Is the Captain coming?' He said. 'When is the Captain coming?'

'You'll have to wait and see,' the soldier said, smiling for the first time and patting the boy's head.

◇

The quarry was dug deep and wide, the road around it pummelled into chevrons by the tyres of earth-moving machinery. Gulls turned circles in the air above. Greg swung his truck round at the edge and James hopped off the driver's step to guide him back, getting the rear wheels as close to the edge as possible without danger of the ground crumbling away beneath them.

'You've still got some crops going then,' Wilkie said, pointing across the excavation to a field of tall stalks.

'Corn,' Greg said. 'Only about fifty hectares. But if I didn't grow something here, I'd go nuts.'

'Will it be edible?' James said, and when the other two gave him confused glares, he added, 'You know, with all this being right next to it.' James waved his hand around, gesturing at the pit.

'Give me a break,' Greg said.

Wilkie picked up a flint, pulled his arm all the way back and grunted as he threw it. The stone flew in a high arc, seeming to take forever to fall, and hit the ground with a soft thud, only a quarter of the way across the pit. Gulls and crows sprung up around the point of impact, complaining, and then settled back into their scavenging, amongst the flecks of pink, blue, white and grey where the clothes of the dead showed through the fine layer of dirt.

'This time last year,' Greg said. 'The government was paying me twice what they're paying now because I had skylarks nesting right here.'

'It won't always be like this,' James said. 'They'll find a weakness. Everyone has a weakness.'

'Who's they?' Wilkie said. 'They think what they're doing now is the best thing for everyone. They're not even looking. This might be as good as it gets. Next year, we might look back to this moment and wish we still had the same freedoms we've got now.'

'Well that's a cheery thought,' Greg said. He unbolted the trailer's tailgate, and grabbed the trouser leg of a man already half falling out. 'Let's get this done.'

'What I was about to say,' Wilkie said, 'is that they aren't going to do jack shit about it. It's down to us.'

◇

While the cakes were baking, the kids watched a film. It was a montage of clips of the Captain set to a heavy-rock track. Some of the clips were high-quality, taken from news broadcasts. Others were jumpy and low-resolution, filmed on home movie cameras and mobile phones.

All of the town hall curtains were drawn. The kids sat on cushions on the floor, heads tilted back to watch the screen above them. They watched the Captain zipping past office blocks, thousands of windows shattering around him. They watched the Captain standing alongside generals at podiums, bathed in camera flashes. They watched the Captain land on a beach, raise his hands in his signature pose, the people in swimsuits leaping up terrified from their towels, feet kicking up sand as they run to the water's edge to gather their children. And then everyone dropping, the whole beach felled in a second. And the children cheered.

'How can you stand this?' Melissa said, watching through the kitchen serving hatch. 'Would you let your kid sit through this?'

'Keep your voice down,' Amanda said.

'How can they watch this?'

'They don't understand,' Amanda said. She opened up the oven door and took out two trays of cakes and set them on the hob, before putting in the next two trays of mixture. Most of the cakes were lopsided mutants, spilling over the edge of their paper cups.

'This can't go on,' Melissa said.

Just then, Amanda noticed for the first time, the ginger soldier who'd eaten their Smarties earlier. He was stood outside the kitchen door, watching them both through the small square window.

Melissa wiped her hands on her apron. 'Would you like one?' she asked him, holding up a cake. 'Fresh out of the oven.'

The soldier wedged open the door with his boot and took the cake from her. He shoved the whole thing in his mouth in one go, severing it from the paper cup with his front teeth, watching Melissa the whole time.

'Good?' she said.

He nodded, chewing, and wiping crumbs from his beard. He looked around the kitchen, around the floor, behind the door, all around the work surfaces.

'Are you looking for something?' Melissa asked.

'No,' the soldier said. He took another cake, then went back into the main hall, shutting the door behind him.

Amanda leaned up against the oven, puffing, shaking her head slowly at Melissa. Melissa came close, wiping cake mixture up

with a cloth. 'Do you think he...' she began, but Amanda shook
her head and pinched her lips together. 'You're going to get the
wrong kind of attention wearing perfume like that,' she said.

The men were down to the last body, that of the big woman who
was loaded onto the truck first back at the farm house. As before,
Wilkie grabbed her ankles, James and Greg an armpit each. Wilkie didn't count this time, but they did swing, and couldn't help
but watch the bulk of her, bouncing down the steeply chiselled
quarry, her slow turns, hair streaming, the sudden acrobatic lunges
when she connected with something jutting from the side, a rock,
an irrigation pipe.

'What time was the party due to finish?' Wilkie asked.

Greg looked at his watch. 'In about half an hour.'

'So it could be happening now,' Wilkie said.

'Will she really do it?' James said. 'I mean...'

'Melissa's got bigger balls than the three of us put together,'
Greg said.

'Yeah, but James is lowering our average,' Wilkie laughed.

James punched Wilkie's arm. 'This isn't the time,' James said.
'Jeez, I can't even think about it. I mean I can't stop thinking
about it.'

Governor Franco-Basoni stood before all the children with the
palms of her hands pressed together. 'I have a special treat for you,'
she said.

The children all jumped up and down on the spot, their hands
in the air, shouting, 'Captain! Captain!'

'Yes,' the Governor continued, 'especially for Sasha's birthday,
and because her family is so loyal, the Captain has come.'

Melissa and Amanda were wiping down the tables and repacking
leftover ingredients into their plastic boxes. They watched the red-

costumed man stride in through the front door. It was not the real Captain, but even a facsimile was enough to set Amanda's hands shaking.

The Captain raised his arms and all the children ran up to him, high-fiving him and calling out his name. 'And where is the birthday girl?' the Captain said. He was wearing a concealed voice changer which gave his speech the unearthly metallic sound of the real Captain.

Governor Franco-Basoni looked across at Amanda, and mimed the action of lighting a candle with a match. Amanda nodded. The two women went into the kitchen and took out an enormous cake from its box. The red, yellow and black fondant icing on top was in the shape of the Captain's logo. Amanda's hands trembled as she stuck one candle into each of the five points of the star, and then three more gathered close together in the middle of the fist.

'You carry it,' Melissa said. 'I'll light the candles.'

Amanda agreed and handed Melissa the box of matches from her apron pocket. They waited at the kitchen door, just out of sight, for the signal.

The Captain began the first note of 'Happy Birthday', and everyone joined in. Melissa struck a match and lit a candle, then plucked it from the cake and used it to light the others before sticking it back in.

Governor Franco-Basoni bade them over with a flick of her hand. A soldier switched off the hall lights.

All the kids, the Governor and the Captain, turning to watch the cake approach, singing the happy birthday song together. Amanda forced a big grin. She could feel the heat of the candles on her face.

The children parted around Amanda and Melissa, so they could get right up to Sasha, who was grinning broadly, the Captain's hand on her shoulder. And beside him, clapping last and loudest at the end of the song was Governor Franco-Basoni.

In the middle of this applause, just as Sasha opened her mouth and sucked in a big breath of air in preparation for blowing out the candles, Melissa stuck her blouse sleeve into the tiny flames.

The substance she'd soaked her clothes with that morning ignited in one explosive whoosh. Everyone gathered around her was lit up by the flash, their terrified faces captured for a second as her blouse, trousers and hair ignited.

In the second that Melissa burst into flames, Amanda dropped the cake, the Captain stumbled back and tripped over his own heels, and the soldiers, suddenly awakened by duty, swung their guns round from their backs. It took a moment for the screaming to start, but already Melissa was charging at Governor Franco-Basoni, yelling out something, some kind of unintelligible valedictory cry.

So stunned was the Governor that she had taken only one step back when Melissa leaped at her, wrapped her arms and legs around her, and gripped tightly. They hit the ground, burning together.

◇

Greg put the kettle on the Aga. Droplets of water rolled down its enamelled surface and fizzed and spat on the hot plate before disappearing in puffs of steam.

'Have you got any biscuits?' Wilkie said.

'There's some flapjack in there,' Greg said.

Wilkie took the square plastic box from on top of the microwave, opened up the corner and sniffed the air inside. James came back from the bathroom. His short fringe and the neck of his t-shirt were soaked where he'd wetted his face.

'Did Amanda know?' James said.

'No,' Greg said. He put out three mugs on the side and threw a teabag in each.

'Aren't you worried that...?'

'Amanda would never have let Melissa do it,' Wilkie said. 'She would have cancelled the whole gig. We would have missed the opportunity.'

'But what if they think Amanda was involved?'

'Give him a break,' Wilkie said. 'Yes Amanda is going to ape shit, but that's what's going to convince them she's not involved. Her natural reaction will be the thing that gets her out of there.'

'You hope,' James said.

The kettle whistled. Greg poured water over the teabags, mashed them against the inside of the cups with the back of a teaspoon. 'Get the milk will you James,' he said.

'And will Amanda know that you knew?' James said. He opened the fridge, took out the bottle of milk, checked the use-by date on the side, and when he set it down on the work surface next to Greg, Greg grabbed his wrist, turned it over and squeezed with a force that caused James to gasp, to drop his shoulder, to grab at Greg's immoveable fist.

'Stoppit!' James said.

'Don't you dare question my morality,' Greg said. 'What have you ever risked? You weasel around with us, sitting at the back, piping up with your naive observations when there's only one or two of us around. Don't you think I'm terrified? On the day you risk something, anything, you get to have an opinion, until then, just shut it.'

'Okay okay!' James said. 'I'm sorry!'

James rubbed at the red streaks Greg left on his wrist.

'This is great flapjack,' Wilkie said. His mouth was bulging with it. Greg poured milk into the tea, squeezed the teabags again, and tossed them in the compost pot. He carried the three mugs to the table. Wilkie raised his mug in a toast and said, 'Death to the Captain', but before James or Greg could return the toast, the phone began to ring.

Amanda's hands were at her face, covered with icing, closing the horrified gape of her mouth. Children were screaming, soldiers pushing them out of the way, sending them skidding across the floor. The soldiers yelled at Melissa to let go of the Governor, their fear at the size and ferocity of the conflagration obvious in their hesitation. In response to Governor Franco-Basoni's screaming, and the thrashing of her legs, they kicked at Melissa, five of them, but Melissa's grip was strong. She was fused to the woman. The fire alarm began. The faux Captain scampered back on all fours to the edge of the hall, his voice changer amplifying his whimpers.

Only after someone had blasted the burning women with a foamy white jet from the fire extinguisher did the soldiers go at Melissa with their hands, peeling her apart from the Governor. There was smoke, and steam, and an acrid stench that made their eyes water. The soldiers yelled at her, spitting out curses, even though she was still.

Amanda was paralysed by all of this, standing in the same spot she'd been when Sasha was about to blow out the candles, the cake broken over her feet, but then the soldiers began thudding Melissa with the butts of their rifles, and Amanda became galvanised.

'Stop!' She yelled. 'It was an accident!'

She took one step towards her fallen friend when a soldier tackled her from the side, his shoulder hitting her thigh with awful force. Her feet skittered in the air for purchase as she fell, crying out, 'I'm pregnant'. The soldier crashed on top of her, crushing her. His elbows pinned her arms. A big metallic-tasting palm covered her mouth, pushed her head to the side. And then there were more around her, pointing their rifles in her face, telling her not to move.

Greg got up from the table and lifted the handset from its cradle. The number calling was unknown. His thumb was on the answer button, but he didn't press it yet. Each ring shook the whole kitchen.

He was at the open door. The heap of bodies only slightly diminished. Now the crows and the magpies had found it, hopping from limb to limb, blinking and squabbling.

There were only two rings left before the answerphone would cut in. Greg was shaking. Inside him, things fell, things froze, things curdled and things woke up startled. Had Melissa succeeded? Had they gone too far? Had the world changed? Had it changed enough to make the sacrifice worth it? Could he live with the consequences?

Under the weight of all the possibilities, Greg pushed the button and took the call.

Biographies

Maurice Broaddus is the author of the novel series, *The Knights of Breton Court* (Angry Robot). His dark fiction has been published in numerous magazines, anthologies, and websites, most recently including *Dark Dreams II & III*, *Apex Magazine*, *Black Static*, and *Weird Tales Magazine*. He is the co-editor of the *Dark Faith* anthology (Apex Books). Visit his site at www.MauriceBroaddus.com.

Monte Cook has worked as a professional writer and game designer since 1988. He has published two novels, numerous short stories, countless articles, and a comic book series for Marvel. Monte was also one of the three principal designers of *3rd Edition D&D* and the d20 system. His d20 game design studio, Malhavoc Press, produced award-winning products including *Monte Cook's Arcana Evolved*, *Ptolus*, and the *Books of Eldritch Might*. Games he has worked on include *D&D*, *Champions*, *Rolemaster*, and more. He also created *HeroClix*, *D20 Call of Cthulhu*, and *Monte Cook's World of Darkness*. He is a graduate of the Clarion West Writer's Workshop and his recent nonfiction book is *A Skeptic's Guide to Conspiracies*.

Named by Gamasutra as one of its Top 20 Videogame Writers, **Richard Dansky** is the Central Clancy Writer for Red Storm/ Ubisoft. His credits include critically acclaimed games such as *Splinter Cell: Conviction*. He's also published five novels, most recently *Firefly Rain*, and has contributed extensively to multiple tabletop RPGs. For a brief time, he was the world's leading expert on Denebian Slime Devils, but he doesn't like to talk about those days. Richard lives in North Carolina with his wife and their inevitable cats.

Graeme Davis was born within spitting distance of London's Heathrow Airport and traveled around the world twice by the age of seven, visiting Australia, Fiji, and other places across the Pacific. He is just old enough to remember airliners with propellors and has a lifelong fascination with vintage aviation. Best known as a writer for roleplaying games such as *Warhammer Fantasy Roleplay*, *Vampire: the Masquerade*, and *GURPS*, he has also written a *Dungeons & Dragons* novel and a few short stories. He has always wanted to write an air-pulp adventure.

Julia Bond Ellingboe is a freelance editor, writer, and roleplaying game designer. Having missed her chance to become an itinerant storyteller, her work often draws on various folkloric traditions, such as African American slave narratives, Japanese kaidan stories, and the Francis J. Child Ballads. Her work includes *Steal Away Jordan: Stories from American's Peculiar Institution*, the forthcoming *Tales of the Fisherman's Wife*, and the short fiction "The Wolf and Death". Julia holds a bachelor's degree in Religion and Biblical Literature from Smith College and lives in Greenfield, Massachusetts.

Peter Freeman was born in London, educated at Oxford and is still alive. He has now been a professional writer for fifteen years, producing over a hundred works on all manner of subjects and under more than a dozen different pseudonyms. His output has varied from writing cartoon strip text for *Punch Magazine*, through fantasy, humour, detective fiction and erotica to non-fiction on everything between recycling equipment and unexpected sexual practises. For him, this story was very much a case of coming home to early influences. (Alexandra Freeman is his daughter and has an imagination perhaps more vivid still.)

Ed Greenwood is the creator of the *Forgotten Realms®* fantasy world-setting, an award-winning game designer, and a bestselling author whose books have sold millions of copies worldwide in more than thirty languages. Once hailed as "the Canadian author of the great American novel", Ed is a large, bearded, jolly Santa-Claus-like librarian who lives in an old farmhouse crammed with more than 80,000 books in the countryside of Ontario, Canada. His most popular series include the *Elminster* books published by Wizards of the Coast, the *Band of Four* series from Tor, and the *Falconfar* trilogy from Solaris.

Kenneth Hite has designed, written, or co-authored more than seventy roleplaying games and supplements, including the *Star Trek Roleplaying Game*, *GURPS Infinite Worlds*, *Day After Ragnarok*, *Trail of Cthulhu*, and *Night's Black Agents*. Outside gaming, his works include *Tour de Lovecraft: the Tales*, *Cthulhu 101*, *Zombies 101*, *Where the Deep Ones Are*, and the graphic illustrated version of *The Complete Idiot's Guide to U.S. History*. He writes the "Lost in Lovecraft" column for *Weird Tales* magazine, and his essays and criticism have also appeared in *Dragon Magazine*, *Games Quarterly Magazine*, *National Review*, *Amazing Stories*, and in anthologies from Greenwood Press, Ben Bella Press, and MIT Press. He lives in Chicago with his wife Sheila, two cats, and many, many books. He blogs at princeofcairo.livejournal.com.

Editor and Stone Skin Press Creative Director **Robin D. Laws** is an author, game designer, and podcaster. His novels include *Pierced Heart*, *The Rough and the Smooth*, and *The Worldwound Gambit*. Robin created the GUMSHOE investigative roleplaying rules system and such games as *Feng Shui*, *The Dying Earth*,

HeroQuest 2 and *Ashen Stars*. He is one half of the podcasting team behind "Ken and Robin Talk About Stuff". Find his blog, a cavalcade of film, culture, games, narrative structure and gun-toting avians, at robindlaws.com.

Adam Marek is award-winning short story writer. He won the 2011 Arts Foundation Short Story Fellowship, and was shortlisted for the inaugural Sunday Times EFG Short Story Award. His first story collection *Instruction Manual for Swallowing* was nominated for the Frank O'Connor Prize. His second, The Stone Thrower, followed in 2012. His stories have appeared in many magazines, including: *Prospect* and *The Sunday Times Magazine,* and in many anthologies including *Lemistry, Litmus* and *The New Uncanny* from Comma Press, and *The Best British Short Stories 2011.* To subscribe to Adam's blog, Twitter and Facebook updates, visit www.adammarek.co.uk

Jonny Nexus lives in Brighton, England, with his wife, their dog, and an array of chew toys that the dog invariably leaves on the topmost step but one. He was the editor, co-founder, and chief-writer of the cult gaming webzine Critical Miss, and wrote the *Slayers Guide to Games Masters* and a regular monthly magazine column for leading British roleplaying publisher Mongoose Publishing. His debut novel *Game Night,* published by Magnum Opus Press in 2007, was shortlisted for a GenCon EN World Award (an "ENnie").

Jeff Tidball is an award-winning writer and game designer with a roiling wake of stories, board games, card games, and roleplaying games in his rear-view mirror. Marquee credits include the *Horus Heresy* board game, the *Pieces of Eight* pirate coin combat game, and the book *Things We Think About Games.* Jeff holds an MFA in Screenwriting from the University of Southern California and lives with his wife, sons, and dog in Minneapolis. His website is predictably located at jefftidball.com and he spews forth on Twitter as @jefftidball.

Monica Valentinelli is an author and game designer who lurks in the dark. Her publications include non-fiction, original and tie-in fiction. Stories range from *Redwing's Gambit*, a novella set in the universe of the *Bulldogs! RPG*, and "Tailfeather" which debuted in *Apexology: Science Fiction and Fantasy*. In addition to her short stories, novellas, articles, and RPG contributions, Monica crafted one of the first enhanced e-books titled *The Queen of Crows*. In her spare time, she dons the role of project manager for horror and dark fantasy webzine, www.flamesrising.com. For more about Monica and her work, visit www.mlvwrites.com.

Kyla Ward is a Sydney-based creative who works in many modes. Her novel *Prismatic* (co-authored as 'Edwina Grey') won an Aurealis Award for Horror. Her short fiction has appeared in Ticonderoga Online, Shadowed Realms, Gothic.net and in the *Macabre* anthology among others. Her short film, *Bad Reception*, screened at the 3rd international Vampire Film Festival and she is a member of the Theatre of Blood, which has also produced her work. Poetry, articles, rpgs, art; if you can scare people with it she probably has, to the extent of programming the horror stream at the 2010 Worldcon. To see some very strange things, try www.tabula-rasa.info.

Chuck Wendig is a novelist, screenwriter, and freelance penmonkey. Chuck is the author of the novels *Double Dead*, *Blackbirds*, and *Mockingbird*. He, with writing partner Lance Weiler, is a fellow of the Sundance Film Festival Screenwriter's Lab. Their short, *Pandemic*, showed at the 2011 Sundance Film Festival, and their feature *HiM* is in development with producer Ted Hope. He has contributed over two million words to the RPG industry, and served as developer of *Hunter: The Vigil*. He currently lives in Pennsylvania with his wife, dog, and newborn heir to the Wendig throne. You can find him dispensing dubious writing wisdom at his website: www.terribleminds.com.

Also from

Stone Skin Press...

Shotguns v. Cthulhu

Pulse-pounding action meets cosmic horror in this exciting collection from the rising stars of the New Cthulhuiana. Steel your nerves, reach into your weapons locker, and tie tight your running shoes as humanity takes up arms against the monsters and gods of H. P. Lovecraft's Cthulhu Mythos. Remember to count your bullets...you may need the last one for yourself.

Relentlessly hurtling you into madness and danger are:

Natania **BARRON** • Steve **DEMPSEY** • Dennis **DETWILLER**
Larry **DiTILLIO** • Chad **FIFER** • A. Scott **GLANCY**
Dave **GROSS** • Dan **HARMS** • Rob **HEINSOO**
Kenneth **HITE** • Chris **LACKEY** • Robin D. **LAWS**
Nick **MAMATAS** • Ekaterina **SEDIA** • Kyla **WARD**

ISBN: 9781908983015

Publication date: October 2012

Available to pre-order from the Stone Skin Press website
www.stoneskinpress.com

The Lion and the Aardvark
Aesop's Modern Fables

These confusing times of Internet trolls, one-percenters, toxic fame, and impending singularity cry out for clarity—the clarity found in Aesop's 2,500 year old fables. Over 60 writers from across the creative spectrum bring their modern sensibilities to this classic format. Zombies, dog-men and robot wasps mingle with cats, coyotes and cockroaches. Parables ranging from the punchy to the evocative, the wry to the disturbing explore eternal human foibles, as displaced onto lemmings, trout, and racing cars. But beware—in these terse explorations of desire, envy, and power, certitude isn't always as clear as it looks.

ISBN: 9781908983022

Publication date: December 2012

Available to pre-order from the Stone Skin Press website
www.stoneskinpress.com

The New Hero
Volume 2

Every generation fits the time-honored constants of the hero tale to its own needs. Today's serial adventurers, whether they burst from re-envisioned histories or ply the humming foredecks of an imagined future, ride a cresting cultural wave. Through thirteen thrilling stories of threatened identity and vanquished disorder, The New Hero 2's diverse cast of top writers slices, dices and re-combines the limits of the form.

Grab camera, medkit or mystic tome and rush to your rendez-vous with the heroes of tomorrow.

ISBN: 9781908983039

Publication date: February 2013

Available to pre-order from the Stone Skin Press website

www.stoneskinpress.com